IN THESE
DISCONSOLATE
WOODS

Also by Michael J. McCann

IN THESE DISCONSOLATE WOODS

A MARCH AND WALKER CRIME NOVEL

Michael J. McCann

The Plaid Raccoon Press
2023

In These Disconsolate Woods is a work of fiction. Names, characters, institutions, places and events are either the product of the author's imagination or are used fictitiously. Any resemblance to actual persons, living or dead, events, or locales is entirely coincidental.

This novel is entirely the product of the author's imagination, hard work, and creativity. No artificial intelligence applications or similar tools were used, nor will they ever be. Organically grown fiction is always the best!

To Erin, Jeff, Hannah,
Noah, and Miles.

Chapter

1

Ontario Provincial Police Detective Constable Kevin Walker paused in front of the sliding doors at the main entrance long enough to remove his sunglasses. Trading them for the wallet in his jacket pocket, he took a deep breath and committed himself to the calculated gloom of the Thousand Islands Casino.

Two people were waiting for him in the reception area. One, a woman in a dark business suit and white blouse, stepped forward as he opened the wallet to display his warrant card and badge.

"I'm Karen Blanchard," she said. "This is Toby Small. I don't think they needed to send a detective."

"There's been an accident just this side of Gananoque," Kevin said, putting away his wallet. "The responding officer and EMS were diverted to the scene. We've got another unit and a second EMS coming down from Brockville, but

I was closer, so. . . ."

"Whatever. Toby will take you back." Blanchard waved a hand and walked away.

"Okay." Kevin followed Small out of the reception area and across the casino floor. The place was filled with noise and flashing coloured lights. It was just past three o'clock on a Saturday afternoon in August, and there were already quite a few patrons at the slot machines and gaming tables.

Kevin wasn't surprised, because he'd counted the cars in the parking lot before coming in, practising his observation skills, comparing the number of Ontario plates to those from Quebec and New York state. It never ceased to amaze him how popular these places were with people from all over the map who seemed to have nothing better to do with their time and money.

He followed Small into a broad corridor. "Seems busy."

Small said nothing. Appropriately, he was short and balding, in his fifties, and he wore the stereotypic black trousers, white shirt, and fancy waistcoat of a croupier, which seemed to be a uniform of sorts for the employees who worked on the floor with the patrons.

If he had a personality, Kevin thought, he was certainly holding it close to his vest.

They reached a row of washrooms at the back. Small stopped at one of the doors where a beefy security guy stood guard.

"Let him in," Small said.

The guy frowned at Kevin.

Kevin badged him with a friendly smile.

The guy pushed open the washroom door and stepped aside.

The man was lying on the floor in front of the sinks. He was curled up into a fetal ball, his elbows tucked in and his hands clasped together between his knees. Drool bubbled from between his lips as he snored.

He was in his late thirties, with thick brown hair trimmed short, a small jaw, and a five-o'clock shadow. He wore vomit-stained green pants and a khaki shirt in even worse condition. His stomach contents, which apparently had included a big lunch and a lot of liquor, were spewed across the floor.

"Is this where he was when you found him?" Kevin asked, ignoring the smell as he cautiously moved forward for a closer look. "You didn't try to move him?"

No response.

Kevin looked around. He was alone. He'd thought Small had followed him in, but evidently the man had more important things to do than stick around while the cops attended to an unconscious drunk.

It was just as well. Kevin had recognized the man on the floor from a photograph he'd seen this morning. Avoiding the mess as much as possible, he knelt and felt the man's neck to check his pulse.

There it was, strong and steady.

He checked the other stalls, but the washroom was otherwise empty.

He took out his cellphone and retrieved the message he'd remembered. It was a lookout bulletin for four inmates of the Collins Bay minimum-security institution who'd commandeered the van in which they were being driven to an Alcoholics Anonymous meeting in Kingston. They'd overpowered the driver, a social worker employed at the prison, and disappeared.

Kevin opened the attached file containing the four mug shots. One of the faces matched the man lying on the floor in front of him: Leonard Peter Smith, a.k.a. Lennie Smith, a.k.a. LP, a.k.a. Long Play.

Kevin had taken a few minutes this morning to look

into the backgrounds of the four men, and he remembered the details of Smith's record. Thirty-four, Caucasian, a string of convictions for possession, drunk and disorderly, and a clumsy attempt to sell a bag full of street drugs to an uncover police officer. Bipolar. Childhood abuse. A history of suicide attempts and self-harm. An alcoholic and a drug addict.

Kevin patted Smith's pockets, felt a wallet, and took it out. Inside was a driver's licence in the name of Harold John Wilson, the social worker Smith and his cronies had bushwhacked and left on the side of the road. There was only a five-dollar bill left in the currency pocket. It would seem that Smith had gambled away the rest of Wilson's cash while guzzling down too much of the casino's booze.

Smith stirred, coughed, and subsided again.

Kevin stared at him for a long moment, remembering that this was someone's son. A human being. An example of what happened when a person with mental health issues crossed over the line from health care into the judicial system. Court appearances and convictions and incarceration changed them from a patient into a criminal requiring correction as defined by the law and the judges who applied it. And although institutions might offer periodic counselling or therapy or even medication to address something like bipolar disorder, a guy like Lennie Smith was now viewed by the system first and foremost as a convict and as a sufferer of mental health problems second.

Kevin decided it might be a good idea to check the rest of the casino in case Long Play's fellow escapees were also hanging around, trying their luck at the slot machines or the roulette wheel. He hadn't seen a Corrections Canada van in the parking lot on the way in, though.

At that moment the washroom door burst open and a paramedic entered.

"His pulse is good," Kevin said, standing up and moving aside.

The paramedic ran through his own checklist as his partner pushed in with a gurney. Behind him was a uniformed patrol officer that Kevin recognized as Provincial Constable Connie Coburn. She hovered just inside the door, watching the paramedics, as Kevin went over to her.

"Relax, Connie, there's no one in here but him."

She rolled her eyes.

Kevin called the contact number on the lookout and spoke to the individual with Corrections Canada handling the escape. The officer confirmed that an arrest warrant had been issued for Leonard Peter Smith and that a team was already on the road in the area. He would direct them to the casino and they'd take custody of the prisoner.

Kevin advised him that paramedics were already on the scene and that Smith might require further medical treatment.

"We'll handle it."

"All right, then." Kevin ended the call. He forwarded the Corrections message to Coburn and opened his mouth to say something to her about the other escapees when his phone buzzed with another call.

"Preston Raintree, Kevin. How's your luck holding out at the blackjack table?"

"The guy's an escaped prisoner, Sarge. Corrections is on the way. Constable Coburn's here. I was about to check around and see if the other fugitives are also on site."

He raised an eyebrow at Coburn, who nodded and slipped out.

"Wow, an escaped con, eh? All right. Look, if everything's under control there I need you to slide up to Lanark ASAP. The powers that be have ordered me to loan you out for a homicide, and who am I to say no to Detective Incredible March?"

"Lanark?"

Detective Sergeant Raintree commanded the Leeds County Crime Unit, of which Kevin was a member, but Lanark was a separate detachment covering the area immediately north of Leeds. Policing five rural municipalities and three towns within 3,000 square kilometres, and with a total population of about 59,000 people, Lanark had its own crime unit. Normally there was minimal crossover between the two jurisdictions.

"Resource depletion, Kev. They don't have enough detectives right now for a game of bridge, so they'd appreciate a helping hand."

"Sounds good to me," Kevin said.

Chapter

2

Ontario Provincial Police Detective Inspector Ellie March was skimming through e-mail in her work account inbox when she heard a knock at her kitchen door.

Her big German shepherd, Reggie, was asleep on the rug next to her desk, but the sound brought his head up, and he began to pound the floor with his tail.

Ellie lived alone in a four-season cottage on Sparrow Lake, northwest of Brockville, Ontario. She'd converted one of its two bedrooms into a home office and stocked it with every kind of communications equipment she could think of, including a satellite phone to back up her cellphone, a desktop radio set connecting her to the Government of Ontario Fleetnet network, a router connecting her through a satellite dish on the roof to the Internet, and a secure encrypted system allowing her remote access to her OPP network account.

An addition to the front side of the cottage had become her laundry room and pantry, the latter stocked with an inventory of food, bottled water, medical supplies, and other essentials that would make a survivalist drool with envy. Not that she was a prepper, though. Not by a long shot. She was merely a believer in redundancy and proactive planning.

The cottage was also equipped with a state-of-the-art security system including video surveillance, motion sensors, and other high-tech elements. It protected her pantry and office, the gun safe in her bedroom, and, of course, Ellie herself.

The best part of her security network, though, as far as Ellie was concerned, was the four-legged, fur-bearing component who'd just jumped to his feet and trotted out to the kitchen door. His ears and nose were easily as reliable as any electronic sensing device currently on the market, and since Reggie was happy to have been disturbed while taking his beauty nap, Ellie wasn't worried about their surprise visitor.

She thought she knew who it was.

"Hi, Dean." She stepped aside to let him come inside.

"Hi. Hi, Reggie!" Dean Othman knelt down and grabbed the dog around the neck to give him an energetic hug. Reggie wiggled happily, knocking Dean's heavy, black-framed glasses askew. Undersized at age twelve, the boy likely weighed less than the dog.

"Want a Coke?" Ellie asked, closing the door.

"Sure."

Reggie led the way into the living room. Dean flopped down on the couch as Ellie dug two cans of Coke out of the fridge and brought them in.

"Mother's working this afternoon," the boy said, scratching Reggie's head, "which means complete silence in the house. I tried skipping rocks off the dock, but it got boring."

"I see."

The Othman family had purchased the cottage next door—a lodge, really—from her former neighbour, Ridge Ballantyne, when the old man had finally given up trying to live on his own in the middle of nowhere. Two serious strokes had convinced him that assisted living in Kingston with close proximity to doctors and hospitals was a good idea, after all. Ellie missed him. And she was still trying to get to know her new neighbours, who'd moved in last fall.

Dean's father, Dr. Luther Othman, was a psychiatrist. He'd relocated to the area from Toronto with the idea of re-establishing his private practice in Brockville, but Ellie gathered that it wasn't going as smoothly as he'd hoped. He was working on-call at the hospital at the moment, one of several psychiatrists in the area, and clients weren't exactly breaking down his office door to see him.

Dean's mother, Mali Pernell, was a painter and illustrator whose work appeared regularly in magazines and on book covers. Also from Toronto, her father was Charles Pernell, a professor of political science at the University of Toronto, and her mother was Aranya Sangthong, a professor of anthropology. Ellie had Googled them all, of course, as soon as she'd learned who was moving in next door.

"What are you doing?" Dean kept his attention on Reggie, stroking his fur with a gentle touch. Ellie had realized early on that the boy didn't like to make eye contact.

"A little work, but I think it's time for a break."

"What kind of work?"

"Boring stuff, really. E-mail. Mostly from our headquarters people. New forms for recording overtime, who's replacing whom on vacation over the next couple of weeks; junk like that."

Dean digested this information in silence for a moment and then shrugged. "I thought being a cop was more exciting than that."

"Sometimes it is, but mostly it's just dull routine. We're a bureaucracy, Dean. One of the largest police forces in North America. A lot of policies and standard operating procedures and forms and memos."

"Don't you ever get to shoot your gun?"

Ellie paused before replying. The boy had talked to her several times before about the fact that she was a detective, and he'd shown a typical young person's curiosity about the various things that police officers might do on the job, but this was the first time he'd brought up the subject of firearms.

"Once in a while," she said. "I have to go to the range and re-qualify on a regular basis. Pass tests to prove I still know how to safely handle a weapon and can fire it with reasonable accuracy."

"Have you ever shot somebody before?"

"That's not a question you ask a police officer, Dean."

The boy flinched. "Sorry."

Ellie said nothing, studying him. He was a very nice kid, and she enjoyed his impromptu visits, but she could see that he had problems that went deeper than just the normal pre-adolescent difficulties children his age had to face. Mali had mentioned they'd left Toronto because of Dean, to get him away from a bad environment and give him a fresh start, but she hadn't gone into detail, and Ellie hadn't pressed. It wasn't any of her business.

Dean patted Reggie on the head and looked around the cottage. "Is it okay to ask another question? Instead of that one?"

"Sure."

"Do you have guns here? In your house?"

"Yes, I do. Why do you ask?"

He hesitated for a long time, long enough that Ellie knew what was coming next.

"Can I see them?"

"No. Sorry."

"What kind of guns? Ones that they give you because you're a cop, or ones you bought yourself because you like them?"

"I don't like guns, Dean. Let's get that clear right up front."

"Okay."

"We consider them tools to do our job. We're authorized to use them whenever it's absolutely necessary in order to enforce the law, but there are very specific policies that spell out when and where use of force is justified and when it's not. The bottom line is that firing a gun should be absolutely the last resort in a potentially dangerous situation. Absolutely. Period. The very last thing a police officer should want to do is discharge their firearm, believe me. It's not fun or a big adventure, like on TV or in a video game. It's a nightmare turned real."

"Okay. But what's it like, I mean, just to shoot it? On the firing range, say."

A wave of irritation surprised her. Despite her normal discomfort with children, she'd learned over the years that patience and kindness helped get her through her interactions with kids, but for some reason Dean was pushing her buttons right now and she wasn't sure why.

She shrugged, suppressing her annoyance. "I don't know. Guns make me nervous, so I feel stressed when I have to shoot. They're loud, so on the firing range you wear ear protectors, like big headphones. They kick back when they discharge, so you have to be ready for that, too."

"Where do you keep them?"

Sighing, she stood up. "All right, I'll show you something. Come with me."

She led the way into her bedroom. Reggie pushed past her so he could make a U-turn along the side of the bed and watch what they were doing.

"This is a gun safe. I store my firearms in here."

It sat in the far corner of the room, a tall metal box resembling a half-sized gym locker. "It has a biometric lock that's keyed to my fingerprints. Which means I'm the only person who can open it. I've set the system so it can never register any other fingerprints than mine. Which means when I'm done using it, it goes to the bottom of the lake. All my firearms and ammunition are in here. Someone could break in and steal all my stuff, but they wouldn't be able to get a single gun, because they're all in here."

"What if somebody breaks in when you're asleep at night? Wouldn't you want to be able to grab your gun and shoot them?"

Ellie shook her head. "First of all, it's best to let a burglar take what they want and leave without causing any violence. If they're looking for trouble, though, I've been trained to take care of myself. It might not be as easy as they think. But," she glanced at Reggie, "you're forgetting that I've got this big guy with me. Anybody stupid enough to come in here in the middle of the night is going to be leaving twice as fast as when they came in, with a Reggie-sized hole in the seat of their pants."

Dean laughed. "Right on! Can I ask—"

Ellie's cellphone began to buzz. She looked at the call display and said, "I'm sorry, Dean. We'll have to continue this another time."

"Is it work?"

"Yeah. See you later, okay?"

"Okay."

Chapter

3

It took Kevin about an hour to drive the eighty-five kilometres from the casino to the crime scene on Concession Road 9A in Drummond, Lanark County. It was a run that was pretty much straight north to begin with, following County Road 15 up to Smiths Falls, and then west to Perth and northwest into the rural township of Drummond-North Elmsley. It was a nice afternoon for a drive, so Kevin watched the scenery as it passed by on either side of the road, thinking about nothing in particular.

It was something he was trying to teach himself to do. Think about nothing in particular now and again. His friend Dr. Ash Latimer, a forensic anthropologist he'd met on a case in the Rideau Ferry area three years ago, was trying to educate him on the benefits of Zen meditation, but Kevin was proving to be a poor student. His mind was far too restless, far too easily stimulated by new information and new ideas, to yield to the nothingness of being without putting up a stiff fight.

Nevertheless, he made an effort from time to time at least to clear his mind, pay attention to his surroundings, and feel in harmony with physical existence.

Or something like that.

Concession Road 9A followed a straight line on a northeast trajectory through farmland and bush. It was a flat, narrow gravel road that would accommodate two vehicles if they slowed down to a crawl and edged over as far as possible before passing each other, but there were no shoulders to provide a safety margin, and if you met an oncoming farm vehicle, like a corn harvester or a tractor pulling a loaded hay wagon, you were pretty much out of luck.

Kevin rolled up to a barricade at the intersection of 9A and Dunlop Side Road. The uniformed officer who studied his warrant card and badge before handing him the clipboard to sign was someone he'd never met before. He passed it back and eased around the barrier.

Trees continued to crowd the road on either side, but now he could see a well-kept snake fence on the right, running through the shrubs and brush beneath the overhead power lines.

Finally he reached a stretch where the undergrowth had been cleared away on both sides. A line of vehicles was parked along the edge of the road close to the snake fence. He eased up to the tail end of the queue and got out.

About a hundred metres up ahead on the other side of the road was a house, set back a few metres with a makeshift lawn in front and a gravel driveway leading to a garage-and-workshop combination.

Almost directly across the road from the house was Kevin's objective, wheel tracks that passed through an opening in the snake fence into a woodlot.

As he approached, he saw coloured markers on the road just beyond the entrance, many of them numbered, and a white-clad forensic identification officer taking photographs of tire treads, he assumed, as well as footprints and other forms of physical evidence that might be there for the collecting.

Mature cedar trees crowded the opening into the woodlot. Walking between them, he saw a clearing that was serving as an ad hoc parking lot. He noted an OPP SUV and several cruisers; a Mercedes SUV that he recognized as belonging to Dr. Linh Phong, the coroner for Lanark-Leeds; a black van operated by a body removal service; a Drummond township fire truck; the big white forensics unit truck; and a grey unmarked Crown Victoria that he knew was assigned to Detective Inspector Ellie March.

Definitely a gathering of the clan.

Kevin had been instructed by Raintree to report to Staff Sergeant Gary Dunn, a name he was familiar with but someone he'd never met before. Staff sergeants sometimes acted as detachment commanders, but here in Lanark County Dunn served as operations manager and second-in-command to Inspector Colleen Galvin. Given the drastic resource depletion currently being experienced within the detachment, however, Dunn was also filling in as commander of the crime unit, a position normally occupied by a detective sergeant, the rung below him in rank.

He found Dunn standing alone behind the OPP SUV, on the phone. Although Kevin didn't know him to see him, the little crown on top of the three chevrons on his epaulettes gave away his rank and therefore his identity.

Dunn hiked his eyebrows and raised a finger. He wrapped up the call and put away the phone. "Welcome to Lanark, Walker."

They shook hands, a custom that was slowly returning

to social etiquette in the aftermath of the COVID-19 pandemic. Kevin had never been a fan of the elbow bump, and usually forgot himself and stuck out his hand, leading to the occasional awkward moment.

"Sorry to drag you all the way up here," Dunn said, "but we're a bit shorthanded at the moment." Dunn was tall and stocky, in his mid-forties, with pale blue eyes and thinning reddish hair.

"Glad to help. What have you got?"

"The guy's some kind of minor celebrity around here." Dunn leaned his hip against the back of the SUV. "Somebody beat the crap out of him with a baseball bat."

"Sounds bad."

"Yeah." Dunn opened his notebook. "Name of the vic's, uh, Burnham. Grant Burnham."

Kevin raised his eyebrows. "Wow. The hockey player?"

"Yeah, I guess so. I don't follow sports." Dunn pushed away from the SUV and started walking down the line of vehicles toward another clearing just beyond. "Guy across the road found him and called it in at fifteen forty-six. Coroner's got him dead for about four hours, so TOD's somewhere between eleven hundred hours and noon."

They rounded the tail end of the body removal van and were met by Identification Sergeant Dave Martin, who was in charge of the forensic identification team. The hood was pushed back on his white Tyvek coveralls and his protective mask was pulled down under his chin.

"Kevin!" he said, flashing a grin, "I heard they might draft you for this one. How's Josh?"

"About to start kindergarten. He can't wait. Neither can Janie."

Martin nodded. "I bet. I remember those days. I'm glad mine are in junior high now. Less stress, believe it or not."

"I was telling Walker this is a bad one," Dunn said.

"Yeah. Brutal." Martin led the way past the opening into the next clearing. "This is where he was doing his woodcutting thing. I'll walk you through it later. First you'll want to see the victim in situ before they pack him up and haul him away."

They followed a short path into the trees. "This peters out a few dozen metres farther in," Martin said. "Probably part of a deer trail or something. Anyway, it looks like he was chased from his woodcutting chores up to here, where he was caught and killed."

They maneuvered around plastic cones and markers. "This has already been processed," Martin said.

They reached a group gathered at the foot of a large maple tree. Martin held up a fist, military style, and they stopped.

People moved aside so that Kevin could see the body.

Martin was right.

It was brutal.

Chapter

4

"The first blow was probably to his right shoulder," said Dr. Phong. "Back at the clearing, I'd say. The humerus has been driven right out of the socket."

Kevin crouched for a closer look, trying his best to ignore the smell and the flies. Dave Martin's team had already processed the body and the immediate area around it, and the removal crew had brought in a gurney. Kevin had apparently arrived just in time to take a look before they carried it out and transported it to Ottawa for autopsy.

The victim wore a black T-shirt, jeans, black cotton sports socks, expensive-looking work gloves, and steel-toed construction boots. Everything was spattered with blood, bone fragments, and grey matter. He could see that the right arm was dislocated.

"The next blow," Dr. Phong continued, "was probably to the back of the legs. Before he reached this tree." She pointed behind Kevin to a spot with a cluster of plastic markers they'd edged around on the way in. "He fell down, got to his knees, crawled up here, and sat down with his back against the tree trunk."

She took a breath before continuing. "The terminal blow took the top of his head off, destroying most of the frontal bone just above the brow."

"Looks like the guy swung from the heels," Martin said.

Dr. Phong nodded. After a moment, she turned to Kevin. "Do you have any questions for me?"

"Not right now." He stood up.

"Come on," Martin said. "Let's go back and look at the clearing."

"Sounds good to me," Kevin said, for the second time that morning. He'd felt his gorge momentarily rise at the mess and the smell, but he'd been able to suppress it. Thankfully.

As they retreated back down the path," Martin glanced over his shoulder. "So I'm guessing you know who he was, right?"

"Sure," Kevin said. "Who doesn't?" Then he remembered that Dunn was right behind him, and he felt his face grow warm.

"Of course, his dad was a lot more famous," Martin chattered on, "but still. Who the hell would want to kill Grant Burnham?"

"That's what we're here to find out," Dunn growled as they left the path and walked into the clearing. "Right?"

"Sure," Martin replied affably. "Don't we always? Find out?"

Ellie March waited for them beside a black Ford F-150 pickup truck.

"Thanks for coming," she said to Kevin.

"No problem."

"Victim's truck," Martin said, waving at the F-150. "Keys still in the ignition. As you can see, there are several bats. The killer grabbed one, used it, and threw it back in here when he was done."

Kevin looked. The box of the truck held a white hard hat; a pair of white Nike sneakers; a big red tool box; several hand saws; plastic bottles of chain bar oil and motor oil; a coil of yellow rope; an orange outdoor extension cord; a red plastic gas can that looked full; a smaller can with "O/G" written on the side with a black permanent marker; several chunks of wood; and four baseball bats, none of which looked as though it had been used as a murder weapon. The bottom was littered with wood chips and stained with grease and oil and other substances.

"Murder weapon's already bagged and tagged," Martin said, reading his thoughts. "Truck's cleared. His cellphone was on the front passenger seat. We'll see if it can tell us anything interesting."

Kevin glanced at a small trailer half-filled with chunks of wood waiting to be split. Evidently the victim sawed them to size in back after cutting down the tree, and then hauled them up here in loads to split.

At that moment a man stepped out from behind a clump of cedar trees, his hand moving away from the fly of his trousers. He walked calmly up to them and nodded at Kevin. "You must be Walker."

"This is Detective Constable Doug Skelton," Dunn said. "He's the primary on this one. You'll be getting your assignments from him or from me."

If it hadn't been for the badge clipped to his belt, Kevin might have mistaken the man for a game warden or conservation officer. The brim of his felt Stetson hat was pulled low over his eyes, the pockets of his green cotton shirt were neatly buttoned, his black denim jeans were well-worn and comfortable looking, and his boots were of the kind that would be worn either while walking a forest trail or crossing a back pasture to find a stray calf.

"You've worked a homicide before?" A small man, Skelton carried himself with remarkable composure, his back straight, his shoulders relaxed, his eyes studying Kevin the way a farmer might size up a steer he was being offered at a price that was lower than normal.

Kevin nodded, glancing at Ellie.

"Good. Then you'll know what to do without having to be told."

"Sure," Kevin said. "Has anyone interviewed the guy across the road?"

Skelton shrugged. "Responding talked to him. Waste of time, other than to confirm the basic chronology. He doesn't know anything useful."

Kevin glanced again at Ellie, who was watching him with what he thought might be faint amusement. "Okay. Mind if I go over and ask him a few questions?"

Skelton nodded curtly. "Be my guest. Let us know if he suddenly remembers something earth-shaking." He turned and walked away.

Kevin looked for Dunn, but he was over with Dr. Phong, watching the removal team wrestle their gurney with its gruesome burden off the path and over to their van.

Dave Martin had already disappeared somewhere.

He looked at Ellie, but she'd taken out her cellphone and was making a call. She raised an eyebrow at him and turned away.

Okay fine, he thought. *Whatever*.

Chapter

5

As Kevin crossed the road, he waved at Identification Constable Serge Landry, who was packing up his evidence case after having finished his work on the shoulder of the road. He hadn't recognized Landry before, as the man's hood and mask had been up and his back partially turned, but now the forensics man gave him a smile and a nod.

Landry was an experienced tire tread and footprint specialist on Dave Martin's team, and the evidence he collected at crime scenes often played an important part in cases brought to court by the Crown attorney.

Kevin had recently picked up a copy of Bodziak's Footwear Impression Evidence, 2nd Edition, but hadn't had a chance to start reading it yet. Maybe this coming weekend he could find some time to—

Focus, Kevin.

Max Macdonald was washing his car in the driveway,

and as Kevin approached he turned off the hose and tossed it onto the lawn, drying his hands on a rag from his back pocket. The car was a black older model Hyundai Elantra hatchback. Macdonald evidently took good care of it. The car looked to be in excellent condition for a vehicle that was at least twelve years old.

"Detective Constable Walker," Kevin said, taking out his wallet to flash his warrant card and badge. "Do you have time for a few questions?"

"Sure. Okay if we sit down?" Macdonald pointed at a pair of lawn chairs on his front porch.

"That's fine." Kevin followed him up a short walkway made of paving stones onto the porch, a small cement rectangle with a clear view of the road in both directions.

Macdonald sat down in the chair on the right, which had a little stand next to it holding an ash tray and an open beer can. Kevin sat down in the other one.

"Does anyone else live here with you, Mr. Macdonald?" he asked, taking out his notebook and pen.

"Call me Max. No, I'm by myself here. Divorced."

Kevin nodded. He was an odd-looking little guy, his fuzzy black hair uncombed, his hairline receding rather severely above a domed forehead, and his beard scruffy and thin. His eyebrows were pointed in the middle, like chevrons, and they gave him a strange, almost satanic look.

"I understand you were the one who found Mr. Burnham's body."

"Yeah, yeah. It was awful. I'm still not sure how I made it back here before puking."

"Did you know him at all?"

"Yeah." His face brightened a little. "Yeah! We talked now and then, pretty much whenever he'd come out to the lot. He's a great guy. Really friendly. Not stuck up at all, for somebody as famous as him. Yeah." His expression fell again. "He *was* a nice guy. Very nice."

"When was the last time you spoke to him?"

"This morning. Like I told the officer."

"About what time would that be?"

"Around a quarter to ten. I'd just pulled out of my driveway when he came along. I was going into town to pick up a few things. We stopped and talked for a minute. I rolled my window down, so he did too. I asked if he wanted some help, but he said no. Sometimes I go over and stack cordwood for him while he's running the splitter, you know, just to be helpful, but he seemed to want to be by himself this morning."

"What makes you say that?"

"I dunno, just his mood. He seemed a little down." Macdonald unrolled a pack of cigarettes from the sleeve of his T-shirt. "Mind?"

Kevin shrugged.

Macdonald stuck a cigarette between his lips, removed a small lighter from the empty side of the ashtray, and lit up. "He was sort of quiet. Like he was thinking about something." He exhaled smoke out of the corner of his mouth, away from Kevin.

"Like what?"

"He never talked about personal stuff. He's very private that way, so I never ask too many questions. I just told him to have a good day and drove off. That was it."

"Tell me about how you happened to find him."

"Yeah." He tapped ash and stared across the road. "I guess I gotta."

Kevin waited.

"I got home a little after lunch. I had something in town, at Burger King. I put my stuff away and went out into the shop to do a little work. I build birdhouses. It's a hobby, but I have a table at the farmer's market and I sell them." He smiled faintly. "I don't make enough from them to get

Revenue Canada all upset with me, though. Like I say, it's more for fun than anything else."

"Where do you work?"

"At the Hyundai dealership in town. I'm the desk clerk in the service department. I answer the phone, book appointments, deal with customers, drive cars around the lot, that sort of thing. The money's not so great, but it keeps me busy and pays the bills."

"So you were in your garage this afternoon."

"Yeah. I threw a cassette into the player and worked on this big bluebird house I got going. Like a hotel for birds, eh? It's almost done. It's funny how the time passes when I'm out there. Anyway, I gave it the first coat of paint and stepped outside for some fresh air and a smoke. Paint fumes are a bitch, pardon the language."

"What time was that?"

"I'm not sure. Let's see. I played both sides of three different cassettes, so, uh, almost three hours, give or take. What time did I go out, again? I guess around twelve thirty. So I guess it would have been about three thirty or so. Does that sound right?"

"You came out for a smoke. Then what?"

"I don't know. I looked at my car and thought it needed to be washed. I like doing it by hand instead of going through the car washes, you know? Sometimes they scratch the finish, even though they're not supposed to. Anyway, right then I noticed I couldn't hear Grant's chain saw across the way. Or the splitter. Maybe he'd gone home already. I wanted to stretch my legs a bit, after sitting at my workbench for so long, so I walked across to see how his firewood was coming."

Kevin raised his eyebrows. "Is that something you normally do? Go onto his property without him knowing about it?"

Macdonald coughed on smoke. "Shit. Sorry. Agh. No,

no, he was okay with me going over there. He told me before he had some trails he'd cut in back, and I was welcome to go over for a walk whenever I wanted to. Just no hunting. He hated that. I told him I didn't even own a squirt pistol, so no worries there."

"You're saying you had his permission? That he didn't consider it trespassing?"

"Not at all. He wasn't that kind of guy, all territorial and shit, is what I'm trying to say. He didn't mind me going over. He was totally easy going about stuff."

"Okay. What happened when you went over?"

Macdonald tapped his cigarette over the ashtray. "First thing I noticed was his truck. It was still there. I was surprised. Like, I was sure he'd gone home already."

They watched the removal service's black van appear in the entrance across the road. It stopped. The driver put on his left-hand turn signal. He looked both ways, eased out onto the road, and accelerated away.

"Shit," Macdonald murmured. "Shit."

Kevin waited.

"Okay. Yeah. Sorry. So I went up to where he'd been working. His chain saw was there, on the ground. His ear protectors, too. It looked like he'd been running the splitter, but it must have run out of gas. The spout was in the gas can, like he was going to refill it."

"The gas can in the back of the truck?"

"No, no. That's his spare. Plus the oil and gas mix for his saws."

"What happened next?"

"Well, I looked around a bit. I went behind the big stack of cordwood, to see if he was lying on the ground or something, but he wasn't there. Once someone gets a little older you start to think about heart attacks and stuff, so I was worried maybe he'd had one. Anyway, I figured he must have gone for a walk, you know, on one of his trails

at the back of the clearing, but I wasn't going to go looking
for him. If he was back there, fine."

"So you decided not to look around anymore?"

"Yeah. I was going to head back, but then . . ."

"Uh huh?"

"I, you know. Smelled it."

"Smelled what?"

"Him. You know. The wind came up and oh, God, I
could smell it. Shit and . . . other stuff. I didn't want to,
Christ, but I had to go look. It was bad. I went up the little
path and . . ."

"I'll need you to describe what you saw, Mr. Macdonald."

"Yeah." He stubbed out his cigarette in the ashtray,
took another one, lit it, and inhaled deeply. "Jesus. He was
sitting, you know, with his back against the tree. The top of
his head was gone. I—" Choking a little, he stopped.

An OPP cruiser came out of the entrance across the
road and headed off in the same direction as the removal
van.

Kevin gave Macdonald a moment to collect himself.

"Sorry, sir. It was just . . . really bad."

"That's all right. I understand. Did you see any vehicles
around when you came home after lunch? Anyone
parked on the side of the road or maybe in the woodlot
entrance?"

Macdonald shook his head.

Kevin watched a dark green Range Rover emerge from
the woodlot and turn in the opposite direction from the
hearse and the OPP cruiser. It accelerated away with Doug
Skelton behind the wheel.

"Tell me again about the conversation you had with
him this morning."

"Sure. No problem." He pulled on the cigarette and
exhaled raggedly. "I said, 'Good morning, Grant' and he

said good morning back. I called him that. 'Grant.' First time it was 'Mr. Burnham,' you know, when we first met, but he got annoyed and told me just to call him Grant, so after that I did. Anyway, I said something lame about him going in to cut more firewood and he said yeah, so I asked if he wanted some help and he said no. I thought he looked a bit upset about something so I asked if everything was okay, and he kind of smiled and said yeah, that he just needed to get away from things this morning and sweat out a problem that was on his mind. He said to me one time that cutting firewood was like therapy for him, or something like that, so I figured this was one of those times. So I said, 'Have a good one,' and he nodded and rolled up his window and drove in. That was pretty much it."

"Do you have any idea what this problem might have been that he mentioned?"

Macdonald puffed out his cheeks. "Hunh! He didn't talk to me about stuff like that. I guess I already said that, but it's true." He frowned.

"There's something else?"

"No. Not really. Just stuff I heard around town lately."

"Oh?"

"Just talk. I heard he had some investments that took a shit-kicking during the pandemic, plus his business had to close for, like, a year or so, so I figured sometimes it was money problems he had on his mind when he came out here. So maybe it was that."

"Something to do with his finances? Or his business?"

Macdonald shrugged. "I don't know. Could be. Like I said, he kept all that kind of stuff to himself, but sometimes you can tell."

He fell silent, and Kevin let him stare across the road for a few moments, smoking his cigarette, before standing up and handing him a business card.

"Thanks for your time, Mr. Macdonald. Give me a call

if you think of anything else I should know."

"It's Max," he said, taking the card without looking up.

Chapter

6

Ellie stood by herself for a moment, looking around the clearing where the attack on Grant Burnham had begun. Ident had pulled the keys from the truck for fingerprinting and trace analysis, but Dunn had ordered a patrol rotation to maintain the security of the crime scene for the foreseeable future, so no one cared if the vehicle remained unlocked.

The same lack of concern went for Burnham's equipment and tools. No one would be coming in to touch them, so they'd remain out here exactly where they sat, rain or shine, until the scene was released. Whenever that would happen.

She waved at Dave Martin as he climbed into the passenger seat of the forensic identification vehicle. As soon as he slammed the door the truck backed up, turned, and disappeared.

Earlier, Martin had sent someone to the edge of the clearing to take a look down the trails that led to the back of the property, but they'd returned empty-handed except for a few dozen photographs they'd taken with their digital cameras. Everything else, as far as Ellie could see, had been thoroughly processed, and now it was up to the lab to tell them whatever story could be told by the physical evidence they'd collected.

It was a process she'd directed many times. It was how she lived her life.

Right now she was by herself, alone in the middle of a crime scene. It reminded her of those moments when she'd be sitting on the back deck, smoking a cigarette, and the wind would suddenly drop and the birds would fall silent, as though the world were hesitating, drawing in a long breath, before deciding that existence was worth continuing on with a little while longer.

She normally felt comfortable with solitude, with the pauses between things, momentarily separated from human activity, by herself, wrapped in aloneness. It didn't bother her. Sometimes, she sought it out. Welcomed a little isolation. There was so much noise and nonsense and horror around her in the world that sometimes she wanted to slip away from it for a bit, like a stick floating downstream that finds its way along a side current to an eddy where it pauses, free from the insistent pull of necessity for a few moments; just a stick, motionless on the surface of the water.

Lately, however, she'd noticed that her mood was tending to sink down into stretches of brown funk. Not prolonged depression, not something she was particularly concerned about, but a definite sense that something was bothering her at a very low level.

It wasn't family-related, she was sure. Her ex-husband and children had moved on from her years ago. She no longer had any contact with them, and she'd dealt with the feelings associated with their loss quite a while ago. She understood that her daughters never thought about her now. She was nothing more than a fading memory, compartmentalized into a back corner of the brain that was never accessed. She was fine with that. She loved them; in her heart she wished them well; but it would never go any further than that.

As for her natural father, Jay Lippincott, he'd struggled with the COVID-19 virus midway through the pandemic and had stayed in intensive care for three weeks. Thankfully he'd recovered and was slowly working his way back to health. They spoke twice a week on the telephone, Thursday evenings and Sunday evenings, and their conversations were always cordial. Occasionally pleasant. They'd overcome the stiffness that was natural when two strangers discovered they were actually family and decided to make an effort to do something about it, and Ellie often looked forward to talking to him.

It was always she who called and Jay who waited for his cellphone to ring.

The brown funk wasn't related to her job either, she didn't think, but she'd found herself growing more impatient and grouchy with others while working. Over the last few years she'd had opportunities to move up in the ranks and had spent a little time seconded into the director's chair in the Criminal Investigation Branch, but she hadn't particularly enjoyed the experience and preferred now to remain where she was. She was a firm believer in the Peter Principle and would rather not rise to her level of incompetence if she could possibly avoid it.

Was it her love life, or lack thereof?

Her good friend Danny Merrick, an assistant commissioner with the Royal Canadian Mounted Police, was beginning the second year of a long-term assignment in Brussels, and while they kept in touch, their relationship had evolved into a long-distance thing that was more a friendship now than a romance.

Since she wasn't the kind of person who needed constant attention or companionship or physical intimacy, she didn't believe her inactivity on this front was the cause of her current funk.

So if it wasn't family, and it wasn't her job, and it wasn't her dormant sex life, then what the hell was bothering her?

She made a sound at the back of her throat. This was ridiculous. Here she was, standing in a clearing in the middle of nowhere, the late afternoon sun in her eyes, fresh air in her lungs, birds calling to one another in the distance. Alive. Still in the middle of her life, dammit. With a long way still to go.

Take it or leave it, Ellie. This is it. Your life. Don't you dare feel sorry for yourself.

She heard footsteps on gravel, walking toward her.

She knew from the gait that it was Kevin, returning from his interview across the road.

She removed the scowl from her face and turned to watch him trudge across the clearing toward her.

Chapter

7

"Talked to Dunn," Kevin said, unbuttoning his jacket and loosening the knot of his tie. "The scene's secure. Everyone else took off, I see."

"Just us chickens left," Ellie replied. "Did the witness have anything useful to tell you?"

"Just that he talked to the victim briefly this morning and that Burnham seemed a little upset. He thought it might have had something to do with money, his business or something like that. Where'd Skelton go?"

"Home. Something about bringing in his sheep before dark. He's a farmer, apparently."

"I thought he was a detective."

She heard the frustration in his voice but didn't react. "Dave Martin's on his way to Perth. The warrant came in to search the victim's factory, and Dave's got SOCOs already there, so that's about to happen. Ditto with Burnham's house at Balderson."

"Okay."

Scenes of crime officers were front-line uniformed constables who were trained and qualified to perform basic forensics tasks such as fingerprinting, photography, and other evidence collection. They provided support to forensic identification units in the OPP when Ident resources were unavailable or spread a little thin. Dave Martin had developed a loyal and motivated cadre of SOCOs in the region, and he often delivered much of their training himself.

They often told Ellie that their forensics responsibilities were the most motivating and challenging part of their job. For her part, she'd never encountered any problems with their work.

"Obviously," she went on, "this crime unit has a serious shortage of people. Apart from Skelton, they have one other detective on strength right now, and she's currently working a nasty home invasion case. I talked to Colleen about it. She's arranged for the regional office to send someone to Balderson to attend the house search and stick around to help out with things. You and she will stay with this for as long as it takes."

"Okay."

As a major case manager, Ellie was a headquarters resource, reporting to the commander of the Criminal Investigations Branch in Orillia. She and her colleagues were mandated to oversee and direct investigations of homicide, attempted murder, kidnapping, and other major crimes within the province while regional management provided local detectives and support staff to conduct the actual investigative work.

Ellie held functional authority over the case, but line authority rested with the detachment commander, Colleen Galvin, and her local staff. Ellie therefore played no role in resource management other than to make sure there were enough qualified people working the case to get the job done.

Hence her conversation with Galvin and her suggestion that there might be a detective in the Regional Support Team working out of Smiths Falls that could be made available. She dropped the name; Galvin made the call; and the detective was ordered to attend.

"Go over to Balderson first," Ellie told Kevin. "Meet with Detective Constable Freeling; make sure everything's under control; and then go down to Perth. Sound like a plan?"

"Sure."

Ellie patted his shoulder. "You'll have to be patient, Kevin. Not all crime units are created equal."

Chapter

8

Kevin pulled over onto the shoulder of the road behind a line of three vehicles. At the front of the line was the white OPP van belonging to forensics; the second was an OPP cruiser; and bringing up the rear was a grey Dodge Charger, signed out of the motor pool, no doubt, by the RST detective Kevin was about to meet.

He walked up to the tape at the end of the driveway and submitted his credentials to another provincial constable he'd never seen before.

Grant Burnham's house on Concession Road 8A sat on a pleasant, five-acre treed lot within a stone's throw of the intersection that constituted Balderson, a hamlet made famous by its cheese factory of the same name.

Dominating the enormous front lawn were two mature willow trees. Behind the trees, set back more than fifty metres from the road, was the house itself. Probably about a hundred years old, it was a three-storey, yellow brick beauty with two chimneys and bay windows on either side of the neat front verandah.

Nice place, Kevin thought as he ducked under the tape. Expensive.

A tall, blond woman stepped forward and held out her elbow. "I'm Sonja Freeling. You must be Kevin Walker."

At six feet, five inches and two hundred and thirty pounds, he towered over her. Remembering the protocol for once, Kevin bumped elbows with her. "Nice to meet you. The warrant got here, did it?"

She nodded. "No signs of a disturbance or any other problems. Strictly secondary."

The decision to treat the victim's home as a secondary crime scene meant that although the murder was judged not to have been committed here, evidence might still be collected that would assist in the investigation in a meaningful way. Best-case scenario would be direct proof of someone's culpability. Also welcome would be background or developmental information that would point to a suspect.

Worst case? A dry hole that told them nothing they could use going forward.

Sonja stepped under the tape and stood at the side of the road. "Right now Ident's going through the victim's home computer, his laptop, and other electronics stuff. I've got a few minutes."

Kevin joined her, and they ran their eyes up and down the road.

"The neighbour on this side," she pointed to her left, in the direction of Balderson, "are the Colquitts. Mrs. Colquitt told Damon," she glanced over her shoulder at the uniformed constable with the clipboard, "that their son walks Burnham's dog for him. Has a key. He took the dog out just before we got here, so Damon told Mrs. Colquitt that when he gets back they should keep the dog with them until we say otherwise."

"Okay."

She pointed at a house across the road, about thirty metres down in the other direction. "No response. Probably at work. I'll follow up on them later."

Kevin nodded. There were no other houses nearby that they could canvass for potential witnesses. Which meant that this particular scene would likely be fairly straightforward and uninformative.

"How about we stroll down and talk to the dog-walker family?"

"Sure."

They started along the shoulder of the road, Kevin moving to the outside as a point of etiquette, something his mother had taught him to do long ago, when she was still well enough for them to take an occasional walk together.

Sonja noticed. She smiled. "So you're Leeds's fair-haired boy."

Kevin snorted. "Hardly."

"Colleen requested you by name, on Ellie's recommendation. Must mean you're pretty good."

He threw her a sharp look. The smile was friendly, he decided, and not mocking or challenging, so he let out a breath. "I've worked a couple of these before."

She pushed her red-framed glasses back up onto the bridge of her nose. She was in her late forties. Her eyebrows were light brown, and her fair hair, streaked with light brown, was showing some grey. The fact that she was on a first-name basis with the Lanark detachment commander and a GHQ major case manager suggested she was part of the network. Or he was supposed to think along those lines.

The Colquitt house was much closer to the road than Burnham's. A nearly-new Mercedes SUV sat in the short paved driveway, a little dusty from having been driven on back-country dirt roads but immaculate inside. The house had a downstairs window looking out onto Burnham's driveway, and another window upstairs, likely in a bedroom, that would also provide a view of the property next door.

Kevin took a photo of the rear tires of the Mercedes before Sonja led the way up onto the front porch.

They badged the woman who answered the door and identified themselves.

"I'm Lona Colquitt," the woman said. "The officer said something's happened to Grant. Is he—"

"May we come inside for a few minutes and ask you some questions?" Sonja asked, her foot already inside the door.

Lona waved them in. The place was as immaculate as the interior of the Mercedes. They followed her through a doorway on the right into a large living room. Sonja sat in an expensive-looking antique armchair, and Kevin chose the end of an oak settee with spotless upholstery. Lona sat down and folded her hands in her lap.

"We understand your son's keeping Mr. Burnham's dog at the moment." Sonja glanced at Kevin as he brought out his notebook and pen.

"Yes, Trace took Buster for a walk on our trail. They should be back in about twenty minutes or so."

"What kind of dog is it?"

"A boxer. Purebred."

Sonja smiled. "Nice breed. My mother has one."

"He's very well trained."

"Is your husband at home right now?"

"He's at work."

Kevin caught a side glance from Sonja, which he interpreted as an invitation to jump in. "What does he do for a living, Mrs. Colquitt?"

"Mack's an aircraft mechanic. He works at YOW."

Kevin wrote it down. "Ottawa International Airport."

"Yes."

"And how about you? What do you do?"

"I'm a cosmetics technician. Currently unemployed. Is Grant badly hurt?"

"I'm afraid he's dead, Mrs. Colquitt."

She made a sound at the back of her throat. "What? What? What happened?"

"Someone murdered him, Mrs. Colquitt."

They gave her a few moments to absorb the news and make an effort to compose herself.

"I don't. I don't. I don't understand. Who would want to hurt Grant? I don't understand. Oh God, what will I tell Trace? He'll be devastated."

"Was he close to Mr. Burnham?"

"Grant was really nice to him. Patient. Paid him more to look after Buster than a professional service would have cost. It gave Trace a good summer job, which was nice. He wasn't able to find anything in town this year."

"How about you and Mr. Colquitt? How'd you get along with Mr. Burnham?"

"Oh, God." She took another few moments to stare at the floor, using the back of her hand to brush away tears. "Fine. We were fine. No problems. Grant's a good neighbour. A really good neighbour."

Sonja took a small packet of tissues from her jacket pocket and passed them over. "Tell us about his comings and goings. What was a typical week for him?"

"Um. Thanks." Lona broke the seal on the pack and pulled out a tissue. "We're not nosy types. We mind our own business."

"I understand. Please tell us whatever you might know. Anything at all could be a help."

"Sure. Okay. He has his factory. In town. He went in

there pretty much every day." She blew her nose and kept the wadded tissue in her hand. "Monday to Friday. Left in the morning and came back in the afternoon. Took the weekends off. Sundays he was usually around, and every now and again he'd set up a big canopy tent thing and have a barbecue on the front lawn. We were invited over, and some of his friends would be there. Saturdays he went to his woodlot, on the next line over. It's only about ten minutes away, so it was really convenient for him. He loved going there."

"Did you know any of his friends?"

"Not really. I met his business partner, Mr. Moore, and a few people who work for them. And of course his dad."

"Bobby Burnham."

"Yes. A real card, that man. They called him Bobby the Buffoon. I never thought it was a very nice name. But you probably know that already, if you're a hockey fan."

Sonja nodded. "I understand Mr. Burnham—Grant—was divorced. Did you ever meet his ex-wife? At any of those barbecues, say?"

Lona shook her head. "Once or twice he had a girlfriend over, but I never got the idea it was anything serious. More like a passing fancy. Willowy blondes; the occasional redhead."

Something in her voice caused Kevin to glance at Sonja. "Can you think of anyone at all," he said, "who might have had bad feelings directed against him?"

She shook her head vigorously. "No. Absolutely not. He was such a nice man. I can't imagine anyone wanting to hurt him."

"We'll want to talk to your son a little later," Sonja said, standing up. "I trust that won't be a problem?"

"I'll talk to Mack about it. My husband." She got to her feet. "I think he'll be able to do it. Trace, I mean. Once he gets over the shock and everything."

"How old is he, Mrs. Colquitt?"

"Sixteen."

"Is he your only child?"

She nodded, tugging at the seat of her beige riding breeches and pulling down the cuffs on her long-sleeved white T-shirt.

"Do you own a horse?" Sonja asked.

"No."

Kevin put away his notebook and handed her a card. "Call if you think of anything else we should know."

"I will. Thanks."

"We'll be in touch to arrange an interview with your son," Sonja said, passing her a card.

Kevin led the way out into the hallway and, opening the door, turned around. Lona stopped, blinking up at him.

"One more thing. Did you happen to see Mr. Burnham at any time this morning? Maybe driving down his driveway? Or anyone else coming or going? Any vehicles other than his?"

"No, I'm sorry. Nothing."

"All right. Thanks."

Out on the paved driveway, Kevin took out his cellphone to check the time. "I'd better hustle down to Perth."

Sonja nodded. "Weird vibes, eh?"

"Yeah."

"If those riding pants were any tighter, she'd need surgery to take them off."

"I didn't notice."

"The hell you didn't." She gave him a friendly smile. "Nice to meet you, Kevin Walker. I'll catch up with you later."

"Sounds good," he said.

For the third time that day.

Chapter

9

It was a little after seven in the evening, or nineteen hundred hours, as Staff Sergeant Dunn would put it, when Ellie arrived home. Rolling down Tamarack Lane, the gravel road that accessed all the cottages on this side of Sparrow Lake, she parked in the little space at the top of her property and got out.

She was bone tired. Standing around a crime scene in the middle of nowhere for almost four hours had taken a bit more out of her than she was used to, and she could feel soreness in her back muscles as she walked down the slope to her cottage. Time to gear up the exercise regimen again, apparently.

Although darkness was still an hour away, the sun had reached the tops of the trees on the other side of the lake, and twilight had begun to leak through the pines around her cottage and the lodge next door, causing her to walk with care down the pathway.

A figure stepped out of the shadows alongside the lodge. Her hand went to the weapon holstered under her jacket and then relaxed as she recognized Dr. Luther Othman, her next-door neighbour.

"Good evening, Ellie."

"Dr. Othman." Ellie walked around to the lakefront side of her cottage. Othman followed her. If he'd noticed the instinctive movement of her hand, he gave no indication.

"I was wondering if you might have a few minutes to talk."

Ellie paused at the bottom of the deck stairs. "What about?"

"Dean." Othman ran a hand over his scalp, as though to smooth down the few remaining strands of hair on the top of his head.

"All right. Come on inside." She went up the stairs and unlocked the glass sliding door that led into her living room. Reggie stood there waiting for her, his big tail whipping back and forth.

She opened the door and stepped in, nudging Reggie back a step with her shin. The dog retreated amiably, allowing them enough room to enter.

Othman moved around the coffee table to sit down on the sofa, which gave Ellie a chance to let Reggie slip outside.

"Have a pee and come right back," she said, knowing the dog would do whatever he wanted to do and before too long would be kicking at the kitchen door to be let back in.

"Coffee?" she asked, sliding the glass door closed but leaving it unlocked.

"Sure. Thanks."

She filled the coffee maker with water, put in a pod, and hit the switch. "Dean came over for a visit this afternoon."

She walked into the bedroom, took off her jacket, and threw it on the bed.

"Yes," his voice came from the sofa, "that's why I thought we should talk."

Ellie opened the gun safe, removed her firearm, dropped the magazine and cleared the chamber, and put everything into the safe. She wasn't surprised at all that Othman had shown up so promptly after Dean's visit. The boy had no doubt answered questions about their conversation, likely after mentioning something that had upset Othman. She closed the safe and locked it, knowing what was on his mind.

"How do you take your coffee?" she asked, walking back into the kitchen.

"Black, please. I'm sorry to bother you like this, as soon as you get home from work. I heard on the news that something happened in Drummond; a body was found. I suppose that's where you've been."

"Yes." She set down the cup in front of him on the coffee table with a napkin and went back to make another one for herself.

"I can imagine how difficult it must be. Your kind of work."

"It has its challenges."

He tried his coffee. "This is good. I think I like your machine better than ours. It makes a lot better coffee. Is this Arabica?"

"Just plain Colombian."

"Well, it's good."

Ellie put a spoonful of honey into her coffee and stirred vigorously. She recognized the tactic of subject avoidance, having come across it so many times while interviewing witnesses and interrogating suspects, but she thought it was faintly amusing to be encountering it now in a psychiatrist. Was it deliberate? Was he stalling until she was sitting down across from him, giving him her full attention, allowing him to take control of the moment and give it the direction he wanted? Or was it just instinctive, the behaviour of an upset next-door neighbour?

She crossed the room and dropped into her recliner, aware again of how tired she was.

"Dean said you were talking to him about guns today," Othman said.

"The subject came up."

"He told me he was the one asking questions about it."

Ellie said nothing. Although the family had lived next door for about ten months now, she still didn't really know Dr. Othman all that well. She'd spent the most time with Dean, and had had several conversations with Mali, but Dr. Othman had remained rather distant. Her initial take was that he was a very focused and intelligent man, but wrapped up in his work and not always accessible. It was this last problem, she believed, that he was trying to correct by moving his family to Sparrow Lake for a fresh start.

"Mali and I are concerned," he went on, "because he hasn't shown a lot of interest in guns before. He doesn't play a lot of video games or watch a lot of television or movies."

"Oh?"

"He plays online chess. He belongs to a club. He likes role-playing games where there's a lot of moving around, exploring landscapes and solving puzzles. Violence upsets him."

"When he visits," Ellie said, "he talks a lot about the woods and the lake. He seems to really like it here. He showed me a journal he's keeping."

Othman brightened. "Yes, that was Mali's idea. He records all the various kinds of birds and insects that he sees, he sketches plants and flowers, and that sort of thing. A couple of weeks ago, though, he started asking his mother questions about what was involved in becoming a police officer."

"Me too," Ellie said. "He wanted to know how the various laws work, procedures we have to follow when making an arrest, whether or not we can go into someone's house whenever we want to. That sort of thing. I explained to him how warrants work, what probable cause is, what 'a man's home is his castle' means and where it comes from in British common law; other stuff like that." She paused. "This was the first time he brought up the subject of firearms."

Othman nodded. "I looked you up. You killed someone in Westport a year or two ago. I'm a little concerned about him spending time with someone who's capable of taking another person's life."

"And yet you went ahead and moved in next door anyway."

Othman smiled sheepishly. "Well, I looked you up today. After talking to Dean. I will say, though, that I saw a lot of other things. Service awards; a commendation from the prime minister. Very impressive."

"What do you want from me, Dr. Othman?"

"I don't know. I'm sorry. We're really very protective of Dean, because he's been through a lot and he's still fragile, still trying to put it back together again."

Ellie put down her coffee and stood up. "Let me show you what I showed him."

She took him into the bedroom and stood in front of the gun safe. "Biometric security. No possibility of programming the lock for anyone else. Impossible to break into by force. The guns stay in there until I go to work, and they go back in there as soon as I get home. You probably heard me putting my service weapon away when your coffee was brewing. I explained all this to Dean, in no uncertain terms, and I made it very clear I don't like guns and I don't like shooting them. They're a tool I carry with me as part of my job. I'm fully trained in their safe handling, and I understand they're a very last resort when use of force can't be avoided. If he's developed a sudden enthusiasm for shooting, he sure as hell didn't get it from me."

Othman went back out to the sofa and sat down.

"Why don't you tell me what's going on?" Ellie invited, easing back into her recliner.

"I don't know if he's actually serious about this interest in police work or if it's just another thing his curiosity has fastened on. Maybe it's something he'll explore for a while and then move on from. He's only twelve."

"When I was twelve, I wanted to be a dancer more than anything else in the world. You can see how that turned out."

Othman laughed nervously. "Exactly. He's got a lot of time to choose a path. Not that police work wouldn't have its rewards, of course. But I expect his interests will take him in another direction. No offence."

"None taken."

"You should understand the situation. He's a victim of extensive, prolonged bullying. It was happening at the school he was attending in Markham. It took Mali and me quite a while to realize what was happening. To our eternal shame. He wouldn't talk about it; he blamed the cuts and bruises on gym class or whatever, but I should have recognized it for what it was a lot sooner. I still haven't forgiven myself."

He sighed. "Much of it was physical, but a lot was also psychological. Taunting, teasing, making fun of his name and calling him Mothman, ridiculing his glasses and poor eyesight, all the sorts of things kids are so damned good at doing. Once we understood what was happening, we did the things parents always do. Met with his teacher, the school principal, even sat down with the parents of a couple of the kids. None of it made any difference. Bullying is supposed to be a hot-button issue these days, but it's surprising how defensive and evasive people get when a real case is actually brought to their attention and they're somehow personally implicated in fixing it."

Ellie nodded.

"I'm a psychiatrist, as I guess you know, but I don't specialize in children. Surprisingly, when it comes to my own son I can screw up just as badly as any other parent. I floundered around with him for a while, making things worse, and then did the smart thing and reached out to colleagues and found someone qualified in the field. She saw Dean half a dozen times before we moved, and she referred us to someone in Brockville who also seems to be good. He's making progress, but there's still a long way to go."

"Progress is important," Ellie said.

"It definitely is, but I'm still walking on eggshells, I have to admit." He folded his hands and squeezed them together. "There was a bit of self-harm, some cutting, and once he hit his thumb with a hammer, deliberately. He cracked the bone, but thank God it wasn't worse." He stared at Ellie. "That's why the sudden talk of guns set off alarm bells in my head. He talks to me a bit more than before, and he seems somewhat better, but if he's still thinking about hurting himself and our new neighbour has a bunch of guns lying around, then my stress level just went through the roof."

"I understand."

"I'm really glad you showed me the safe and explained how you handle your weapons. Maybe I can sleep a little better tonight. Actually," he tried to smile again, "we thought it was great when we learned we were moving in next door to a police officer. Mali and I both thought it was a plus; it made us feel more secure about living in a rural environment instead of the city. And we hoped that you might be a positive influence on Dean. We still do, most definitely. So I didn't mean to come off as hostile or critical of you. I'd hate to think I've spoiled Dean's opportunity to make an important adult friend."

Ellie shook her head. "No problem there. But if you'd rather that he have no further contact with me, I'll understand. It's been his choice up to now, but I'll respect whatever decision you make. He's a nice kid. I like having him around, but it's up to you folks how you want to handle things."

"As I said, I'd like you to be a positive influence on him. If he's not bothering you, and it's okay, I'd like him to continue talking to you from time to time."

"If that's what Dean wants," Ellie said, "then I'm game. Plus, Reggie really likes him. They're already best buddies."

"Thank you, Ellie."

She nodded. "No problem, Dr. Othman."

Chapter

10

The Burnham & Moore Wood Working Company occupied a former warehouse on North Street in Perth. Kevin admired the look of it, all brick and glass and steel, as he opened the front door and stepped inside.

The card in the window said that the little showroom at the front was open on Saturdays until nine in the evening, no doubt to maximize purchasing opportunities for people too busy working on weekdays to make it in before six. This particular Saturday, however, was a failure. Armchairs, benches, live-edge side tables, dining room sets, and kitchen islands with high stools, all arranged in attractive groupings, were without potential customers, like deserted little oases of finely crafted utility.

Music played faintly from speakers overhead. Light jazz of some kind, with a high-pitched English horn and an orchestra in the background. Kenny G or someone?

A young man in a grey suit and brown shoes approached with a mournful expression on his face. "I'm sorry, we're closed. I should have put up a sign."

Kevin badged him.

"Oh yeah, sure. Sorry. Everyone's in back. This way."

"You left the music on?"

"Damn, I forgot. Mr. Moore asked me to turn it off, but then an officer started asking me questions and it slipped my mind."

Kevin followed him to a uniformed constable standing in front of a pair of swinging doors. Finally, someone he recognized.

"Shawn."

"Kevin."

The swinging doors opened into the factory proper. Kevin looked at a row of enclosed offices on the right and wondered if they were located there to help insulate the showroom from the noise of the manufacturing area, which dominated the rest of the building.

A white-garbed man stepped out of the largest office in the row and shoved back his hood. "Kevin, you made it." It was Dave Martin.

"How's it looking?"

Martin stripped off his gloves and dropped them into an evidence bag. "Same old same old. Some computerized files but a lot of paper. As old-fashioned as this building, I guess. Sully's plowing through it all right now."

Identification Constable Cole Sullivan was the member of Dave Martin's team who specialized in financial records, business documents, and similar forms of evidence. While an expert forensic accountant would be called in to analyze his findings when something significant turned up, Sullivan's training ensured that the team wouldn't miss important files related to the financial aspect of the investigation while executing their search warrant.

Typical of Martin's team, he was also a qualified document examiner, handwriting specialist, and, for something completely different, he knew a thing or two about bugs. In an entomological way. Someone else was up to speed on the electronic kind.

Behind Martin, Kevin could see a SOCO finishing up her fingerprint collection tasks in Burnham's office. "I need to talk to the partner," he said, more to himself than anyone else.

"I think he's up front somewhere." Martin strolled off to point out something to the SOCO.

Their search warrant for the premises was similar to the one they'd executed in the Brockville offices of the Clinics for Kenya charity four or five years ago. It covered Burnham's office, the board room, a kitchenette and cafeteria, and other common areas of the factory where Burnham might have spent time. It also covered the factory's security setup, including the key card entry system and video security.

The woodworkers and labourers were all at home today, since the manufacturing portion of the business operated on a Monday-to-Friday basis, so everyone Kevin saw around him worked for the OPP. He returned to the front, where he found the salesman looking out the window at the early evening traffic passing in the street.

"Where's Walter Moore?" Kevin asked.

The salesman turned around. "Oh, he's just in here." He led the way toward a doorway on the far side. "This is our little office, where we write up the deals."

"I heard my name," a man said, coming out of the office before they reached it.

Kevin badged him. "Are you Walter Moore?"

"Wally. Just Wally." He ran a hand through untidy, light-brown hair. "I've been trying to stay up here, out of the way."

"I'd like to ask you a few questions."

"Sure. No problem. We can do it in here." Wally led the way into the tiny office space. He sat behind a desk and gestured to a visitor's chair across from him. He frowned at his salesman. "Keep an eye on the front door, will you, Todd?"

"Sure, Mr. Moore." The salesman disappeared.

Kevin sat down and took out his notebook. "Any chance you could turn off that music?"

Wally blinked. "What? Oh, yeah. Sure." He reached behind him to a compact disc player on a shelf and punched the power button. The music stopped. "I completely forgot it was on. After a while, you don't hear it anymore, know what I mean?"

"I'm sorry for your loss, Mr. Moore. Were you and Mr. Burnham close?"

"It's Wally. We were business partners, not friends, and from time to time there was a bit of friction there, I guess, but at the end of the day he was a very likeable guy. A little introverted, which was sort of surprising for a former professional athlete, and what you could call self-absorbed, which is not surprising at all, but overall he was pretty hard to dislike."

"How did your partnership work?"

"Grant originally started this business with a woodworker named Westerman. They made baseball bats. They spun their wheels on that for a while, and then Grant bought out Westerman and brought me in as his partner. We completely overhauled the business, getting rid of the bats and going into cabinetry and high-end furniture. Things took off right away. Changed the name from Burnham and Westerman to Burnham and Moore. As you no doubt figured out from the big sign out front."

"What happens to Mr. Burnham's half of the partnership?"

"We have it arranged so that everything passes to the

surviving partner in the event of a death, and the company converts to a sole proprietorship. It's my understanding that Grant's father's his only beneficiary. I don't know for sure, because he never talked to me about his will, but he didn't have kids and he wasn't going to leave anything to his ex-wife, I know that for a fact."

"Oh?"

He shrugged. "She's done very well for herself. Remarried. Moved on. And Grant couldn't stand her."

"I see. Were they in contact very often?"

"Nah. Grant would rather have his fingernails pulled out with pliers than be in the same room with that woman. God, I shouldn't talk like that, should I?"

"So this becomes all yours." Kevin looked around the tiny office.

Wally laughed without humour. "Yeah, well, once everything clears probate or whatever I'll be looking for another partner. I'm not really a cabinets and furniture guy. I've got a lot more irons in the fire than this company, although I have a few ideas I guess I'll still follow through on here."

"What's your role?"

Wally glanced down at his large stomach. "Well, I'm not the celebrity athlete, that's for sure. I made a pretty good investment in this place, but I figured out right away that Grant had relied on Westerman for the day-to-day operational stuff and that I was going to have to step up and be an active partner until I could hire someone to take it over. Ended up liking it, I guess. The operational part. Not that the products get me particularly excited. Anyway, I'm the shop manager, and I keep everything moving. There are two salesmen, three certified woodworkers, and five labourers who all report to me, along with an administrative assistant and a part-time bookkeeper. I'm responsible for pretty much all the changes that've happened here to turn this thing around."

"I see." Kevin was taking notes.

"But you have to keep in mind that Grant always signed off on everything before it was implemented. Production changes, new product lines, hiring and firing, whatever. If he didn't like it, we didn't do it."

"Can you account for your whereabouts today, Mr. Moore?"

"Wally. God." He rubbed his fleshy jowls. "It really is true, isn't it? It really happened. Jesus."

Kevin gave him a moment.

"I live the next block over, on Foster. Above the Red Anvil Cafe. I own the building and my wife and I are partners in the business. We live in the apartment upstairs. Judy goes downstairs at five thirty to get ready to open at seven, and I'm usually down at seven thirty for breakfast. I try to time it so most of the early morning commuters have already gotten their coffee and bagels and hit the road. This morning it was a little closer to eight. I brought my food over here instead of eating it there at my table in the front window because I was running late and I knew Todd would be waiting for me on the sidewalk. He doesn't have a key. Anyway, I ate breakfast in my office, which is the one next to Grant's; I surfed around on my phone for a while, reading the news; and then I made a few calls. Actually, that used up the rest of the morning. As I said, I have other business interests. I'm in venture capital, and I like to keep my money moving. I'm always working on new investments. Just my own stuff; though. Nothing to do with Grant or this place."

"What about lunch?"

"We ordered something in. Pizza. Todd locked the front door and we ate in the lunch room. He's a nice kid, actually has a brain in his head, and I like to listen to him chatter on about this and that. Is this the sort of thing you want to know?"

Kevin nodded. "After lunch, did you leave the premises?"

"No. Judy says I should go for walks, even if it's just around the block, but I can't get up the energy for it. I spent a little time with Todd, and a few customers came in, but they were only browsers so I went back to my office and made a few more calls."

"Were these calls on the landline or your cellphone?"

"Cell. I do all my business on it. Everything. Grant likes a landline, so we had them installed in the offices, but I don't bother with it." He leaned forward, grunting, and took his cellphone out of his pocket. "You can check through it if you want."

Kevin shook his head. "We'll file for a warrant first. But I caution you not to tamper with it in any way beforehand."

"No problem." Wally leaned over the desk and held the phone out to Kevin.

"Take it. I insist."

Kevin hesitated before removing one of the evidence bags he always kept in his jacket pocket when on a call out. He held it open and Wally dropped in the phone.

"Now you'll be able to see I'm telling the truth," Wally said. "Not just the call log but the GPS tracker app. I haven't left the building all day."

Kevin nodded. The fact that Wally had voluntarily offered his phone to prove his whereabouts while someone was unloading on Grant Burnham was a point in his favour, of course, but he didn't bother mentioning to Wally that they'd also get a warrant for the landline phone in his office. At this point, they weren't about to take anyone's word for anything. Besides, the GPS information might show that the cellphone had remained in the factory, but wouldn't necessary prove Wally Moore had stayed here with it.

"Did Mr. Burnham come in today?" he asked.

"He dropped by around ten or so. He usually doesn't bother on the weekend, but we're putting together a buyout offer on a small outfit in Prescott that makes a really nice line of concert guitars. That's one of the ideas I said I was going to move forward on. The pandemic really hit them hard, and the luthier who owns the business wants to get out from under all the debt. The best part is that he wants to stay on, and he's willing to relocate up here to Perth. His work is considered high end, and he's won a number of awards. Any way I look at it, it's a win-win. So I asked Grant to stop in this morning and check out the final draft of our offer. He signed off on it and left. Said he was going to go cut wood." Wally smiled sadly. "That was Grant."

Kevin frowned, thinking about what Max Macdonald had told him earlier, that he thought Burnham was worried about money. "It sounds like things have been going well here. Financially."

Wally lifted his eyebrows. "Are you kidding? We're in terrific shape. The pandemic was tough, yeah, but we did a lot of online stuff to get through it and moved what inventory we could, using whatever contact-free processes we could manage. There was always enough cash on hand to pay ourselves at the regular rate each month and cover the salaries of the staff as well, once the place reopened."

"What about Mr. Burnham himself? Was he having personal trouble, financially?"

Wally looked surprised. "Not that I was aware of. He took care of himself and wasn't much of a spender. A few times he'd ask me for advice on an investment or something, but overall he managed his money pretty well, from what I could see."

"What about personal problems unrelated to his financial situation?"

"No clue. He kept personal things to himself. Sometimes he got a little broody, like there was something going on in the background, but all in all he was a pretty even-tempered sort of guy. Oh shit."

Kevin frowned. "What?"

"I was supposed to fax the offer to the guitar guy this afternoon. I forgot. And the fax machine's in my office."

"It'll have to wait," Kevin said.

"Yeah." He bit his lip. "Ah, crap."

"What now?"

"I just thought, 'I'll call and let him know I'll get it to him on Monday,' then I realized I just turned over my cellphone. Damn."

Kevin stood up, putting a business card in front of him. "Is there somewhere else you can call him from?"

"Yeah, from home. I'll Google his number."

"Stick around in case we need to talk to you again," Kevin said.

"Yeah. Okay." He picked up the business card. "This is really happening, isn't it?"

"I'm afraid so," Kevin said, walking out.

Chapter

11

It was late when Kevin got home, after ten o'clock in the evening, but Janie was still up. He went into the kitchen and stuck his head through the doorway into the living room, where she was sitting cross-legged on the couch, watching TV.

"Hey. Whatcha watching?"

She said nothing, staring at the screen. The sound was off, and as far as he could tell it was some kind of Christmas-in-the-summertime movie. Not her usual fare.

He found a plate of leftover pork and beans in the fridge. Stripping off the plastic wrap, he smothered it with barbecue sauce and stuck it in the microwave. He grabbed a can of ginger ale, drank half of it while he was waiting, and then took his meal into the living room.

"Where are the kids?" He dropped into his recliner and, balancing his plate on his lap, dug in.

"Josh is asleep. Cait's in her room. Brendan's downstairs on the computer."

"How'd it go today?"

"Wrong question."

Kevin spooned beans into his mouth, waiting. She wasn't the kind of person who would keep things bottled up inside herself for very long.

The movie went to a commercial. She grabbed the remote and turned it off. She threw the remote at the arm of the couch. It bounced into the air and landed in a wastepaper basket beside the TV.

"Goddamned little weasel. I'd like to wring his goddamned skinny little neck."

Kevin chewed and swallowed. "Who are we talking about?"

"Harry. That's. Who. We're. Talking. About."

Harry Bridges owned the building in Sparrow Lake where Janie ran her hair salon. Actually, it was owned by Harry and his wife, Summer Chadwick. They lived in Brockville and, if Kevin remembered correctly, they were partners in a number of businesses and property investments in the surrounding area, including the building and one or two others in the village. Janie's salon occupied one half of the ground floor. At one time, the other half had been rented out to a guy who did appliance repairs, but he went out of business several years ago. Upstairs was a three-bedroom apartment that had been vacant since the beginning of the pandemic. Janie was the only tenant Harry had left in the place.

Kevin gave it another mouthful before taking his life in his hands. "What's wrong?"

She leaned forward suddenly. "It's Saturday, right? I've got a full slate of appointments. I get there first thing this morning and all the goddamned locks have been changed."

"Changed? Why?"

"So I go see Peggy. She tells me there was someone messing around the place last night. Out front and in the back alley. She was going to call the cops, but then she saw Harry strutting around like the goofball he is, giving orders."

Peggy Swarbrick and her husband owned the mom-and-pop hardware store next to Janie's building. They lived upstairs over their shop and were inveterate gossips. Peggy spent half of her free time at the windows, checking out the action. Such as it was.

"Then I talked to Sarah. She saw the same thing, plus a locksmith truck in the back alley. Some Brockville outfit. Son of a bitch, sneaking around changing the locks on me."

Kevin didn't know who Sarah was, but it didn't matter. Janie had obviously canvassed the area, drumming up witnesses, and put two and two together. Harry had evidently come up from Brockville last night with a professional locksmith and secured the building against unwanted entry. The question was, Why? Janie paid her rent faithfully at the end of every month, like clockwork.

"Doesn't make sense," he ventured, getting up to return his empty plate to the kitchen.

"So I called Doris. She knows Harry's lawyer and she put in a call. Took all afternoon for the bastard to call her back."

Kevin rinsed off his plate and spoon and left it in the dish rack on the counter to dry. Doris Winston was Janie's lawyer, also in Brockville. She'd handled Janie's divorce, she'd counselled Kevin when he adopted Caitlyn and Brendan, Janie's two children from her first marriage, and she helped Janie with legal questions related to her business. In Kevin's opinion, she was solid and reliable. He sat back down in his recliner and put up his feet, ready for the rest of it.

"Turns out Summer's divorcing the worm. She threw him out and changed all the locks on their house. She's taking him for everything he's got. He was messing around with their dog groomer and she caught them behind the kennels in a tree hammock."

"Doris told you all that?"

"Damned right she did. Harry's lawyer's a total idiot. Tried to play the sympathy card with her. What a fool."

"I don't understand. Why change the locks up here?"

Janie got up to retrieve the TV remote from the wastepaper basket. "Looks like Summer stashed a bunch of valuable antiques in the apartment upstairs after some estate sale in Athens last fall. I had no idea they were up there. She was storing them in the village instead of hauling everything down to Brockville, I guess. Stuff's worth between ten and twenty thousand, from what the lawyer said. Harry wants his cut."

She turned the television back on and reset it to mute. "The goddamned moron forgot all about me. He changed the lock on the doors going upstairs, the appliance place next door, and both of mine, front and back. 'Hello, Dickhead? I still work here?' What the hell's wrong with people?"

"So he's going to bring you up a key, right?"

She brushed at her cheek. It was a measure of how upset she was, that she'd allow a few tears to undercut her anger. Janie, who never cried.

"No. That's just it. The lawyer says the building stays locked up until there's a settlement. It's that damned back staircase behind my washroom. Some moron could still access the upstairs that way if they felt like walking through my shop, moving my stuff, pulling out the damned sheet of wallboard they nailed back there to block off the stairs, and trooping on up. Christ. Doris is gonna do her best, but right now I'm shut down. Again."

During the pandemic, barbershops and hair salons were forced to close down for months at a time in Ontario, along with other businesses, and it had had a devastating effect on Janie. She'd applied for one of the economic relief packages available to small businesses, and once she began to receive the funds she was able to keep up the payments on her rent and utilities. Unfortunately she had to let her two part-time hairdressers go, including her best friend Lauren Foley, but the money kept her afloat while she waited it out. Unfortunately, there was no relief available from the government for her state of mind.

Janie was a doer. She was happiest when she was working. Her salon was her little world, a place where she could be herself, make her own decisions, determine her own fate, and be successful on her own terms.

While the schools were shut down, she'd stayed at home with the kids. Before the pandemic, her mother, Barb, had often looked after the children while Janie was busy, but after developing heart trouble she'd sold her house and moved into a condominium in Brockville, and they were still avoiding contact with her for COVID-related reasons.

Janie loved her kids, and she was a good mother. Conscientious, caring, responsible. But she needed external things to occupy her mind, and staying home around the clock during the lockdown with nothing to do except housework, fixing meals, and refereeing disputes nearly drove her insane.

Kevin thought she'd done an admirable job, all things considered, but everyone was vastly relieved when the schools finally reopened last year. When the province moved to Step 3 in the recovery process and hair salons were allowed to resume business, Janie thought she was finally out of the woods. It had all been worth it. The wait, the boredom, the aggravation. She'd paid her dues, and now it was time to get back to her life.

Clear the tracks.

Now, with only a few weeks left until another school year began, Josh would be heading off to kindergarten, Brendan would be entering Grade Eight, and Caitlyn would be a sophomore at high school. Cait had watched Josh over the summer so that Janie could work without worrying about what was going on at home. Everything was finally getting back to normal.

"Now this," she said, staring at the TV.

"We'll think of something."

"It was so humiliating," she said, "having to call everyone and cancel their appointments. Humiliating."

"I'm sure they understood. They've been coming to you for years. They waited through the pandemic. They'll still be there after this."

She leaned back and closed her eyes.

"I just don't know what I'm going to do."

Chapter

12

The following morning, which was Sunday, Ellie walked into the little meeting room in the Lanark detachment office in Perth and sat down in the empty seat at the head of the table.

Constable Rachel Townsend laughed at something Dave Martin was saying on the speakerphone.

"I'm sorry, Dave, I missed that." Ellie took her tablet out of her handbag and powered it up.

"Hi, Ellie. Nothing important. I was just talking about the kind of things that keep me awake in the middle of the night."

"Oh?"

"Well, for example, last night I was thinking about the fact that they sell cigarettes in packs of twenty-five."

"Okay." Tapping on her tablet, Ellie opened the case file that had been created for the Burnham investigation.

"Twenty-five's an odd number, right? So that means one side of the pack has thirteen cigarettes. Doesn't that bother people? I couldn't stop thinking about it. I don't smoke, so it never occurred to me until last night. What about you, Ellie? You smoke. Does it bother you?"

"I buy the packs of twenty. Avoids the problem altogether."

Polite laughter rippled around the table.

Rachel Townsend was attending the meeting as the regional media liaison officer assigned to the case. She and Ellie had already written a press release that had gone out to the news outlets last night, and Rachel would handle all other public communications. Ellie avoided speaking directly to the media whenever she could.

Each major case manager usually had a preferred media liaison officer to work with, co-ordinating statements, press releases, Crime Stoppers web pages, and all other public contacts requiring official communications, and Rachel was always Ellie's first choice. She was calm, professional, and possessed an intuitive ability to anticipate how Ellie would want to handle any given situation.

Sitting on either side of Rachel were Kevin Walker and Sonja Freeling. Across the table from them were the Lanark detachment people—Staff Sergeant Dunn, Skelton, and a nervous-looking young man Ellie had never seen before.

"I don't think we've met," she said to him.

Dunn cleared his throat. "Constable Downey's filling in as file co-ordinator for us."

"I'm Ellie March. What's your first name, Constable?"

"Uh, Stephen, ma'am."

"Do people call you Steve or Stephen?"

"Uh, Stephen, ma'am."

"Stephen it is. Gary, I thought Constable Perreault was going to be our file co-ordinator."

Dunn grimaced. "Ah, yeah. Well, first thing this morning

her husband called. She was rushed to the hospital for an emergency appendectomy. So she's out for a while, looks like. I tapped Downey here to sit in for her."

"I see." Ellie looked at the young constable. "Is this your first time participating in a major case?"

"Yes, ma'am."

"Don't call me that. I hope you've completed the training."

"That's affirmative," Dunn interjected. "He's passed the OPC case management software course, as well as the General Investigation training course. He's taking more courses this fall. Isn't that right?"

Downey nodded. The Ontario Police College offered complete training in major case management, and the MCM, the computerized system used by police services in the province, was a key information management tool. The role of file co-ordinator was very important, as this person controlled the flow of information and ensured that everything was entered into the system and kept up to date. Ellie was a little perturbed that Dunn had made a last-minute substitution without consulting her.

"We'll talk about it later." She leaned forward, her eyes moving to the speakerphone. "Dave, why don't you start us off?"

"Yes, ma'am."

Ellie rolled her eyes.

"Warrants have been executed," he said, "and evidence is being collated and analyzed even as we speak. Where would you like to begin?"

"You choose."

"Oh, very well. I always like to talk about Serge's specialty, tire tread marks, but I'll keep it simple this morning. It's a Sunday, after all, and we should really be in church instead of at work. Amen and et cetera. Anyway, our report has already been filed in Constable Downey's system, so you can read it there at your leisure."

Ellie frowned at her tablet. "Yes, I see it."

"The victim's truck tires are duly recorded, and they're not very interesting. The tracks we found on the shoulder of the road are worth mentioning, though. Firestone Destination LE2 all-season tires, size 225/65R17. Bad news is that they're extremely common and sold all over the place, including Walmart and everywhere else, for a lot of different vehicles. Good news is we also found partial marks left by them in the parking area used by Burnham. They'd mostly been driven over by Burnham's truck, several times, which means they're old, predating the homicide, but it also means the person who parked along the side of the road and walked in yesterday to kill our victim had been present at that woodlot before."

"Were the Firestones found elsewhere? The house at Balderson or at the factory?"

"Negative, Ellie. Kevin, the picture you sent me yesterday wasn't a match. Sorry."

"Oh well." Kevin had forwarded the photo of Lona Colquitt's tires to Martin in case she might have been involved, but it seemed she hadn't been to the crime scene. Not in the Mercedes, at least.

"I see you've also reported on the footprint evidence," Ellie said.

"Yeah. Boot prints of the victim and the guy across the road are present and accounted for. Size thirteen for the victim, size nine for Macdonald. The hiking boots that tried to scuff out the tire treads on the shoulder of the road, walked in to remove a bat from the back of Burnham's truck, which I'll get to in a minute, confronted Burnham while he was splitting wood, chased him to the kill spot, and then walked back out are size eleven. Thanks to our handy-dandy footwear database, we know this individual was wearing Salomon Quest 4 Gore-Tex boots. They cost two hundred and fifty dollars plus tax and shipping if you order them online. I'm thinking of asking for a pair for Christmas."

"He could have bought them second-hand," Skelton said. "Or they could be stolen property."

"Sure," Martin said, his voice sounding a little testy, "and that's your job to figure out. I'm just telling you what he or she was wearing on his or her feet when he or she killed our victim."

"Understood, Dave." Ellie wondered if Martin had dealt with Skelton before and hadn't enjoyed the experience. "Anything else on the footprints?"

"Yeah." The sound of tapping came through the speaker. "We found partial prints of the Gore-Texes, older prints, along with our victim's but on different days from the looks of it, going up and down one of the trails toward the back of the woodlot. Again, the person we're looking for had been there before."

"You were going to tell us about the murder weapon," Ellie prompted.

"Yeah, the baseball bat. The handle and knob were wiped clean, so nothing wonderful coming from there. The gore was left on the sweet spot, though. Samples have been sent to the lab. The main thing to know about it was that it's the same make and model as the other three bats in the back of the truck. Maybe you noticed the label? 'B-ampersand-W, Perth, Canada, Model M272, Jack Inglis, Cleveland Indians.' Ash bat, natural colour, varnished, et cetera."

"The victim's company," Kevin said, "or its original iteration, anyway. Burnham and Westerman."

"Once again," Martin said, "our boy from Sparrow Lake's been doing his homework."

"They stopped making bats five years ago," Kevin said, "so it would have been old stock he was carrying around in the truck. That's why it says 'Cleveland Indians' instead of 'Cleveland Guardians' or whatever they're called now."

"Sounds like a weapon of opportunity," Dunn offered.

Kevin nodded. "Exactly. Everything looks unplanned, disorganized."

"Some kind of FBI profiler now, are you?" Skelton asked.

"No, not at all." Kevin flushed again. "It just seems to add up that way."

Ellie wondered if Skelton might be deliberately putting the needle into Kevin to see how he'd react.

"Fingerprints aren't really telling us anything at this point," Martin threw in. "Most samples collected at the residence belong to the victim, and the rest we're in the process of tracking down. Same thing at the factory. It'll take a day or two to sort through them all."

"How about his cellphone?" Ellie asked.

"Well, y'know, Ellie," he drawled in a fake country accent, "them big-city service providers like to drag their feet sometimes, but we're hopeful that tomorrow, it being a business day and all, we might see them comply with the warrants without us having to raise a fuss, like."

"All right. Thanks."

"Personally," Skelton said, "as far as I can see, whoever did this made a clean getaway. I think this is all going to be a waste of time and taxpayers' money."

"We're just at the beginning," Ellie said, aware that her own voice now sounded a little testy. "Kevin, what was your takeaway from the interview with the witness across the road?"

"Macdonald strikes me as a hero worshipper and a fan more than anything else. Even though it looks like an unplanned and spur-of-the-moment thing," he glanced at Skelton, "I think we need to find someone stronger willed than him. I didn't get the impression he'd be capable of the fury we saw at the scene."

"What about the next-door neighbour?"

"Kevin and I interviewed Mrs. Colquitt," Sonja Freeling said, "and she was pretty shook up by the news. I think we'll probably talk to her again. And her son." She glanced at Kevin. "We'll bring Mr. Colquitt in here too, don't you think, Kevin?"

"Yeah."

"And Burnham's partner?" Ellie asked.

"Moore's alibi looks solid," Kevin said, "but there's always the possibility of murder for hire. We'll have to look at him more closely."

Skelton made a rude noise. "I know Wally Moore. You're wasting your time."

"We'd have to look at his personal financial records," Kevin said, doggedly.

"Yes." Ellie looked at Dunn. "Have your warrant writer start preparing the paper for them. We're already getting the business records, correct?"

Dunn nodded. He looked at Kevin. "Can you give us enough for probable cause on Moore's personal records?"

Kevin grimaced. "I don't think so, not right now."

"Work on it," Ellie said. She paused and put down her tablet. "Are you taking minutes of this meeting, Stephen?"

"Uh, no ma'am. Sorry, um, Detective Inspector."

She shot a look at Dunn, who grimaced. Taking minutes of investigative team meetings was one of the responsibilities of the file co-ordinator, and it was an error on her part not to have ensured that young Downey knew what he was supposed to do before the meeting began. At the end of the day, it wasn't entirely Dunn's fault for having improperly briefed his officer; it was also hers.

What the hell was the matter with her, anyway?

"See me when we're done," Kevin told Downey, holding

up his notebook. "You can copy from mine. Okay?"

"Thanks," Downey said gratefully.

"All right," Ellie continued, "thanks, everyone. It looks to me like there's a lot of work in front of us. Let's get busy. Thanks, Dave."

"You're very welcome, ma'am," Martin replied, his disembodied voice booming from the speaker in the middle of the table.

The room quickly emptied, but Ellie didn't move. "Staff Sergeant Dunn, a word with you, please?"

Dunn stopped in the doorway and bumped shoulders with Downey, who was behind him. They shuffled around each other, and Dunn edged back into the room.

"Close the door, please." Ellie powered down her tablet and put it into her bag. "Sit down."

Dunn sat.

"I understand we're in the middle of a resource crunch. Other detachments are feeling it as well, but Lanark's been hit especially hard. I get that. But we're going to make some changes to this investigative team, and they'll go into effect as soon as we leave this room."

Dunn nodded, waiting for it like a chastened schoolboy.

"Kevin Walker and Sonja Freeling will be the lead field investigators. Sonja will assume the duties of primary, but she'll also have to fill in on some of the investigative duties in the absence of other bodies to pick up the load."

"Yes, Ellie."

"What's happening with the other active detective? Hope, is it?"

"Heather Hope. Uh, she's working a series of home invasions right now. I also had to send her out on a stolen motorcycle report this morning. She's stretched pretty thin at the moment."

"You're commanding the crime unit right now and you

report to Colleen, not me, but if I were you I'd assign Doug Skelton to property and see if Hope could be freed up to work on Burnham instead. She's worked violent crimes before, hasn't she?"

Dunn nodded. "Actually, the latest home invasion involved assault on an elderly couple. She's working that one particularly hard."

"Can Skelton handle it?"

"I guess so."

"I want him off Burnham. Right now. And get that damned kid Downey up to speed on file co-ordination. I don't care if you have to read him bedtime stories about the three bears, Collect, Collate, and Disseminate. Make it happen."

"Yes, Ellie."

"Inform Colleen of the changes, and tell her I'll follow up with her later. We need more bodies, period."

"Will do." He paused, and when there was nothing else, he hurried from the room.

Ellie hadn't felt this annoyed and aggravated by a case in quite some time.

Chapter

13

After the team meeting was over, Kevin followed up on some homework and tracked down Grant Burnham's ex-wife, Roxanne Lansing, whose maiden name was Rechelbacher. She and her second husband, Pete Lansing, ran a gas bar and restaurant on Highway 7 near Maberly, and he made arrangements to interview them early in the afternoon. He then called Bobby Burnham, the victim's father, who agreed to see him at his home in Smiths Falls in an hour.

It was a bit of an awkward arrangement, as Smiths Falls lay twenty kilometres to the east of Perth while Maberly was an additional twenty-five kilometres back the other way, but Kevin wanted to get both interviews into the books today, so he reconciled himself to the driving.

When he ran it by Sonja she expressed a desire to go with him, and as she was now acting as the primary he agreed to the arrangement, suggesting they could travel in his motor pool Ford Fusion. Sonja seemed content to let him do the driving.

They stopped first at Tim Hortons for coffee, since they had a bit of time before Bobby Burnham would be expecting them. There was a table free in the lobby, so they sat there and worked through the kind of get-acquainted conversation Kevin had experienced countless times before.

He hurried through a thumbnail sketch of his past, a Brockville boy with dreams of playing professional hockey; his realization that becoming a police officer was far more important to him when the time came to make a choice; his experiences as a patrol constable and detective for the now-defunct Sparrow Lake Police Service; and his transfer into the OPP when they assumed the contract for the municipality.

It was old hat to him and he didn't like talking about it much, since some people within the force looked down on small-town cops lateralling in at an equivalent rank, as Kevin had done, but Sonja seemed to be interested.

When it was her turn, Sonja talked more about her family than herself. Her husband, Tom Finnegan, was a geologist who worked for the federal government. Their twin daughters were second-year university students, one majoring in physics at the University of Waterloo and the other studying visual art at the Ontario College of Art and Design in Toronto.

"As different as chalk and cheese," she said, smiling. "If you closed your eyes and listened to them gabble on, you'd never guess they were twins."

Sonja and Tom had met in Kirkland Lake, she explained, where she started out as a provincial constable before working her way up to a spot in the North East Region crime unit. She acted for a while as detective sergeant, and when her husband accepted a high-level managerial job at national headquarters in Ottawa, an opportunity he couldn't possibly turn down, she remained behind with the twins for two years until a transfer to East Region came through. They bought a house just north of Carleton Place, and while Tom commuted east into Ottawa each day she made the drive south to RHQ in Smiths Falls.

And here she was.

When their coffee was finished they got back into the Fusion and Kevin headed east on Highway 43. On the way, Sonja talked about last evening's search of Grant Burnham's home.

"Definitely no signs of any conflict. A ton of fingerprints, but none of them will probably lead us where we want to go. It was a single man's house, Kevin. Furnished mostly with stuff from their factory and arranged indifferently, as though he'd gone through the motions without really trying to make it look like a home. The dining room and living room in particular were virtually untouched, like showrooms for the furniture. The same with two guest bedrooms upstairs."

She brushed at a lock of hair that had fallen over her glasses. "There were a few stray items in the bedroom closet and bathroom cabinet that were female, but the sort of stuff left behind after an overnight stay rather than by someone living in. Overall, as I say, the place was very male."

Kevin nodded, keeping his eyes on the road. Highway 43 was a typical two-lane eastern Ontario deathtrap, a seemingly endless series of hills and curves and blind spots peppered with traffic that almost unanimously ignored the 80-kilometre-an-hour speed limit and passed each other with the freedom of spirit one would associate either with immortality or a latent death wish. He wanted to be polite and let Sonja know he was listening to her, but he also wanted to make sure they stayed alive to make it to Bobby Burnham's house.

"The finished basement had a rec room," she went on, "which had the usual stuff—a bar, pool table, juke box, and a vintage pinball machine in really good shape, but there was also a trophy- and memorabilia-room down there that was a collector's paradise. Tom's into that kind of stuff, so we have a room in our house like that, filled with collectibles, although not the trophies, of course. Anyway, Grant apparently played on a Calder Cup championship team in 1987-88, and he was the league's most sportsmanlike player that year, too. Not to mention the minor hockey trophies and awards and so on."

"I didn't know that," Kevin said.

"Oh? I thought you were a hard-core hockey guy."

He smiled. "Who told you that?"

"What are your first impressions of this whole thing? Who would want to kill this guy with so much anger and hatred pumping through their bloodstream?"

Kevin thought for a moment. "It was an argument or conflict murder. The scene was spread out because of the movement by the victim and killer. The body was left where it was and no attempt was made either to hide it or stage it in any way."

"You're thinking of the *CCM*," Sonja said.

"Yeah, I guess so." Kevin had read the FBI's *Crime Classification Manual* several times, and he tried to make use of its insights into criminal behaviour whenever it seemed relevant. The authors categorized argument or conflict murders as those resulting from a dispute not involving family or household members. Victims often knew their killer, and Kevin remembered reading that the crime scene was often spread out, reflecting a lot of movement and signs of a struggle.

Skelton had already ridiculed him once as "some kind of

FBI profiler," and he had no desire to feel the needle again, so he closed his mouth and kept his eyes on the road.

"You think the bat was a weapon of opportunity."

He nodded.

"And the victim knew the killer? Not some stranger?"

"Definitely, he knew them."

"This argument or conflict, do you think it was something spontaneous, or was it something that was long-standing between them?"

"Good question. If it was spontaneous, then we're looking for someone with a bad temper, a very short fuse, and a history of sudden violence, aren't we? Not necessarily someone he'd known for a long time, though. And possibly an issue that had just cropped up between them."

"Unlike a long-standing dispute, where it could have been festering for a while, until the killer reached a point of no return."

"Yeah." Kevin was pleased. They were having a serious discussion without bringing personalities into it, without sarcasm or disparagement or dismissal. Sonja seemed sincerely interested in his thought processes and how they might help solve the case. Kevin was surprised to realize how much Skelton had gotten under his skin. And Dunn, as well, through non-verbals he probably wasn't even conscious of showing.

Not that Kevin was unusually sensitive about these things. It was just that, as an outsider in Lanark, he was acutely aware of the differences in culture and temperament between this crime unit and the one in which he'd been working for the past decade.

"When we talk to Bobby, take the lead, Kevin."

"All right. Will do."

Chapter

14

Bobby Burnham lived in a modest ranch-style house on Vincent Street in Smiths Falls. It was a quiet neighbourhood of bungalows, well-kept lawns, and mature shade trees.

There was nothing modest about the car sitting in the driveway in front of the garage, though. It was a tangerine Porsche sports car that looked like it was worth a lot of money.

Sonja paused for a long look. "Nice. This is a 1967 Targa. A flat-six engine, two-point-seven litres, up to one-fifty horse. These things sold for about seventy-five hundred new, and now they're worth at least a hundred and sixty grand."

"You sound like you know what you're talking about."

She shrugged, reluctant to take her eyes off the vehicle. "I'm a car aficionado. I rebuild engines in my spare time. As a hobby."

"Wow."

"Yeah, well, we all have to have a hobby, right? You probably collect hockey cards or something like that."

"Not really. A few bits of memorabilia, but nothing serious."

"Oh? You don't collect stuff as a hobby?"

"No. I read a lot, though. I guess you could call that my hobby."

"Okay."

The man who opened the screen door and waved them inside was an elderly echo of the celebrity who'd entertained countless hockey fans across North America a lifetime ago, but he still had the big nose, the twinkling blue eyes, and the famous handlebar moustache that drew people to him for autographs in the grocery store, the health care centre where he kept his regular appointments, and the local arena where he still loved to attend minor hockey games in the winter.

"We're very sorry for your loss," Kevin said as they sat down in the living room. He'd half-expected to see more Burnham and Moore furniture, but the couch and recliners were ordinary big-box store items purchased years ago, the upholstery faded and a little worn in spots but still clean and tidy, like everything else seemed to be in Bobby's home.

"Thanks." Bobby dropped into his La-Z-Boy with the rubbery carelessness of a much younger man. "Hell of a shock. My only boy, but you probably know that. Leaves a great big damned hole right here." He thumped his chest with the edge of his fist.

"Is there someone you can talk to—"

"Never mind that." Bobby waved a hand in the air. "I'm all right. Pretty much everybody I know's dead and gone by now. You get used to bad news once you reach your eighties, so that gives you something to look forward to, eh? Ah, shit. Forgot to offer tea or coffee or whatever. Damn."

"Don't get up," Kevin said. "We're fine."

"Okay. I'm not as used to dealing with people as I was when I was still doing the card shows and stuff. That sort of thing gets you out and talking to people, remembering their name long enough to write it down on the pictures they're paying twenty bucks for or the hockey cards or whatever, but I haven't done them for a couple years now. The pandemic kind of shot the shit out of that end of the business."

Kevin had his notebook and pen out, jotting down all the essential preliminaries at the top of the entry, including the date and time, the location of the interview, and the names of everyone present, but he looked up for a moment and smiled.

"Yeah. I've been to a couple of them. Years ago, now. But you know, you and I have met before."

Bobby lifted an eyebrow. "Oh?"

"Yeah, you were playing with the NHL Alumni against a police team in Brockville, and you gave me your autograph after the game, outside the dressing room. On a hockey stick I brought with me. I was thirteen."

"No kidding. I'm sorry, I don't remember. Although you know what, I do remember that game. Ninety-seven, eh? Just after New Years. The cops had ringers with them from the Braves who were a little nasty with the stickwork when they thought nobody was looking."

"I remember you mixing it up a bit with a couple of guys, but I thought it was all part of the act."

"Not that night, it wasn't. You were thirteen, eh?" He shook his head. "Sorry. Too many kids, and too many years ago."

"That's all right. We want to ask you a few questions about Grant. Are you sure you're okay to do this now?"

"Yeah. There was a couple of nice ladies came around last night from, uh," he picked up a business card on the side table next to his recliner, "community services, and we had a talk. I had my little cry then and got it over with. Anyway, my pastor's coming around tonight and we'll do some praying together." He looked at Sonja. "I'm a born-again Christian. And a reformed drinker."

Sonja smiled sympathetically.

He shook his head. "Who would have thought, eh? Bobby the Buffoon, a humble Christian teetotaller." He put the business card back on the table and tapped a fat cigar sitting in an ashtray. "Just these big boys left over from the old days. But what can you do? They're my trademark."

Kevin crossed his legs, balancing his notebook on his knee. "Was Grant a drinker?"

"Nooo, no, not at all. He never touched the stuff. Drugs neither. Smart kid. Looked after his body and his health like you wouldn't believe. Unlike his old man. You can imagine how upset he was when he blew out his knee in eighty-nine. He tried for two years to rehab that thing before he finally gave up and left the game for good."

"He was divorced?"

"Yeah. He and Roxanne got married in eighty-eight, about six months before he got hurt. He was only twenty-one, can you believe it? He was playing down in Muskegon, this was after getting drafted by the Penguins, and she was a local girl used to hang around the rink and talk to the players. She was three years older than him. Anyway, when he got hurt he came back up here to get the surgery done and do his rehab. She got her citizenship or whatever it was, I don't know much about all that stuff, but anyway they lived here in town for years until they finally got sick of the sight of each other and got the divorce."

"Were there any children?"

"One, a girl. She died from the crib death. What do they

call it again?"

"Sudden infant death syndrome," Sonja said. "SIDS."

"Yeah. A low blow for both of them. They decided they wouldn't try to have any more after that. The beginning of the end, I always thought. Anyway, Roxanne was a lush, and the drinking didn't help none, that's for sure."

"After he retired, Grant went into business?" Kevin asked.

"Yeah. But you know what? If it hadn't been for the knee, he might have made it to the Big Show. Hell of a shot, and a good skater. Don't get me wrong; he liked being in Muskegon. Had his head on straight. Just loved playing the game."

"A guy from the I," Kevin said.

Bobby laughed. "Yeah, that's right! That's what he was." He looked at Sonja. "That's what they used to call guys who played in the International League, back when it was still operating. Say, did you know the guy who owned the team when Grant played there bought it for a dollar? Renamed it the Lumberjacks from the Mohawks. Imagine, a buck. Hell, even I could have afforded that! Then I would have been an owner instead of a retread. Oh well."

Sonja smiled again, and Kevin could see that she already knew about the International League and Grant Burnham's career but was letting the old man speak freely not only as a courtesy but also to encourage him to keep talking.

"After he retired," Kevin said, turning the page in his notebook, "he went into business?"

"Yup. And you know, I always thought that son of a bitch who laid the knee-on-knee hit on Grant that night did him a favour in the end. He would have been a decent NHLer, probably good for twenty goals a year, but he was a helluva businessman. Had a head for it. Not like me. Blew all my money on bad investments, horses, and a lot of booze. That baby in the driveway out there's the only thing I've got left to show for it all. And I can't even drive it anymore. I just back it out of the garage on nice days and let it sit there where I can look at it. Anyway, Grant had a way with the dough."

"How did he and Westerman get together?"

Bobby picked up the cigar, looked at it fondly for a moment, and then put it down again. "I can only smoke when I'm by myself. People get upset at the smell. Anyway, as soon as Grant decided he had to leave the game behind for good, he went and got himself a job at the Ford dealership here in town. He was only twenty-two, mind, but right away he was their top salesman. People knew who he was, or he reminded them if they didn't, and he was one of those low-pressure guys who was a good listener. Didn't force anything on them, just got them talking. Listened to what they wanted in a car or truck and pointed them in the right direction."

He touched the cigar again, his eyes down.

"Go ahead and smoke," Sonja said. "I don't mind. Kevin?"

"No, it's fine."

Bobby lit the cigar and sighed, the smoke obscuring his face for a moment. "Thanks. You wouldn't believe how calming this is."

They waited as he took a few additional puffs.

"Some guy came in one day to get work done on his car, and he and Grant got jabbering. The guy was a drummer for Bauer, sold their skates and other stuff to stores in the area, and he told Grant he was leaving the job and going out west. Suggested to Grant he might want to talk to Bauer about taking over for him. By this time Grant was what, twenty-five? So Bauer took him on, and he did that job for a couple of years. Well, six years or so, I guess it was."

He put the cigar back in the ashtray. "It'll go out by

itself. Where was I? Oh, yeah. How he met Westerman. Typical Grant, that was. I've told this story before. You know, that's why the newspaper guys always came around even after I retired, because I could always tell a good story. Kept them scribbling stuff down just like you are, young man."

Kevin smiled.

"They don't come around anymore, so I don't get much of a chance to get chatty. And you'd be surprised how little interest them PSWs and nurses have in listening to an old geezer babble on. Anyway. Grant was making a sales call in a sporting goods store up in Ottawa one day when this tough-looking little twerp came in to sell some bats he was making. The owner said he bought his bats from Bauer, you know, pointing to Grant standing right there, and the little guy went through this loud song and dance that just ended up pissing off the owner, pardon my French, who told him to get the hell out. Grant stepped up and asked to look at the bat he'd brought in as a sample. I guess it was high-quality stuff, and Grant had a good eye for products even then, and so he asked the guy, Westerman, for his business card. Well, the owner hands Grant the card Westerman had given him, saying he had no damned use for it anyway, and Westerman stomped out. Grant called him up later, arranged to get a tour of Westerman's shop, and made him an offer to go into business together."

"So that's how they started the company," Kevin said.

"Well no, son, not right away. Westerman told him to go to hell. Said he had no interest in taking on a partner." Bobby chuckled. "Grant gave him a week. Meanwhile, he lined up a really good lease-to-own agreement on that old warehouse in Perth, talked to his bank about the whole thing, and then the following weekend paid a little visit to Westerman at his house in Carleton Place. Turns out the little dickhead's wife was very nice. She took an instant liking to Grant, the same as pretty much every woman he ever met, and once he found out she was born and raised in Perth and wanted to go back there to be close to her family again, Grant knew he had Westerman by the balls. Pardon me."

"Did they get along? Grant and Westerman?"

Bobby snorted. "Nope. Fought like cats and dogs all the time. Bert Westerman has got to be the most contrary, foul-mouthed, wretched human being ever born. I'd drop into their factory now and then to say hello to Grant, and that guy'd practically run me out the door. Said I was distracting his workers. Could I help it if they wanted autographs and pictures and stuff? Grant thought it was funny, but Westerman must have been jealous of all the attention I got."

"You've mentioned a couple of times that Grant was popular with women," Kevin said. "Anyone specific? Anyone recently?"

"Oh, gosh, there was always at least one. Right back to when he was a kid, he was always popular with the girls. Inherited his mom's looks instead of mine, thank God. He got real serious with this one girl in high school, I can't remember her name off the top of my head. This was when he was playing Junior B for the Bears here in town. I thought they might stay together, but when they graduated he got drafted by the Penguins and she went away somewhere to university and that was it. Wish I could remember her name.

"Anyway, yeah, there was always someone. After he and Roxanne divorced, to answer your question, I don't think there was ever anybody serious. He liked the fair-haired ones, and the odd redhead. Couldn't give you names, though. He never talked about them to me, and he sure never introduced any of them. When he came here to visit, he was always by himself. And I didn't go over to his place much; oh, a couple of times when he had one of his barbecues, but the girl of the day didn't pay me any attention at all. He tended to favour the ones who had no interest in hockey, I guess. Shoot, they all looked like models out of a magazine."

"Do you have other family, Mr. Burnham? Someone you could talk to, or someone who should be called?"

He shook his head. "My wife's been gone for years, now. Our daughter Katrina went out west and passed away six years ago. I have a sister-in-law. I try not to talk to her if I can possibly help it."

The old man's voice had grown a little husky as he spoke, and Kevin suddenly noticed a tear trickling down his cheek.

Kevin looked at Sonja, who nodded and stood up.

"I think that's good for now," he said, putting away his notebook.

Sonja found a box of tissues on a side table and put it on the arm of Bobby's La-Z-Boy. He nodded gratefully and, pulling out a handful, blew his famous nose.

Kevin leaned over and put a card on top of the one that the officer from community services had given Bobby last night. "If you think of something, call me."

"Yeah. Sorry about this."

"No need to apologize. Will you be okay? Should we call your pastor now?"

"Nah, I'm all right." Bobby dropped the wad of tissues into a wastepaper basket next to his recliner and grabbed his cigar. "I'm just gonna smoke the rest of this bad boy and I'll be okay."

As Kevin turned to leave, Bobby leaned forward.

"Say, kid. Sorry, I forgot your name again."

"Kevin Walker. It's right there on the card."

"Yeah. I haven't got my glasses on right now. Tell me something, will you?"

"Sure."

"You still got that stick I signed for you back then? When you were a kid?"

"You bet I do."

Bobby grinned and sagged back into his chair.

"That makes me feel a little better, at least."

Chapter

15

They hit a drive-through in Perth for some lunch before heading west on Highway 7 toward Maberly, about twenty minutes away. As they drove, they went over what Bobby Burnham had told them about Grant.

"Definitely a ladies' man," Kevin said.

"Yes. We'll see if the fingerprints we collected from his house will give us a name or two."

"Maybe it was trouble with a woman."

"We seem to be moving further away from the trouble-with-money theory," she said. "Bobby was pretty definite that Grant was a solid businessman. Which confirms what the partner, Moore, was telling you as well and contradicts Max Macdonald's theory."

"We'll see what the ex-wife has to say." Kevin swerved slightly to avoid something in the middle of the road. "Maybe there's still trouble between them."

"Could be. I—"

There was a sudden loud bang, and the car dropped down on the front passenger side. Kevin fought the wheel and feathered the brakes, glancing in the mirror to make sure no one was behind them, trying to lose as much speed as possible before moving off the pavement onto the gravel shoulder.

When they were finally stopped, he shifted into park, hit the hazard lights, and shut off the engine. They got out for a look.

"Flat," Kevin said, disgusted.

They were out in the middle of nowhere, halfway between Perth and Maberly, just past a bend in the highway, not far from a speck on the map known as Brooke.

"There should be an emergency spare in the trunk."

Kevin stared at the tire, hands on his hips. "Yeah. There is."

"You should call CAA."

"It'd be quicker to do it myself," he said. "Unless you'd like to, since you're the car aficionado."

"I don't change tires. Anyway, there are health and safety considerations."

Kevin shrugged. "I've changed a tire before. If you don't tell, I won't."

As Kevin popped the trunk to get the spare, an OPP cruiser zipped by in the opposite direction. The driver hit the brakes, pulled a U-turn, and came up on the shoulder behind them, light bar flashing.

The constable got out and approached them, hand on his sidearm. He was young and muscular, and he moved with the easy confidence of an athlete. "Licence and registration."

"For crying out loud." Kevin took out his ID wallet and showed him his badge and warrant card.

"I still need to see your driver's licence and registration," the constable said, glancing at Sonja. "There's been fake OPP IDs floating around lately."

Aware that Sonja was trying to suppress a smirk, Kevin dug out his personal wallet and handed over his driver's licence. "Registration and insurance are inside the car. Want me to get them?"

The cop, whose nameplate identified him as McGill, glanced at the photo on Kevin's licence and handed it back. "Nah, it's good." He nodded at Sonja. "Sergeant Freeling. We've met before. I was a rookie when you were commanding the North East crime unit. The road rage murder just outside Kirkland Lake."

"I remember." She smiled. "I'm back to my substantive right now. Detective constable. It's Brad, isn't it?"

"That's right. Aren't you at RHQ?"

She nodded. "On loan to Lanark at the moment."

While they were busy catching up on old times, Kevin removed his jacket and left it carefully folded on the front seat. Rolling up his sleeves, he pulled the emergency spare tire out from under the trunk insert and propped it against the back fender. He grabbed the jack and tire iron and, reluctantly getting down on his knees in the dirt, slid the jack into place under the front axle.

"You should call for service," Constable McGill said.

"Where have I heard that before?"

"Don't jack it up until you've loosened the lug nuts."

"Yeah, I know." Kevin removed the hub cap and started in on the lug nuts. The first one he tried refused to budge, so he tried another one. Same result. He gave it a really good reef and the tire iron slipped off, causing him to bang his knuckle painfully against the rim.

"Hold on," McGill said, "I've got a better one." He went to his cruiser and came back a moment later with a heavy-duty torque wrench and socket set. He waved Kevin out of the way and knelt down. In a matter of a few seconds he had the first lug nut loosened nicely, and the others followed suit as meekly as lambs.

McGill checked the placement of the jack and used the tire iron to crank it up. As Kevin stepped back to watch, the tire came off, the spare went on, the jack came down, and the lug nuts went on, snug but not too tight.

McGill grinned as he tossed the flat tire into the trunk, followed by the hub cap. "That should do to get you back to the pool."

They watched him trot back to his cruiser, pull a U-turn onto the highway, and disappear around the next bend.

"I think he likes you," Kevin said to Sonja, dabbing at his bloody knuckle with a tissue.

Chapter

16

Pete and Roxanne Lansing owned and operated a cluster of businesses at the junction of Highway 7 and County Road 36 where the highway bypassed Maberly less than a kilometre to the south.

Kevin pulled into a broad parking area that provided access to a roadhouse-slash-restaurant on the right, a convenience store in the middle, and a gas bar-slash-service garage on the left. A large sign identified the place as "Lansing's Corner." When he'd called earlier, Pete Lansing had told him that he'd be available in his office inside the garage, so Kevin parked on that side of the lot and got out.

"Looks like a going concern," Sonja said.

A man came out of the convenience store and began walking toward the garage, peeling the cellophane from a pack of cigarettes. He glanced up and slowed, looking them over.

"You the OPP folks?"

Kevin badged him. "Mr. Lansing?"

"Come on in." Lansing nodded toward the garage. "I was just grabbing some smokes." He stopped and stared at the Fusion. "What happened there? Flat?"

"Yeah. A few kilometres back."

"Tsk tsk. Just a puncture, or did it shred on you?"

"Just a puncture, I think."

"In the trunk?"

"Yeah."

"We can take a look at it for you, if you want. While we talk."

"Sure. If you take our card." Kevin tapped his wallet, which contained an OPP Fleet Vehicle credit card supplied for use with the Fusion by whomever signed it out of the motor pool. Kevin had had it refused by a few gas bars who didn't take fleet cards of any kind, so he always made a point of asking first.

Lansing made a noise. "Are you kidding? Where else do you think your patrol boys get their gas around here?" He held out his hand for the key fob. "Since it's Sunday, things are quiet, so we can get it done right away. Lucky you."

"Yeah. Lucky me."

They followed him through an open garage bay door, where Lansing handed the fob to a mechanic.

"In the trunk. Let me know if there's a problem, otherwise repair it and put it back on."

"Yes, Mr. Lansing."

Kevin watched the man trot outside to the Fusion before following Sonja and Lansing up a flight of stairs into an office that overlooked the garage. The place was clean and tidy, with a large desk covered with files and parts catalogues and other assorted items, an electronics rack in the corner with a flatscreen TV and DVD player, and a large map of the area on one wall.

Inhaling the familiar smell of grease and oil, metal, and stale cigarette smoke, Kevin glanced down through the glass at the two bays below. There was a car up on one of the hoists, but the other one was free. He sat down across from Lansing and took out his notebook.

"We're investigating the death of Grant Burnham," he said, sensing that Sonja once again preferred him to take the lead in the interview.

"Yeah, jeez. Heard about that on the news. Terrible."

Kevin nodded. Lansing was tall and skinny, middle-aged, with a receding hairline and bright blue eyes. He stared at Kevin from the comfort of his leather office chair with the stillness of a lizard basking in the sunshine.

"Your wife, Roxanne, was formerly married to Mr. Burnham."

"That's right."

"Is she available to talk to us when we're done here, Mr. Lansing?"

"I don't see why not. She's over in the store right now. She looks after it while I cover the garage and the gas pumps."

"I see. How did you two meet, Mr. Lansing?"

"Let's see, that was ten years ago now, I guess. You want the full story, or just the *Reader's Digest* version?"

"The full story, if you don't mind."

"Okey doke. Well, she stopped in for gas, and I saw she'd been crying. I asked where she was headed, and she was so confused she didn't really know. So I took her next door for a cup of coffee. Somebody else owned the place back then and the coffee wasn't nearly as good as ours is now, but she was grateful for small kindnesses, I guess. So we sat and talked for a while. She told me she was in the process of divorcing her husband. I said I'd been down that road a couple years ago and I knew it wasn't much fun. She said her lawyer was a hockey fan and took at face value whatever Grant's lawyer fed him. She'd just signed the papers settling for a piddly little amount and didn't know what the hell she was going to do. He got the house and most of everything else, and she didn't even know where she was going to spend the night.

"Once she'd settled down, I got her to call a friend of hers in Perth, and this lady told Roxie to come right around and she could stay with her for a while. You know, until she got things sorted out. I figured I'd never see her again, but damned if she didn't drive all the way out here again a few days later for more gas. I guess it went from there."

Kevin nodded. He was sitting next to the glass wall, and through his peripheral vision he saw the Fusion roll into the empty bay downstairs. "She must have felt a lot of resentment toward her ex-husband for how she'd been treated during the divorce process."

Lansing barked a short laugh. "Hell, yeah. She was a handful for the first while, I gotta admit. And Job One was getting her off the booze. Easier said than done. But once she was into recovery and the backsliding was behind her, she brightened up a whole hell of a lot. It helped that I'd gone ahead and bought the store. It gave her something to do. Turns out she'd worked as a cashier when she was a teenager and didn't mind it, so after a few months of that we were able to move her into the manager's job instead of Mary Jane, who looks after the restaurant now. Roxie kind of found her groove, I guess you could say. She's got a good head for business, and we're turning a nice profit all around."

"What's her attitude toward Mr. Burnham?"

"You mean how did she feel when we heard the news?" Lansing shrugged. "She shed a little tear and then moved on."

"What about before his death? Did she still harbour

bad feelings toward him?"

"Are you asking me if she still hated him? Enough to kill him? You're barking up the wrong tree there, buddy, with all due respect. She's not the person she was ten years ago, and she never was that kind of person. Anyway, almost all of her anger is self-directed."

Sonja stirred. "Can you tell us where you were yesterday morning, Mr. Lansing?"

He blinked at her. "Huh? Where I was? Oh Christ, yeah. I get it. Sure. I was here. Where else? We open the gas bar at six o'clock every morning in the summer, and that's my job. I get here at five thirty to unlock the doors, turn on the pumps and the lights, check the prices and reset them, usually up from yesterday, if you know what I mean, and I stay here pretty much all day. Go next door for breakfast. Same thing for lunch. We get takeout from the restaurant to eat when we go home, which is usually about nine."

"Did you leave here at any point during the morning?"

"Shit, no. Actually, you can ask Terry. The kid fixing your tire. He comes on at six when we open for business, and he'll tell you I was driving him nuts all morning. Maybe you didn't notice that car in the other bay. Mercedes. Terry's gotta learn how to fix them, and I'm his teacher. God help him. Anyway, he'll vouch for my whereabouts, as you guys would say."

Sonja crossed her legs. "How about your wife, Mr. Lansing? Where was she yesterday morning?"

He snorted. "She's the one gets me out of bed and into the shower at five, then drives us both over here. She would have been in the store all day."

"Can you be certain of that?"

"No, ma'am, I can't. But the store has surveillance video up the ying-yang if you need to verify her whereabouts."

Sonja nodded.

"Can you think of anyone who might want to harm Mr.

Burnham?" Kevin asked.

"Well, look. I'm not the kind of guy who likes to point a finger at someone else, but I have to wonder if you've talked to his old partner. Westerman."

"Why would Mr. Westerman be someone we'd want to talk to?"

"Come on. Everyone knows how much that old fart hated Burnham for cheating him out of his half of the business. It was all Roxie could talk about for a month after it happened."

Kevin raised an eyebrow. "Was she staying in touch with Mr. Burnham?"

"Nah. She and Westerman's wife were chummy for a while, that's all. Naomi would call up and talk Roxie's ear off about how awful her ex was treating poor Bertie. What a laugh. Westerman's a mean little snake. Kick him and he comes back at you, hard."

Chapter

17

Roxanne Lansing walked over from the convenience store to talk to them in Pete's office while her husband went down to check on his mechanic's progress with the flat tire.

She was short and on the heavy side, with tinted hair and a smoker's cough, and she spoke in sentences that were bitten off and expectorated like chunks of rind from a slice of watermelon. However, she was direct and to the point. She admitted she was a recovered alcoholic, she freely acknowledged she'd borne a grudge against Grant Burnham for several years after the divorce, and yes, while she'd initially been saddened by news of his death, she'd quickly put the whole thing in perspective and moved on with her day.

She went through her movements yesterday morning, beginning with her bedside alarm at 4:30 AM; the difficult task of getting Pete up and moving around at that early an hour; their departure from their house in Maberly and the five-minute drive to work; opening the convenience store, the arrival of her regular clerk and a quick inventory of the dairy cooler in anticipation of the day's delivery; and the sporadic busyness that followed as people showed up for their cigarettes, lottery tickets, and to pay for their gas.

When Sonja informed her that someone would be around with a warrant for the store's surveillance video, Roxanne couldn't have cared less.

She echoed her husband's belief that Bert Westerman was a likely suspect they ought to be talking to, and she added that while she'd never gotten a dime from Grant after the divorce settlement went through, he certainly wasn't hurting for money, despite the impact of the pandemic on everyone's bank accounts. Not that she gave a flying whatever, because she and Pete were raking it in, out here in the middle of nowhere with no competition for miles and a surprisingly steady stream of traffic seven days a week.

They wrapped it up soon after that, and while Roxanne returned to work they went downstairs to check on the Fusion. The mechanic had already replaced the repaired tire and returned the car to the parking lot. While Kevin paid the bill, Sonja stepped outside with Terry, the mechanic, who confirmed Pete's story of not having left the garage all morning.

Before they left, she went over to the restaurant for take-out coffee while Kevin made a couple of calls. The first was to the motor pool manager, whom he'd texted beforehand, to let him know the tire had been repaired and the bill was within expectations. The manager told him to bring the car in before close of business so that it could be inspected and serviced. They'd line him up an alternative vehicle when he got there so he wouldn't be stuck without a ride.

His second call was to the number he'd written down in his notebook earlier for the residence of Bert Westerman. Westerman's wife, Naomi, answered and said that her husband was currently in Toronto and would be returning tomorrow morning. She reluctantly gave him Westerman's cellphone number.

His next call was to Westerman's cell, which rang through to voicemail. Kevin left a message identifying himself and asking for a call back.

Sonja got in the car and handed him a cup of coffee. When he brought her up to speed on what he'd been doing, she told him she'd return to RHQ for the rest of the day while he took the Fusion to the garage.

Back in her office, Sonja took a few minutes to catch up on things. She answered e-mails, watered her plants, checked her voicemail, returned a few calls, and took a moment to freshen up in the washroom at the end of the hall before sticking her head into the outer office of her boss, Staff Sergeant Joe Fleishman.

The administrative assistant told her that Fleishman was on the phone but would probably be free in a few minutes. Sonja sat in a chair and chatted with the assistant, whose name was Rick, until Fleishman's door opened and her boss emerged, dropping a file folder into Rick's in-basket.

"Come on in," Fleishman said. "How's it going?"

Sonja sat across the desk from her boss. "They're definitely in a bind, resource-wise."

"How's Dunn doing?" Fleishman ran a hand over his greying brushcut.

"He's trying, but his lack of experience in criminal investigation shows. He hasn't done a very good job putting together a functional team for Ellie."

"Because they're short-handed."

"Yes, mostly. But also because he's not really up to

speed on major case management and how the team needs to work. He brought in a last-minute file co-ordinator, for example, who has no experience and is clearly out of his depth. And a primary investigator who's completely disinterested in finding a murderer."

"Which one are we talking about?"

"Doug Skelton."

"What about the loaner from Leeds?"

Sonja took off her glasses, polished them with a tissue, and put them on again. "Walker. He's good. If not for him, we'd be completely out to sea right now."

"I was just talking to Colleen," Fleishman said, glancing at his desk phone. "The sergeants' list is coming out in a week or so. We've both heard the same thing—you're at the top."

"That's wonderful." Sonja looked at her hands to hide her pleasure at the news. She'd written the examinations, endured the interviews, and waited through the interminable reference checks more than three months ago, trying to put the whole thing out of her mind while the bureaucratic wheels slowly turned. Now, finally, here was the reward for her hard work and patience.

"She agrees with your assessment of Staff Sergeant Dunn—a fish out of water." Fleishman paused. "She's faxing over a secondment agreement as we speak to slot you into the crime unit command vacancy so Dunn can go back to his regular duties. Rick probably has it in his hands right now, waiting for you. Sign it, and you'll act in the job until she can staff you into it permanently from the list. Interested?"

Sonja didn't hesitate. "Yep."

"Fine." Fleishman got up and opened his office door. "Rick?"

"Got it," he called out from his desk.

"Sign it and get out of here," Fleishman said. "Go home

and get some rest. "You're going to need it."

On her way out, Sonja paused. "Oh. By the way, could you do something for me?"

"Something else?" Fleishman snorted. "Sure. What?"

"Walker's turning in his Fusion to the motor pool right now for servicing. Could you see if you could pull some strings and get him assigned a nice, sporty Charger instead?"

Chapter

18

The following morning, which was Monday, Ellie drove to Ottawa to attend the autopsy of Grant Burnham. It would be conducted by Dr. Geneva Kalman of the Eastern Ontario Forensic Pathology Unit, which was located at the Ottawa Hospital. While Dr. Phong, the coroner for Lanark-Leeds, often sent sudden death cases in the Leeds County-401 corridor to Kingston, where Dr. Carey Burton was the pathologist most often responsible for the autopsy, Lanark's closer proximity to Ottawa made it more desirable to direct cases in this county to the EOFPU facility.

Ellie had dealt with Dr. Kalman before, and while she found her a bit curt and occasionally ill-tempered, she trusted her work and respected her judgment. As a pathologist, Dr. Kalman had worked on a number of high-profile cases including airplane crashes in northern Ontario, a pharmaceutical product-tampering case, and several murder investigations, two of which were overseen by Ellie as major case manager. Her work was painstakingly careful and detail oriented, and when she was called upon to testify in court, she was miraculously able to put aside her brusque nature and answer questions simply and directly, in terms a jury would find easy to understand. At the end of the day, what more could you ask for?

Also attending the autopsy this morning would be Staff Sergeant Dunn, Doug Skelton, Dave Martin, and Provincial Constable Ray Joyce, who'd been one of the first responders to the scene and had stayed with the body on its journey to Ottawa Hospital in order to ensure chain of custody. Skelton had tried to duck the assignment, but Dunn had seen the look that crossed Ellie's face and insisted, citing Skelton's presence at the crime scene as primary investigator when the body had been found and prepared for transport.

As she drove, her thoughts strayed from the difficult eccentricities of Doug Skelton to young Dean Othman, her next-door neighbour. Her conversation with the boy's father on Saturday evening replayed itself in her head, and she found herself second-guessing some of the things she'd said. Had she been too aggressive? Challenging him on having decided to move next door to a police detective while knowing she'd shot someone, and lecturing him on her gun safety practices in a starchy way that probably came off as defensive.

She knew it was appropriate to leave up to them—Dean and his parents—the decision as to whether or not he'd continue to visit her in the future, but she began to ask herself whether there was something more she could do to help the boy. Being passive, allowing situations to fester or stagnate or otherwise twist in the wind, just wasn't in her nature.

She grappled with the question for several kilometres.

Dean seemed to be quite interested in law enforcement, and up until this thing about guns, which he'd soon realized had been a misstep, he'd asked intelligent and relevant questions about legislative authorities, procedures, and so on. Passing fancy or not, it was a subject he wanted to understand and explore.

Maybe if he had a chance to see what the job was like first hand, experience a little bit of the boring routine, and the caution and attention to detail necessary to stay safe, plus the patience required to deal with the public, he'd lose interest in the subject and move on to something more acceptable to his parents.

A ride-along?

The OPP as an organization was not particularly keen on the idea of allowing civilian members of the public to accompany uniformed staff while on duty, given the health and safety risks and attendant liability headaches that could result if something went awry. Occasionally they granted ride-alongs to journalists covering a particular story or writing a book or a magazine profile, as well as to students following police foundations programs at the college level, but it wasn't something the force went out of its way to encourage.

She remembered an incident that had occurred during a ride-along more than a decade ago in West Region that had scared the virtual crap out of everyone involved. A police foundations student had been out on a ride-along in an OPP cruiser when an Indigenous police force called for backup during a domestic dispute call out. A number of OPP units responded, including the constable conducting the ride-along. When shots were fired by the man at the centre of the incident, one of the bullets struck the cruiser containing the student. Thankfully, he wasn't harmed. However, it gave everyone involved a bit of a scare, and no one wanted to see the situation repeat itself.

Offering a ride-along to a minor was even more problematic. Each detachment had its own policy on the subject, but it was general practice that the minimum age for participation was twelve, and not only would parental approval be required, but a parent would accompany the child during the ride-along.

She mulled it over. Would Dean be at all interested? Would his parents approve? What about the detachment commander? Would he give it the green light? And if these boxes were checked off, whom would Ellie trust enough to allow them to take Dean out on the road?

It might be a good idea, she decided. It might be the experience of a lifetime for the boy, something that might help his self-confidence while satisfying his avid curiosity about policing. And, of course, it might lead him to decide that his future lay in some other direction, which would please his parents.

Impulsively she thumbed the hands-free button on the steering wheel and called the Leeds County detachment office.

Chapter

19

While Ellie was driving to Ottawa and chatting about her idea for Dean Othman with Inspector Kirk Rousseau, the recently installed commander of Leeds detachment, Kevin and Sonja Freeling were driving on Highway 7 toward Almonte.

"Man, this is great!" Kevin rapped the steering wheel. "What a car. I thought I'd just get another Fusion, but this is amazing."

His newly assignment vehicle from the motor pool was a three-year-old Dodge Charger Pursuit, charcoal grey and, of course, unmarked. It drove like a scared rabbit and handled like a dream.

When he'd turned in the Fusion, he cleaned out all his personal items from the trunk and glove compartment, and the Charger was now fully equipped with his go bag, a tool kit, a digital camera and charging unit that plugged into the cigarette lighter jack, and a small evidence collection kit including extra gloves, fingerprinting supplies, and footprint plaster. It was like moving into his own little portable work space.

"I can't believe they had this one just sitting there."

"Mmm."

"You drive one too, don't you? Do you like them?"

Sonja nodded. "A 5.7-litre Hemi V-8 with 345 cubic inches of displacement and all the other specs that make it a bit of an upgrade over your old Fusion."

They drove under the Cemetrey Side Road overpass, dedicated to the memory of OPP Constable John A.C. Behan. The constable had been with the force for exactly three months in 1956, after having served in the RCMP, when he was killed in a car accident on Highway 7.

Sonja glanced over at him. "So, what do you know about this town? Or should I ask?"

Kevin laughed, aware that she was pulling his leg. "Almonte? Let's see. Population of just over five thousand, forty kilometres west of Ottawa, now part of the amalgamated municipality of Mississippi Mills. Formerly known as Shipman's Mills and Ramsayville. Subsequent to which, for some obscure reason, they decided to name the place after a Mexican general, Juan Almonte."

"Weird."

"You've never been here before?"

"Nope.

"The textile industry was pretty big in the area at one time. In part, I guess, because the land's so rocky and the settlers decided it was better for raising sheep than growing crops."

"You sound like a history buff."

"I guess so." He rubbed the steering wheel with the palm of his hand. "I was up here a couple of years ago, before the pandemic, for a summer fair. They had border collie herding demonstrations going on next to the woollen mill museum, so I watched the dogs for a while and then took the tour inside." He shrugged, embarrassed. "It was interesting."

"Before we get there, I need to tell you. I've been seconded into the sergeant's spot, and Dunn's going back to his regular duties. I'm commanding the crime unit as of this morning."

"Congratulations!"

"Thanks. I've talked to Ellie about it, and short term I'm going to do double duty and continue with the responsibilities as primary investigator for this case as well as handle the supervision of the unit as a whole."

"Are there many other active cases right now?"

"No, thankfully, we're in a bit of a lull, crime-wise. Speaking of which, the home invasion case Heather Hope's been handling had a sudden ending. An estranged son-in-law came forward and confessed, so she's going to be able to give us a hand with Burnham. Skelton's going to cover property crimes."

"I don't think I've met her before."

"She's nice. You'll like her."

Kevin wove his way into Almonte and parked in the lot in front of Westerman's studio. As they went inside, he could see right away that this factory bore very little resemblance to the one in Perth where Bert Westerman had formerly partnered with Grant Burnham.

He followed Sonja across a broad reception area filled with artwork—large wooden sculptures three metres tall and smaller ones on pedestals or behind glass display cases. The few pieces of furniture Kevin looked at were also made of wood and designed to look like works of art in their own right, stylish and attractive. Arranged in between the display pieces were tall plants flourishing in the natural sunlight streaming down from skylights in the ceiling far above their heads.

They identified themselves to a young woman behind a curved reception desk.

"Good morning, detectives," she said. "Welcome to the Westerman Studio. I'm Kendra. Let's get you checked in."

She came around the desk and tapped the screen of a wireless monitor, accessing a visitor log-in app. "Use your camera phone to take a picture of the QR code, and all you have to do is fill in the blanks."

Sonja stepped forward and snapped a photo of the code image on the monitor as Kevin watched over her shoulder. A dialogue box opened on her phone, and she tapped in her name and organization; selected Bert Westerman's name from a list as the employee she was visiting; clicked boxes for coffee, regular, cream, and sugar; declined to have her picture taken; and then tapped Done.

A hand-sized printer next to the monitor spat out a visitor's sticker. Sonja put it on the lapel of her jacket and looked at Kevin. "Your turn."

"Have you seen one of these systems before?" Kendra asked, calling up a fresh QR code.

Kevin shook his head, fumbling for his cellphone.

"Don't worry, it's very simple. It really has enhanced the arrival experience of our visitors." She blushed. "Sorry. I didn't mean to sound like an advertising brochure."

As Kevin filled out the dialogue box, a man walked through a doorway. "Detective Constable Freeling, I'm Thijs Westerman."

He was in his mid-thirties, small and thin, with unruly brown hair and a trimmed beard. He pronounced his name "tice," with a faint Dutch accent. He didn't offer to shake hands, but sketched a congenial little bow and turned to Kevin.

"You must be Detective Constable Walker."

Picking up his visitor's sticker from the printer, Kevin

nodded.

"Did the system notify you of our arrival?' Sonja asked.

"Yes. All my dad's notifications are sent directly to me. He doesn't have much patience for this kind of stuff."

"He's available to speak to us this morning, though, right?"

"Yes. He knows you're coming and will meet us in a break-off room. I told him you were here."

Thijs led the way across the reception area to a doorway on the far side.

"Nice place," Sonja said.

"Thank you. It's a former woollen mill, a smaller one than the one they turned into the museum. It was run for many years by an old Scottish bachelor named Angus Dawson. He died in a dentist's chair while under chloroform in 1909, apparently. The property passed through several hands and fell into disrepair before we bought it."

They trailed after him down a short hallway to a break-off room. As they sat down at the meeting table, Kevin looked around at pieces of wood sculpture on corner shelves.

"You have some nice artwork here," he said, bringing out his notebook and pen.

"Thank you. It's all ours, of course."

Kevin turned to a fresh page and began writing.

"My dad and I are partners. I design, and he carves. And turns, and builds, and so on. He's the master craftsman."

"And you're the artist."

"I guess so. We have a wide variety of offerings. Some of our clients come to us for limited-production bespoke furniture, but where it's really taken off is in the field of original carvings and sculpture. We have a list of private collectors who invest in our work on a regular basis, plus corporate clients who are always looking for something to display in their offices, reception areas, and boardrooms."

"Impressive."

"Thank you."

They looked up as Bert Westerman appeared in the doorway, hands on his hips. "I don't got a lot of time for this," he announced. "I got a lot of work to do."

Thijs stood up. "Papa, come and sit down just for a minute. Kendra's bringing you a cold drink, all right? It won't take long."

"Sure. All right." Westerman wiped his hands on the hem of his streaked and sawdust-covered apron. "As you say."

He dropped into a chair next to Kevin and frowned at Sonja. "Who are you?"

Sonja showed him her badge and warrant card. "Detective Sergeant Freeling. This is Detective Constable Walker. We're investigating the death of your former partner, Grant Burnham."

Westerman ran a hand over his round, balding head. "Ya, sure. Bad business, that."

The receptionist came into the room with a tray. She put a large mug in front of Sonja and a bottle of water in front of Westerman.

"This is my wife, Kendra," Thijs said.

Sonja smiled. "I see. Family business all around."

"Yes." Thijs blushed as Kendra tapped him lightly on the shoulder and left the room.

"Okay, okay," Westerman said, removing the cap from his bottle of water. "Let's cut the chit-chat. What do you want from me?"

Kevin glanced at Sonja, who nodded for him to proceed. "First of all, Mr. Westerman, can you tell us where you were on Saturday?"

Westerman pulled at the water and wiped his ragged moustache with the back of his hand. "Sure. We were in

Ottawa. Thijs and me. Seeing a client. They decided they didn't like the piece they bought and wanted something else. We showed them some other stuff. Pain in the damned neck, you ask me."

"Here's their business card," Thijs said, sending it across the table to Kevin.

"Thanks." Kevin looked at it without picking it up: Edwards, Collins and Delancey, Attorneys at Law. Thijs seemed to have prepared for this interview beforehand.

"Were you consulting them on a legal matter?" He looked at Westerman as he asked the question, but knew that Thijs would reply.

"No. As my father said, they're clients of ours. Mr. Collins in particular is an avid collector."

"As I understand it, Mr. Westerman, there were bad feelings when you and Grant Burnham parted ways. Is that correct?"

"He—"

Westerman held up a hand, interrupting his son. "Ya, correct. He did business with me in bad faith. We argued about everything, all the time. I didn't like that drafty old place he set us up in and I don't like that town. I wanted to stick with the baseball bats because we were making a name for ourselves with them, but he got all restless and insisted we switch to other stuff. Stubborn son of a bitch."

"Maybe I can give you a little background," Thijs put in. "Mr. Burnham first wanted to make hockey sticks, being a former hockey player, but the market had already moved on from wood sticks to composite graphite, which is not what we do. Sam Holman, the Ottawa guy, had introduced his maple bats a few years before and he was already getting some high-profile attention for them, from Barry Bonds, Manny Ramirez, and other players like that, but my father preferred the traditional ash, which had the greater market share in the professional leagues at that time. So that's what Mr. Burnham agreed to go with."

"After much bullshit argument," Westerman muttered.

"Mr. Burnham did a good job selling them," Thijs plowed on. "He had good connections to distributors selling bats to the professional minor league teams, and the company made a decent living with them."

Westerman shrugged. "Too bad that all good things must come to an end, eh son?"

"Yeah, that's true." Thijs looked at Kevin. "After eighteen years maple bats had taken over three-quarters of the market, and our sales dropped right off."

"Burnham wanted to start making kitchen cabinets and commercial junk like that," Westerman groused. "Stuff you can train a chimpanzee to do. I had other ideas but Grant, dear boy, didn't want to listen. Then he comes to me with this balance sheet and financial stuff I don't know nothing about and tells me we're going under. He offers to buy my half before we have to declare bankruptcy or whatever, and I believed him. Thijs was still at school, and there was no one else I knew who could tell me different, so I sold."

"I was just finishing my MBA," Thijs said. "I'd already done my Fine Arts degree and I thought I had time for grad school before Dad would need me. I had no idea Mr. Burnham was going to pull such a dirty trick."

"Not your fault," Westerman said. "Your studies were much more important than my problems with a lying snake."

Kevin edged back from the table and crossed his legs. "You must have been very angry when you found out he'd taken on a new partner and the company was doing well after all."

"You're damn right I was." Westerman's eyes flashed. "I don't like being cheated. Nobody does, eh? That was a rough time for Naomi because I didn't know what to do with myself and I was cursing and swearing all the time and breaking stuff around the house. I was a damned mess."

He looked at his son. "It wasn't until Thijs came home from school that summer with his studies all finished and his head filled with great things that I could get a grip and find a new way to do my work. I was talking about suing and all that crap, but he had better ideas."

Thijs was smiling. "I had a bunch of sketch books filled with concepts for wood sculpting projects, furniture design, and all that. It took a while, but Dad finally sat down with me and went through them. He could see what I wanted us to do, and he agreed with my proposal to form this company to make it happen."

"Best decision I ever did in my life." Westerman shrugged. "Dear Grant made out fine with his new partner, that Moore guy, as you say. Bought the drafty old warehouse and put a lot of cash into it. Moore's apparently a good money man. Maybe almost as good as my boy, here."

Kevin had written down in his notebook the information on the business card Thijs had passed over to him. "So if we call these people, Mr. Westerman, they'll confirm you were in Ottawa meeting with them when Grant Burnham was killed?"

"Sure. Ya."

Kevin saw a look of calm assurance on Westerman's face. He also noticed that Thijs's jaw was tight and his eyes were down, staring at the table.

"Now it's my turn to ask you a question," Westerman said.

Kevin raised his eyebrows.

"Tell me, how did they kill him? Whoever did this?"

"They beat him to death with a baseball bat."

Westerman grunted. "Ironic, eh? What model?"

"Jack Inglis," Kevin quoted from memory. "The M272."

"Hunh. How about that. The last model I did before he bought me out. Karma really is a bitch, ain't it?"

Chapter

20

The Lanark office manager, a grumpy, middle-aged civilian named McGregor whose temperament seemed a perfect fit for the detachment as a whole, had set Kevin up in a cubicle conveniently located right outside the men's washroom.

Its previous occupant had apparently vacated the premises some time around Valentine's Day, leaving behind a red, heart-shaped ceramic dish with a broken lid, several unsigned paper valentines intended for children, and a drawer filled with red foil wrapping stripped from chocolate balls, which, for whatever reason, the person had not bothered to toss into the wastepaper basket. Along with the rest of the junk.

The cubicle was equipped with an older model desktop computer and monitor that afforded him access to the detachment's local area network. Through it, he was able to process his e-mail and type up his reports for attachment to the Burnham file in the case management system. The computer was so slow he wondered if he should check to see if it might be using a dial-up modem.

Once he'd cleaned up the refuse in the cubicle and managed (after several attempts) to log in to the network, Kevin got busy typing up an interview report covering their meeting with Bert and Thijs Westerman. After he finished the report, documenting all the information provided by them—including their whereabouts on Saturday—he intended to call the Ottawa law firm the Westermans had mentioned in order to confirm their alibis.

"Hey."

Kevin looked over his shoulder at Sonja, who was standing in the cubicle doorway with several paper bags of takeout food in her hands.

"Lunch break."

He glanced at his watch and was surprised to see that it was almost twenty minutes past noon. "I didn't realize it was so late."

"I got us sandwiches from the Red Anvil. That is, if you still have an appetite." She looked behind her at the washroom door, which was closing behind someone hurrying in to take care of urgent business.

He shrugged. "Pleasant neighbourhood."

She made a face at the lingering odour. "Aren't there other empty cubicles you could use?"

"Not according to McGregor. He was doing me a special favour, apparently, fitting me in here on his crammed floor plan."

"Bullshit. Come on."

He saved his report, logged out, and followed her through the maze to an empty meeting room on the far side of the floor, just down from Staff Sergeant Dunn's office. The table was bare, chairs neatly parked around it, and the two rolling whiteboards had been wiped clean. Kevin suspected that Sonja had tidied up beforehand.

She dropped into a chair and slid one of the bags across the table. "I got you Montreal smoked meat. Mine's a Reuben. You can have it if you don't like yours."

Kevin sat down and tore open his bag down the middle of the Red Anvil logo. "No, this is great. Thanks."

She opened another bag and set out cans of Coke, ginger ale, and iced tea, followed by napkins and disposable utensils. "Help yourself."

Kevin grabbed the iced tea and popped it open. "So, how about you? Got your new office yet?"

She shook her head. "There's something wrong with the air duct. They're fixing it today, so I thought I'd just work in here for now and stay out of their way." She took a big bite, looking around the room.

"Hopefully not a dead raccoon or something stuck in there."

She snorted.

"We need a team meeting," Kevin said. "Pool what we've got so far. It feels like we're stuck in the mud right now."

"I thought we could make this a working lunch," she said, eyeing her sandwich critically.

Kevin wiped his fingers and got up. He grabbed one of the whiteboards and rolled it over. "I feel better with a chart in front of me."

"Me too. Eat first."

"Okay." Kevin sat down and greedily resumed his attack on the sandwich. It was exceptionally good.

"This crime unit needs to be rebuilt from the inside out," Sonja mused. "Traffic and patrol are in good shape. The detachment as a whole is in good shape. Dunn's a good administrator, and he makes Colleen's life a lot easier. He'll have his own detachment before very long. But he wasn't comfortable commanding the crime unit, particularly where it's so shorthanded, and it showed. A murder case just tipped the scale a little too much." She raised the last bite of her sandwich and sniffed it. "I'm supposed to be eating and not talking."

Kevin laughed. "I—"

"Excuse me, Detective Sergeant Freeling?"

A young woman stood in the doorway, one hand on her hip and the other resting on the strap of a blue canvas messenger bag. She wore jeans, hiking shoes, and a yellow T-shirt with Felix the Cat on the front, strutting along and whistling a tune.

"You must be Heather," Sonja said, finishing her sandwich. "Come on in."

Kevin stood up as the woman rounded the table and shook his hand with a firm grip. Apparently she wasn't an elbow-bumper.

"You must be Kevin Walker. I'm Heather Hope. As in, 'I hope we get her and not Skelton.'"

Sonja barked a short laugh. "Take a seat. We're just finishing lunch. Have you eaten?"

"Yeah, thanks." She unslung her messenger bag, dropped it on the table, and sat down in the chair on Kevin's right.

"I think I mentioned," Sonja said to Kevin, "that Heather's going to be able to give us a hand with Burnham."

"Yes."

"I've worked a few major cases before," Heather said, taking her cellphone from her pocket, "but not a homicide. I understand you're the guy with all the expertise in that area."

"I've worked a couple," Kevin replied.

"Good. Then consider me an apt pupil."

"If you're finished eating," Sonja said, "maybe we could get busy on the whiteboard. It'll be a good way to bring

Heather up to speed."

Kevin still had a bite left of his sandwich, but he took the hint and got up. Picking up a dry erase marker, he wrote "Grant Burnham" in the middle of the whiteboard and drew a circle around it.

"Our victim."

"The hockey player," Heather said, not looking up from her cellphone.

"Yes. You know about him?"

"Yeah. Who doesn't?"

"Okay." Kevin drew a line from the circle to the top right corner of the whiteboard and wrote "Roxanne Rechelbacher Lansing" and "Pete Lansing." He drew a circle around them. "The victim's ex-wife and her second husband. They run a couple of businesses out on Seven, at Maberly."

"Wait, Lansing's Corner? I get my gas from them."

"Is that right?"

"I live on Bolingbroke Road, just down from there."

Kevin wasn't familiar with the area, but he nodded anyway. "No love lost between the exes, but we got a warrant for video surveillance recordings that will probably put both of them there at work on Saturday morning when the victim was getting beaten to death with one of his own baseball bats."

Heather winced. "Detective Sergeant Freeling gave me the rundown on the scene and the body. Sounds brutal."

"Yeah, it was brutal, all right," Kevin said.

"Murder for hire?"

Kevin shrugged. "Possibly, but I doubt it. Everything points to a crime of passion using a weapon of opportunity, the bat coming from the back of the victim's truck. Someone being paid to kill someone for money would probably bring their own weapon and not invest nearly as much emotion in it."

Heather smiled at him. "Sounds like you've put a lot of thought into this already."

Kevin drew another line from Burnham to the top left corner of the whiteboard and wrote "Colquitts," then below that "Lona," "Malcolm/Mack," and "Tracy/Trace." He drew a short line below them and said, "Next-door neighbours. They live on Concession Eight A, just east of Balderson."

Heather make a sound at the back of her throat.

"Sorry? Something?"

"No, just a private joke. Don't mind me."

"Do you know these people?"

"Never heard of them."

Kevin glanced at Sonja before continuing. "We talked to the wife, Lona, Saturday afternoon. Something a little off about her, maybe. She was very upset by the news."

"Uh oh. Hanky panky?"

He shrugged. "Hard to say. The victim was definitely a ladies' man. The husband, Mack, is an aircraft mechanic at YOW. He and the son, Trace, are at the top of our interview list."

"As I mentioned on the phone," Sonja said, "we've been a little shorthanded."

"I imagine Señor Skelton's been a big help, though."

Sonja said nothing.

Kevin drew a line from Burnham's name to the left of the whiteboard, wrote "Max Macdonald," and drew a little star beside it. "Lives across the road from the victim's woodlot on Nine A. Found the body. Lives alone. Comes off as introverted and anxious, a hero worshipper who thought it was great he could talk to an ex-hockey player."

"Burnham never made it to the NHL, did he?"

Kevin shook his head. "Spent three years in the minors, blew out his knee, and that was it."

"Okay."

Kevin tapped Macdonald's name with the end of the marker. "He put us on a bit of a side track by saying he thought Burnham was worried about his finances, which has been contradicted by other witnesses, but I don't really think it was deliberate. I think he's just a little clueless, is all."

"Speaking of finances," Sonja prompted.

Nodding, Kevin drew a line from Burnham's name to the far right and wrote "Wally Moore." He circled it and looked at Heather, who had put her cellphone down and was giving him her full attention.

"Current business partner. Venture capital guy; invested in Burnham's factory and ended up stepping in as shop manager. Saw the victim Saturday morning not all that long before his death, got him to sign a couple of documents, and has an alibi for the rest of the day. Possible murder-for-hire suspect as well, but I still don't like that theory very much."

"What about other family?" Heather asked. "Isn't his father still alive?"

Kevin drew a short line immediately below Grant Burnham's name and wrote "Bobby Burnham." He put the cap on his marker and shrugged. "Not a suspect. Pretty broken up about it. Too old; no motive; not physically able to swing a baseball bat with the kind of exceptionally violent power it took to kill the victim."

"Brothers? Sisters?"

"Only one sibling, a sister who predeceased him. His mother's also dead; breast cancer, about ten years ago."

Heather studied the board. "Is this it, then? Our field of possible suspects?"

Kevin uncapped the marker and drew a line past Bobby Burnham's name, where he wrote "Bert Westerman" and "Thijs."

Heather frowned. "This?"

"He pronounces it 'Tice.' It's Dutch. Bert's the former partner, scammed by Burnham to sell his half of the business. Crotchety old goat. Despised the victim and doesn't apologize for it. Thijs is his son and current partner. Their factory in Almonte seems to be making money hand over fist, so I'm not sure yet about motive, but the emotion definitely seems to still be there."

Heather used her phone to snap a photo of the whiteboard.

Someone rapped on the open door.

Kevin turned around as Doug Skelton walked into the room.

Chapter

21

"Doug," Sonja said. "How did your appointment go?"

"I guess I'll live. A1C numbers are pretty good." He pointed behind him with his thumb. "These two young fellows are looking for you."

"Thanks, Doug. Come on in, gentlemen. Glad you could make it."

Skelton gave her a two-fingered boy scout salute and left, closing the door behind him.

The two new arrivals were polar opposites. The older one, tall and immaculate in a neat suit and repp tie, shook hands all around before sitting down.

"This is Detective Constable Bob Pierce," Sonja said. "He's going to help us out for the next few days with the paperwork and other administrative stuff. He'll also take Stephen Downey under his wing and bring him up to speed on the file co-ordination responsibilities."

"Boy," Heather drawled, "we're sure glad to see you."

Pierce smiled at her.

The other new arrival was a dishevelled and shaggy young bear in an ill-fitting tan jacket and polyester trousers. He looked as though he might be five to ten years younger than Pierce. He ambled over to Sonja and shook her hand. "Nice to see you again. I hear congratulations are in order."

"Thanks." Sonja pulled out the chair next to her. "Sit here, Alaric. Everyone, this is Detective Constable Alaric Quinn."

"Hi." Quinn sat down and opened his battered briefcase. Removing a handful of stapled documents, he passed them over to Sonja. "There should be enough copies to go around. I know some people still like paper. It's all in the case file, anyway."

Sonja took a copy and, leaning over, gave the rest to Pierce. "Thanks, Alaric. How was your drive?"

"Nerve-wracking. I don't like two-lane highways, and Seven's particularly awful." He ran a hand through his uncombed brown hair and, leaning forward, began to struggle out of his jacket.

"Alaric works in the Ottawa detachment office," Sonja said.

Quinn looked around. "Detective Inspector March isn't here?"

"She's attending the autopsy."

"Dang, that's too bad. I've only met her once before. Impressive. Really impressive."

Kevin took a copy of the documents and handed the rest to Heather Hope. He scanned the top page and saw that it was a report on the financial status of the Burnham & Moore Wood Working Company. "That was fast."

"Not really." Quinn draped his jacket on the back of his chair and loosened his tie. It was a red flowered monstrosity, far too wide, but it was actually a decent match, colour-wise, with his yellow shirt and gold-framed glasses. "I took receipt of the files early Saturday evening. More than enough time."

"What does this tell us?" Sonja asked.

"That the company is in very good shape. Remarkably good shape, considering."

"I hate numbers," Heather grumbled.

"Not to worry," Quinn said. "That's why I'm here. Let me start with the company's balance sheet. Generally you want to look at three things. First, you check out their working capital, which is their current assets, including cash and accounts receivable, plus inventories of raw materials, in this case pretty expensive wood, metal fittings, and so on, and also their finished goods on hand, waiting to be sold. You subtract their current liabilities, like debts and accounts payable, and that gives you their net working capital. These guys are in really good shape."

"Halfway down the first page," Sonja said.

"Yeah. That's right. Second thing, you check out their asset performance. So, what's their net income divided by the total value of their assets? The building which they own, the machinery and tools, several design patents, and so on; these things all have a dollar value, right? So, are they using these assets properly to generate a decent level of income? In this case, Hell yeah. They sure are."

"Bottom of the page," Sonja said.

"Third thing, capital structure. So, equity from company shares and debt in the form of loans, bond issues, that sort of thing. How they fund overall operations and growth versus how much borrowed money is due to be paid back at some point, plus interest. Isn't this fascinating?"

"Riveting," Heather murmured.

Kevin turned the page and saw the figures Quinn was referring to. He cleared his throat. "Your takeaway is that the company's balance sheet is very healthy."

"An understatement!" Quinn adjusted his glasses. "Think about it. These guys were shut down for seven months, from June the first, 2020 to January fifth, 2021. Because of the pandemic, right? They applied for government assistance to cover overhead, taxes, and loan payments during that time, but really it was more because it was there to make use of, I imagine, than because it was an urgent necessity. Their cash reserves were good, more than adequate, and they've already paid it all back. This is an extremely well-managed company."

"How about Grant Burnham's personal finances?" Sonja asked.

"My next handout." Quinn reached into his briefcase for another sheaf of documents. "I'll give you a moment to pass these around. You know, I've always sort of believed the stereotype that professional athletes are a bunch of muscle-bound cement heads. Not that I'm jealous, of course." He gave Sonja a side glance. "Believe it or not, I've invested in a gym membership."

She grinned. "Good for you!"

"My goal is twenty-five pounds to start with. Then maybe Dad will stop referring to me as his plump young son and just settle for large-boned or something."

"How is Pat, anyway?"

"Unhappy."

"Oh?"

"He just lost a patent case. He's trying to decide whether or not to appeal."

Sonja winked at Kevin over the top of her glasses. "Alaric's dad is an inventor. Kitchen gadgets, green energy devices, exercise and hiking gear, you name it."

"I see." Kevin accepted the next batch of reports from Pierce, kept one, and passed the rest to Heather.

"As I was saying," Quinn said, wiping perspiration from

his forehead with a linen handkerchief, "your victim gave the lie to the blockheaded athlete stereotype. His chequing and savings accounts, four in total, all have six-figure balances. His investment portfolio is very impressive, almost all blue-chip dividend generators. His assets include the Balderson property, a house in Tofino, a condo in New Orleans, and a waterfront property on South Caicos in the Turks and Caicos Islands."

Kevin frowned. "Disproportionate lifestyle?"

"No," Quinn said, "no signs of questionable activity whatsoever. Income and expenses balance out. Several of his larger acquisitions he financed through his main bank, as you can see on the third page, and his loan payments were as regular as clockwork. No big-time deposits of mysterious money; nothing like that at all. He was just a really, really good money manager."

"Maybe he's just good at hiding stuff," Heather said.

"From me? Surely you jest. Believe me, I know how that game works, and I'm not finding any indicators whatsoever of malfeasance. I went over the numbers a dozen times, and every which way you look at them, they all add up."

"Do we know who stands to inherit all of this?"

"According to the will found in his residence," Quinn said, "everything's going to be liquidated and disbursed to a number of different charities. Except for a million dollars that's already sitting in an account held in trust for his father, Robert John Burnham. The account was set up to pay for his father's living expenses, medical bills not covered by OHIP, and funeral costs."

"Nothing for the ex-wife, or any other individual?"

"Nope. Doctors Without Borders, a couple of area hospitals, the Humane Society, a cat rescue organization in Ottawa, stuff like that. The attorney who prepared it for him is the same one who handled all his real estate transactions."

"Oh? What's his name?"

"Her name. Clarisse De Witt. Here in Perth."

The name meant nothing to him. Kevin asked, "How are we coming on the phone records?"

"It'll take another day or two," Alaric said. "The usual rigmarole."

"Okay." At that moment his cellphone vibrated. He slipped it out of his pocket and saw that it was a text message from BMankewicz:

Call me. Urgent.

Bill Mankewicz was a provincial constable who worked out of Elizabethtown-Kitley, Kevin's home base. They were friends, and when Kevin had played hockey, before Josh was born, Mankewicz was a teammate. If he was texting him out of nowhere and saying it was urgent, Kevin knew he'd better respond.

"Excuse me," he said, getting up. "I need to take this."

Out in the hallway he leaned against the wall and called Mankewicz's number. It was answered on the second ring.

"Kev. Thanks for calling. What's your twenty?"

"I'm at the Lanark detachment office right now, Mank. Perth. What's up?"

"Shit. How fast can you get to the village?"

"The village? Sparrow Lake?"

"Yeah, yeah. You need to get here ASAP."

"Why? What's going on?"

"It's Janie, Kev. I've got her sitting in the back of my vehicle right now, and unless she cools down and smartens up I'm going to have to arrest her."

"What? What the hell for?"

"Too much talk and not enough driving, pal. Get here."

Chapter

22

The village of Sparrow Lake was a small cluster of homes on either side of the county road that ran right through it in a straight line. With a population of about seven hundred people, it was normally a quiet, sleepy little place that seldom saw anything in the way of action or excitement. At this time of year, its shops and sidewalks saw more cottagers, many of them Americans vacationing on the lake itself, than local residents.

As Kevin approached the village, coming from the west, he could see ahead of him the flashing light bars of two cruisers in the middle of town. His heart sank as he realized they were parked in front of the Bridges building, where Janie ran her hairdressing salon.

All the parking spots along that block of Main Street were occupied, but a uniformed constable waved him over and motioned for him to double park behind his cruiser. It was Mankewicz.

"What the hell's going on?" Kevin demanded, jumping out of his car.

"Christ, Kevin," Mankewicz said, "she's madder than a goddamned hornet. You need to get her calmed down right away."

"What happened?"

"Dispatch says they got a call from a guy coming out of the coffee shop down the street." Mankewicz pointed. "Said he saw a man and a woman fighting on the sidewalk."

Kevin ran his eyes around the scene. A second cruiser was parked on an angle in front of the first. A uniformed officer, whom he recognized as Brent Long, was directing traffic around the obstructed lane, motioning impatiently as drivers rubbernecked on their way past. Another officer was encouraging the bystanders on the sidewalk to move along, while a fourth, Brenda Dalton, stood between the two cruisers, hands on her hips.

In the back of Mankewicz's cruiser Kevin saw the shape of someone's head.

Janie.

Someone else was sitting in the other patrol car. Janie's sparring partner, no doubt.

"Witnesses say they saw Janie take a swing at the guy," Mankewicz said. "She missed. The guy swung back and missed, but Janie lost her balance and fell. She hit her face on the sidewalk. You can see the bruise coming. Jack and Louise happened to be here on a coffee stop, and they checked her out. She's okay. No signs of concussion or a fracture or anything."

Kevin shook his head in exasperation. Jack and Louise were paramedics who worked in the area. He was relieved that they'd been on the scene and had examined Janie, but it did very little to offset his growing anger.

"The guy's name is Harry Bridges. Says he owns the

building."

"Christ. Not him."

"Apparently she's locked out. Someone called her at home and said the landlord was here; she drove over; and they had a confrontation and exchanged whiffs. Witnesses stepped in and broke it up, and that's where we're at right now."

Kevin saw Janie's apple-green Pontiac Vibe parked in a spot down the street.

"If you could talk to her," Mankewicz said, leaning forward and lowering his voice, "we could maybe call it a draw, get them to apologize to each other, and you could take her home. We don't want to lay charges for something like this. Honestly, there's a lot better shit for us to do than dick around here."

Kevin nodded and walked up to the cruiser. Janie was in the back seat on the driver's side, staring straight ahead. He walked around the vehicle and Brenda Dalton opened the door for him.

"Good luck," she said.

Chapter

23

She looked at him sideways and bared her teeth.

"If they let me out of here, I'm going to rip his balls off and stuff them down his goddamned throat."

Kevin looked at the red mark on her cheekbone and swallowed. "What happened?"

"Peggy called, said the slimy little prick was here, strutting around. I came in and ripped him a new one. He didn't like it and called me a bitch. 'A fucking know-it-all bitch,' to be exact. I tried to take his head off but I missed, goddammit. I want another shot at him."

As far as Kevin knew, Janie had never hit anyone in anger before in her life. Even during the darkest days of her first marriage, when Doug Warrick would get drunk and take out his frustrations on her, she never retaliated in kind. She'd insisted to Kevin, repeatedly, that it was something she'd never done and something she'd never do. She didn't believe in physical violence. She'd smack the kids on the bum when they were small to make them mind, but it was always fairly mild and short-lived. God knew she had a temper, and it flared with little provocation when she was tired or frustrated, but this was something new to his experience.

"Bill says if you apologize to each other, it'll be over and we can go home."

"Not a shittin' chance."

"Did you ask him to give you a key so you could get back in?"

She rolled her eyes. "What do you think, Kevin? Do you think I came over here to invite him for a cup of goddamned tea? Jesus H. Christ almighty."

"What did he say to that?"

"Oh for crissakes, all he did was vomit a bunch of bullshit about Summer's antiques stash and I must be in cahoots with her and taking a cut and blah blah frigging blah. The guy's loony tunes."

"I think you made a reasonable request. You just want to get back to work."

"Reasonable? Reasonable? I'm sick and tired of trying to be reasonable with a bunch of goddamned sons a bitches, Kevin. It's time to crack a few heads open."

"No, it's not."

"Yes, it is. Let me at him."

"Janie."

"What?"

He looked at her.

She closed her eyes and screamed, as loudly as she could. It was pure, unadulterated anger.

Outside, Brenda Dalton took a step forward but Kevin caught her eye and shook his head. Dalton stepped back, her face grim.

He gave Janie a moment.

After a while, she opened her eyes and looked out the window. "I'm not apologizing."

"Maybe if you apologize to Bill and Brenda for causing a disturbance? And promise to go home and cool down?"

"No. The bastard tried to clock me. I want another shot."

"What if I ask Bridges nicely to give you a key? So you can get back to work?"

"No. I don't need you fighting my battles for me."

He sighed. "It should never have gotten to this point, Janie."

"I know." She reached up to wipe at a tear rolling down her cheek.

Her wrists were cuffed together.

The mother of his son. And his two beloved step-children. His life partner. He thought, at that moment, his heart would break.

"Give me a minute, darlin'." He rapped on the window, and Brenda let him out.

He waited for Mankewicz to join them, then folded his arms and looked from one to the other. "What's your feeling on this?"

"I already told you we got better shit to waste our time on," Mankewicz said.

Kevin looked at Dalton.

"He tried to physically assault her," she said.

Kevin was very well aware that attempted assault was still considered a criminal offence under the law, despite the fact that a blow had not been struck. Technically, they could both be charged.

"She swung on him first," he reminded her.

"Kevin, for God's sake."

"I know. I know." His jaw tightened. "I'd like a piece of the son of a bitch myself. Nobody takes a swing at my wife. Nobody." He took a breath. "However. The primary objective here is to keep the peace, right? Defuse the situation. Exercise discretion." Kevin looked over at the other cruiser. "What's his state of mind?"

"He's scared shitless. I have a feeling it's not the first time he's swung on a woman."

"He's in the middle of a messy divorce process. That's why he's changing the locks and getting all shitty about it."

Mankewicz looked at the building behind them. "That's her place? *Skizzors*?"

"Yeah. Look, I'll deal with whatever you guys decide. It's your call."

Dalton shrugged. "It all goes into the occurrence report. Names and addresses, a blow-by-blow description, everything."

"Which goes into the system," Mankewicz added, "and stays there. We're not saying anything you don't already know."

"I know." What they were telling him was that if Janie's name were ever run again by law enforcement, this incident would appear as a hit. Even if no charges were laid, it would still be there as a precedent that might lead to a different outcome another time around.

Dalton frowned at him. "You'll take her home? Talk some sense into her?"

"Immediately," Kevin said. "And stay with her. She's not a talker, at least not the two-way-conversation type of talk, but we'll work it out."

Dalton gave him a wan smile and shook her head. "Good luck," she said for the second time.

Chapter

24

The following morning, which was Tuesday, Ellie was driving from her cottage on Sparrow Lake to the Perth detachment office when a call came in from Dave Martin.

"Good morning, Ellie. Sounds like you're en route to somewhere."

"Perth. What can I do for you?"

"I'm just checking in to make sure you're in the loop on this."

"On what, Dave?" She could hear the irritation in his voice. Normally he was a very easy-going sort, with a dry sense of humour and a streak of irreverence to go with it, but something was obviously bothering him this morning.

"I'm sending a team to Lanark village," he said. "Partridge Small Engine Repair, to be exact. On Princess Street."

"Okay, Dave. I'll bite. Why?"

"Apparently our lovely dear colleague Doug Skelton has found evidence connected to the Burnham case in Hollis Partridge's shop and wants us there ASAP to take possession and process it. God bless his incompetent little heart."

"Skelton?"

"You weren't aware, I take it."

"No. Do you know exactly what the evidence is?"

Martin snorted. "Nope. Guy's too important to share details with the hired help. The SOCOs will have to deal with it when they get there."

Ellie sighed. "Okay, Dave. Thanks for the heads-up. Keep me posted."

"I don't like the guy, Ellie. I'm sorry. I just don't. Anyway, that's got nothing to do with anything. Talk to you later."

The line went dead, and Ellie punched the button on her steering wheel to disconnect.

She did a slow burn, falling in behind a line of cars waiting for an opening to pass a large, slow-moving tractor. As a major case manager, she was responsible for ensuring that sufficient resources were deployed to work the investigation, and in this specific instance she'd faced a personnel crunch right from the beginning. Her first move had been to engineer the loan of Kevin Walker from the Leeds crime unit, followed by the acquisition of Sonja Freeling from the regional office, first as a detective and then as Staff Sergeant Dunn's replacement as acting detective sergeant. Detective Constable Heather Hope had cleared her home invasion case and would partner up with Kevin. Following Ellie's request for further assistance, Colleen Galvin had secured the temporary loan of Detective Constable Pierce from the region, with a promise of other constables to conduct interviews and to process information coming in from Alaric Quinn and other sources.

All of which to say, despite having to scramble for hands to work the Burnham case, she hadn't hesitated to make sure that Doug Skelton was moved off to the sidelines. He clearly lacked the temperament and skill set to function as a field investigator in a homicide, despite his decent record in other cases worked by the crime unit.

Now here she was, getting a phone call about the apparent discovery of important evidence from Dave Martin, for crying out loud, rather than from Sonja, the crime unit commander and de facto primary investigator.

As soon as her turn came and the oncoming lane was clear, she swung around the tractor and hit the accelerator while thumbing the green hands-free button on the steering wheel.

"Call Freeling."

When Sonja answered, Ellie didn't mince words. "Are you aware that Doug Skelton has called an Ident team to Partridge Small Engines in Lanark village?"

"No, Ellie. Skelton?" She sounded as baffled as Ellie had been when Martin had called her.

"I thought he was off violent crimes and exclusively working property."

"He's supposed to be. Where did you say he is? Lanark?"

"Partridge Small Engines. Look, I'm just about to hit Port Elmsley, so I'll be there hopefully before the turn of the damned century. Find out what's going on, will you?"

"I'll call him," Sonja said, her voice tight. "Kevin and Heather are here. I'll send them out right away to handle it."

"Thank you." Ellie ended the call. She put her foot on the brake pedal, reducing speed as she reached the hamlet of Port Elmsley, a cluster of buildings where Highway 43 was intersected by Station Road on the right and County

Road 18 a hundred feet or so past that on the left.

It wasn't that she was an absolute stickler for hierarchy, but she felt that chain of command was important in major case investigation, and someone like Doug Skelton couldn't just thumb his nose at it and do whatever the hell he wanted.

Ellie chafed as she followed several cars that were conscientiously adhering to the posted speed limit.

After all, she fumed, this wasn't a university environment, where someone could take a bright idea and hare off along their own personal line of research, hoping for a big discovery of some kind. Or a news organization, where journalists could freelance in the field, hunting for their next big scoop.

Sure, she valued creativity and out-of-the-box thinking as much as anyone else, and she'd often seen detectives and analysts make intuitive leaps when working with evidence that moved an investigation forward in unexpected and fruitful directions.

She also understood the reality that patrol officers learned quickly when working alone in the field or with a single partner, that they would face situations in which they'd have to make their own decisions on the spot, weighing discretion and social responsibility with the need to enforce the law. Often they were required to choose quickly, without the luxury of consulting with their sergeant, who was often elsewhere and juggling more balls than just theirs.

Still.

Just the same.

Everyone's mind had to be focused at all times on the concept of reasonable grounds and what a court of law would rule, after an arrest was made and charges were laid, in terms of the admissibility of evidence discovered during the course of an investigation. Decision-making layers, not only within a team of detectives but with the primary investigator, the commanding sergeant, and the major case manager, served as filters to ensure the proper conduct of the case at each point along the way.

What had led Doug Skelton to show up at a small engine repair shop in Lanark village and suddenly discover evidence relative to Grant Burnham's murder? Did he have probable grounds to go there in the first place, to demand to see something in particular, and then to seize it as evidence to be turned over to Ident for processing? Would his actions, and the evidence itself, stand up to scrutiny down the road?

Ellie had no idea. Neither did Sonja Freeling, or Dave Martin, or anyone else other than Skelton. Which was the entire point.

Her foot went down a little too heavily on the accelerator as she left Port Elmsley. Once again, a promising morning had turned sour for her, and her mood was anything but light.

Chapter

25

"I'll drive," Heather said as they walked out into the parking lot behind the detachment office.

Kevin followed her to a dusty Ford Fusion not unlike the one he'd turned in to the motor pool yesterday. She thumbed her key fob, and when he opened the passenger door he found the seat littered with stuff.

"Sorry," she said, getting in behind the wheel and leaning over to toss handfuls into the back.

They were, he saw, comic books: *Daffy Duck*; *Uncle Scrooge and the Beagle Boys*; *Star Trek*; and even a *Thundercats* issue he remembered from long ago.

"Reading material," she said, gunning the engine and backing out of the parking space as he hastily fastened his seat belt.

She swung out into the street without looking and took a quick right onto Highway 511, which would take them north to Lanark, about eighteen kilometres northwest of Perth.

"We haven't been properly introduced," she said, dropping the sun visor and throwing on a pair of Ray-Ban Wayfarer sunglasses. "I'm Heather Hope, from Keene. Know where that is?"

"Yeah, actually I do. Up near Peterborough. How long have you been with the crime unit?"

"Since forever, man." She smiled at him, her cheeks dimpling. "Three years. Having a ball."

"You guys have been drastically short staffed."

"Tell me about it. I've worked so many doubles I'm starting to see double."

She was a very fast driver, and they were already only a few minutes away from Balderson.

"If we have a chance when we come back," Kevin said, "you can turn onto Eight A and we'll take a look at the victim's house."

"Yeah, okay."

Her tone was light, careless, and Kevin wasn't sure whether she was kidding around or if she was actually being sarcastic and had no interest whatsoever in the particulars of the case. He was finding the Lanark staff took a lot of getting used to.

She barely slowed down as they reached Balderson. As they passed the cheese outlet, she snorted.

"What?"

She shook her head, not bothering to answer.

Very soon they arrived at Lanark village. Heather turned left at the T-intersection and then swung a quick right as Highway 511, referred to locally now as George Street, ran in a northerly direction through the village.

She waved her hand at an abandoned limestone and cement block factory on the left as they crossed the little bridge spanning the Clyde River. "Shame to see that place falling apart."

"That was the Kitten Mill, wasn't it?"

Heather nodded. "My grandmother had a pantsuit from them that she used to wear at Christmastime. Shocking pink with flared trousers. Looked godawful, but she loved it. It was her favourite."

The village that had grown up around the Clyde in the 1820s prospered for more than a century and a half on logging and a thriving textile industry rivalling that of Mississippi Mills to the northeast. Its bright future ended in 1959 when a fire wiped out most of its commercial buildings, many of which were uninsured. A subsequent flood of cheap imported goods from China and southeast Asia finished the job. The Glenayr Kitten Mill, which produced sweaters, skirts, and yes, pantsuits, continued to operate and to sell their merchandise into the 1990s before closing their doors for good.

Partridge Small Engine Repair occupied a small, single-storey frame building just around the corner on Princess Street. Heather drove past the van that had been driven to the scene by the SOCOs and parked in front of it. As they walked back to the shop, they looked at Doug Skelton's dark green Range Rover.

"He's still here," Heather said.

Kevin wasn't sure if that was a good thing or a bad thing.

She opened the door, jingling a bell suspended above the lintel. She nodded at a uniformed constable standing inside. "Hey there, Pete. What's happening?"

"Heather." The constable looked over the top of her head at Kevin. "You are?"

"Oh, this is the famous Kevin Walker," Heather said with a wave of her hand. "Gracing us with his presence from the Leeds crime unit. Lucky us, eh?"

Pete's eyes narrowed, but in a way that caused the laugh

lines at the corners of his eyes to deepen with amusement. He reached over Heather's shoulder, offering his hand. "Pete DiNardo. SOCO-at-large."

Kevin shook his hand and looked around. The place smelled of motor oil, gasoline, and ozone. The floor space was filled with snow blowers, lawn mowers, and several dirt bikes propped up on their kickstands. An older uniformed officer, no doubt the other scenes-of-crime officer, stood at the back counter arguing with Doug Skelton while the owner of the business listened from behind the counter with his arms folded and a grim expression on his face.

"Sergeant Martin said we should wait for you," Pete explained, leading the way back to the counter.

"Okay," Heather said easily. "Doug. Whatcha got?"

"I don't know why the hell they called you out," Skelton complained, glaring at Kevin. "I got this covered."

Heather leaned her hip against the counter. "Got what covered?"

"I'm the one who called," said the man behind the counter.

"Called me," Skelton added.

"Why'd you call Doug, Hollis?" Heather asked.

"Every so often some goofball comes in trying to sell me stolen property. I call Doug and he comes over to check it out."

"This is Hollis Partridge," Heather told Kevin, "the owner of this fine establishment. He fixes up my snow blower every fall and does a pretty good job of it for not too much. Isn't that right, Hollis?"

"Look, Atkins," Skelton said to the older SOCO, "this is very simple. You take the chain saw to your lab as evidence, you dust it for prints and swab it for DNA and whatever the hell else you guys do, and I'll run the serial number and see if it matches up with our vic. Is that too complicated for you?"

"You look, Skelton." Atkins poked a finger at the detective. "I don't bow and scrape whenever you open your mouth and say something. My orders, from my sergeant, are to wait for the arrival of these two detective constables before taking this chain saw into evidence. Is that too complicated for you, Farmer Brown?"

"Okay, okay," Heather said, stepping between them. "Dispense with the personalities and let's hear what you got. Mr. Partridge? You're up to bat."

"Yeah, sure. Well. Guy comes in, Max Macdonald to be exact, with this chain saw and wants to know if I'd sell it for him on consignment."

Kevin bent over to look at a Poulin Pro chain saw sitting on the corner. Its green paint was chipped and scraped, but its sixteen-inch blade was wiped clean and the chain itself looked sharp and well cared for.

"I said maybe," Partridge continued, "because I've sold a few things for Macdonald before and they were okay. But I said, 'Just a minute,' and gave it a look over. That's when I saw this."

He picked up the chain saw and pointed at initials scratched on the underside of the handle—GSB—and what looked like a pair of crossed hockey sticks below them.

As Kevin caught his breath and Atkins winced, Heather casually asked, "You've been handling the saw like this, picking it up and everything, since Mr. Macdonald brought it in?"

"Sure, yeah. Of course. How else was I supposed to know if it was good enough to sell?"

"You'll have to let Constable Atkins here take your fingerprints before we leave, okay? For elimination purposes. Understood?"

"Huh? Uh, yeah. Oh, okay. I get it. Since I've been touching it. Anyway, I knew right off it was one of Grant Burnham's saws because he bought a new one from me one time and I watched him scratch that stuff onto it with his jack knife, right there where you're standing now, while I was running his card."

"So these markings are going to be on his other chain saws too?" Heather lifted an eyebrow at Atkins, who nodded.

"I'd imagine," Partridge said.

"So what did Mr. Macdonald tell you about the saw, Hollis?"

Kevin saw Partridge glance at Skelton, who was fuming and shaking his head. This was his seizure and his story, and Heather was crowding him out.

Kevin heard him mutter something that sounded like "Damned butterball."

"Well, Heather, he handed me this bullshit line that he'd picked it up through an online auction and thought he could flip it to make a few extra bucks. Said he had no idea who'd owned it before."

"You didn't believe him?"

"He was stammering and falling all over himself, and I couldn't see Mr. Burnham's stuff turning up in an auction like that. Don't make sense. Right?"

Heather said nothing, waiting for him to go on.

"So after he left I called Doug and asked him what he thought."

"And you came right over," Heather said, looking at Skelton.

"Shit. I am working property crimes now, aren't I? You know, as in stolen goods? Since we swapped places? Or am I in the damned penalty box and not supposed to do bugger all?"

"Did you handle the saw, Doug?"

"Why is everybody treating me like a damned moron all of a sudden? Of course I didn't."

"Take it," Heather told Atkins, "and do your thing.

Photographs, fingerprints, you name it. Hollis, are you willing to give us a written statement of what you just said?"

"Sure, of course. Why not?"

Heather looked at Kevin. "I'll call Sonja with a quick update."

Kevin nodded. He moved aside to let her pass, but not quickly enough to avoid her hip, which bumped against his thigh.

"Sorry," she said over her shoulder as she went out the front door, cellphone pressed against her ear.

Kevin watched the two SOCOs begin to process the chain saw. They both photographed it, then DiNardo produced a large evidence bag from his kit and Atkins helped him ease it into place around the handle and engine portion of the saw. They closed up the bag to seal in trace evidence that might be of interest. After slipping another bag over the blade, DiNardo put a cardboard evidence container on the counter, which he unfolded and set up so that Atkins could ease the saw down inside it. They secured it in place with zip ties, closed the box and sealed it with evidence tape, and while DiNardo carried it out to the van, Atkins got out his fingerprinting kit and smiled at Partridge.

"If you don't mind, sir?"

Heather came back inside, putting away her cellphone.

"Sonja's sending out a car to pick up Max Macdonald," she said.

"He's mine," Skelton said, hands on his hips. "This is mine. I'm the one who's going to interrogate him."

"Whoa, partner. Rein up, now. That'll be Sonja's call. She's sitting in the commander's chair now, don't forget."

"Don't remind me," Skelton fumed, turning on his heel and walking out.

Chapter

26

It was uncomfortably warm in the detachment office.

Ellie asked McGregor, the office manager, to check on the air conditioning, and he reported back that it was fine. She didn't believe him, but she didn't have time to find the thermostat and look at it herself. She'd have to take his word for it that the equipment was operating and that cool air was being pumped out somewhere in the building.

Just not where she happened to be, obviously.

The video observation room was larger than the one at the Leeds detachment office, but it was crowded when she got there. Sonja was pressed up against the edge of the computer desk with Skelton in her face, arguing about something, while Kevin and the other detective constable, Hope, both tried to out-talk him.

"What the hell's going on?" Ellie thumped her bag down and took off her jacket.

"This is mine," Skelton repeated, turning on her. "I made this happen. This is my suspect, and I'm going to question him."

Ellie looked at Sonja.

"Macdonald's prints are on the chain saw," Sonja said, pushing away from the desk. "The repair shop owner, Partridge, has given us a signed statement that Macdonald brought it in to sell it on consignment, and the initials scratched on it match those on the other saws in Burnham's truck."

"Excuse me." Ellie deliberately stepped between Skelton and Sonja in order to separate them. Pulling out a chair and draping her jacket over the back, she looked at the monitor and saw that Max Macdonald was already in the room, a cup of coffee in his hands, his eyes down and his jaw clenched.

"I've been in there," Skelton said, "questioning criminals and losers and riff-raff more often than both of these two put together." He glared at Heather and Kevin. "I know how to handle this guy."

"Do you."

"Yes, ma'am, you're damned right I do."

Ellie sat down, feeling out of breath, hot, and grouchy. "No. Sonja?"

"You got the call about stolen property," Sonja said to Skelton, "and that's fine. But it's now evidence in the Burnham investigation and you're not working the case anymore. So Kevin Walker will interrogate Mr. Macdonald. End of story. Please return to your normal duties. Write a report on the discovery of the stolen chain saw and file it. Understood?"

Skelton's eyes went from hers to Ellie's and back again. "Unbelievable. Just unbelievable."

He stalked out of the room, slamming the door behind him.

Sonja looked at Kevin. "Well? You're up."

Ellie watched him leave the room. She recognized the look of grim determination on his face and knew that his mind was busily sorting through the optional approaches available to him with Macdonald, given the man's change in status from witness to suspect.

"Sorry about that," Sonja said, taking a chair in front of the computer and switching on the audio feed. "Skelton's going to be a challenge."

Ellie didn't reply, watching Kevin on the monitor as he entered the interview room and closed the door.

She forced herself to settle down and listen attentively as he walked Macdonald through the preliminaries, informing him of his rights and getting him to state his full name, date of birth, and current address for the record before moving on to questions about his home and how long he'd lived there, where he'd grown up, when his wife had divorced him and why, how he felt about living alone, and other questions along those lines.

Kevin had chosen to follow the Reid Technique, an approach that began with a behavioural analysis interview before moving to a more intense interrogation. The idea was to ask a series of non-confrontational questions that would establish a baseline of truthfulness and willingness to answer without evasion or deflection. It was a technique that required patience and subtlety, both of which Ellie knew Kevin possessed in abundance.

Macdonald was very nervous. His answers were low-toned and disjointed at first, as though he'd lost the ability to speak in complete sentences, but Kevin's calm demeanour soon brought his chin up, allowed him to establish eye contact despite his fear, and increased the tempo and substance of his responses.

After fifteen minutes or so it had become more of a conversation than a question-and-answer session, and it helped that Kevin had been the one who'd interviewed Macdonald on the day the body had been discovered. While it had been a stressful and upsetting day, Macdonald seemed to have connected with Kevin as someone who was honest and trustworthy, and he was now able to hold up his end of things.

Ellie watched as Kevin asked a few more routine questions and then suddenly shifted his body language. His tone of voice became sharper and less friendly.

"Describe your relationship with Grant Burnham."

"Huh? Relationship? We were friends, I guess."

"Did he have you over to his place? For dinner maybe, or his weekend barbecue parties?"

"No, no. Not like that. He was friendly. We talked."

"When?"

"When he was at the woodlot. Sometimes he'd come over to use my washroom. Sometimes I'd go over to help him pile wood. Stuff like that."

"Did you ever ask him for his autograph?"

"Uh, no. Well, one time he gave me a signed puck. He had it in his glove compartment."

"In his truck?"

"Yeah."

"He just gave it to you? Just like that? Without you asking for it?"

Macdonald wiped his face with his hand. "We were talking about the card shows and stuff. I asked if he liked doing them, liked signing stuff for people. He said 'Not really.' I said something about having his dad's autograph on a hockey card, and that's when he gave me the puck. 'Now you've got the Burnham set,' he said. Or something like that."

"Ever take anything out of his truck?"

"No. Of course not. And I didn't take the puck. He gave it to me."

"Where'd you get the chain saw you asked Hollis Partridge to sell for you?"

"Huh? The saw? From an auction."

"What auction? Where was it held?"

"It was an online auction. The guy who has them every week in Smiths Falls."

"What'd you pay for it?"

"Uh, I don't remember. Twenty-five, or something."

"Twenty-five? That's all?"

"Stuff goes cheap sometimes on those sales. Depends on who's paying attention during the week. Stuff slips through every now and again."

"How'd you pay for it?"

"Cash. When I picked it up."

"Got a receipt?"

"I think I threw it out."

"Why'd you buy it in the first place? You don't cut wood. You've got an oil furnace. I saw the oil tank at the side of your house."

"I don't know. Thought it might be good to have one, in case I need it."

"It was Grant Burnham's saw. You took it from his truck."

"No, I didn't. I swear."

"You're lying, Max. Why are you lying?"

"I'm not lying. I swear."

"Burnham scratched his initials and a pair of hockey sticks on the handle of all his saws to identify them. You didn't see that?"

"I don't know what you're talking about."

"You're lying, Max. Jeez, that's upsetting. Come on, Max. It was Burnham's saw. You stole it from the back of his truck."

Macdonald didn't answer.

"Did you kill him, Max? Did you kill him and steal the

saw as a souvenir?"

"No!" Macdonald half-rose from his chair. "No, it's not true! I didn't kill him!"

"Sit down," Kevin snapped.

Macdonald sat.

"Tell me about it, Max," Kevin suggested.

"There's nothing to tell."

"You took a bat out of his truck too, didn't you?"

"No."

"You took a bat out of the back of his truck and you beat him to death with it. Didn't you?"

"No!"

"The evidence is going to prove that you did."

"No, it won't! I found him, yeah! I already said that. But he was dead. It was awful. I already told you what happened. The day I found him. When you came over and we talked. I ran home and threw up, then I called nine-one-one. That's what happened."

"You left out the part where you stole the saw from the back of his truck."

"Okay, okay, okay! I took the saw. He was already dead and he had a bunch of them. He wasn't going to need one beat-up old Poulin anymore. Nobody would miss it."

"Did you steal it before or after he was dead? Was he still alive? Did he see you taking it and try to stop you? So you grabbed a bat and killed him?"

"No, no, no! I swear, he was already dead. It was awful, sir. Just awful. You gotta believe me. You saw him, right? Who'd do that to him? It was awful."

"Did you do it? Did you beat him to death like that?"

"No. Honest. I'd never. I liked him. We were friends."

"Come on, Max. Tell the truth."

"I am." His eyes went down. "I'm telling the truth. I took his saw, but he was already dead. I didn't kill him. I didn't."

"On Saturday you told me you'd talked to him that morning."

"Yeah, I did."

"Did you have an argument with him, Max?"

"No, no, no, of course not."

"Tell me again what you said to him."

"It's just like I told you. I asked him if he wanted help with his wood today and he said no. I said something like it was a nice day to be out in the bush and he said 'Yeah,' or something, but he didn't seem to want to talk, so I pretty much left it at that and drove into town."

"What time was this? That you talked to him?"

"About ten or so. Quarter to ten."

"Where'd you go in town?"

"Uh, grocery store. Lumber yard to get more stuff for my birdhouses. Beer store."

"Do you drink a lot, Max?"

"No way. Not at all. My parents were really bad alcoholics and I got into it after I left home. Cost me a couple of jobs. I've been sober nearly eight years now."

"I don't understand. Why'd you go to the Beer Store then?"

He grimaced. "They give me trays that I use to keep my birdhouse parts organized when I'm painting them."

"Trays?"

"Yeah, you know. When they cut down the boxes the cans of beer come in and then stack them on the shelves in them, like trays? A friend of mine who works there saves a bunch of them for me."

"What's this friend's name?"

"Terry Finucan."

"So when we ask this Terry Finucan if you stopped in for trays on Saturday, is he going to lie for you or is he going to tell us the truth?"

"It's the truth, man! He'll tell you. I was there. Around

noon. He'd just gone off for lunch. I met him at the loading dock. He stacks them back there for me before they get thrown in the recycling dumpster."

"What time did you go across the road to see what Burnham was doing?"

"I'm not sure. Later in the afternoon, like I told you before. I was painting and I took a cigarette break. Before four o'clock. Three thirty or so."

"When you went across the road, was Burnham still cutting wood?"

Macdonald shook his head vigorously. "No, please. Like I said. I found him dead, down that little pathway. Please. You gotta believe me!"

"Did you kill him, Max?"

"No!"

"Did you use one of the bats from his truck to chase him down and beat him to death?"

"No! No! I really liked him! You gotta believe me!"

Ellie sat back, eyes on the monitor, as Kevin stood up and left the room.

Chapter

27

The following morning, which was Wednesday, Kevin drove to Perth through a steady rain that showed no sign of letting up. Although the Charger didn't seem to be having any problems on the wet pavement, he kept his speed down and one eye on the rear-view mirror for tailgaters just the same. Some folks refused to believe that it was necessary to adjust their driving habits in bad weather, and Kevin was in no mood this morning to get tangled up in a traffic altercation.

His thoughts lingered on Janie. Not only was she still dealing with the unpleasant reality of being locked out of her business once again, but she was now also trying to get over the after-effects of having been forced to sit in the back seat of a police cruiser—handcuffed—while she waited for her husband to "rescue" her.

Last evening when she called Doris Winston, her lawyer,

expecting to stir up a storm of righteous indignation, she received instead a dressing-down, as Doris chastised her for getting into a dust-up with Harry Bridges and complicating what should have been a simple issue. Janie took it meekly, somewhat consoled by Doris's assurances that she'd make some calls today and try to get her back into her shop.

It wouldn't happen right away, though. Maybe tomorrow. More likely next Monday.

Two of Janie's friends from the village, Peggy Swarbrick and Sarah, whose last name turned out to be Coburn, were dropping by the house this morning to keep her company. Janie had reluctantly agreed to give Sarah a haircut in the kitchen, after which they planned to eat the nice lunch Peggy would bring and watch a couple of sappy movies in the afternoon with a bottle of wine.

Caitlyn had agreed to take Josh over to a neighbour's house for a play date, and Brendan planned to entertain himself on his laptop computer down in the basement rec room.

Kevin was very grateful Janie had friends, even if they were a little on the gossipy side. He appreciated being able to head off to work without the guilt of leaving Janie to her own devices while so deeply upset. Which was never a good scenario, in his experience.

As the wipers beat rhythmically in front of him, sluicing off the heavy downpour, he tried once again to clear his mind and think about nothing in particular. He told himself that the sound of the windshield wipers, the steady patter of the rain, and the hissing of the Charger's tires on the wet pavement were relaxing and peaceful. What had Ash said this was called? He searched his memory for the terms. *Wu-hsin*. And there was another one. Uh . . . *wu-nien*. That was it. No-mind and no-thought. What you can accomplish when you learn what Ash had described as the art of leaving your consciousness alone, easing up on all the pressure you put on yourself to figure things out and process information and all that sort of stuff. Giving your mind a break. Clearing the deck.

Other than having lied about stealing the chain saw, Macdonald had remained consistent in his story about finding Grant Burnham. The intense emotions he still felt about the murder weren't coming from guilt or remorse, as far as Kevin was concerned, but from grief and sorrow at the loss of someone he'd looked up to.

Kevin knew he could have continued with the interrogation, trying to break the man down until he was ready to confess to everything under the sun from jaywalking to treason, but he'd reached a point where he knew in his heart that Macdonald was telling the truth, that he hadn't killed Burnham. Macdonald was just a pathetic little guy with low self-esteem and an almost complete lack of assertiveness. Kevin couldn't see him as the type of person who'd grab a baseball bat, chase someone he admired—and, well, fawned over—and beat the daylights out of him in a savage rage.

An oncoming truck in the other lane bounced through a pothole and splashed water across his windshield. Kevin's foot instinctively came up off the accelerator as the wipers took a couple of beats to restore visibility. As he eased back up to speed he realized he'd lost the thread of his Zen mindfulness or whatever it was called. Thoughts of work had snuck back in, like a cat slipping through a tear in a screen door, and wiped out his *wu-hsin* before he even got close to it.

Oh well. It probably wasn't meant to be.

Instead of driving straight to the detachment office, he was on his way to the Burnham and Moore factory, where he intended to show Max Macdonald's photograph around in case someone had seen him there before the murder.

It was routine work, the sort of thing he'd hoped one of the borrowed constables would take care of while he followed more important leads. Sonja, however, had decided that Macdonald's confession, which had led to a charge of theft under five thousand dollars being laid against him, was the kind of leverage they could use to convince him to admit to the murder as well. Facing a sentence of up to two years in prison on the theft charge, Macdonald might be willing to work with the Crown attorney on a plea agreement for the murder. Or so their thinking went.

Kevin had been a little surprised when Ellie had gone along with the idea. A search warrant had been obtained for Macdonald's home, workshop, and car on the basis of his theft of the murder victim's property, and Sonja had sent Heather to oversee the execution of the warrant.

He supposed that Ellie wanted to ensure that the investigation was thorough, that it covered all the bases one by one. But he wasn't buying in. Not at all.

What would Macdonald's motive have been? A chain saw? An autographed hockey puck?

Burnham had struck Kevin as the kind of guy who would have waved off that kind of pilfering by someone who meant little to him on a personal basis. Rather than get upset and confrontational, he would have told Macdonald to keep the stuff and afterward turned a cold shoulder on the guy as someone not worth spending further time on.

Kevin's opinion was that they were fishing for motive right now with the search warrant, but no one was asking him what his thoughts on the subject might be, so he was keeping them to himself.

It was all pensionable service, after all.

They were finished with the factory as a secondary crime scene, having thoroughly processed it for evidence according to the parametres of their warrant, which had subsequently expired. Given that the pickings had been slim, other than the financial records and physical evidence gathered in the victim's office, Ellie had seen no need to apply for a new warrant, and so the property had been released.

Kevin found the place busy when he arrived. Several customers were browsing in the showroom up front, and Todd the salesman appeared to have his hands full. Kevin caught his eye and nodded as he made his way over to the little office where he'd interviewed Wally Moore before. It was empty.

Kevin caught Todd's eye and shrugged. Todd pointed to the back. Kevin nodded.

Wally Moore was in his office, the one next door to the victim's.

"Detective, what can I do for you?"

Kevin showed him the photograph of Max Macdonald. "Know this man?"

"Nope. Who is he?"

"Haven't seen him around here before, maybe looking for Mr. Burnham?"

"Nope."

"Mind if I show it to your staff?"

"Nope. Help yourself."

Kevin circulated around the shop area, mindful of the yellow safety lines laid out on the floor around the saws and lathes and other tools and machinery that were in operation, as production had evidently geared up in a serious way. He waited until a worker was finished with whatever task he was in the middle of, badged him, and held up the photo. He nodded when the worker shrugged or shook his head or otherwise indicated that he didn't know who the guy was, and then he slowly and deliberately moved on to the next candidate.

When he was done, having drawn a blank all around, he made his way back to Wally Moore's office.

Wally looked up from his cellphone, which was a replacement for the one he'd voluntarily turned over during the search. "Any luck?"

Kevin shook his head. "Dry hole. That's okay. I—"

"Sorry, Wally," someone said behind Kevin, "I'm a few minutes late."

As Moore stood up, Kevin moved aside.

"Wolf," Wally said, shaking hands with the man. "No problem." He glanced at Kevin. "This is Detective Constable Walker. He's looking into Grant's death."

"Wolf De Witt," the man said, offering his hand. "We're all very upset about this. I really hope you find out who did it."

Kevin shook hands. "How did you know Mr. Burnham?"

"Oh, we go back a long ways. Went back, I guess I should say."

"I see. Mind if I ask you a few questions?"

De Witt ran a hand through his white hair, which looked as though he'd slept the wrong way on his pillow and gotten up in the morning to discover his comb was missing. "Perhaps when Wally and I have done talking?"

"Wolf's putting together an offer to buy into the company," Wally said. "We have a couple of details to discuss. Shouldn't take, what?" He looked at De Witt. "Fifteen? Twenty minutes?"

"About that." De Witt's eyes slid back to Kevin. "Do you mind waiting?"

"Not at all."

"Fine. It'll make me late for another meeting in Smiths Falls, but if you'll give me a moment, Wally, I'll call and reschedule it."

"No problem," Wally said. "I've got the files all ready for you."

"Perfect."

"You two can use the lunch room if you like," Wally said to Kevin.

"Thanks."

Kevin wandered off to let the two men do their thing. He'd heard the name De Witt before, very recently, but the memory eluded him. He went up into the showroom, where Todd was handing out his business card to a woman who was on her way out the front door.

"Our hours are printed on the back," Todd said as the woman waved and disappeared down the street.

"Busy morning?" Kevin asked, running his fingers over the finish on a beautiful handmade side table.

"Browsers. Sightseers, actually. All they want to talk about is Mr. Burnham. 'Was he murdered here?' 'Was he shot?' 'I heard he was stabbed.' It's depressing."

Kevin showed him the photo. "Do you know this man?"

"Yeah, sure. Uh, what's his name again. Mark? Give me a sec." He snapped his fingers. "Service department. The guy on the desk. At the Hyundai dealership. Mike? No, wait. Max. That's it. Max."

"Have you seen him around here lately?"

"Him? No. Why would I? I just, no, um, I see him when I take my car in for servicing. An Elantra. Piece of crap, but it's still under warranty, so I take it to the dealership. Why would this guy be coming here?"

"When you take your car in, does he ever talk to you about where you work?"

"He doesn't really talk about much of anything. He's that kind of guy. Surly."

"Oh?"

"Well, maybe that's not the right word. Taciturn. Something like that. Anyway, his interpersonal skills suck, is what I'm trying to say. I'm in sales, so I know you have to pretend to like everybody and be interested in whatever they have to say, because it helps you understand what they want and maybe it gets you a sale or two, but this guy never took that course. Not by a long shot."

"I see."

"Actually, it was Mr. Burnham who taught me that. He did my training when he hired me. He said he'd sold cars and sporting goods at one time and learned by trial and error what works and what doesn't. He showed me a lot of valuable stuff about salesmanship and customer service."

Kevin waggled the photograph. "Did this guy, Max, ever mentioned Grant Burnham to you?"

"We don't have a conversation. I tell him what's wrong; he takes my keys; he calls my name out when it's done; we do the paperwork; and I get the hell out of there. Excuse my language." Todd rolled his eyes. "Next time I'm buying a Ford."

Kevin put the photograph back in his pocket. He strolled up to the picture window and looked out onto North Street. The rain had eased off, to the point that only a fine drizzle was still falling. He watched a man across the street hurry down the sidewalk, holding an umbrella over his head. The man turned the corner and was gone. A delivery van passed, tires spurning water as it bounced through a pothole.

Kevin's phone vibrated.

He took it out and saw Prez Raintree's name in the call display. He looked behind him. Todd had disappeared, probably into the little office.

He thumbed the button to answer the call.

Chapter

28

"How's the weather up there, Kev?"

"Same as what you're looking at right now, Sarge." Kevin could picture Raintree standing behind his desk, staring out at the rain falling in the parking lot behind the building, his preferred spot when he was on the phone. Not that there was much to look at. But it seemed to calm him, since whenever Prez's phone rang it was likely something stress-inducing on one level or another.

"Yeah. Great for the farmers, I guess. Listen, I had a little convo with Stevens this morning. He's got a bug up his ass about this thing with Janie on Monday."

"Shit. Sorry, Prez." Sergeant Lee Stevens commanded Traffic, having backfilled for Raintree after he'd taken over the crime unit, and he was a difficult man to get along with. Kevin was well aware that he resented Raintree's arrival from the South Porcupine detachment straight off the previous sergeant's list, and Kevin had overheard talk that he often grumbled about certain individuals getting preferential treatment because of their Indigenous status.

He was also one of those who still complained from time to time about Kevin's transfer from "the bush leagues" into the OPP at the detective constable level, even though it had happened ten years ago. Stevens was the kind of guy who seemed to enjoy nursing a grudge, and it wasn't much of a surprise that he'd jump on something with the Walker name attached to it.

"Yeah, don't worry about it. A bunch a crap about one of my guys putting pressure on his people to look the other way, preferential treatment and a possible professional standards complaint, blah blah blah. I told him I'd already heard what happened from Brenda Dalton, and hey, how about he copy me on the reports she and Mankewicz filed? He hemmed and hawed, but I'd already seen them and knew he was full of bullcrap. So, to make a long story short, nothing's gonna come of it. Other than this guy just isn't gonna be our friend, Kev. As much as it breaks my heart to say it."

"Sorry to hear that."

"So take me through what happened."

Kevin described the incident, starting with Mankewicz's phone call during his meeting on the Burnham case, his hasty departure and hurried drive to the village, the witness statements to Brenda Dalton and Mankewicz as they'd described them to him, and Janie's initial refusal to calm down while sitting handcuffed in the back of a police car.

"She's tough stuff, Kev."

"Yeah."

"What'd you say to them? After you had your little chat with the missus?"

"I asked them what their feeling was on it. Mank said

a couple of times they had more important crap to waste their time on; Brenda was upset that the landlord had taken a swing at Janie; I said it sounded like Janie swung first; I asked what Harry's state of mind was; Brenda said he was scared shitless and that she figured it wasn't the first time he's hit a woman, or tried to. She was a bit steamed. Then I said I'd deal with whatever they decided."

"Meaning if they arrested her."

"Yeah."

"And what else did you say?"

"Not much, really. Brenda asked if I'd take her home right away if they released them both, and I said I would. I said I'd stay with her for the rest of the day. Brenda said, 'Good luck.' That was basically it."

There was silence on the line for several moments as Raintree digested it. Then he exhaled noisily. "Jibes with what Brenda told me. Okay, fine. Just forget about it and make sure Janie's all right, hm? I've taken a liking to her. Lady's got a lotta spunk."

"Okay, Prez."

"Stevens has got a soft underbelly, my friend, and I don't mind handing him a little payback, you know, just to remind him which one of us is the mastermind and which one the gristle-brain, but it's got nothing to do with you from this point on, and you can just ignore it. Okay?"

"Yeah, sure, Sarge."

"While I've got you. You might be interested to know that Corrections has rounded up their four runaways and returned them to the friendly confines of Collins Bay. Apparently the way it worked was the ringleader, a forger named Dubassie, was the one who overpowered the social worker and commandeered the van. They dropped your guy, Long Play, off at the casino and then headed straight for the border. Dubassie was gonna use the social worker's ID to try to get through U.S. Customs, but he didn't realize

Long Play had already lifted the guy's wallet until it was too late. The man with the plan, 'til it all hits the fan. Fish in a barrel, eh?"

"Kind of depressing," Kevin said.

"Yeah, I hear you. But funny, too, don't you think? In a nihilistic, laughing-into-the-abyss kind of way."

"I suppose."

"You've got a tender heart, Kev. I sometimes wonder why you became a cop. Then I see you in action, and that answers that question."

"Thanks. I guess."

Raintree laughed. "Stay out of trouble, son. Make me look good up there."

Chapter

29

"Detective Walker?"

Kevin put his phone in his pocket and turned around.

"Ready when you are," Wolf De Witt said.

They went back to the lunch room and, after closing the door, Kevin asked to see some identification. De Witt opened his briefcase, took out his wallet, and handed over his driver's licence.

Kevin sat down at one of the lunch tables and took out his notebook. De Witt's full name was Wolfram Gustav De Witt, his residence was in Perth, and his date of birth told Kevin that he was seventy-two years old.

"You're retired, Mr. De Witt?"

"Hardly." He pulled out a chair and sat down across from Kevin. "I'm a lawyer. De Witt, Paulin, and De Witt. I still have a full slate of active clients."

"You said you'd known Grant Burnham for a long

time." Kevin handed over the driver's licence and accepted a business card in return.

De Witt leaned back comfortably and crossed his legs. He wore a grey suit, a black shirt open at the neck, and expensive-looking black leather shoes. He studied Kevin with calm grey eyes.

"Yes. I first met Grant when he was eighteen. I owned the Bears back then. I'd just bought the team and got them back on the ice after, what was it, nine years in limbo? Grant was our star player. He dated my daughter for a while."

The Smiths Falls Bears played in the Central Junior Hockey League. Their name and original uniform colours were inspired by the Hershey Bears of the American Hockey League, in large part, no doubt, because the Hershey chocolate factory was the dominant business in town at the time. Junior hockey was important to communities such as Smiths Falls, even at the level of the CJHL, which was a rung below what was known as Major Junior A back then, and if Grant Burnham was the teenaged star of the team it would have been an equally big thing. Particularly if he was dating the owner's daughter.

Something nagged at Kevin. It wasn't coming to him right away, so he said, "Did you stay in contact with him all these years?"

"When he was drafted and moved down to Muskegon, I lost touch with him for a while. Clarisse went off to university, and that was it for a few years. I followed him in the *Hockey News*, which covered the 'I' a little bit back then. That was it, until he came back to Smiths Falls."

Clarisse. That was it.

"Clarisse De Witt is your daughter?"

"Yes, she is."

"She was Mr. Burnham's attorney?"

"Grant's? Yes, that's correct." De Witt folded his hands over his knee. "She handled his personal business,

including his divorce, and also his real estate transactions."
He looked around. "Including this place."

"Oh?"

"It's a bit of a story."

"I know you're pressed for time, but I'd like to hear it."

De Witt nodded. "Grant is—was—very important to
me. I loved him like a son. He knew I was very active in
real estate and came to me for advice. He wanted to start a
business, this business, and he needed a place to set up his
factory and get to work. I happened to own this property
and was looking for a tenant, so we talked about it. Grant
showed me his business plan. I liked what I saw, and I
made him an offer."

He stopped abruptly and got up. He opened the fridge
behind them and took out a bottle of water. "Want one?"

"No thanks."

Sitting down again, De Witt opened the bottle and
drank half of it. Kevin noticed that there was a piece of
masking tape on the bottle with someone's name written
on it.

"Sorry." De Witt screwed the cap back on the bottle.
"I'm still upset. Anyway, the deal I pitched him was a
lease-to-own arrangement that would see him acquire full
title to the property, building and lot, over a twenty-year
period. He managed it in nineteen, paying off the balance
in 2017."

Kevin flipped back a page in his notebook. "That was
when Mr. Burnham bought out his former partner, Bert
Westerman."

"Yes, I suppose it was. I wasn't following the business
all that closely by then. Grant had more than proven to me
that he had an exceptional head for business."

"Did you know Wally Moore when he bought into the
company?"

"Oh sure, everyone knows Wally. Venture capitalist;

top notch. Started making connections almost from the day he got here. I sold him a very nice piece of land on the edge of town that I'd gotten bored with and couldn't see the upside on. Damned if he didn't turn it over two years later and double his money. Why do you think I'm interested in buying into this operation? He's a genius."

"Do you know anyone who'd want to kill Mr. Burnham?"

De Witt shook his head. "It's terrible. No one should do a thing like that to their fellow man. It's outrageous."

Kevin closed his notebook. "Thanks for your time, Mr. De Witt. If I have any more questions, I'll be in touch."

"Don't hesitate. Whoever did this needs to be caught and punished to the fullest extent of the law. It won't bring Grant back to us, but at least it'll be something. To balance the scales, if you know what I mean."

Kevin stood up. "I know what you mean, Mr. De Witt."

Chapter

30

Ellie hadn't slept well the night before, so she decided to spend the morning at home. She worked her way through a pot of coffee as she re-read the transcript of the Max Macdonald interrogation, looking for holes in his story. At this point she couldn't see any, other than the obvious problem the man had caused himself by lying about the chain saw in the first place.

She started to read Dave Martin's report on the search of Macdonald's house, but stopped after a page and got up to make more coffee. Her eyes felt like bags of grit, her leg muscles ached, and she was having a little bit of difficulty concentrating. She started the new pot and detoured to the washroom.

That was another thing. Her bladder seemed to be working overtime, as though her body was processing the coffee as fast as she could drink it.

She was confident it wasn't the virus or one of its variants. She was fully vaccinated, and she'd tested herself the day before yesterday with the free kit the government had distributed through the pharmacies. It came up negative.

There was something going on, though. She felt like ten pounds of dog crap in a five-pound bag. Maybe it was the weather. It had been raining hard when she got up, and although it had slacked off to a fine drizzle, it was still wet and dark outside. Depressing.

She worked through the noon hour and then took a break for lunch. She was trying to eat more healthy stuff, so she'd bought an assortment of pasta and vegetable bowls that were supposed to be high on nutrients and low on bad cholesterol and fat and other nasty ingredients. She heated one up in the microwave and took it back to her desk to eat while she was reading.

Reggie lifted his head as she sat down. His big nose twitched as he considered her choice of food before deciding it wasn't worth getting up for. His head flopped down with an audible thump and he went back to sleep almost immediately.

As she ate, she thought about the ability of animals to sleep whenever they felt like it. She'd never been bothered much by insomnia before, but it was starting to become a nightly thing. There was no specific reason for it that she could put her finger on, no particular stressors she was brooding about at three o'clock in the morning, nothing she was upset about or worried about. It was damned annoying.

After finishing her lunch, she logged out and, grabbing her cigarettes from the cupboard, went out onto the back deck for a quick smoke.

The wind coming off the lake had a freshness about it that never failed to lift her spirits. The blue jays and sparrows were still under cover, waiting for the storm to dissipate, but out on the water she could see a loon bobbing around, not seeming to mind the weather at all.

She put her hand on the railing and looked over at the lodge next door, wondering how Ridge was making out. They exchanged the odd text message or e-mail, but he wasn't one for regular correspondence, no matter what the form, and he didn't like to talk about his health anyway, so she felt a little out of touch.

Both cars were parked beside the lodge, meaning that both Dr. Othman and Mali were currently at home. Putting out her cigarette, Ellie went over and knocked on the side door.

"Come in, Ellie," Mali said, opening the door. "How are you doing today?"

Ellie stepped inside. "All right. How about you?"

"I'm very well, thank you so much for asking." She led the way into the kitchen, where Dr. Othman looked up from his cellphone.

"Ellie."

"Dr. Othman. Is Dean around?"

"He's upstairs on his computer," Mali said. "Did you need to see him about something?"

"No, I wanted to talk to the two of you."

Mali pulled out a high stool, and Ellie sat down on it across the island from Othman, who put his phone aside and made an effort to smile.

Not for the first time, Ellie was struck by the differences between husband and wife. Othman was almost fifty, balding, and he'd skipped shaving this morning, giving him an untidy, tired look. His wife, on the other hand, was small and neat, blessed with delicate features inherited from her Southeast Asian parents.

Folding her arms, Mali leaned against the counter. "Could I get you something? Tea or coffee?"

"No, thanks. I just had lunch. I thought of something that might help Dean with his current interest in law enforcement. I spoke to the local detachment commander, and he's willing to offer Dean a chance to go on a ride-along to get a sense of what—"

"No." Othman's hands balled into fists. "Absolutely not."

"Luther," Mali began, "I—"

"Wait." Luther glared at Ellie. "Did you mention this idea to Dean before you brought it to us? Fill his head with a lot of nonsense?"

Ellie stood up and started for the door. "You must think I'm a complete idiot, Dr. Othman. I'm sorry I've wasted your time."

"No, please." Mali waved her arm at her. "Just a moment. Luther, can we please listen to what Ellie has to say?"

"A cockamamie idea like this? Are you serious?"

"Luther. You're being very rude."

He startled, as though she'd slapped him. "You're right. I'm sorry." He looked at Ellie. "I apologize."

"Please tell us what you have in mind," Mali said.

Ellie hesitated. This whole thing had nothing to do with her, really. It was their son, not hers, and their problem, not hers. She was tired of Othman's histrionics and his disrespectful attitude toward her. For two cents—

"Please," Mali repeated.

Ellie slowly sat back down on the stool.

"What exactly is a ride-along?" Mali asked.

"It's when a civilian is permitted to ride with a police officer during a shift, to see what the officer typically does on the job. It's something journalists often do when they're researching a story, or police foundations students who want to get a sense of what they're studying for; that sort of thing."

"I see." Mali glanced at Othman, but he was staring at his hands. "And you are thinking that if Dean went on such a ride-along, he might change his mind about wanting to follow a career in policing?"

"I don't know about that. What he decides is up to him, and you as his parents. I'm just offering an opportunity for him to experience what it's like. To help him make a decision when the time comes."

"I think our main concern," Mali said, glancing at her husband again, "would be Dean's safety."

"Of course. Some detachments have an age limit, but Inspector Kirk Rousseau, the Leeds County commander, would be willing to allow a ride-along in Dean's case if he were to be accompanied by a parent."

"I see."

"Actually, police work can be pretty boring. A lot of routine, a lot of paperwork; dull, repetitive stuff. But what I had in mind wasn't riding in a patrol vehicle or with a constable working traffic, but rather with a detective I know."

Mali frowned. "A detective?"

"Yes. Detective Constable Dennis Leung has four daughters of his own, he's got a level head on his shoulders, and he's very, very smart. Dean would be in good hands with him."

Mali looked at Othman. "Luther?"

"I don't know. Maybe."

Ellie stood up again. "Anyway, I'll leave it with you to think about." She gave Othman a look. "I won't mention it to Dean if I'm talking to him again, unless you've already discussed it with him and he brings it up first."

"Thanks," Othman said.

"If you're interested, I can give you Dennis's number and you can give him a call. If you're not, well, no harm done."

"We'll discuss it," Mali said, as she followed Ellie out of the kitchen to the side door.

"Thank you," she added, lowering her voice, "for going to all this trouble for Dean's sake. It means a great deal to me."

"No trouble at all. He's a nice kid."

"You're a good neighbour. I'm glad you're next door to us." She pushed at strands of long, straight dark hair that had fallen in front of her eyes.

Ellie looked at her hands, her thin, bony fingers, small knuckles, and smooth skin. There were crescents of orange and blue rimming her nails at the cuticles—paint, no doubt, from her morning session in the studio. Her dark eyes almost pleaded for understanding.

"I'll go along as well," Ellie said, knowing she'd regret the impulse later. "You or your husband will be with him, but I'll be there with Dennis. Dean will be well taken care of."

"You're very kind." Mali gently closed the door.

Chapter

31

The following morning was Thursday, and Kevin was chafing at the lack of progress they were making in the Burnham investigation. The search of Max Macdonald's house and car had been completed, and all the evidence had been processed, catalogued, and analyzed. In Kevin's opinion, it had all added up to a big fat zero. Unless Macdonald confessed, which didn't seem likely at this point, the case they were building around Max Macdonald seemed to have crashed and burned.

He poured himself a cup of coffee from the carafe in the lunch room and wandered over to Heather Hope's cubicle. She was typing away at something, lost in thought. He wrapped his knuckles on the edge of the divider.

"Oh!" She glanced over her shoulder, continuing to type. "It's you. You scared me."

"Sorry about that. Busy, I see."

"What can I do for you?"

"I thought I'd run up to Burnham's house and take another look around. Care to join me?"

She swivelled around to look at him. "Why would you bother doing that?"

"I don't know. There's something missing, a piece of information, something I can't put my finger on right now. I thought I'd go back to the beginning; see if something jogs loose."

She turned back to her computer and logged off. Grabbing her bag from under her desk, she stood up.

"I'll drive," he added.

Rolling her eyes, she followed him out.

Today's T-shirt featured Marsupilami, a cartoon character Kevin remembered watching as a kid. Her brown denim jeans and tan-coloured Skechers were a good match for the marsupial's bright yellow fur, he thought, as they got into his Charger and pulled out into traffic.

"Is the warrant still open?" she asked, putting on her sunglasses despite the dullness of the day. At least the rain had stopped.

"Yeah, on the house, it is. Maybe it'll help having a fresh pair of eyes look it over."

"Sure. It' a time-honoured trope, like in the old TV series. You know, *Rockford Files* and *Barnaby Jones*. So who knows? A 'fresh set of eyes' can be a good thing."

He gave her a sidelong glance. "Have you actually seen those shows?"

"Are you kidding? I'm a veteran binge-watcher, mister."

Having noticed before the wedding ring she wore on her left hand, he said, "What does your husband think about them?"

"He didn't watch a lot of TV. Of course, neither did I, back then."

Noting her use of the past tense, Kevin kept his mouth shut, sensing that he'd made a mistake.

"It's okay, Kevin. Loosen up on the steering wheel before you put us in the ditch. He was killed eight years ago by an IED in Afghanistan. Two months into his tour."

"I'm sorry."

"It was a gigantic bummer. Still is, but we learn to live with this shit, don't we?"

Kevin slowed down as they approached Balderson, anticipating his turn onto Concession 8A. Looking out the window, Heather gave an audible snort.

"What? What is it? You did that the last time we came through here."

She snorted again. "'Village Cheese Store.' What a joke."

"You don't like Balderson Cheese?"

"It's a long story. I'll regale you with it some other time."

Kevin turned into the Burnham driveway and drove up to the house. As he got out and cut the tape sealing off the verandah stairs, Heather stood back, arms folded, looking over the place.

"Nice. I can see what Quinn means about him not having money problems."

Removing the padlock, Kevin unlocked the front door. She trotted up the stairs and followed him inside.

They started in the living room, with its sterile show-room feel. Kevin watched Heather as she walked around, eyes moving constantly, taking everything in.

"I recognize this stuff from their online catalogue," she said.

"Not very personalized, is it?" Kevin remarked, interested that she'd shown the initiative to look at the company website.

She led the way into the kitchen. "You can tell this is

a guy's place. All tidy and squared away. Obviously not used to cooking meals. No kitchen gadgets or appliances like a food processor or juicer or anything. I'll bet the coffee machine got more work than anything else in here, including the stove."

She opened the refrigerator. "Beer. White wine. Milk. Kombucha. Fruit juice. Hummus. Look at all these containers of chopped vegetables. Hot sauce. Salsa." She opened the freezer door. "Not much here. A lot of ice cube trays. Couple of frozen pizzas. This guy was obviously a grazer."

"A healthy one."

"Yeah, more or less."

They toured the rest of the house without finding anything revelatory. Outside on the front lawn, Kevin pointed at the house next door on the left.

"The Colquitts. The son, Trace, was Burnham's dog walker."

They strolled past the Charger, on their way to the road.

"No car in the driveway," Heather said, looking over.

A few more paces improved their angle so that they could see into the Colquitts' open garage. There was no car inside.

"In town," Kevin guessed, "doing her shopping."

"Yeah, or taking dancing lessons."

Kevin pointed at the ranch-style bungalow across the road. "They were at work on Saturday—they're both vets with an animal hospital in Carleton Place—when I was here with Sonja. Someone interviewed them later. Zero to offer, other than the usual. Burnham was a good neighbour. Nice guy. Great barbecues. Et cetera, et cetera."

"There's a car in the driveway now."

"Yeah."

As they stood there, a woman emerged from the side

door and walked around to the back of the vehicle, a black Honda SUV. Heather checked for traffic and trotted across the road. Kevin followed.

"Excuse me, ma'am," Heather called out, holding up her badge. "OPP. May we have a moment of your time?"

The woman opened the hatch and put the plastic bucket she was carrying into the back before turning around. "Yes? What is it?"

"Detective Constable Hope; this is Detective Constable Walker. Do you live here, ma'am?"

"No. This is one of my clients."

"Clients?"

"Housekeeping. What do you want from me?"

"We're investigating the death of the man who lived across the road. It happened last Saturday. Did you know him?"

She shook her head. "I live in Fergusons Falls. I don't know anyone around here other than clients."

"What's your name, ma'am?"

"Marianne Pacquette. You say he died last Saturday?"

"It was all over the news."

"I don't watch TV. Too upsetting. What happened to him?"

"Someone killed him."

Kevin saw surprise flash across her face.

"His name was Grant Burnham," he said. "Are you sure you didn't know him?"

"Burnham? Oh, I knew the man to see him. I mean, this is right across the road, isn't it? But I didn't know his name. He wasn't a client, and he certainly wasn't a friend of mine."

Kevin glanced at Heather, who'd also heard the edge in the woman's voice. Looking over his shoulder, he said, "What about the woman next door? Mrs. Colquitt? Know her?"

Pacquette made a rude noise. "No. Other than to watch her flit back and forth from her place to his like a little bumblebee."

"When are you here?" Heather asked.

"Twice a week. Mondays and Thursdays."

"And you've seen Mr. Burnham and Mrs. Colquitt together?"

"I'll say. Any time he was outside doing something in his yard in his T-shirt and shorts, flexing his muscles, she was over there like a shot, hands all over him. Sometimes they'd go inside and she'd be out after an hour or so, scurrying back to her place. Disgusting."

Kevin frowned. "You saw all this while you were cleaning this house?"

"I'm not blind, am I? See those front windows? I clean them twice a week. And I'm back and forth to the car with my cleaning stuff. Plenty of time to see what's going on over there."

"Was this recently?" Heather asked.

"Since the spring, I guess. But not for the past couple of weeks. Maybe he told her to get lost or something."

"Did the people who live here, the Bordens, not mention anything to you about what happened? The guy across the road being murdered?"

"I never see them. They're always at work. I let myself in with a key. So, no. This is a surprise to me."

"Okay." Heather cocked her head. "Do you have a business card?"

Pacquette took out a small wallet and gave her one. "If there's no answer, just leave a message."

"Thanks." Heather gave her one of hers. "If you remember something you think we should know about, call."

They watched her slouch back into the house for the rest of her cleaning supplies. Heather said, "Let's see if

Mrs. Colquitt's home. Maybe the car's off getting fixed or something."

As they crossed the road, she added, "Boy, that's one uptight lady. And nosy, too."

"She's probably just tired," Kevin said, leading the way up the driveway. "Cleaning houses all the time must be pretty exhausting work."

Heather smirked at him. "Why do you think I got her card? I wonder if her rates are any good."

There was no answer when Kevin pounded on the front door. They could hear a dog barking somewhere at the back of the house. Probably Buster, Grant Burnham's dog.

As they stopped at the intersection in Balderson on the way back to the detachment office, Kevin waited for the snort, but Heather was apparently too preoccupied to direct further disdain at the cheese store.

After a kilometre or so, she stirred. "You know, I'm not above the odd TV trope myself. I gotta say, I don't think Macdonald's our guy. He's a red herring being dragged across our path to distract us, as the Sherlockians in the crowd would say. Sonja's giving it a lot of play, but I just don't think it's Macdonald we want. You said yourself you thought something's off. Something's missing from this picture."

"Yep."

"Maybe it's Mrs. Colquitt. I read your interview report on her. She sounds like a flake."

Kevin shrugged.

"I'd like a shot at her."

"Oh?" Kevin glanced over.

"I'm an empath," she grinned. "Didn't anybody tell you? People like to talk to me. It's my super power."

Once again, Kevin had no idea if she was serious or pulling his leg. Would he ever get used to these Lanark people?

"Let's bring her in," he said, seeing the merit in the idea. "See what she has to say in a different setting."

Heather rubbed her hands together. "Now you're talking, Kevvy. Let's do it."

Chapter

32

Kevin sat in the video observation room on a hard plastic chair, watching the monitor with Sonja Freeling and Ellie March as Heather Hope walked into the interview room and closed the door behind her.

After arriving at the detachment office, she'd changed out of the Marsupilami T-shirt in favour of a green polo shirt and dark blue jeans, and she now wore her badge on a lanyard around her neck. It was a somewhat more professional look that she no doubt hoped would convey enough authority that Lona Colquitt would co-operate with her and answer her questions truthfully.

There were two chairs in the interview room, both of them bolted to the floor, with a metal table between them. Heather dropped her file folder on the table and sat down.

She ran through the preliminaries with Lona just as

Kevin had with Max Macdonald, reminding her that she was not under arrest and that she had the right to speak to counsel at any time, that the interview was being recorded, and that she was here on a voluntary basis and could leave whenever she felt like it. It was all very friendly and non-threatening.

Lona had been given a cup of tea when she first arrived at the detachment office, and Heather politely asked if she'd like a refill. Lona declined.

"How did you get along with Grant Burnham, Mrs. Colquitt?"

"Oh, he was nice. Very nice. We were friends. Trace walked his dog. Buster."

"Were you upset to hear that he'd been murdered?"

Lona nodded, her jaw working. Then she began to cry. She picked up the napkin that had been provided with her tea and patted her cheeks, but it soon became a sodden mess.

Heather handed her a cellophane packet of tissues. Kevin wondered where she and Sonja were getting them. There seemed to be an unlimited supply. He wondered if he should start carrying some around as well.

Lona tore the packet open and pulled out a tissue. Heather waited, projecting patience and compassion, until Lona had the tears under control.

"Sorry."

"Please don't worry about it, Mrs. Colquitt."

Lona nodded.

"Good neighbours are hard to come by," Heather said. "Believe me, I know from experience. I've lived next door to some real trolls in my time."

Lona nodded again, trying to smile.

"So, what about your husband? Mack? Did he get along with Mr. Burnham as well? Maybe spend time with him doing guy stuff together?"

"Oh, no. Mack's not that sort of person. He keeps to himself. He has a few friends at work, but he doesn't socialize very much. He hardly ever spoke to Grant at all."

"What about the barbecues Mr. Burnham liked to have on the weekends? Wouldn't he go to those?"

Lona shook his head. "He doesn't like going to parties. And he doesn't like grilled meat."

"Not even for a beer?"

"He doesn't drink."

Kevin thought that Mack Colquitt sounded like a pretty joyless soul, at least according to his wife's account. He leaned back and crossed his legs. Heather seemed to be off to a good start.

"So you went to them on your own, then?"

"Yes."

"You probably had to come up with some kind of excuse to explain why Mack wasn't with you, I guess."

"At first, yeah. But after a while people understood and stopped asking about him."

"Mr. Burnham wasn't offended? He didn't think Mack was snubbing him or being stuck up?"

Lona tried to laugh, but she was still very upset and it came out more like a wheeze. "He knew what Mack was like. There was no love lost."

"Oh? Did they argue?"

"No, no. They were never in the same place at the same time, so how could they? No, Grant didn't have much use for Mack. One time he called him a little household martinet. I had to look it up later to know what he was talking about. But he was right. Mack wanted me and Trace to follow all of his rules, all the time."

"Was one of his rules that you shouldn't socialize with your next-door neighbour?"

"I suppose so."

"But you went over to his barbecues?" Heather frowned,

as though having difficulty understanding.

"Yeah. Mack usually works the weekends."

"So you wouldn't say anything to him about having gone next door for a hamburger and a glass of wine."

Lona wheezed again. This time it sounded a little more like a sad laugh. "No. What he didn't know wouldn't hurt him."

"You went over to visit Mr. Burnham quite a bit, didn't you? Other than just the barbecues?"

Lona looked at her hands.

"I've looked at a lot of pictures of Mr. Burnham," Heather said. "Going back to his hockey-playing days, then after when he became a successful businessman. He was very handsome. I wish I had a next-door neighbour who looked like that."

Lona said nothing.

"He was a looker, wasn't he, Mrs. Colquitt?"

"I'd rather that you call me Lona."

"Sorry. Sure. You thought he was really good looking, didn't you, Lona? In a middle-aged Kurt Russell kind of way?"

This time the laugh was genuine. "Oh, yeah. Kurt Russell in the flesh."

"During the pandemic, you know, we all had time on our hands, so I watched a lot of movies and TV. Escape from New York; Stargate; Tombstone. George Clooney and Tom Selleck have always been number one and number two for me, but Kurt Russell's a very close third."

Lona's smile faded slowly.

"Did you have an affair with him, Lona? Did you sleep with Grant?"

Lona hesitated.

"I should explain something, Lona. You passed up on the opportunity to talk to a lawyer before we started this chat. I went over all your rights with you, and reminded you that this conversation was voluntary on your part and that you could get up and leave at any time, and I'll remind you of that again. But I need to add right now that it's a criminal offence to lie to a peace officer like me. You have to keep that in mind as we talk. Just tell me the truth. That's a girl."

Wringing her hands, Lona failed to make eye contact, but she eventually whispered, "Yes. I did."

"You slept with Grant Burnham?"

"Yes."

"Okay. It's so, so important to tell me the truth, Lona. Okay. Fine. When did you sleep with him?"

"Oh, God. Is this going to get back to Mack? Will he hear this? You said you're recording what I say. Are you going to play it back to him so he'll know I screwed Grant Burnham six ways to Sunday and enjoyed every second of it?"

Heather acted as though she were startled by the very idea of squealing on her to her husband. "Uh, well, uh, I'm not sure at this point why we'd want to share this with your husband, Lona. Yeah, of course it's part of the official record of this investigation, but so's a lot of other stuff that will never see the light of day outside our files. What's more important right now is that you answer all my questions to the best of your ability and not worry about a lot of other extraneous stuff. Okay?"

"My husband's not exactly 'extraneous stuff,' detective."

"Yeah, I know. Sorry. What I meant was that I need your honest answers to my questions. For example, when did you start your affair with Mr. Burnham?"

"Shit. I hate this. I really do."

Heather waited.

"A few months ago."

"Oh?"

"Not like I hadn't sent him all the signals long before that. Christ, I was about to learn semaphore to try that one out on him. I ended up going into his bedroom and stripping and whistling at the top of my lungs. How's that for humiliation?"

"I'm sorry, Lona. How long did it last?"

"I don't know. God. Only a few weeks. A couple of months? Six times. Six glorious times. God, what a man. Crazy, crazy, crazy sex. You have no idea."

"Did Mack find out?"

"No! Hell, no. I wouldn't be sitting here, still breathing air, if he had."

"Oh, really. Is he violent?"

"Well, he's hit me before, that's for damned sure. But he's a goddamned hypocrite."

"Why do you say that?"

"Because he's got a girlfriend of his own, in Ottawa, that he sees at least once a week and talks to online, like, every day."

"Oh?"

"He announced quite a while ago that as soon as Trace heads off to university he's divorcing me. Obviously he and Cherry have been planning their future together for some time."

"Her name's Cherry?"

Lona rolled her eyes. "Typical, eh? I hope she dribs him of all his money and leaves him on the side of the damned road. It'd serve him right, the bastard."

"After the divorce, you mean."

"Well, yeah."

"What's Cherry's last name?"

"I don't know. Jones or Johnson or Jackson. Something like that."

"She's in Ottawa?"

"Barrhaven, yeah."

"Tell me where you were last Saturday, Lona."

"I was at home, all day. Reading. House cleaning. Trace can tell you."

"What about Mack?"

"He was in Ottawa. All day. He worked. If you think he killed Grant, you're barking up the wrong tree. He's a mean, vindictive bastard, but he doesn't have the balls to stand up to a real man like Grant. He's a goddamned passive-aggressive prick who'd rather make everyone's life miserable than take action like that. Sorry."

"Did you kill Grant Burnham, Lona?"

"Oh, God. No. Of course not. No, I didn't." She looked up at the camera in the corner of the room. "DID YOU GET THAT? I DIDN"T KILL HIM! I LOVED HIM!"

"Thanks, Lona. We'll give you a ride home now."

Chapter

33

As it turned out, today was Colquitt day at the Lanark detachment. The constables who took Lona home encountered Mack Colquitt turning into his driveway after a long shift at Ottawa Airport. Since the cruiser was blocking his way, he had to park on the shoulder of the road, which spiked his irritation level rather significantly.

While one constable got out with Lona and attempted to keep the peace, the other constable called for instructions. Sonja ordered them to bring Mack in. Which spiked his irritation level well into the red zone.

Trace also happened to be there, having been dropped off by a friend after a lunch date, and the constables brought him along to the detachment as well. Father and son sat in the back seat together without saying a word to each other during the drive into town.

"We'll do Colquitt first," Ellie said to Sonja as they

moved them into separate interview rooms. "That'll give us time to get a public defender here to counsel the boy."

Once again, Kevin was up to bat. He barely had time to close the door before Colquitt started in on him.

"This is ridiculous. I just worked a twelve-hour shift and I'm fucking exhausted. What the hell is this for? Burnham? Didn't know the guy, don't know who offed him, end of story. Done. Take me back home so I can get some sleep."

Kevin patiently covered the preliminaries with him, tolerating his relentless outbursts and interruptions, until Colquitt had declined to speak to an attorney and the stage was set to begin asking questions.

"What do you do for a living, Mr. Colquitt?"

"I'm an aircraft mechanic. Who gives a shit? I don't know anything you need to know about."

"Where were you on the morning of Saturday, August thirteenth?"

"At work."

"Can someone confirm this?"

"Are you fucking kidding me? My foreman, my co-workers, the guy who drives the lunch truck. The punch clock. Are you insane?"

"This will go a lot quicker if you just answer my questions calmly and politely, Mr. Colquitt."

"Yeah, sure. Whatever."

"You said you didn't know Grant Burnham, but that's not true, is it? He was your next-door neighbour."

"Look. The guy was an ex-hockey player or something. Local celebrity. Think I care? Think I give a shit? I'm harder than that to impress."

Kevin waited. Sometimes silence was better at encouraging talk than asking questions.

"I didn't like the guy, okay? I'd go over there and he'd have all these incredible women, models or whatever, hanging off his arm. And it didn't stop him from hitting on

Lona while he was at it. Turned my stomach."

"Do you have a problem with sex outside of marriage, Mr. Colquitt?"

Colquitt laughed.

Kevin paused for a moment, as though considering his options. Finally he said, "Are you currently having an affair, Mr. Colquitt?"

"What's that got to do with anything?"

"Please answer the question."

"Lona must have whined to you about it. Well, yep. Dipping the wand. Got one tucked away. Actually, I may marry this one after I dump Loser Girl."

"I'll need a name and telephone number."

"Go fish, dickhead."

"Is Lona also having an affair?"

Colquitt laughed again, but not with the same level of amusement.

"Do you and Lona have an open marriage? Is that it?"

"That's not it at all, mister. She should know better than to step out on me. But can you tell that bitch anything? No. So, yeah. I knew she was sneaking over next door to ride the stick with Mr. Hockey. Whatever. She'll pay for it in the end."

"Oh? How will she pay for it?"

Colquitt made a fist and rapped it on the table. "She's getting zip in the divorce. I'm taking the house and property, the cars, the stocks, everything. She'll get half of the bank accounts and that's it, man. She's already given verbal agreement, which I recorded, and by damn I'm going to hold her to it."

"You seem to have a lot of hostility built up toward Lona. Why is that?"

"Are you kidding? You've talked to her, right? You should know what I mean. She's a loser from the word go."

This was his wife Colquitt was talking about. Kevin was having difficulty tolerating it, given his relationship with Janie, but he'd encountered it before and would no doubt see it again, so he asked the next logical question.

"Why do you say she's a loser?"

He sighed, a martyr's expression settling across his face. "Shit. I should never have married her in the first place, but I had no idea what a total screw-up she was. My mistake. I admit it. But after the first time she was hospitalized for an overdose, I started to get a clue."

"Overdose?"

"Prescription meds. The first time, I found her in bed with pills all over the carpet and booze on the sheets. Fucking mess. The next time it was pills and booze, but this time she tried to slash her wrists. Stupid bitch didn't know that if you want to do it the right way, you go vertically up the arteries and not across the wrist like you're trying to saw off a tree branch. Whatever. Anyway, after three or four episodes like this, I knew I had to start making contingency plans."

"What plans were those?"

"My future away from this fucking loser, of course. Took me a while to find someone, but eventually I did. Like they say, there's plenty of fish in the sea. Just a matter of hooking the right one."

"You didn't try to help Lona? Figure out what was wrong and try to help her?"

"You must have been a Boy Scout, sonny. That's not how the real world works. And, you weren't there when I had to drive into the grocery store in Perth and try to defuse shit with the manager and convince him not to call the police."

"Oh? What happened?"

"She went in to get some groceries. Ran into some guy she'd had an affair with a few years ago. Some one-night stand thing, as I understand it. They argued; she grabbed a bottle of mayonnaise from the shelf and threw it at him. Missed, like the loser she is, and it smashed on the floor. He took off. She chased him, slipped in the mayo, fell and hit her head on the floor. Ended up with a concussion. Total loser. They took her to the hospital; I paid for the jar of mayonnaise; and the store decided not to have her charged with anything."

Kevin waited for a couple of beats, giving Colquitt a chance to think about what might be coming next. His own alibi would be simple enough to confirm. Colquitt knew his son was also going to be questioned, but the focus would be on the boy and his mother, not on his father, who was apparently in the clear. There wasn't much left to cover here.

"Do you think your wife killed Grant Burnham?"

"No idea. You'll have to ask her."

"We're going to be questioning your son. Do you wish to be present?"

"He's not my son. Biologically speaking. My bitch wife coughed up that little factoid one night when she was really drunk. So, no, I won't be present. Do whatever the fuck you want. When the kid graduates and goes off to university, I've agreed to pay the bills as long as I never have to lay eyes on him again. How's that sound?"

Unable not to think of Brendan, who was not his biological son but whom he loved with every ounce of his being, Kevin couldn't respond.

Instead, he left Colquitt sitting there and went to find himself a cold drink of water.

Chapter

34

Although she was now the acting commander of the crime unit, Sonja Freeling continued to perform the duties of primary investigator in this case, given the ongoing shortage of detectives and lack of supervisory experience in the unit when it came to criminal investigation. Since the primary's responsibilities could include handling a portion of the tasks that needed to be carried out during the case, and since Ellie was confident in her abilities, Sonja was chosen to conduct the interview of Trace Colquitt.

While Kevin was interviewing the boy's father, Ellie called the assistant Crown attorney for Perth, David Rochester. She explained the situation and asked him to recommend a public defender who could come over on short notice and represent Trace. He suggested that she try Pamela Herbert first.

Ellie knew Mrs. Herbert fairly well. Although they

weren't friends—Ellie could count on the fingers of one hand the people she considered to be a friend—she liked Pamela and respected her ability as a criminal defence lawyer. She thought she'd be a good choice.

Fortunately, she was available. Ellie explained that Trace had already been advised by Sonja Freeling about his right to counsel, and that he was a little confused about the situation, saying he didn't know any lawyers and didn't understand why he would need one.

"Give me time to call his mother," Pamela said, "and I'll be right over."

Sonja went back in to explain to Trace that Mrs. Herbert was coming to meet with him. He didn't have to see her, but Sonja said she thought it might be a good idea if he talked to her before he answered any questions.

Trace, being a generally courteous young man who was anxious to please—unlike his father—agreed to see her. Sonja made sure that he phrased it as an actual request for representation.

Ellie breathed a sigh of relief. Since the right to counsel lay with Trace himself, and not with his parents, she felt it was extremely important that Pamela Herbert would be in the room with him when Sonja conducted the interview. There was a small chance—very remote, really—that Trace had murdered Grant Burnham, and if he incriminated himself in any way it would be essential to demonstrate in court that Trace had been properly informed of his rights and that counsel had been present during questioning.

Somewhat more likely in Ellie's view was the possibility that Trace might tell them something that would incriminate one of his parents. In that situation, his potential testimony as a witness would be useless if defence counsel could show that Trace's interview had been improperly conducted.

Mrs. Herbert arrived only minutes after Mack Colquitt left the building. Ellie met her in the observation room, where she could see that the audio and video feeds from the interview room holding Trace were currently live. As she described the situation, Ellie leaned over and turned off the A/V. Then she walked the lawyer out to the interview room and opened the door.

Before Mrs. Herbert was barely inside, Ellie heard Trace ask, "Is this going to cost a lot of money?"

As she closed the door and leaned against the wall, Ellie felt a strong urge for a cigarette to calm her nerves and help pass the time.

Pamela Herbert put in countless hours as duty counsel, providing emergency legal support to people with criminal and family-related problems who couldn't afford a lawyer. She was also an expert in the *Youth Criminal Justice Act*, as David Rochester had reminded Ellie when they spoke. The *YCJA* was the legislation that provided the structure for a youth criminal justice system in Canada alongside the *Canadian Charter of Rights and Freedoms*, focusing on young people between the ages of twelve and seventeen, inclusive. Ellie was somewhat familiar with the legal needs of young people and how the legislation applied to them, but Mrs. Herbert was now the expert in the building, and Ellie felt confident that, whatever the outcome, Trace's legal rights would be respected and protected.

Mrs. Herbert's duty counsel service was paid for by Legal Aid Ontario and so wouldn't cost the Colquitts anything. Before agreeing to take the case, she would have verified with Lona that there wasn't a family lawyer who could represent her son. Ellie remembered reading somewhere that over 700,000 people a year in Ontario received the assistance of duty counsel in one form or another.

After an eternity, the door opened and Mrs. Herbert stuck out her head.

"Let's go," she said.

Chapter

35

"How did you feel when you found out last Saturday that Mr. Burnham had been killed?"

"Horrible. Just really awful."

Sonja nodded sympathetically. "You and he got along all right, didn't you?"

"Yeah. He was a great guy."

"You walked his dog for him? What's its name again?"

"Buster. Yeah. I treated it like a part-time job, cuz that's how he wanted it."

"It's a boxer, right?"

"Yeah."

"My mother has a boxer. Jarvis. Beautiful dogs."

Trace managed a small smile. "Yeah."

"So how often did you walk Buster? Every day?"

"Yeah. Once in the morning and once just after supper."

"How did you get in?"

"I have a key for the kitchen door. Buster has the run of the house, but he knows when I'm coming over and he's always waiting for me in the kitchen when I get there. I keep him on a leash until we get to the trail behind the house, and then he can run free because he's trained to come back when I call."

"So was Mr. Burnham always away when you went over to get Buster?"

"No, sometimes he was home, but it didn't matter. I always knocked before I unlocked the door, and when Mr. Burnham was home, Buster would bark. So he knew I was there."

"I see. Okay. Ever see anyone else in the house when you went over there?"

Trace blushed. "Yeah. Sometimes in the morning a lady would be there, making coffee or breakfast."

"Someone you knew?"

He shook his head. "One lady, she had long red hair. She'd been there a couple of times and knew my name. She was nice. But I didn't know who she was or anything."

"So last Saturday afternoon, why were you out walking Buster when we were there, if you only walk him in the mornings and evenings?"

"Uh," he glanced at Mrs. Herbert, who gave him a little smile of encouragement, "when I took him out in the morning I noticed he had, uh, the runs. So I came back after lunch to take him out again. He'd already made a mess, so I wiped it up and then we went for another walk."

Sonja made a sympathetic face. "Unpleasant stuff."

Trace laughed, starting to lose his nervousness a little. "Oh yeah. Awful. After I cleaned up his mess, I took the trash out and put it in Mr. Burnham's metal garbage can behind the garage. Repulsive, but it's all part of the service."

Kevin made a note to check in Ident's report on the search of Burnham's house for evidence of the dog's incontinence and Trace's clean-up efforts. It would help substantiate the boy's statement if Martin's SOCOs had documented it.

"What else did you do for Mr. Burnham?"

"Well, I groomed Buster and clipped his claws—the vet lady who lives across the road showed me once how to do it properly—and I kept his food and water dishes filled up. They're in the kitchen. Stuff like that."

"Did you ever have any problems with Mr. Burnham? Things you did that he didn't like? Times when he chewed you out or something?"

"No, no way. Never. He was always super nice to me." He looked down at his hands. "We were friends."

"Okay, Trace." Sonja glanced at Mrs. Herbert, who seemed to understand that she was about to shift gears. "What about your parents? How did they get along with Mr. Burnham?"

"All right, I guess. Dad's not very sociable. He doesn't like many people. He grumbled a lot about him, but it was all just a bunch of static, as far as I was concerned."

"Problems with the property line between your places, or noise, or other neighbour disputes like that?"

Trace thought for a moment. "Not really. Oh, he crabbed about Mr. Burnham's weekend barbecues, the smell and the noise, but nothing serious."

"Do you know if they ever got into an argument or had any kind of confrontation like that?"

"No, ma'am. Dad's a passive aggressive, in a big way." He frowned. "If you're wondering if he'd hurt Mr. Burnham, you're wrong. He doesn't have it in him."

Mrs. Herbert shifted in her seat, but said nothing.

"How about your mom, Trace? Did she and Mr. Burnham get along okay?"

"Yeah. They were good."

"She's more sociable than your father, is she?"

"Yeah." A small, embarrassed smile told Sonja that the boy had a good idea what had gone on between his mother and their next-door neighbour.

"Same question as with your father, Trace. Did your mom have any arguments or disagreements with Mr. Burnham?"

He shook his head. "She went over there a lot. A couple of times she came back and was crying, or at least I could hear her crying in the bathroom after, but I don't think it was because of arguments or fights with him or anything like that. She never argues with people. Not even Dad, which as far as I'm concerned makes her some kind of superhero. I sometimes wonder how she does it."

"Where was your mother last Saturday morning?"

"At home. She belongs to this book club; they meet every other week, and she'd just gotten a new one, so she was reading that. She wondered if maybe Mr. Burnham had given Buster something bad to eat that had given him the diarrhea. I said I couldn't tell." He shrugged. "She was home all day."

"What about your father?"

"He was at work."

"Do you drive, Trace?"

"No, I don't have my licence yet."

"Oh? Why not?"

"Dad wants me to wait."

"So you have to get rides everywhere?"

"Yeah. Sucks, but what can you do? It is what it is. Can I ask a question?"

"Of course."

Trace looked at Mrs. Herbert, his eyes filled with concern. "What's going to happen to Buster? Will he be taken away and put in an animal shelter?"

Sonja raised her eyebrows. "No decision's been made on that yet, Trace. We may want a vet to examine him, but that's only a possibility at this point and not something definite."

"The reason I ask," he said, "is that I want to know if it's okay for him to stay with us. With me. I can't stand the thought that he might be stuck in a cage somewhere and maybe put to sleep. For no good reason. When he could just go on staying with us."

"Well," Sonja replied, "I don't see why that would be a problem right now. If your parents continue to agree with the arrangement, I think it would work, short term. As for later, I don't really know. We'll have to cross that bridge when we get to it."

"That's okay." He looked again at Mrs. Herbert. "I'll sign papers to adopt him, or whatever I have to do. Will you help me?"

Mrs. Herbert smiled. "I'll do what I can, Trace. Detective Sergeant Freeling and I will stay in touch, and she'll let me know what's going to be done with the dog. How's that?"

"That's good. Thank you."

"You're welcome."

"That's all for now," Sonja said.

Chapter

36

The following morning, which was Friday, Kevin arrived early at work. Janie had several errands to run in Brockville, including an appointment with her lawyer, and Caitlyn had agreed with surprisingly good humour to watch Josh again, so Kevin was able to hit the road early, as soon as he'd showered, shaved, and dressed.

Having decided, at least for the short term, to shelve his attempts to focus on the stillness of a quiet mind, or whatever Ash would call it, he spent the drive mulling over details of the Burnham case. After yesterday's interviews, Ellie had decided that the Colquitt family was a collective dead end. Mack Colquitt's alibi was rock solid, and despite the fact that he was a despicable human being who had a motive for wishing Grant Burnham harm, thanks to his wife's infidelity, he was an unlikely suspect at best. Ellie thought they'd be wasting their time trying to shake his tree any further, and Kevin agreed.

As for mother and son, no one was particularly comfortable with the fact that they were serving as each other's alibi, but Lona had clearly been infatuated with Grant, and Kevin didn't believe she fit the profile of a woman scorned. He felt strongly that she was the kind of person who'd direct anger and rejection inward onto herself rather than grab a baseball bat and brutally murder someone she clearly believed she'd fallen in love with.

Trace, for his part, lacked opportunity. Without a licence, he couldn't drive himself to the woodlot. Could he have taken a car and driven there anyway? It lay within the realm of possibility, Kevin acknowledged, but he thought he had a good enough sense of the boy's character by now to doubt that he would do so. Plus, like his mother, he worshipped the ground Burnham walked on. He didn't seem capable of the fury displayed by the killer. However, once again Kevin was forced to concede the remote possibility that Trace had confronted Burnham at his woodlot in an act of protectiveness, enraged at the way his mother had been treated.

No one, however, supported that theory. Ellie agreed that a canvass of the boy's friends might turn up something, perhaps someone who'd given him a ride out to Concession 9A last Saturday morning, but given their chronic shortage of resources she decided the theory should be parked for now in favour of other, more promising, lines of investigation.

As far as Kevin was concerned, Ellie's take on the situation was the right one. The Colquitt family was a dead end.

After a quick breakfast at his desk, Kevin spent a couple of hours re-reading the case files stored in the Major Case Management (MCM) system on the departmental network. While hard copies of key documents were still generated and filed away in the big grey cabinets in the records room, Kevin preferred working in the computer-based system. Without having to tote armloads of file folders to and from his desk, he could browse through interview reports, witness statements, transcripts of tips received through the Crime Stoppers hot line, telephone and social media transcripts, and canvass reports generated by investigators working the case. He could also jump over to reports posted by Ident as they processed the physical evidence they'd collected and analyzed. It also had a portal through which he could access the autopsy report and other key documents filed by the coroner and the forensic pathologist assigned to the case.

The system had been developed and implemented in Ontario after the judicial review of the Paul Bernardo investigation by Justice Archie Campbell in 1996. Bernardo was a sadistic psychopath who raped and murdered numerous women in the Scarborough, Peel, St. Catharines, and Burlington areas between 1987 and 1992. Individual investigations by local police in those municipalities suffered from a lack of co-ordination and information sharing across jurisdictional lines that could have been remedied by a comprehensive case management system, had one been implemented at the time. The existence of such a system likely would have led to an earlier arrest and conviction. As it was, Bernardo kept moving around when police in one city came close to finding him. As Justice Campbell wrote, "He might as well have moved to another country for a fresh start."

Kevin, being Kevin, had read the report several times. He'd also read *Forsaken*, the report written in 2012 by the Honourable Walter Oppal as a result of a commission of inquiry into missing and murdered women in British Columbia. Oppal examined the investigations of almost seventy missing and murdered women in the province between 1997 and 2002, including those connected to the notorious Robert Pickton case, and concluded that major case management practices and principles hadn't been followed by the various police agencies nearly as well as they should have been. The province was slow to implement the recommendations of Justice Campbell, which had been issued the year before the time frame of the BC killings, and while Kevin understood it took more than a year to develop and implement complex techniques and computer-based systems from scratch, Oppal pointed out that MCM systems and training had actually been available in Canada since 1994.

Of course, the focus of the Campbell and Oppal inquiries had been on serial murders in more than one jurisdiction, for which the need to co-ordinate information coming from multiple directions over a period of time was essential, particularly when a serial offender moved around the way Bernardo had.

However, MCM training in Ontario also emphasized the need for individual homicide investigations to be entered into the system as well, in case they might end up creating a match in ViCLAS, the Violent Crime Linkage Analysis System, triggering a multi-jurisdictional investigation of a serial predator.

Finishing his English muffin with sausage and cheese, Kevin re-read Ident's report on the contents of Wally Moore's cellphone. The call list, contacts, social media activity, and everything else on Wally's phone had been gone through with a fine-toothed comb. Charts and lists highlighted his most frequent activities and his favourite contacts, none of which lit the red light behind the hockey net for Kevin.

Browsing, he spotted a backgrounder on Wally that had been compiled by Bob Pierce shortly after joining the team on Monday. Kevin had passed over it before, but now he read it with interest.

He was surprised to learn that Wally had a record in the province of Quebec, where he was born and raised. Six years ago he'd racked up a DUI in Montreal after hitting another car, the driver of which suffered a serious neck injury. His licence was suspended and he was sued in civil court, resulting in a heavy settlement. A year later his wife filed for divorce, and he was arrested for cocaine possession. The charges were dropped when the police failed to prove possession.

Kevin leaned back in his chair and folded his arms behind his head, trying to ignore the smell wafting into his cubicle from the washroom behind him. The door banged, and he reflexively looked over his shoulder.

Doug Skelton sauntered past his cubicle, the corners of his mouth curled up. He threw Kevin a two-fingered salute and disappeared from view.

Kevin forced his attention back to the information on his monitor. Wally Moore had come across to him as an affable, co-operative, and sensitive guy who'd been very upset by the loss of his business partner. A close look at his background, however, started Kevin wondering if there were darker aspects to his personality hidden below the surface.

So far, their second time through the persons-of-interest list had yielded nothing conclusive. Max Macdonald was going to be charged with theft under five thousand dollars, but he was a long shot at best for the murder. And everyone agreed none of the Colquitts made a viable suspect. Was it Wally Moore's turn for a more intensive second look?

There was also the Westerman father-and-son combination. Bert had the temperament, as far as Kevin was concerned, to have swung the bat at Grant Burnham, and Thijs was definitely uneasy about something.

Kevin opened up a report filed by a constable from the

Ottawa detachment who'd been helping out on Tuesday. Sonja had tasked him to follow up with the Ottawa law firm the Westermans had visited on Saturday. The report was very brief and short on details. The officer spoke to a receptionist who confirmed that Bert and Thijs Westerman had attended a meeting with one of the partners, Richard Collins, on Saturday. The meeting involved artwork purchased by the law firm from the Westerman factory.

That was it. The time of the meeting, the names of attendees, and its outcome were not included in the report.

Kevin made a note to get in touch with Collins himself later in the day to fill in the blanks.

Meanwhile, however, he decided he wanted another crack at Wally Moore.

Chapter

37

"Tell me again about your relationship with Grant Burnham."

"Sure." Wally Moore edged forward a little on the bolted-down chair and ran a hand through his thinning, tawny hair. "What do you want to know?"

"How did you two first meet?"

"He was a regular at the Red Anvil. A toasted everything bagel with cream cheese, large coffee, two napkins. This was when I was spending a lot of my time there, clearing tables, cleaning up spills, that sort of thing. Helping out Judy and keeping an eye on Ti-Paul."

"Ti-Paul?"

"Yeah. Paul Gagnon. Ti-Paul. Our baker. I'd only brought him in a couple months before, and we still weren't sure if he was going to work out. It's a long story."

"Talk to me about Grant Burnham first."

"Yeah. Sure. How'd we meet? Well, as I say, he was a regular that summer. This is five years ago I'm talking about. Sometimes he'd sit in the front window and eat his breakfast, watching the traffic on the street, and sometimes he'd take it to go. The mornings he stayed, we'd have the usual chit chat, small talk about the weather and so on. Judy had told me he was a former hockey player who owned a factory in town, but Grant never really talked about that sort of personal stuff at all. Just the usual good-natured bullshit people get into when they want to be friendly but not too friendly, if you know what I mean."

"I know what you mean."

"So this one morning, maybe late July, early August, he seemed a little down, so I asked him how things were going. He surprised me by starting in about his business and how his partner had more or less stopped talking to him. At first I just gave him the usual polite comments. You know: 'That's too bad' and 'Sorry to hear it,' that sort of stuff. But he obviously wanted someone to talk to, so I got us fresh coffee and sat down with him. Poor guy started pouring his heart out to me."

Wally slid back a little in the chair, trying to find a comfortable spot, which Kevin knew from experience was impossible in rooms like this.

"His partner, Westerman, wanted to keep making baseball bats, but Grant had tried to convince him the market for ash bats had evaporated before their eyes. He wanted to get into commercial stuff like kitchen cabinets and dining room tables and occasional furniture, but Westerman was a surly prick and wouldn't talk to him about it. Grant didn't know what to do."

Kevin nodded, encouraging him to keep going.

"So I asked him, as politely as I could, what the market was like for the kind of wood-crafted stuff he wanted to do. Come to find out he'd done a lot of research, and there was money to be made. He'd hooked up with a few contacts in the home construction business in Ottawa; you know, developers building new subdivisions with hundreds of housing units, and they were interested in seeing if he'd work out as a supplier. For products like cupboards, cabinets, banisters, woodworking, all that kind of stuff. It'd mean retooling the factory, and Westerman didn't even want to talk about it. He was stuck in his niche and wouldn't budge."

Wally shrugged. "I told him I was a venture capitalist. If he wanted, I'd be willing to look the situation over. If he was interested in finding an investor, I'd at least give it some thought. No promises. Just an opinion.

"He dropped off a file box that afternoon, and I spent a week going through it, making calls to people I know, doing my due diligence. Once I was done, I was convinced it would be a pretty solid investment. He'd done his homework on the retooling and redirection of the business, and I had to agree with him. There was money to be made. So I called him and set up a meeting. In the Red Anvil, after closing time, so we'd have privacy. I told him I was interested in coming on board as an investor, if he'd be willing to make a few adjustments to his proposed business plan.

"I gave him a four-page list, and he read it while we were sitting there. 'This is all fine,' he said when he was done. 'What I need, though, is a new operating partner. Would you be interested in that sort of arrangement, rather than just being an investor?'

"I said, 'You've already got a partner.' He said he'd already put together a buy-out offer he was ready to make to Westerman. He wasn't specific on the details, and I really didn't care. All I was interested in was his acquiring full ownership of the business and then selling half of it to me. Well, forty-nine per cent. That's why I told you before he had the final say on all the decisions. Anyway, that's what happened. He bought out Westerman, and I bought in. I didn't know until later that he'd told Westerman some kind of dire story based on what would happen if they stuck to baseball bats and let the business stagnate. Not that it was a lie, of course. He was right; they were a slowly sinking ship. It's just that there were options, but Westerman was too stubborn even to consider them."

"Did you ever speak to Bert Westerman at any time about this?"

"Westerman?" Wally frowned. "No, I never talked to the guy. Everybody I spoke to about the company had only negative things to say about him, so I stayed clear. Why would I waste my time with a troll like that?"

"And you haven't communicated with him recently?"

"No, I haven't. Like I said, why would I bother to?"

"You've had problems in the past with the police," Kevin said.

"What?"

"Tell me about the DUI, Wally. And the coke."

"Oh, God." He closed his eyes and tugged at his hair.

"Talk to me. Let's clear up a few things."

Wally said nothing, chewing on his lower lip.

"You were born and raised in Montreal, is that right?"

"Yeah."

"You went to school at," Kevin made a show of searching his memory for the information, "Vanier College, an English-language CEGEP in Saint-Laurent, correct?"

"Yeah."

Exclusive to Quebec, a collège d'enseignement général et professionnel, or CEGEP, was similar to a junior college, from which a diploma must be earned before a student could be admitted to university in the province to pursue a bachelor's degree.

"It used to be a convent, didn't it?"

Wally opened his eyes. "I don't know where you're

going with any of this."

"Just answer my questions, Wally. Please."

"Questions. Sure. Okay, yeah. It used to be a convent, and a private college for women after that. Great place. Lots of tradition."

"Sounds like it. So, what'd you take?"

Wally sighed, making an effort to calm down. "Computer science technology."

"Really? Wow. Just in general, or did you specialize in something?"

"Graphic user interfaces."

"Impressive. And after that?"

"McGill. Same thing."

"How'd you get into venture capital?"

"Long story."

"Another one. I'd love to hear it."

Wally thought about it for a moment before shrugging. "Fine. Okay. After I finished at McGill I was hired by Ubisoft Montreal."

"Holy cow." Kevin was familiar with the basics of Wally's employment history from the backgrounder Pierce had written for the file, and he'd been impressed at the time to see that Wally had worked for the famous video game development company responsible for such classics as *Rayman*, *Assassin's Creed*, and *Prince of Persia*, among others.

"Yeah." Wally's face relaxed a tiny amount. "Holy cow."

"What was that like?"

"It was cool." Wally folded his hands in his lap. "Very cool. I was twenty. A bit of a prodigy, I guess. Heady stuff for a kid."

"How long were you there?"

"Five years."

"Why'd you leave? A great job like that?"

"Why, indeed. I guess you could say a little hubris set in. 'King of the world!' I led a little clique, and we got it into our heads to set off on our own, with our own company, calling our own shots. Myself, two other developers, and a couple of capital investment guys I'd made friends with along the way. We called our new empire BerniSoft. Catchy, right? We took over an upstairs loft in a building on rue Bernard, only a few blocks from Ubisoft. BerniSoft. Made sense at the time."

"How'd that go?"

Wally smiled, now caught up in telling the story. "In the first three years we brought five games to market. One of them, *Penny Soldier*, was a hit. Made us a ton of money. Even better, it brought us a buyout offer we couldn't refuse. My cut was ten million dollars. Ten million! I was twenty-eight."

"A lot of cash," Kevin said. He had no idea what it must have felt like to have been that rich at that age.

"Yeah. It was. But you know what? It changed my life in a bad way, which you obviously know about, but it also changed my life in a good way. I realized that anybody could do software development—there were dozens of geeky stiffs cranking out code and scripts all over the place—but not everyone could work the money side of it. I'd been the one on our end of the buyout, you see, and once I had a taste for it I couldn't back off. I switched hats to capital investment and never regretted it."

"And walked right into a lifestyle change that screwed it all up."

"Yep. Drinking and snorting and driving. It caught up to me not long after my thirtieth birthday."

"You hit another car, and the driver suffered a serious neck injury. You were convicted of driving under the influence, and the guy sued you."

"Sued my ass off. I had to agree to a seven-figure

settlement to make him go away."

"But the drug consumption continued."

"It did. Do we have to talk about this?"

"What about now? Are you still using?"

He grunted, as though in sudden pain. "God. No. Thank God."

"Really? If we compelled you to take a drug test, how would that come out?"

"I'll pee in as many bottles as you like, Detective Walker. I'm an addict who no longer consumes. Not for the past five years, four months, and . . . sixteen days."

"How'd you get off it?"

"Rehab. A six-month stint and a three-month follow-up. I've stayed clean ever since. Unlike most other people, I was lucky enough to have it work the first time."

"All of this in Montreal. How'd you end up here?"

Wally barked a short laugh. "Yet another story. Are you sure you've got time to sit here and listen to all this? Shouldn't you be off somewhere catching the guy who bashed Grant's brains in? Oh, wait, you think maybe you're looking at him right now. I keep forgetting."

"Just answer the question, Wally. Let me worry about the rest."

Once again Wally took a few moments to get his emotions back under control. "Okay," he finally said, "to make it short and sweet, I was on my way from Montreal to Oshawa for a job interview. After that, I was going on to Toronto for another one. I decided to go Highway 7 instead of the 401 because I don't like driving on the Trans-Canada unless I absolutely have to. Too many trucks and nut jobs. Anyway, my Jag broke down a couple of kilometres before I got to Perth. I had to call CAA and get it towed here."

Kevin's eyebrows went up. "A Jaguar?"

"Yeah, yeah. I know. No better than a tricked-up Ford, right? That's what everybody says. Well, I love the damned thing anyway, so there you go."

Kevin already knew that Wally owned a 2011 Jaguar, which he bought new not long after starting BerniSoft, and that was still registered in his name as a personal vehicle. He'd wanted to see how he'd react to being prodded about it. Wally seemed to be recovering the mild, self-deprecating sense of humour Kevin had seen in their earlier interview at the factory.

"So, continue. You were on your way to a job interview."

"Yeah. My income was zip at that point, and my savings were starting to get a little low. None of my capital contacts were interested in talking to me, and nobody in Montreal would hire me. My reputation was shot. But I was able to wrangle an interview for a programming job with GM in Oshawa and another one with a security software company in Toronto. Sweatshop stuff, but honest-to-God work with a salary and benefits. I needed to start over."

"So your car broke down."

"Yeah. They towed it to a garage here in town, and I had to sit and wait for more than an hour before the place opened. It was still early in the morning. When the guy finally showed up and got it on the hoist for a look, he said he couldn't get the parts until the next day, because it was a Jag, right? Manufactured on Mars, apparently. And once he did get the parts, it wouldn't be ready until the day after that. Great. So I had to make some phone calls to reschedule my interviews, which was not a very good look for a guy essentially begging for a job. And I had to figure out what I was going to do for the next two days in a town I'd never been to before in my life."

"Big change from the big city," Kevin said, wanting Wally to keep up his half of the conversation. Sometimes when people started talking about themselves they ended up saying too much. Would Wally Moore turn out to be that kind of guy?

"I got a room in the Best Western and wandered around downtown. I was kind of surprised to see so many interesting shops and restaurants. A lot of limestone buildings and a funky historical feel to everything. I had lunch in the Red Anvil and exchanged small talk with the woman running the place. Sound familiar? Nice lady. Spent the afternoon wandering some more, had an early supper in an Irish pub place, and spent the night watching TV in my motel room.

"The next morning I had breakfast again in the Red Anvil and hung around to talk to the lady a little more. Her name was Judith Landers. Judy. I told her my sob story about the car and having to reschedule my job interviews. She sat down to commiserate and told me her own tale of woe. She owned the business and the building, which she'd taken over after her husband had died five years ago. But the taxes had gone up, costs were going through the roof, customers were peeling off in droves to the Tim Hortons and McDonalds on the highway, and she was about to default on the bank loan that was keeping everything afloat. She was thinking of selling but didn't know whether to make the jump or not.

"I'm a money guy, right? It's what I do. It's instinctual. Like a cat that curls up in a patch of sunlight in the middle of the floor. Drawn to the warm, comfortable feeling that a good business opportunity brings."

Kevin nodded.

"The building itself looked like it was in really good shape," Wally continued, "and it had upstairs apartments that were sitting vacant because she was having trouble finding good tenants. The kitchen was clean and well run. As far as I was concerned, the whole thing was passing the eyeball test up front. I was interested. You've already heard me tell the same basic story when it came to Grant

Burnham. It was the same process with Judy before that. I told her I might consider getting involved, and I asked her if she would show me around the place.

"The apartments upstairs were all hardwood floors, high ceilings, big windows looking out on the street. Clean and neat as pins. The kitchen, like she said, was really good. It even had a large, industrial-type oven for baked goods, but she said that had been her husband's job and she didn't know how to do it. She was sticking to making sandwiches, fixing up fresh bagels from a supplier in Carleton Place, and that sort of thing.

"I asked if I could see the books. She called her lawyer, and after a few minutes, put me on. I said I'd be willing to spend the time looking them over in his office, if that's what he and Judy wanted. He asked me to put her back on the phone, and when she hung up she said I could go over to his office at ten the next morning and he'd let me see the files and the accounts.

"So that's what I did. After a couple of hours, I knew I wanted to do a deep dive, so I called my lawyer in Montreal—thankfully he was still taking my calls—and had him set me up with a lawyer here in town who could give me a hand. Turned out to be Wolf De Witt. A couple of days turned into a week. That Friday I made Judy an offer, and told her to take the weekend to think about it. We could meet the next Monday or Tuesday and do whatever negotiation she wanted."

Kevin frowned. "I thought you said you were broke."

"No, I said I wasn't generating any income and my savings were getting low. I still had a couple of small but healthy investments I hadn't blown up yet, and believe me when I tell you that a half a million in the bank is low, for me. I had more than enough to swing a deal with Judy—cash on the barrelhead and financing for the rest with the investments as collateral. Man, I was all in."

"What about your job interviews?"

Wally snorted. "Long forgotten! The road not taken, eh?"

"You didn't bring in anyone else on the deal? A silent partner? Someone in Montreal from your past life?"

"No, of course not. Why would I?" He stared, and after a moment the penny dropped. "No. Definitely no. Look, I never had any connections to the underworld. Not in Montreal, and not now. Not ever. Never. Never. Yeah, I had a guy I bought the coke from, but he was just some meathead asshole I met on a street corner once a week when I was using. A few blocks from the old Forum."

He paused to take a breath. "If you think I'd bring in someone like that, inflict some dirt bag horror on Judy like that, you're completely wrong. No disrespect intended. I mean, look. I married her, didn't I? She's my full partner, in the Red Anvil and in my life. Fifty-fifty. Best thing—best thing!—that ever happened to me. I'll never do anything to jeopardize that. Not ever. Not for anything. Ever."

"You mentioned someone named Ti-Paul," Kevin said. "Paul Gagnon. You were going to tell me about him."

"Ti-Paul? Sure." Wally laughed without humour. "Not an underworld figure, in case you're wondering. Not some hit man for hire or an ex-boxer enforcer or whatever. Nope. Sorry. Just a baker."

Kevin waited.

"Part of the business plan I'd put together for the bank included reintroducing fresh baked goods made right on the premises, using the industrial oven I think I mentioned. Ti-Paul was a guy I knew who used to have his own bakery on rue Bernard, a couple doors down from us during the heyday. Best scones on the planet. For a while there I was living on them, with cold cuts from the deli across the street. And his danishes were incredible. Plum. Blackberry. All with fresh fruit from the south shore. Don't talk to me about gooseberry. Christ! Interstellar stuff.

"Anyway, I digress. I'd heard he'd fallen on hard times. I made a few calls, tracked him down, and reached out. He was working in the bakery section of a Walmart in Laval, God help him. *Incroyable*. An absolute genius like that. It was like the winner of the Kentucky Derby pulling a snow plow. Anyway, I made him an offer. He talked to his girlfriend and her two kids, and made the move a week later."

"Have you ever cheated on your wife?"

"On Judy? Are you insane? Haven't you heard a word I've said?"

"Did you kill Grant Burnham?"

"No, I did not."

"Did you pay someone, or offer someone another form of compensation, in exchange for the murder of Grant Burnham?"

"Murder for hire? Same answer. No. No. No."

"That's all for today," Kevin said, standing up. "We'll give you a ride home."

"With all due respect, detective, this has been a waste of time. I understand you need to do your job, but while you've been questioning me the real killer's been getting away with it, scot-free."

Kevin led him up to the front exit and told him someone would be there shortly to drive him home. He left him there and went to the observation room, where Ellie gave him a look.

"You've got jack on that guy. Nothing at all that'll get us his financials. He's another dry hole. Find something else on him, Kevin, or find someone else. Period."

Kevin nodded.

"He's right," she added. "Time's a-wasting."

Chapter

38

"Good morning, this is OPP Detective Constable Kevin Walker with the Lanark County Crime Unit, calling from Perth. Your receptionist, Peter, said you might be able to help me with something I'm following up on."

"Yes, Detective. What can I do for you?" The voice at the other end was a plummy baritone with a hint of an Ottawa valley accent. Perfect, Kevin thought, for a successful, middle-aged lawyer. Or a CBC radio host.

"Am I speaking to Mr. Richard Collins?"

"You are indeed." A partner in the Ottawa law firm Edwards, Collins and Delancey, Richard Collins was the avid collector of wood sculptures the Westermans had given as their alibi for last Saturday.

"Mr. Collins, did you have a meeting last Saturday, August the thirteenth, with Mr. Bert Westerman and his son, Thijs?"

"Call me Rick. Everyone does. Uh, just a second. I'll double-check my calendar."

Kevin listened to the sound of pages flipping.

"Old-school Day-Timer. Can't seem to shake the paper. Here we are. Yes. I've been acquiring some artwork from them on behalf of the firm. Great tax deduction, don't you know."

"You've done business with them before?"

"Yes. We have some very nice pieces of theirs in our upstairs boardroom, and I was looking for something a little larger—eye-catching—for our front lobby."

"Is that what the meeting was for?" Kevin asked. "To buy something new?"

"Yes. Well, no. Not exactly. You see, we'd already acquired a piece from them which they'd delivered a couple of weeks ago, but one of our clients took objection to it and we decided to have the Westermans replace it with something less . . . provocative."

"What was wrong with it?"

"Well, I didn't think there was anything at all. I kind of liked it. But the client thought it was too . . . phallic. To be honest with you, I hadn't noticed the, ah, resemblance until it was pointed out to me." He chuckled self-consciously. "I thought it was supposed to be someone's arm or something."

"I see."

"Guess that shows you how much I know about modern art."

"So that was the purpose of the meeting? To choose a replacement piece?"

"Yes, exactly. They brought in a portfolio and I went through it. Looking for something a little more, um, innocuous. I picked out three possibilities and had Steve and Chris come in to look at them. That's my partners I'm referring to. Stephen Edwards and Christine Delancey. We settled on one and worked out the details. I'm expecting to take delivery this Saturday, as a matter of fact."

"How long did this meeting last?"

"Seventy-five minutes. Everything you've read about lawyers and billable hours is true, Detective Walker. We're notorious clock-watchers. Time spent with the Westermans, no matter how interesting and amusing, is time that can't be charged to a client."

"Did you finish up before lunch?"

There was a pause on the line. "I don't understand what you mean."

Kevin frowned, tapping his notebook with his pen. "You said it ran for an hour and fifteen minutes. I was wondering if it carried on into the noon hour, or if you finished up before then."

"That's what I thought you were asking, but I was confused for a moment. The meeting wasn't on Saturday morning, it was Saturday afternoon. From two o'clock to three fifteen."

"It was?"

"Yes, of course it was. Saturday mornings I play golf. Without fail. I'm a lapsed Catholic, detective, and the golf course is where I commune with God's natural world in all its wonder and glory."

Kevin thought quickly. The Westermans had clearly misled him and Sonja when asked about the Ottawa meeting that had provided them with an alibi for the time frame in which Grant Burnham had been murdered. And a punctured alibi was like a fire alarm suddenly going off inside Kevin's head, loud and insistent.

"I'm going to have to have the names of the people you played with. Or people who saw you there and can provide a statement to that effect."

"Oh? Really? Sounds like there's a problem of some kind. Well, I can certainly do that for you right now. We're a regular foursome. Got a pen and paper?"

"Ready when you are."

Collins recited the names, along with their telephone numbers and e-mail addresses. Kevin scribbled them down and read them back to verify their accuracy.

"I'll also need to have someone come to your office for the Day-Timer, Mr. Collins."

"I was wondering. Unfortunately, I'm afraid you're going to need a warrant for that. Not that I want to be an obstructionist, since the Westermans aren't clients and there's no confidentiality there, but information related to my actual clients is in there and I'm not comfortable releasing it to you at this time. I hope you understand."

"I'll have a warrant drawn up for it."

"That's fine. I understand. In the meantime, I'm more than willing to provide a signed statement covering everything we've just discussed, if that will suffice."

"Someone will be there within an hour," Kevin said. "Please stay in the office until they get there."

"Oh, I've got plenty to keep me occupied. I'm not going anywhere for the next several hours, trust me. One thing, though. You haven't told me what exactly it is that you're following up on, and how it connects to the Westermans."

"It's an active homicide investigation."

"Oh my goodness. And the Westermans are somehow involved? I can't believe it."

"At the moment we're trying to account for the whereabouts of everyone who knew the victim."

"I think I'd better bring my lawyer in on this."

"Of course, Mr. Collins. As you wish. As I said, someone will be at your office within the hour to get your signed statement."

"I'll be here."

After ending the call, Kevin found Sonja in her office. He explained that he'd just punched a hole in the

Westermans' alibis and that Richard Collins had agreed to provide a written statement. He asked if someone could be sent from the Ottawa detachment to sit down with Collins and take care of it. Since the offices of Edwards, Collins and Delancey were located about twenty minutes away from the detachment in the Kanata suburb of the city, it made sense to have someone from that location secure the statement. Once they had it in hand, Kevin hoped they could use it as the basis for a warrant for the Day-Timer, meeting notes, and any other corroborating evidence that might be necessary to build a case around Bert Westerman and his son.

Sonja picked up her phone and made the call.

Kevin went back to his desk to wait for confirmation that Richard Collins had come through as he'd promised he would.

Chapter

39

Armed with a sworn statement from Richard Collins that the Westermans had not arrived at his Kanata office until ten minutes before two o'clock on Saturday afternoon, between two and three hours after the murder took place, Kevin convinced Ellie that the two men should be brought in for further questioning.

After discussing it with Sonja, Ellie decided that Kevin would conduct both interviews, and Heather Hope would sit in the observation room with them.

Kevin felt strongly that he should interview the son first. He'd noted in his earlier report that Thijs's behaviour had been off, and he thought that, of the two men, Thijs would be more likely to crumble under pressure.

As well, he wanted Bert to sit by himself in the other room for the duration to marinate in his own bile. Given Westerman's volatile personality, Kevin was willing to bet it wouldn't take much for him to lose his composure, blow up into little pieces, and say things he might later regret.

As it turned out, Thijs insisted on exercising his right to speak to counsel, and he was allowed to use a telephone in a secure and private room to call his lawyer in Almonte. The call lasted almost twenty minutes, after which Thijs informed Kevin that the lawyer, Tom Gibson, had agreed to come down to Perth to be present while Thijs was being questioned.

Kevin was surprised that Gibson would make this promise to a client who was about to be interrogated in an ongoing homicide investigation. He had to admit that he liked the young man, despite the possibility that Thijs might have murdered his father's former business partner. As a result, he decided to take it easy on him at this point and explain how the system worked.

In 2010, he said, the Supreme Court had ruled in *R. v. Sinclair* that section 10 (b) of the *Charter*, which guarantees a person the right to retain and instruct counsel without delay, does not mandate the presence of counsel during interrogation. Once he'd been given his phone call, his rights had been fulfilled and questioning would proceed without his lawyer being in the room with him.

Thijs objected. He'd obviously been influenced by American television shows and movies in which people detained for questioning would demand a lawyer under the so-called Miranda rule, bringing investigative proceedings to a halt in order to safeguard the person's Fifth Amendment protections against self-incrimination. Just as many ill-informed protesters in the so-called trucker "freedom convoy" that occupied Ottawa in early 2022 had bitterly complained about infringements on their "First Amendment rights to free speech," Thijs was badly confused about the differences between American and Canadian laws and procedures.

As he calmly went through his explanation, Kevin could tell by Thijs's expression that his lawyer had already gone over the same points with him. Gibson had probably added that his presence wasn't especially welcome in an OPP detachment while questioning was underway, and any attempt on his part to interrupt or curtail proceedings on Thijs's behalf might result in a charge of obstruction against the lawyer.

Eventually Thijs threw up his hands and agreed to answer Kevin's questions.

"Take me through what you did last Saturday, Thijs. What time did you get up in the morning?"

"About eight or so. I sleep in on weekends, because I'm up at six every morning on weekdays."

"Was your wife already up, or does she sleep in too?"

"She was up. Making breakfast. Waffles and maple syrup."

"What did you do when you finished breakfast?"

"Went back to bed."

"Oh?"

He lowered his eyes, blushing furiously.

Kevin waited.

"We're . . . trying to start a family."

"I see. All right. What time did you leave the house?"

"I guess around ten."

"Where did you go?"

"To the factory. I had to get our material ready for the meeting with Richard Collins."

"What vehicle did you drive, Thijs?"

"Uh, the Buick."

"That's a 2020 Buick Envision, right?"

"Uh, yeah."

"Does your wife drive this vehicle as well?"

"No, she has her own."

"A 2017 Audi Technik, correct?"

"Yeah. I think it's a 2017."

"And she doesn't drive the Buick?"

"No. Just me."

"When did you last change the tires on the Buick, Thijs?"

"The tires?" He frowned, confused. "I don't know. Uh, they're in pretty good shape. Wait, I guess in April. I had the winter tires taken off and the summer ones put on. Well, they're all-season, but I switch them for winter tires in early November."

"Where'd you get that done?"

"At the dealership in Carleton Place."

"What brand of tires?"

His frown deepened. "I don't know. Firestones. I don't pay much attention to car stuff, but I remember the guy telling me the tires on the Buick were new Firestones. When I bought it."

"What size are the tires?"

"I have no idea. Why are you asking me about the tires on my car?"

Kevin shuffled the papers in the file folder in front of him. He'd run Thijs and his father through the vehicle registration database maintained by the Ministry of Transportation to find out what they were driving, and had added Kendra and Naomi Westerman as afterthoughts. Once he had their vehicles and plates, he'd called Dave Martin and asked him to check them out against his tire tread systems.

Dave had reported that only Thijs Westerman's vehicle, the Buick Envision, used Firestone Destination LE2 all-season tires, size 225/65R17, the same type of tire that had left prints at the crime scene.

"What time did you get to the factory?"

"Uh, I don't know. Between ten and ten thirty, I guess."

"What did you do when you got there?"

"Like I said, I had to get our presentation material ready for the meeting. We have a couple different portfolios that we use, but I wanted to mix and match because I had a few ideas what the law firm might want instead of *Arching Grace*. So I went through them and put together a fresh one we could take with us."

"*Arching Grace*?"

"The piece they originally bought. That they wanted to exchange."

"Oh, right. The phallic one."

Thijs blushed again. "It's not phallic! It's abstract expressionism. Only someone whose mind is in the gutter would think it's phallic."

"Okay. All right. So how long did that take you to do?"

"About an hour, I guess. Then I showed it to Dad, and he got me to switch out a few pieces."

"Your father was there? At the factory with you?"

"Yeah, of course. He was there when I got there."

"Oh?"

"He likes to come in on Saturday mornings and putter around, organizing his tools and cleaning up, stuff like that. He finds it very relaxing. The machines are all turned off and there's no one in the building except him."

"And you."

"Yeah. And me."

"What time did you leave the factory?"

"I guess around one o'clock."

"What did you do for lunch?"

"I ordered in. Dad likes pizza on Saturdays, so I called Stuffy's. They deliver."

"Stuffy's?"

Thijs shrugged. "A local restaurant."

"What kind of pizza did you order?"

"Large all dressed, double cheese. Dad's favourite."

When Kevin raised his eyebrows, Thijs shrugged. "You saw his belly, didn't you? He's never going to lose weight eating like that, but you can't tell him anything."

"What about you? Did you have pizza, too?"

"No way. Chicken caesar salad."

"What time did your order get there?"

"I don't remember. Quarter after twelve? Twelve thirty?"

"So you ate and then you left to go to Ottawa?"

"Yeah. About one, quarter after one. Dad hates being late for anything, so I have to build in a little safety margin. It's about a half-hour drive, but sometimes the Seven is very slow. Especially if the cops are out, which they usually are on Saturdays. You guys, I mean. The OPP."

"So what time was the meeting scheduled for?"

"Two."

"You got there in time?"

"A few minutes early."

"How long did the meeting last?"

"About an hour and a half."

Kevin turned a page in the file. "Tell me something, Thijs. On Monday when Detective Sergeant Freeling and I met with you and your father at the factory, you led us to believe that you were in Ottawa on Saturday morning when Grant Burnham was killed. Why did you lie to us?"

"I didn't lie!"

"Your father lied, and you failed to correct him. A lie of omission, Thijs. It's never a good idea to lie to the police during a homicide investigation. I'm sure Mr. Galvin counselled you on that very point when you spoke to him. Right?"

"Dad didn't lie. He didn't have a clue what time of day it was when Burnham was killed. He didn't care. All he knew was that he didn't do it."

"You wanted us to believe you were in Ottawa that

morning, didn't you?"

"No."

"You let your father make a false statement and did nothing to correct it."

"No!"

"I asked him specifically, after you gave me the business card, that if we called them, would they confirm he and you were in Ottawa when Grant Burnham was killed, and he said, 'Sure, ya.' He lied. And you knew it was a lie."

Thijs hung his head and said nothing.

Chapter

40

Bert Westerman was surprisingly calm when Kevin walked into the interview room and sat down. His eyes fluttered as Kevin opened his prop file, rustling the papers for the one he wanted on top, and it was apparent that the man had been dozing.

"Can we get you anything to drink, Mr. Westerman? Water or coffee?"

"No, I'm fine. Maybe later. I take it you talked to Thijs first."

"Yes, we did. He called your lawyer, Mr. Gibson, and I know you waived your right to counsel earlier, but you can speak to him now if you want to."

"He's not my lawyer, he's Thijs's. And he looks after the business, the legal stuff. But I never need a lawyer for nothing. Let's get this over with."

"All right then, how about we jump right to the heart

of the matter. When we met at your factory on Monday, you told Detective Sergeant Freeling and me that you were in Ottawa when Grant Burnham was murdered. We now know that's not the case. Why did you lie to us?"

"Lie? I didn't lie. We were in Ottawa. We met with the lawyer guy about another sculpture. You can ask him if you like. He'll tell you."

"We did ask him, Mr. Westerman. He confirmed that you and Thijs met with him Saturday afternoon. But Grant Burnham was murdered Saturday morning. You had plenty of time to drive to his woodlot, kill him, and still get to Ottawa with Thijs in time for the meeting that you wanted us to believe was your alibi."

Westerman sat there, his mouth slightly open. "In the morning?"

"That's correct, Mr. Westerman. The murder happened between eleven o'clock and noon on Saturday morning. As it stands right now, you have no explanation of your whereabouts at that time."

Westerman sputtered. "But I was at the factory! All morning! I thought, I don't know, I thought he was killed in the afternoon. Who pays attention to stuff like that? I didn't even know he was dead when we went to that meeting. I never heard until Naomi told me afterward. That night. It was on the news or something. I don't know. She never said what time. Did they say what time in the news? If they did, nobody ever told me."

"Are you saying you were at your factory all morning on Saturday?"

"Yah, yah, man. Of course that's what I'm saying."

"Can you prove it?"

Westerman scowled. "I don't have to be no lawyer to know I don't have to prove nothing. The burden of proof is on you guys, not me. I'm not a total idiot."

"If that's going to be your attitude, Mr. Westerman—"

"Attitude! Attitude?" He was finally getting worked up. "We got a security video system there, don't we? Cost a hell of a lot, I know that much. Thijs put it inside and outside to catch any idiots who might try to break in and wreck stuff. Why in hell don't you look at that? It'll show you I was there! This is just bullshit. A waste of time."

"What size of shoes do you wear, Mr. Westerman?"

"Shoes? What is this now?" He shook his head. "I don't know. Naomi buys them for me. And clothes and other stuff. Like for Christmas and my birthday and that." He leaned down, removed one of the Nike sneakers he was wearing, and looked inside. "Eleven." He put the shoe back on.

"Do you own a pair of Gore-Tex boots, Mr. Westerman?"

"How should I know?"

"Did you kill Grant Burnham?"

"You gotta be out of your mind."

"Did you and Thijs drive to Burnham's woodlot, confront him there, and murder him?"

"No. You're really starting to piss me off here. You got my answer. Now stop wasting my time so I can go back to Almonte and get some work done."

Kevin stood up and moved to the door. "Not just yet, Mr. Westerman. We've only just started."

Chapter

41

"Thijs, tell me about the security system installed at the factory."

"Uh, sure. Well, you saw part of it when you checked in."

"Yes. The visitor management system your wife's so proud of. What else does it do?"

"The overall system? It ties into our landline voicemail, for one thing, and it also integrates all the video cameras on site."

"Tell me about that. The video surveillance."

"Uh, well, we have four external cameras and seven internal. They cover three sides of the factory, including two different angles on the parking lot and front entrance. There's nothing on the river side, because there's no way to access the building there."

"And internal cameras?"

"There are two in the reception area, one in the freight elevator, one in the upstairs corridor, and one in the showroom we have up there to display our work for visiting clients. Uh, one in the downstairs corridor and one in Dad's workshop. Covering the factory floor."

"And the video surveillance connects to the visitor system, is that what you're saying?"

"Yes."

"When you and your father check in, do you use the system, the same as visitors?"

"No. The external doors have a key card system. Dad and I, and Kendra, swipe in. Why do you want to know this?"

"What about when you leave?"

"We swipe out."

"Pretty elaborate system. I'm surprised your father has the patience for it."

Thijs shrugged. "He gets grumpy, but we have a lot to lose if someone breaks in and robs us, so he tolerates it."

"So the system would know when you and your father entered and left the factory last Saturday, is that correct?"

"Oh. I see what you're getting at. Normally, yes."

"Normally?"

Thijs closed his eyes and took a breath. "The system was down."

"It was down? Why?"

Thijs rubbed his face with his hands. "Every night at midnight the system uploads the day's data to the cloud for storage and then does a purge. That way we don't have to store terabytes of information on site, right? Storage is hardware, and hardware is expensive. So that's how the system works."

"What happened to Saturday's data?"

"Apparently that night, well, technically Sunday morning at one second after twelve midnight, the upload failed. None of the day's data was copied into our cloud account. But the purge worked. Everything was deleted."

"Deleted."

"Yes, that's what a purge is, Detective Walker. It deletes everything so there's room for the next day's data. Gone. Wiped out."

"Is there a restore function?"

"Look, I didn't realize it had happened until Monday when you called to tell us you were coming around to question us after Burnham's death. Before you got there I logged on, and when I went to check on Saturday's footage it wasn't there. The folder was empty. I couldn't believe it. I called the company and that was the first question I asked them. Could they restore the missing data? They said the drive had been completely overwritten on Sunday, and then the whole process started again on Monday morning, so no. Gone. Forever."

"Why did the upload fail, Thijs?"

He sighed. "I'm not a computer expert. They told me that there's a password protocol or something that's supposed to happen when our system logs on to the cloud for the upload. Apparently there was a glitch at their end and it didn't recognize our password. It sent back an error message to our computer and then ended the upload routine. Our system's programmed to initiate the purge automatically when it receives the message that the upload's finished. Unfortunately it ignored the error message that came back first."

"Has this ever happened before?"

"No. We've had the system two and a half years, and this is the first time it's screwed up like this. I've already filed a complaint."

Kevin wondered if Thijs had the ability to sabotage the upload himself somehow, but he decided not to pursue it any further at the moment. They could turn the question over to Ident, and Dave Martin's expert could chase it down for them.

He stood up and was about to open the door when Thijs cleared his throat.

"Can I go now?"

"Not yet." Kevin turned. "By the way, what size shoes do you wear?"

"What?"

"Your shoes. What size are they?"

"Uh, nines."

Kevin had noticed that Thijs was wearing black lace-up Vans today. "Do you have hiking boots?"

"I guess so. In the hall closet."

"Are they nines as well?"

"I'm not sure. They might be size ten. It varies, depending on the shoe. Or boot. I don't really wear them. Kendra bought them for me when we were going to starting walking together, as exercise, but that didn't work out. You know."

Chapter

42

Kevin went for a little stroll through the parking lot behind the detachment office to call Janie. It was past four o'clock in the afternoon, and he knew he wouldn't be able to get home until late in the evening. He didn't want her to worry, but more importantly he was worried about her and didn't want her to feel like she was being left to her own devices right now.

"I've been talking to Doris," she said after a quick update on the kids, who were all doing just fine. "She's trying to get me in there so I can get my stuff out."

"Is that possible?"

"Well, that's what I'm trying to find out, Kevin."

"Sorry. I don't know how this sort of thing works."

"It's all mine, right? I mean, the chairs, the mirrors, the cabinets and shelves, even the damned wash tubs in back. Doris thinks I'll probably have to leave them because they're attached or whatever, but I want the rest of the stuff out of there ASAP."

"What'll you do with it?"

She sighed, the weight of the world on her shoulders. "I'm going to have to rent a storage unit some place and throw it all in there until I can figure out what to do next."

Kevin didn't like the sound of an extra expense for a storage unit without income from her business to pay for it, but he thought they could probably swing the cost from their personal account for a month or two. Wisely, he didn't offer an opinion one way or the other.

"Well, at least it's something. When will she let you know?"

"Monday, I guess. Nobody works on weekends anymore except you and me, Tiger. Crazy world, eh?"

Kevin agreed that it was. He let her go and walked slowly back into the building. He was a few steps from his cubicle when he met Sonja in the narrow aisle between the cubbyholes.

"Zana's coming over to write up the warrants. He can't be here until seven, and I want you to sit down with him and walk him through everything we have, so it's going to run a little late tonight."

"Understood." With no alibi to explain their where-abouts at the time Burnham was murdered, plus tire tread marks consistent with Thijs Westerman's vehicle found at the crime scene, Ellie believed they had enough to apply for arrest warrants and warrants to search their residences and factory for physical evidence tying them to the killing. Because of the chronic staff shortage, the region was being tapped for another resource, Detective Constable Zana Jaharah, to fill in as warrant writer for the investigation. He was yet another person Kevin hadn't met before.

Back in his cubicle, Kevin got busy writing his interview reports, knowing that Jaharah would rely on them while building the case for probable cause in his applications. He was deep into it, concentrating on the chronological flow of events, when he became aware of a disturbance elsewhere on the floor.

Voices. Exclamations. Laughter.

His name, repeated several times as the noise grew louder.

Someone rapped their knuckles on the frame of his cubicle and he tore his eyes from the screen, swivelling around in his chair. A uniformed constable grinned at him and stepped aside, making a sweeping motion with his hand as though ushering the prime minister of Canada into his workstation.

It was Bobby Burnham, hands on his hips, an unlit cigar clamped between his teeth.

"Jeez Louise, boy, looks like they gave you the prime location for sure. It always stink this bad?"

Kevin stood up. "Mr. Burnham! Good to see you. What can I do for you?"

"I was just down here on some business and thought I'd drop in and say hi. Actually, I got a question for you."

Kevin minimized the MCM window on his monitor and spun his seat around, offering it to Bobby. There was no visitor's chair in the cubicle, so he sat on the corner of his desk and folded his arms.

"Ask away, Mr. Burnham. I'll answer if I can."

Bobby eased himself into the chair, his eyes wandered around the workstation for a moment. There wasn't much to see.

"Not a family man?"

"Yes, I'm married. Three kids."

"I wondered. Don't see any pictures or kids' drawings or that."

"This isn't my normal place of work. I'm on loan from the Leeds detachment."

Bobby nodded.

Kevin looked up as someone walked by his cubicle doorway, slowing down for a moment to stare in at the celebrity.

"What did you want to ask me?"

"I just come from a meeting with my lawyer and this other lawyer, De Witt. She's in charge of Grant's will— De Witt is, I mean—and we had some questions. Well, I did. Grant left me a bunch of money in a trust I've been drawing on for a while, which was incredibly generous of him, and he also left me title to his woodlot. The one on Nine A. Where he was, uh, found. Anyways, this De Witt told me there was some restrictions had just been placed on it keeping me from going out there to take a look."

"Restrictions?"

"Yeah. Is that your doing? The police, I mean?"

Kevin frowned. "I don't think so, Mr. Burnham. As far as I know, we've released it. Let me just make sure."

He picked up his cellphone and punched in a number. "Sonja, we're not still controlling the crime—um, we've released the Burnham woodlot, haven't we?"

He listened for a moment and then nodded. "Yeah, okay. That's what I thought. Thanks."

He ended the call and put the phone back down on his desk. "We're all done out there, Mr. Burnham. I don't see why you wouldn't be able to have access to it now, whenever you want."

Protection of a crime scene by police investigators usually lasted until the autopsy of the victim had been conducted, after which the coroner, in this case Dr. Phong, could direct the police to release the scene whenever Identification Services had finished with their collection of physical evidence. Burnham's post mortem had been held on Monday, Dr. Phong had received the preliminary report from the pathologist, Dr. Kalman, on Wednesday morning, and control of the woodlot had been relinquished that afternoon. Kevin couldn't understand why Burnham's executor was telling Bobby and his lawyer that the site remained off limits.

"Did they say why you couldn't go out there?"

"Something about a species at risk or some kind of stuff like that."

"I'm confused."

Bobby laughed without humour. "That makes two of us, son. De Witt said it was government doings. Some kind of report was filed saying Grant was damaging the environment and putting species at risk or some damned thing."

"I don't understand. It looked to me like he was managing the woodlot okay. Just culling some trees and cutting them up for firewood. And a few walking trails in back."

"Well, you know how it is. Only takes one swivel servant to frig everything up beyond all recognition. No offence intended."

"None taken."

Bobby stood up. "So I guess there's nothing you can do for me."

"I can—" Kevin suddenly realized he'd been thinking about the wrong lawyer. "Wait, you said 'she.' You're talking about Clarisse De Witt."

He'd forgotten that Wolf De Witt had already told him that his daughter was Grant Burnham's lawyer.

"Yep. A bit of a history there with her. I may have mentioned it before, when you came around to see me."

"Please, if you could give me just another moment or two."

Bobby sat down. "Sure, but my ride's due in another few minutes."

Kevin searched his memory, replaying in his head the

interview he and Sonja had conducted with Bobby five days ago. He'd talked at length about Roxanne, the ex-wife, but hadn't really been specific about any of the other women with whom Grant had been intimate. Except—

"His high school girlfriend," he blurted. "Clarisse De Witt."

"The very same. Couldn't remember her name at the time, but it came back to me after you left."

"You and your lawyer met with her today, and she told you the woodlot was off limits?"

"Yep. Was pretty firm about the whole thing, too."

Kevin remembered that Wolf De Witt had talked about his daughter representing Grant Burnham for his real estate dealings and his personal legal needs, including his divorce.

"What else did she say about the restrictions placed on the woodlot?"

"Well, damned little, when it came right down to it. She gave Jimmy—that's my lawyer—some kind of government form, saying that access was restricted to blah blah blah while they did some study of some kind. Or they'd already done the study and were doing their report. I didn't understand it. But I understood enough not to like it much, I'll tell you that."

He stood up again. "I better go. Jimmy's probably out there waiting. He gets a little short on patience some-times."

Kevin followed him out of the cubicle and guided him up the narrow aisle toward the front exit. Near the security door they were stopped by the office manager, McGregor, who held out an eight-by-ten glossy photograph that Kevin suspected he'd just printed off the Internet.

"Bobby, would you mind signing this for me?"

"Yeah, sure." Bobby took the Sharpie McGregor thrust out at him and scribbled on it.

They were suddenly swarmed, uniformed officers and civilians alike crowding around for autographs and selfies with the famous hockey great, laughing and joking as the old man did his best to accommodate everyone's requests. Bobby seemed to enjoy the attention, but after giving it a few minutes Kevin stepped in and cleared a path for him to leave.

"That's Jimmy there," Bobby said, pointing at a black Lexus parked in front of the building.

As they walked across the lot, Bobby looked at him and grinned. "That was fun. Glad I came."

"So am I. I'll look into what's going on with the woodlot."

"Thanks. Jimmy said he'd check it out, but it couldn't hurt having a cop ask questions, too."

"One swivel servant to another," Kevin joked.

Bobby nodded. "You're all right, kid."

Kevin figured that was probably better than getting an autograph.

Chapter

43

The following morning, which was Saturday, marked one week since Grant Burnham had been murdered. At eight o'clock they gathered in the meeting room that had been taken over by the investigative team as soon as Sonja had moved into her new office, across the corridor from Staff Sergeant Dunn.

The whiteboards were now covered with names, photos, lines, arrows, and question marks. A coffee carafe had been wheeled in with paper cups and packets of sugar and cream, and Sonja had filled a basket with fresh muffins from the Red Anvil.

As Kevin took his place at the table, he immediately sensed that the mood in the room was dark. Pierce and Heather Hope were busy on the cellphones, while Sonja was confirming that Rachel Townsend and Dave Martin were conferenced in on the speakerphone.

He took out his notebook, glanced at his watch, and wrote down the time.

Ellie set aside her tablet and put her hands flat on the table.

"I thought I made it clear that only Rachel would be making statements to the public about this case. Did I not?"

No one spoke. It was obvious from her tone that she was furious.

"Is it also understood by everyone in this room that information about a major case investigation should not be shared with outside parties unless it's specifically cleared with me first?"

Silence. All eyes were down or up or anywhere other than on her.

She smacked the table with the palm of her hand, making everyone jump. "Who's responsible for this? Which one of you?"

Someone shifted uneasily, shoes scuffing on the floor, but otherwise the room remained silent.

Ellie took a breath before continuing. "Rachel, why don't you bring us up to date on this ridiculous nonsense?"

"Uh, all right, Ellie." Rachel could be heard over the speakerphone tapping away at something, her tablet or cellphone. "As you may be aware, a local Ottawa television news program aired a segment last evening about the Burnham case. The member of provincial parliament for the Lanark-Frontenac-Kingston riding, Bill Hollingsworth, gave an interview critical of the investigation, and he shared information that has not been disclosed through any of our media releases. When the reporter pressed him, he admitted that he'd been in contact with someone, quote, inside the Perth detachment, unquote."

"Eeep." Heather Hope quickly raised her hand to cover her mouth.

Ellie shot her a look.

"I contacted the reporter after the first broadcast," Rachel went on, "and she admitted that the MPP had shared more information with her than what made it onto the air. I then spoke to the producer, who agreed to remove the segment from their late news broadcast in exchange for an updated statement. Ellie and I put one together last night, which they ran instead of the tape from the evening broadcast."

Ellie was still staring at Heather. "Do you have anything to say, Detective Constable?"

"Yes, uh, no. Um, just that according to the investigative standards established as government policy by the Solicitor General and set out in the *Ontario Major Case Manual*, the media relations officer—that would be Constable Townsend—is the designated spokesperson for the release of information, and no one else, quote, shall release information unless authorized to do so by the major case manager. Unquote."

Ellie kept her eyes on her until she was sure there was nothing else forthcoming, then she slowly looked around the table. She noticed that Constable Downey's eyes were on his tablet as he busily tapped away, presumably taking minutes of the meeting.

"Anyone else care to say something?"

Silence.

"Come and see me when we're finished here if you'd like to get something off your chest. Say, a life-long friendship with that worm Hollingsworth and a case of verbal diarrhea. In the meantime, how about we find out where this 'deeply flawed and misdirected investigation,' quote-unquote, is currently bogged down?"

Without having planned to do so beforehand, Kevin stood up and went over to the whiteboards. He picked up a dry erase marker and, leaving the cap on, tapped Bert

Westerman's name.

"At this point he's our main focus, and/or his son." He tapped Thijs's name. "But the pieces just aren't fitting together. The son's Buick has the same tires as the vehicle that was at the crime scene, the father wears the same size shoe as the killer, they misled us on the timing of their supposed alibi, and they had a convenient system screw-up that makes it impossible to confirm their alibi. Dave, were you able to make an exact match between the Buick's tires and the prints lifted from the scene?"

"Sorry, Kevin. The tread pattern's the same; they're both Firestones; but there are very small differences in the wear of the tires, so I wouldn't be able to swear in court that these are the ones we're looking for."

"And when you searched Bert Westerman's house and the factory, did you find Gore-Tex hiking boots matching the footprints left at the scene?"

He knew the answers to these questions already, having read Ident's reports as soon as they were filed in the system, but he was asking them anyway so they'd be recorded in Constable Downey's minutes.

"We collected a lot of shoes and boots," Martin said, "but no Gore-Tex. None from the son's residence either, irrespective of size."

"There's no doubt the prints at the crime scene were made by that brand of hiking boot?"

"No doubt, Kev. Next question."

"Right. And you've confirmed that the factory's security video for last Saturday morning is gone?"

"Yep. Purged, overwritten, irretrievable."

"So they can't prove their whereabouts," Ellie said, "but we can't put them at the scene either. Damn."

She leaned forward, staring at the speakerphone. "Did we ever get any DNA off the baseball bat other than the victim's?"

"As I mentioned before, Ellie, the handle and knob had been wiped clean before it was tossed into the back of the truck along with the others. We sampled everything we could and it's all at the lab, waiting in the queue to be processed. You'll know the results as soon as I do."

"Wiped clean with what?"

"I don't know. We collected cotton fibres from the bat handle that suggest a cloth of some kind, an article of clothing maybe or a towel or something, but whatever it was they took it with them. It wasn't at the scene."

"And you haven't found it in any of the places we've searched so far."

"No. Not at Max Macdonald's, not at the Westerman factory, and not at either of their residences. Not at the victim's home, either, for what it's worth."

"Without a confession from one of these guys," Ellie said, "we're a long way from home on this one."

Kevin nodded, knowing he'd given it his best shot in the interview room with Max Macdonald, Wally Moore, and both Westermans without success. He searched the whiteboard for inspiration. Pete Lansing and Roxanne Rechelbacher, the ex-wife and her current husband, had video alibis that were unshakable. The Colquitt family had been ruled out. Bobby, of course, loved his son and—

Wait a second.

He uncapped the marker and drew a line from Grant's name in the middle to the only bare spot left on the board. He wrote "Clarisse De Witt" and "(Wolf De Witt)" underneath it.

"Wolf De Witt's a lawyer here in town," he said. "He sold Grant Burnham the factory building on a lease-to-own arrangement and has been friends with him over the years. Like a father figure."

Heather Hope nodded. "Nice guy. He's handled a few things for me."

"What about his daughter? Do you know her too?"

"Nope. Can't say that I do."

"Bobby Burnham came in late yesterday afternoon," Kevin explained to Ellie, "and wanted to know if we'd released the woodlot because his lawyer was being told there was a restriction being placed on it and he wasn't being allowed access."

He saw Sonja nod, remembering his call to her yesterday to check on the status of the crime scene.

Ellie frowned. "What kind of restriction?"

"He was pretty confused about it. Said something about a species at risk investigation, or something like that. Sounds like it has to do with the government."

"The only species at risk out there as far as I can see right now is homo sapiens," Heather said.

Ellie gave her another look.

"I mention it now," Kevin plowed on, "because Bobby reminded me that the lawyer handling Grant Burnham's estate is Clarisse De Witt, Wolf's daughter. She's the one who told Bobby and his lawyer about the restriction. When I interviewed Wolf on, uh, Wednesday it was, he'd said that his daughter had dated Grant when they were in high school. Wolf owned the Smiths Falls Bears at that time, and Grant was their star player. But once he was drafted they went their separate ways."

"Until they hooked up again as lawyer and client?" Heather asked.

"Looks like."

"I think you need to talk to Clarisse De Witt," Ellie said.

Kevin nodded. "At the very least, she might be able to explain what's happening with the woodlot."

"I hope to God we get a little more out of her than that," Ellie growled.

Chapter

44

When the meeting was over, everyone filed out of the room except Sonja, who stopped at the doorway and looked back at Ellie.

"He's here."

"Bring him in."

Doug Skelton ambled into the room and sat down at the far end of the table. He wore an olive-coloured safari jacket, khaki trousers, and his usual hiking boots (size nine). He leaned back in the chair, folded his arms, and watched Sonja close the door and return to her place at the table.

"We have a few questions for you, Doug." She glanced at Ellie, who was letting her handle this because she was the man's immediate supervisor.

"Sounds ominous."

"If you were watching the Ottawa news on television

last evening you may have seen a report on the Burnham investigation."

"I don't watch the TV much. Too much work to get done before bedtime."

"The local MPP, Hollingsworth, gave an interview in which he divulged information about the investigation that has not been made public. He stated that he'd received the information from a source inside this detachment."

"I see." Skelton looked from Sonja to Ellie, giving it some thought.

"Do you have any idea who might have passed on case information to Mr. Hollingsworth?"

"Nope. Sure don't."

"Isn't it true, Doug, that you and he are neighbours?"

"Yep. He lives on the same road, a few lots down."

"Are you friends?"

"I suppose you could say. Stop and talk on the road when we're driving past each other. Belong to the same curling club. I see him at the Rotary Club meetings too. We're friendly. He seems all right. For a politician."

"Have you discussed the Burnham case with him, Doug?"

"No, Sergeant, I have not."

"Maybe a few words in passing about having been moved off it in favour of a less experienced detective, or how you think it's going in the wrong direction and overlooking obvious suspects?"

"No, Sergeant."

"There's a leak in this detachment," Ellie said. "This kind of breach in policy won't be tolerated. When we find out who it is, the repercussions will be severe."

"So they should be." Skelton looked from her to Sonja. "We don't want Grant Burnham's killer to be out there watching the news to see how close we're getting to him."

"Do you have any idea who might have been talking to

your neighbour about this case?" Sonja asked.

"No, Sergeant, I do not."

"If you find out who it is, we'd appreciate hearing about it."

"I don't tell tales out of school about other members. It's just not in the playbook. Sorry."

Sonja sighed. "All right, Doug. That's all for now."

He got up and strolled out of the room.

"Shit," Ellie muttered.

"That's what I say," Sonja agreed.

Chapter

45

Kevin spent the rest of the morning working on his reports. After a quick lunch, which he ate at his desk, he checked online for the number of the De Witt law firm and called them up.

"This is Detective Constable Kevin Walker, OPP. Would Clarisse De Witt be there?"

"I'm sorry," the receptionist said, "she's in Ottawa for the day. May I take a message and have her return your call later?"

"Sure, that would be fine."

"What did you say your name was, again?"

"Kevin Walker. OPP." He recited his cellphone number.

Apparently she'd didn't find it unusual for the police to call, looking to speak to one of their attorneys.

"How many lawyers do you have there?" he asked.

"Five altogether."

"Mr. De Witt, Ms. De Witt, and three others?"

"Yes, Mr. Paulin and two associates. Ms. Ryder and Mr. Belcher."

"You'll have her return my call as soon as possible?"

"As soon as possible."

Kevin put down the phone and thought for a moment. The De Witts seemed to be connected to the case at several different points, but he couldn't really say whether that was important or not. His interview with Wolf hadn't raised any suspicions about the man himself, but had led to his awareness of Clarisse, the daughter. Wolf's negotiations with Wally Moore to buy into the furniture company once Grant Burnham's estate was settled didn't seem to raise any red flags. And Moore had already jumped through several hoops and landed safely on the other side.

Then out of the blue, Bobby Burnham walked in and raised an issue about the victim's estate that was brought to his attention by Clarisse De Witt. Somehow she'd been informed of a restriction placed on the woodlot by the government, and Kevin's curiosity was immediately aroused. Where on earth had this restriction suddenly come from? The timing bothered him. Had Clarisse been surprised by it, or had she known before he was killed, as Grant's lawyer, that it was coming?

The fact that she'd been Grant's girlfriend when they were teenagers also nagged at him. Had one of them, or maybe both, continued to carry a flame for the other, or had their personal relationship evolved into a business association with no emotional overlap from the past?

Kevin shut down his computer and went looking for Heather, but her workstation was deserted and she was nowhere in sight. He stuck his head into Sonja's office.

Turning away from her computer monitor, she looked at him over the top of her glasses and raised an eyebrow.

"I'm going to follow up on Clarisse De Witt," he said, not bothering to mention that he knew she was out of town.

"All right. Keep me posted."

The offices of De Witt, Paulin and De Witt were located in a small, two-storey commercial building at the far end of Gore Street. According to the directory in the front lobby, the basement was occupied by a dance school and the main floor by doctors' offices and a dentist. The law firm was located on the top floor. As he trudged up two flights of stairs, Kevin wondered why they hadn't put the dancers on the top floor, since they were presumably more physically fit and wouldn't mind the climb as much as De Witt's miscellaneous clients.

He went through heavy glass doors into a reception area that was as quiet as a church. Nicely upholstered armchairs lined the walls on the far side. The walls held original oil paintings styled after the Group of Seven, and the floor was carpeted in dark burgundy.

Kevin realized that if the dance studio was above them, there'd probably be a lot of walking and jumping and thumping and what not going on over the course of the day that would wear on the nerves after a while and detract from the concentration of their clients.

A middle-aged woman with natural red hair and a crisp white blouse looked up from behind a mahogany counter. "Good afternoon, sir. May I help you?"

It was the woman he'd spoken to earlier on the phone.

He held up his badge and warrant card. "I called earlier for Ms. De Witt."

She frowned. "I believe I explained that she's in Ottawa today."

"Yes, that's right, you did. I thought I'd come over and take a look around. Nice place you have here."

"Thank you. I sent Ms. De Witt a message that you'd called, but she hasn't had a chance to view it yet. She's been in a meeting all afternoon and—"

"Kevin! Nice to see you again." It was Wolf De Witt, coming around the edge of a set of filing cabinets. "What brings you down here today?"

Kevin shook his hand over the counter. "Actually, I was looking for your daughter, but I understand she's out of town."

Kevin's cellphone buzzed with an incoming text message, but he ignored it.

De Witt turned to a young blond woman standing behind him with an armful of file folders. "Just leave them on my desk, Katy Ann, and then you can take your break."

The woman looked at Kevin, then nodded to De Witt and disappeared, presumably to his inner office in the back somewhere.

"Yes," De Witt said, "she's meeting with clients in Ottawa. A development company looking to clear all the legal hurdles for a new project here in town. Exciting stuff, eh?"

"Does she travel out of town a lot?"

"No, very seldom, actually. Her health isn't all that good. But she never complains, does she, Moira?" He turned to the redhead.

"No sir, not that I've ever heard."

"Did you message Clarisse that the detective constable is looking to have a word with her?" De Witt asked her.

"Yes, sir. I'm waiting for a reply, but I expect she's still in the meeting and—"

"That's as much as we can do for you right now," De Witt interrupted, showing Kevin an apologetic face. "She's very scrupulous about returning calls and following up on things, so I'm sure you'll hear from her very soon."

Kevin tapped the counter lightly with his badge wallet before putting it back in his inside jacket pocket. "I'll look forward to it. Sorry for the intrusion."

"Not at all, not at all. Glad you stopped by." De Witt shook his hand again and disappeared around the filing cabinets, presumably on his way to his inner office in the back somewhere.

Out in the parking lot, Kevin got into his car and took out his cellphone. The text message he'd received was from Janie:

Going to buy some stuff. You okay with that?

Smiling, he called her number.

"You didn't answer right away," she said without pre-amble, "so I went ahead and bought it. We're at The Bay now, and there's some other stuff in my cart. You caught me just before I went through the checkout. You're not going to have a stroke if I go a little wild here, are you?"

Janie and Sarah Coburn had decided to indulge in a Saturday shopping trip to the Bayshore Centre in Ottawa. In anticipation of ultimately making a fresh start with her business in another location in the near future, she'd decided to invest in a new wardrobe so that she'd look good for her customers. At least that was the pretext. She'd enlisted Sarah as a splurge partner, and off they'd gone this morning, giddy with excitement. Although he was a little nervous about the upcoming hit on their bank balance, especially where she'd already rented a storage unit on the edge of town for the next three months, he knew that shopping was sometimes good therapy. Within limits, of course.

"How wild is a little wild?" he asked, tentatively.

"Couple hundred. Maybe three. New jeans, some tops, and a couple pairs of shoes."

"Okay."

"So far."

"Okay."

"Stuff that's on sale, Kev, so don't freak out."

"Sale stuff's the best stuff."

"You got it, big boy."

Someone rapped on the window a few inches from his temple, startling him. It was the blond woman from De Witt's office. He nodded and held up a finger to ask her to wait for a moment.

"I have to go," he said to Janie. "Someone wants to talk to me."

"All right. Sarah's already gone through, and she's waiting for me. Later."

The line went dead.

Kevin put his phone away and lowered the window. "Yes?"

"You're from the police, right?"

"That's right."

You want to talk to Clarisse."

"Yes, that's right."

"Maybe you should talk to me first."

Chapter

46

She got into the front passenger seat and closed the door, staring straight ahead.

"I don't know if I should be doing this."

"Doing what? Talking to me?"

She nodded.

"You may not have caught my name inside. I'm Kevin Walker."

"Katy Ann Ryder." Her fingers tapped lightly on her thighs in a nervous rhythm. "Clarisse and I went to high school together."

Kevin considered taking out his notebook, but she was clearly agitated and he didn't want to do anything that would change her mind about talking to him, so he decided to make notes after the conversation was done and she'd gone back inside.

"How long have you worked for the De Witts, Katy

Ann?"

"I guess about eight years now."

"So it was like a reunion of old high school friends."

She made a noise. "Not exactly."

He waited for her to decide what she wanted to say.

"In Grade Eleven Mr. De Witt visited our school to give a talk on the law and the legal profession. It was a big deal because he was Clarisse's dad, and everyone in her little circle fussed over her and made her into a bigger star than she already was, but I kind of made a fool of myself. I couldn't stop asking him questions. I hadn't realized until then how interesting the law was, and how it seemed like exactly what I wanted to do with my life, so I went on and on. The kids treated me like I was a total ass, but he was very kind and patient, answering all my questions. When it was over, he actually gave me his business card and told me to call him if I was interested in a summer job."

"Wow."

She made eye contact with him for the first time since getting into the car. "Yeah. He's a really nice guy."

Kevin nodded.

"So that's what I did. I called him up, and he hired me as a summer intern. I did a lot of clerical stuff and answered the phone when the receptionist—the one before Moira—went on break. I loved it. Not because of the work, which was grunt stuff any moron could do, but because I got to ask everyone questions and be like a sponge. It was great; the best experience of my life."

She shrugged. "Of course, she was there that summer too. We hardly spoke. I thought maybe she was jealous of the attention I was getting from people at the firm, but whatever. When we graduated, she went off to U of T and Osgoode Law School to get her degrees and I had to settle for Carleton. I mean, not that Carleton's a bad school or anything. It's just, well, I guess you'd say it takes second place when it comes to law schools. Toronto being number one, of course."

She glanced at him. "You don't want to hear my life story, do you? You're just interested in Missy Clarisse."

Her bitterness was unmistakable.

"No, I'm very interested. Please, go on."

"Well, there's not much more to say. When I got my degree and passed the bar, I reached out to Mr. De Witt but he didn't have an opening for an associate right then, so I had to stay in Ottawa and shop around until I found something at one of the bigger firms. I ended up working there for five years before Mr. De Witt offered me a spot back here. Needless to say, I jumped at the chance to come home. I hate Ottawa with a passion."

"Was Clarisse here by then, working for her father?"

She nodded. "Oh, she was all fakey nice to me and glad to see me again and to have a chance to work with me, yadda yadda, but I knew it was all manufactured bullshit for her father to hear. I don't know what she's had against me all these years, because I never said boo to her, like, ever. It's just one of those things, I guess."

Kevin thought that Clarisse likely had picked up on Katy Ann's own jealousy and resentment a long time ago and decided not to make an effort to break through it.

"And of course you saw me in there doing grunt work like I was a summer student intern all over again. Wonderful, huh? Our paralegal quit during the pandemic and Mr. De Witt hasn't been able to find a replacement. There's a shortage right now, you know, just like there are shortages in personnel everywhere, and so he asked me to fill in and handle the extra duties. 'Sure,' I said. Anything for Mr. De Witt. But now I'm ten per cent associate and ninety per cent paralegal-slash-administrative assistant-slash-clerk, and it'll probably stay that way because now they don't need a para, do they? They've got me."

"What kind of law do you practise?"

"Family law," she said, a note of pride in her voice. "Clarisse is mainly real estate, since there's more money there, but Mr. De Witt's been covering the clients that would have been mine while I'm filling in, so like I say: ten per cent associate."

Kevin had remained patient while she talked about herself, but he wanted to hear what she had to say about Clarisse, so he showed her a little frown, as though he were confused about something.

"It's my understanding that she was Grant Burnham's attorney when he got his divorce. Wouldn't that normally have been something you would handle?"

She snorted. "I've done a bunch of divorces since I've been here—can you believe it's been twenty years? Incredible. But no, not that one. No way."

"I don't understand. Why not?"

She gave him an incredulous look. "Are you kidding? Grant was her client. Period. For everything. They were like this." She held up her hand with two fingers crossed.

"I knew they'd dated in high school—"

"High school? As soon as he started his business here in Perth—when was that again, in ninety-nine?—they started getting together again. Mr. De Witt set him up with the factory, but it was Clarisse who handled the transactions and the incorporation and everything. Business and pleasure, both."

"They had an affair?"

"Didn't seem to matter they were both married at the time. I could see they were an item, if nobody else did."

"How was that?"

She gave him a look. "He'd stop by on some pretence, with documents for her to review or something, then they'd take off for a two-hour lunch. It was a bit gross, if you ask me."

Kevin tried to hide his surprise. His sense that Clarisse De Witt had been an unsuspected and unexplained factor throughout the investigation had just been validated by Katy Ann. He decided to push the idea forward.

"What's she like? Does she have a temper? Maybe get really angry and throw things?"

Katy Ann laughed. "No, not a chance. She's extremely moody and impossible to please, but people call her the Ice Princess behind her back because that's exactly what she is. She's small and frail, a haemophiliac to boot, and frankly I've never been able to figure out what a hunk like Grant saw in her. She's pretty, yeah, and she must be better between the sheets than I've given her credit for, I mean, for him to keep coming back to her all the time the way he did."

Kevin glanced at her left hand. No ring. "Why didn't they just move in together, then? Especially after Grant got his divorce?"

"Yeah, I don't know. Her husband's very quiet and he really dotes on her, from what I've heard. Waits on her hand and foot. Treats her like she's made of fragile crystal or something. I guess she gets off on that. Anyway, she's got a good thing going there, so I guess she figured she could have it both ways."

"What about her husband? You said he's quiet?"

"Kind of a wimpy nerd type. Works as a consultant for some firm with a lot of government contracts."

"What's his name?"

"Dexter Trowbridge. She calls him Dex, but everyone else calls him *Dex*-ter."

She said it in a sing-song voice that made it sound like a pejorative.

"Did anything happen recently between Clarisse and Grant? Something that might have cooled things off a bit?"

"Your guess is as good as mine. The last time I saw them together was a week and a half ago. About three days before he died. He came into the office with papers and they met in her office for thirty minutes or so, and then he left. By himself. No lunch date this time."

"Was there any indication of an argument between them? Voices raised? Banging around?"

She shook her head. "I think I'd have a heart attack and die if those two ever had an argument. They were like a pair of characters from a Brontë novel or something. Star-crossed lovers. Melancholy personified."

"Okay." Kevin dug out a business card and gave it to her.

"Call you if I think of anything else, right?" She smirked at him. "Just like on TV."

"Yeah, something like that." He watched her get out of the car and cross the parking lot to the rear entrance of the building without looking back.

Then he dug out his notebook and started scribbling.

Chapter

47

That evening someone knocked on the kitchen door just as Ellie was stacking her supper dishes in the dishwasher. Reggie trotted over, his ears up and his posture alert.

"It's okay," Ellie said, closing up the dishwasher and punching the button to start it.

Reggie retreated a few steps, his ears swivelling to her and back again, but his eyes never left the door.

Ellie wiped her hands on a dish towel and nudged him aside with her shin. "Dennis. Come on in."

Dennis Leung edged into the kitchen as Ellie closed the door behind him, showing a policeman's traditional caution when confronted with an unknown dog.

"Friend," Ellie said to Reggie. "Dennis. Friend. Go and lie down."

The dog gave Leung a long look, shook himself, and trotted off to curl up on the carpet in Ellie's office.

They shook hands. "Thanks for doing this," Ellie said.
"No problem. Glad to."

Ellie grabbed a light windbreaker off a hook and threw it on. It was something she occasionally wore to a crime scene when she wanted a break from her usual suit jacket and slacks, and it had the additional benefit of being waterproof. It was navy with OPP shoulder flashes and "POLICE" printed in large letters across the front and back.

Leung glanced down at himself. He was just coming off a shift and was wearing a glen plaid suit, white shirt, and black tie. "Should I take off the tie?"

"No, you're good."

They went outside and around the cottage to the lodge next door. Ellie knocked, using her knuckles instead of the side of her fist as she would have done in other circumstances. Mali opened the door right away and showed them in, hanging up Ellie's windbreaker before leading them into the great room that faced out onto the lake.

Ellie's eyes automatically went to the large picture windows, embossed with reflections of the room against the darkness outside. It had been a while since she'd been in this room, to say goodbye to Ridge on the morning of his final departure to Kingston. Once more she felt a pang of loneliness at the loss of a good friend. It was a reminder that she should call him tomorrow. Hopefully he'd be up to a short chat.

She turned as Dr. Othman rose to greet them. The furniture was all different, of course, and arranged in patterns new to her, according to the preferences of the Othmans. She forced herself to accept the fact that nothing was wrong, that this was now their home, and that change was always inevitable.

She shook hands formally with Othman. "This is Detective Constable Leung."

"We spoke on the phone," Othman said, shaking his hand. "Thanks for coming up tonight to meet with us."

"Glad to."

Mali moved toward a large chesterfield with an unobstructed view of the lake. "This is our son, Dean."

The boy stood up and came over. He smiled at Ellie, rather nervously, she thought, and held out his hand to Leung.

"*Nín hǎo*," he said, shyly. "*Hěn gāoxìng jiàn dào nǐ.*"

Leung grinned. "I'm very glad to meet you as well," he replied in Cantonese. "Have you been learning to speak the language?"

"I'm sorry, that's all I know how to say." Dean shoved his hands into his pockets. "I looked it up this afternoon."

"Well, I think that's great. Your accent is pretty good. You should take lessons."

"Shall we sit down?" Mali gestured and they all took seats, Dean and his father on the chesterfield, Ellie to their left in a comfortable leather armchair, and Leung in a recliner on the right.

"I've made tea and coffee," Mali said, moving to a sideboard. "Ellie?"

"Coffee, please."

"A teaspoon of honey and no cream; am I remembering correctly?"

"Yes. Thanks."

"Detective Constable Leung?"

"Tea would be great. Black, thank you. No sugar."

She served them their beverages, gave her husband a cup of coffee with cream and sugar, and then sat down on the other side of her son.

Leung sipped his tea and set it down on the side table next to his chair. "Very good." He smiled at Dean. "So. Your mother tells me you're interested in going on a ride-along with me. Is that right?"

Dean nodded. "Is that okay?"

"Yes, of course. That's why I'm here. I thought we should talk about it, so I know what you want to learn and so I can tell you what to expect. Sound good?"

"Yes."

Ellie looked at the boy. He was staring at the big picture windows, but his eyes were shining with anticipation.

"Let me tell you a bit about myself, first." Leung glanced at Mali and Othman to include them in what he was going to say to Dean. "I'm a detective constable in the OPP, posted to the detachment at Elizabethtown-Kitley. Spring Valley. On the way to Brockville. If for some reason you or your parents ever need to call the police, it'll be constables from our office who'll come out to help you."

"You?"

"No, normally it'll be what we call provincial constables, the people who wear the uniforms you've seen before. I'm a detective constable, so I have a separate set of responsibilities."

"A detective, like Ellie?"

"That's right. I'm assigned to the crime unit, which means when a crime is reported I'm sent out to investigate. Uniformed constables also go out on those types of calls, as what are referred to as first responders, and when a detective's needed for an in-depth investigation, that's when I go out, too. I hope I'm explaining this okay."

"Yes. And Ellie goes there, too?"

"Sometimes. She's several ranks above me, you have to remember, and she's only called out to what we call major crimes. The very serious incidents that we always hope never happen, but sometimes do."

"Like murder."

"Yes. Ellie and I have worked together a couple of times."

Mali leaned forward. "You have a family, Detective Constable Leung?"

"Please, everyone just call me Dennis. You too, Dean. Yes, my wife's name is Lily. We have four daughters. May is a second-year student at the University of Toronto; Lucy is a senior at the high school in Brockville; Lan's in Grade Eleven; and Meilin's right around your age, Dean."

"Does she speak Chinese?"

"Yes, she does. Cantonese. We all do. My wife wants them to appreciate the traditions and values of our families."

"Were you born in China?"

Leung shook his head. "Toronto. Just like you. My parents, though, were born in Guangdong Province in China, where most people speak Cantonese. My father speaks some Mandarin, but we've always just spoken English and Cantonese at home."

"Is he still there? In China?"

"No, he and my mother immigrated to Canada two years before I was born. He was a doctor back in China, a surgeon, but he couldn't get a licence here, for several reasons, and he decided to open a store on Spadina Avenue to sell traditional herbal remedies and tea and that sort of thing. He still opens every morning at nine and closes promptly at four."

"We've been to Chinatown before," Mali said to Dean. "To go shopping."

"I know!" He made eye contact with his mother, smiling. "I love the grocery stores. I love the smell. The fish, and the vegetables."

"I love them too," Leung said, matching his smile.

"I hope I'm not asking too many questions."

"Ask whatever you want, Dean. It's quite all right."

"Why don't you tell us about the ride-along," Dr. Othman said, finally breaking his silence.

"Sure. I thought we could spend an afternoon together, Dean, so you can see what the office is like, meet some of the uniformed constables, and then take a ride with me to see the sort of things I do on a typical day."

He looked at Ellie and laughed. "Mostly what I do is really boring. I mean, I love my job and wouldn't want to do anything else, but someone your age might find it a little, uh, less than totally exciting. But anyway, I thought I could show you a few places where we were called out one time and tell you the story of what happened."

"Okay."

Leung looked at Othman. Ellie had briefed him on the father's reluctance to allow the ride-along, and now was the time to be direct and forthcoming with him, his wife, and their son.

"My job in the crime unit covers drug enforcement and organized crime. I handle cases that involve trafficking of drugs in our county, for example, and importation across the border. Also drug production."

"Like grow ops," Dean said.

"That's right. Often these crimes are being carried out by organized crime groups and their various members and associates, so I have to stay up to date on who's who and where they're at. I work on task forces and other multi-jurisdictional teams with the RCMP, Canada Border Services, and police in Brockville, Kingston, and Ottawa. I know a lot of people on our side of the law who are working on these things, and they know me."

He glanced at Dean, who was staring at him with wide eyes, and turned back to Dr. Othman. "If you have a concern about Dean's being exposed to this kind of thing, please say so and we can see if there's someone else who can take Dean out."

"I have to think about this for a moment," Dr. Othman said, looking at his wife.

"Of course." Leung reached for his tea and took another sip.

The pause gave Ellie a chance to try her coffee. Othman was right; her machine was better than theirs.

Mali squeezed her hands together in her lap. "Detective—Dennis—you wouldn't be taking Dean on a raid of a biker hideout or anything like that, would you?"

Leung looked shocked. "Good heavens, no. That would be a very bad idea." He set down his tea. "I thought we could go for a short drive around the area after we're done at the office, Dean, and I could give you an idea what rural policing is like. You and I grew up in the big city, and police work there is quite different in a lot of ways from what we do here. The environment's different, the people are different, and our procedures are sometimes different. I could show you a few places where crimes happened before and explain what we had to do to enforce the law."

"Nothing dangerous?"

"No, ma'am. Places where the dangerous elements have already been cleared out and it's no longer an active crime scene."

"Can we think about this?" Othman asked. "And call you in a few days?"

"Of course." Leung stood up and gave him a card. "My home number's written on the back. Call any time."

Everyone stood up except Dean, who remained on the chesterfield, eyes down.

"Dad, I really want to do this."

"I know, son. But your mom and I need to talk about it first."

"I thought you already talked about it."

"We need to talk about it more."

Leung shook Othman's hand, Mali's hand, and made a small gesture to Dean for him to stand up. When the boy complied, Leung shook his hand and held it for a moment.

"It's been a pleasure to meet you," he said in Cantonese, "and I think you're a fine young man."

Although he didn't understand, Dean smiled. He slipped his hand out of Leung's and put it in his pocket, but the smile remained.

"Your father or mother will call me about the ride-along," Leung said in English, "and if the decision is not to do it, you must accept their judgment with good grace and dignity. They're your elders, and you must always treat them with utmost respect, as I treat my parents."

Dean nodded.

"One other thing. No matter what they decide, if you're interested and your parents concur, my wife's best friend is an excellent tutor in Cantonese, and I could arrange for you to take lessons with her. If you're interested."

Dean broke into a rare grin and nodded at his father, who shrugged. "We'll see."

"There would be no cost," Leung said. "Mrs. Chou is a person of, shall we say, independent means, and she never charges to tutor children. She does it for the love of the language, and for the benefit of those who want to learn while they're still young enough for it to take hold."

"It sounds like something you'd enjoy," Mali said to Dean.

"I sure would."

"Thank you," she said to Leung.

"My pleasure." He glanced at Ellie, winked, and they headed for the door.

Chapter

48

"This was on sale for only thirty-five dollars," Janie said, swirling into the living room in a knee-length summer dress with cap sleeves, a modest neckline, and colourful flowers on a white background.

"That's really nice," Kevin said, balancing his plate of microwave pizza on his knee so that he could reach for his can of ginger ale. "You could wear it for special clients."

"Well," she said, looking down at herself, "I thought about having a little wine and cheese thing when I reopen, you know, invite clients to come around and meet me and Lauren, see the new place, that sort of thing."

Kevin swallowed and set the can aside. He could have pointed out that she needed a new place for her business before she could have a grand reopening event, but instead he said, "That sounds like a really good idea."

So far he'd seen three long-sleeved T-shirts in different

colours, brown and black denim jeans, a new pair of comfortable-looking work shoes, and a white blouse and denim skirt combination that looked quite smart on her.

She moved up close to him. "Smell. Do you like that?"

He grabbed his plate, which she'd accidentally nudged with her hip. For a moment all he could smell was pizza. Then he caught a whiff of citrus and cinnamon.

"Nice."

"It's Gordon St. Vincent. Beyond Paradise. Reduced to clear. Ten bucks."

"I like it."

"You better. It's my new favourite." She stepped back and flicked the hem of her dress. "Anyway, that's the fashion show for tonight. I'm going to go hit the shower."

He smiled up at her as she leaned down and kissed his forehead.

"Thanks for being so patient," she said before disappearing into the dining room and down the hall to their bedroom.

Kevin ate his pizza, relieved that Janie was rallying from her funk and trying to focus on moving forward. He doubted that she was going to be able to find another suitable location in the village to reopen her salon, so she'd likely be forced to look elsewhere. Unless it was another village, like Athens or Mallorytown, she'd find her rent would be a lot more expensive. Brockville would be out of the question. Even Smiths Falls, which wasn't much of an option given the distance she'd have to drive every day. In fact, he hated to see her have to drive much at all, particularly in winter. Having her place of business just a few blocks away from their home had been a luxury she was going to miss.

As he picked up his last piece of pizza and took a big bite, his thoughts moved to Ellie. She clearly wasn't herself these days. Her anger this morning during the meeting was uncharacteristic, although he could see how it was justified, given the egregious breach in protocol that had been committed by whomever had leaked information to the politician. Still, it wasn't like her to show her emotions so openly.

He wondered what might be wrong. Should he say something? Maybe ask her if there was anything he could do? To help her out. With whatever it was.

He finished the pizza and got up to take his plate out to the kitchen. *Bad idea, Kev.* As fond as he was of her, and as much as he might think of her as a friend, sort of, he knew that their relationship wasn't the kind where a senior commissioned officer might share her personal life with a constable, detective or not. It just wasn't going to happen.

As he began to tidy up the kitchen, he heard Janie go into the bathroom and start up the shower. If he ran the water in the kitchen to do the dishes, it would affect the supply of hot water to the bathroom. Janie hated cold showers, so he began with a basic tidy-up, piling dirty plates and silverware into the plastic basin in the sink and putting stuff back into the fridge and the overhead cupboards.

As he gathered up Caitlyn's dishes, he saw that she'd left her notebook open next to her dinner plate. She was in her room, reading. Brendan and Josh were downstairs playing video games. The house was quietly humming in its evening routine, and he was all alone for the time being.

He finished clearing off the table and moved behind Caitlyn's chair. In Canadian common law, the principle of plain view evidence dictates that a person has no reasonable expectation of privacy when they expose something to public view, and a peace officer is permitted to seize evidence when observing it from a lawful vantage point. Well, here was Cait's notebook in plain view, and here he was, lawfully able to look at it. Right?

On the page in front of him she'd written a poem:

> Thoughts are knots on a string
> I pull through my head.
> And when a knot gets caught
> It's a thought,
> I think.

Bless her heart. He'd never been any good with poetry, or any of the other creative arts, for that matter, so he had no idea if it was good or bad poetry. It made him smile, though, and he figured that was a good thing, at least.

He was still alone and undisturbed, so he decided to venture out onto more shaky legal ground. He turned to the previous page. She'd written:

Story idea

> A hockey goaltender who tries
> to save other people from their
> problems and sadness but can't save
> himself from his own sadness and
> depression. Canadian Catcher in the
> Rye. Hockey as a metaphor for the
> relentless blows life deals people.

Well, now. Kevin thought that was a rather mature theme for her to be working with, but he had to remind herself that she was fifteen, in Grade Eleven, and reading far above her age group. More surprising was the fact that she was showing an interest—a very strong interest, apparently—in creative writing. He'd had no idea.

Footsteps sounded in the hallway. Janie was still in the shower, so it was probably Caitlyn. He flipped the page over and moved off to the kitchen sink.

As she came into the kitchen, he folded up the empty pizza box and put it into the recycling bin.

"Have you seen my—oh, here it is."

Kevin heard the shower turn off in the bathroom, so he picked up the dish detergent, squirted a healthy amount into the basin, and turned on the hot water. From the corner of his eye he saw her gather up the notebook and tuck it under her arm.

"What are you reading tonight, Cait?"

"A book of poems I found in the school library."

"Poems, eh? By who?"

"Whom. Judith Wright. She was Australian. 'Silence is the rock where I shall stand.' She has some really vivid imagery."

"I never heard of her." He began to drop dishes into the basin.

"I'll give it to you when I'm done. It was in the sale cart for a quarter last April. Imagine."

"Sounds like a heckuva buy."

She didn't answer, and when he turned around, she was gone.

As he started to wash off the first plate, he thought about her story idea, the goalie enduring life's relentless punishment. Had the Burnham case somehow drawn her attention and negatively affected her frame of mind?

He followed a general rule not to talk about active investigations at home, and he knew he hadn't said anything to her about it, or to Janie that Caitlyn might have overheard. It was in the news, of course, and while his name was never mentioned she always knew when he was working a murder case, despite his best efforts to maintain an even disposition around his family.

Was it something he should worry about? That his job was starting to affect the children, now that they were getting older and more aware of what was going on around them?

He started to worry that it might be.

On the other hand, his passion for playing hockey, only recently set aside for the sake of family responsibilities, was something Caitlyn had always viewed with amused tolerance. She'd occasionally attended his games with Janie and had cheered for him more loudly than anyone else in the building, but she'd otherwise never expressed an interest in the sport, or any other sport for that matter.

Kevin wondered if somehow her story idea had been inspired by watching him crash people into the boards, block shots and limp off the ice to recuperate for a shift, and otherwise patrol the ice with the grim determination of an oversized amateur playing for the love of the game.

Did he appear to her as sad and depressed?

He plunged his hands into the hot, soapy water and told himself not to overthink the whole thing.

Chapter

49

The next day was Sunday, so Kevin took the morning off and spent it mowing the lawn. The sun was out and the air was hot, so he stripped off his T-shirt and worked in his shorts and sneakers, enjoying every moment. When he was done, he put the lawn mower away and went inside for a tall glass of iced tea, which he drank outside on the back deck while he made a few phone calls.

When his glass was empty, he went in and ate a quick lunch. Janie chattered away to Caitlyn about a late movie they'd stayed up to watch after Kevin had gone to bed. Everyone seemed to be in a good mood. When the cat jumped up onto Caitlyn's lap to examine the remnants of her lunch for an appetizing snack, Janie held her temper and suggested Boo Boo might go back down under the table where she belonged. She wasn't a cat person and barely tolerated Caitlyn's beloved pet, so the absence of an explosion of anti-cat sentiment was a welcome change for everyone.

After lunch, Kevin showered and dressed. He put on a clean pair of blue jeans, a white dress shirt, a cordovan tie, and polished brown cowboy boots. He topped it off with a navy sports jacket and checked himself in the mirror. It was similar to a look he'd admired before on Tommy Lee Jones in *U.S. Marshals*, a version of business casual that he thought would at least get him inside the door on a quiet Sunday afternoon, and after stuffing his jacket pockets with his badge wallet, his notebook and pen, his cellphone, and a few business cards, he said goodbye to everyone and headed off to Perth.

Clarisse De Witt lived in a large stone house on Mill Street in the centre of town, close to City Hall and Stewart Park. Passing through an open pair of wrought-iron gates, he walked up a long flight of moss-covered stone stairs, admiring the blue spruce trees, hydrangea shrubs, and rose bushes on the front lawn. The verandah extended across the full width of the house, and when he rang the door bell the two-tone chime echoed loudly inside. He waited, and eventually he heard the sound of approaching footsteps.

Given the old-school, classical look of the place, Kevin half-expected the door to be answered by a butler or housemaid, but the woman who appeared in front of him could not be anyone other than Clarisse herself.

She was just as Katy Ann Ryder had described her: small and thin, almost frail, with very pale skin and shoulder-length, frizzy brown hair showing threads of grey. Kevin decided instantly there was no way on earth this woman had wielded the bat that had killed Grant Burnham. She just wouldn't have had the physical strength to do the kind of brutal damage that had been inflicted on Burnham.

He showed her his badge and warrant card. "Detective Constable Walker. Are you Clarisse De Witt?"

"I am." She stepped back, opening the door. "Please come in."

She closed the door and led him into a sitting room with beautiful antique furniture, a stone fireplace, and oil paintings on the walls. Kevin walked up to a large canvas depicting a horse-drawn sleigh in a wintry landscape. He leaned forward to look at the signature.

"This is a real Krieghoff, isn't it?"

"Yes. Please, sit down. Would you like something to drink?"

"No, I'm fine, thank you. I just had lunch." He sat down in a sturdy-looking armchair whose frame was made of dark wood that he thought might be mahogany. "Thank you for seeing me."

"It's my day off."

"Is your husband at home? Dexter Trowbridge?"

"He's out, doing his thing." She waved a hand casually. "I seldom see him on Sundays. He's a botanist, you see. He works for a consulting company and spends the week at his office in Ottawa. The curse of middle management. He squeezes in a little outdoor work on the weekends. You can take the man out of the field, but you can't take the field out of the man, I suppose you could say."

Kevin nodded, opening his notebook. "You have a beautiful home, Ms. De Witt."

"Thanks."

While his expectations had been shaped by Katy Ann, his first impression of her was taking a somewhat different form. She bore a disturbing resemblance to the woman who'd played opposite Harrison Ford in *Blade Runner*, the replicant he fell in love with. What was the actress's name? Sean something. Young. She had the same doll's mouth, the large, dark eyes, and the thick hair. She also had the same lack of expression and ineluctable sadness that seemed to surround her like a gentle mist.

Kevin was puzzled. He thought about Grant Burnham and the composite image of the man he'd constructed as a victim profile: the fit, well-muscled, former professional athlete; the careful, hard-nosed businessman who'd outmanoeuvred his partner and found a much better replacement; the divorced bachelor who liked to throw barbecue parties on weekends with a different woman on his arm each time.

Matching the image of that man with the woman sitting across from him was, on first impressions, quite a stretch. Was Katy Ann wrong that they'd been carrying on a secret affair all these years? Was her judgment clouded, perhaps, by jealousy and her own attraction to Burnham?

According to Katy Ann, Clarisse was a haemophiliac. It was a condition more prevalent in males than females, yes, and it often presented in childhood, resulting in a careful, sheltered upbringing. And yet Wolf had told him that Clarisse and Burnham were a couple in high school. He mentally rolled his eyes at the cliché, but was it true that in this case opposites did attract?

The athlete and the fragile, lovely ice princess?

"You were Grant Burnham's lawyer," he began tentatively.

"Yes."

"You handled his real estate transactions?"

"Yes, I did."

"What did these include?"

"Well, let's see." She plucked at the pleats of her long white skirt and crossed her legs. "I helped him set up the lease-to-own arrangement with Dad on the North Street factory. I handled the purchase of his first house, and then the sale of that property and the purchase of his present home at Balderson. He bought two different woodlots, one on Ennis Road and the other on Eight A. He sold the Ennis Road lot after finding out that it flooded in the springtime and stayed damp until late June. He kept the other one and used it as his woodlot."

Kevin took notes while listening to her, conscious of the monotone in which she spoke. He'd developed a pretty good ear over the years, and he wondered if she might be affecting it as a way to pretend she didn't care one way or the other, that talking about the man she'd loved since she was a teenager, the man who was now dead, didn't bother her at all.

"You also handled his divorce."

"Yes."

"Why did you do it instead of the lawyer who practises family law for your father?"

A tiny smile crept into the corners of her mouth, and her large, dark eyes glittered at him. "You've already talked to Katy Ann, haven't you?"

"Yes, I have."

"I handled it, as you put it, because he asked me to."

"Oh?"

"As a personal favour."

"I see. You and he had a long history, as I understand it. Your father told me you and Mr. Burnham dated when you were in high school."

"Yes, we did."

"After which you went your separate ways?"

"Yes."

Kevin let his eyes wander to the painting of the horse-drawn sleigh for a moment. He remembered reading that a Cornelius Krieghoff around the same size had sold at auction a few years ago for more than four hundred thousand dollars. Yet she'd dismissed it with a virtual wave of her hand. Was life really that tedious for her?

"Mr. Burnham was married when he retired from hockey and came back to Smiths Falls." he plunged on. "As I understand it, they'd only been married for about a year at that point, and they stayed married for more than twenty years before the divorce."

"Yes."

"They didn't get along very well, so I've heard."

The tiny smile again. "No. They didn't."

"Why would they stay together that long, then? I don't really understand."

"She was an alcoholic. He felt . . . sorry for her, I guess. He'd talk her into rehab, she'd stay sober for a few months, and then she'd relapse. It happened over and over. When she was drinking, she wasn't faithful to him, but he stuck with her, trying to help her straighten out. Eventually he just . . . got too tired of it."

"What about him? Was he seeing other women as well?"

"It's not really something for me to comment on."

"Were you aware there was an issue with Grant's woodlot, before his death?"

"Yes."

"Did you discuss it with him?"

"Yes."

"What was his reaction?"

Her lips parted in a faint smile. "Anger. Frustration. Contempt."

"What can you tell me about the restriction?"

"Nothing. Not at this time."

Kevin took a moment to look down at his notebook. He felt he'd finally reached the point where he could ask her bluntly whether she had carried on an affair with Burnham before his death. He was choosing his words when he heard the front door bang. Footsteps approached.

Kevin turned around. A man stood in the doorway, staring at Kevin as he stripped off his windbreaker. He was small and wiry, with a greying beard and pouchy, dark eyes.

"What's going on here? Who are you?"

Kevin put away his notebook and got to his feet, displaying his badge and warrant card. "Detective Constable Walker, OPP. Dexter Trowbridge?"

"Are you all right, Clarisse?" He moved to her side and put a hand on her forearm.

"Yes," she said, gently slipping out from under his fingers. "He's just asking me a few questions about Grant Burnham."

"Burnham?" He shot Kevin a look. "Why?"

Before Kevin could respond, Clarisse sighed and said, "I'm a witness, Dex. I was his lawyer."

"What about lawyer-client privilege?"

"We're not talking about anything that was confidential. Only things that were essentially public knowledge."

"May I have a few minutes of your time, Mr. Trowbridge?" Kevin asked.

"No. Please leave. I can't have you tiring Clarisse out. You can see she's not well. And I don't have anything to say that would be of interest to you."

Kevin looked at Clarisse. She stared back at him.

"A chronic condition," she said. "Haemophilia. Dex worries about me more than he should, but he's right. We've basically exhausted our supply of useful information, Detective Walker. So if you don't mind?"

Kevin put a business card on the side table next to her chair. "Please call me if you think of anything I should know."

She picked it up and nodded.

"I can show myself out."

"Please do," Trowbridge growled.

Outside, the sun came out from behind a cloud and blinded him. Kevin patted his pockets and remembered with regret that he'd left his sunglasses in the car.

Chapter

50

Back at the detachment office, Kevin went looking for Heather. She wasn't at her desk, but when he checked the lunch room he found her sitting alone, drinking coffee and reading a comic book: *Classics Illustrated, Lorna Doone.*

"Let's go for a ride in my new car," he said.

She turned the page. "Where to?"

"Burnham's woodlot. I don't understand why Bobby Burnham was told he couldn't go on the property. I want to take a look around."

She glanced up at him and screwed up her face. "Do I have to?"

"No, but I thought—" He saw that she was smirking behind her comic book and stopped talking.

"Let me finish my coffee first."

"Okay. I'll wait in the car."

She turned another page. "Won't be long."

Ten minutes later, Kevin was sitting in the Charger with the engine idling, watching wasps stitch random patterns up and down the brick wall in front of him, when she opened the passenger door and got in.

"Let's roll, Kevvy." She'd changed into a long-sleeved T-shirt with a *Magic: The Gathering* design on it, khaki cargo pants, and hiking boots. She tipped her sunglasses down, gave him a look, and pushed them back up again.

As they drove north up County Road 511, Kevin said, "I've never read *Lorna Doone*. Is it a good story?"

"It's not bad. Of course when I picked it up and saw Richard Blackmore I thought it was the guy from Deep Purple. Bit of a disappointment, but that's life."

In a few minutes they were slowing down to enter Balderson. Heather snorted, and Kevin looked over. "Okay, that's it. You need to tell me what your problem is with that cheese store."

"What cheese store?"

"Very funny. What gives?"

"Oh, all right, then. Kevvy, here's my deep, dark secret. I'm a cheese girl."

"A cheese girl?"

"Yeah, and I'm proud of it. We're a cheese family, don't you know. My father, Harry Hope, and my mother, Delta, owned and operated the best damned cheese factory in central Ontario, bar none. Better than Stirling, and a helluva lot better than Baldieguts, who don't even make their cheese here anymore. We won awards too, although Mom and Dad didn't like tooting their horn all the time."

"Cheese. I love cheese."

"Many people do, Kev. It's what makes the world go round. Anyway, they sold out a couple of years ago and retired." She laughed. "To Bermuda."

"No kidding."

"I kid you not. The big dairy corporations have been

buying up the smaller operations for years, but Mom and Dad held out until they were darned good and ready to kiss it all goodbye. Meanwhile, they were making the best cheese you ever tasted. Cheddar, primarily."

"Curds?"

"Are you joking? How do you think I got stuck with this girlish figure from the time I was eight? I see big bags of curds when I close my eyes to go to sleep at night."

"Sounds like a great way to grow up."

"Yeah, it was. We made it traditionally, in big, open vats which give it that certain something when it comes to flavour. And all-natural, my man. No preservatives. The cheese maker that took over for Mega-Corp after my parents sold kept all our traditional methods. Want to hear something great?"

"Sure."

"When Dad negotiated the sale, he included a clause saying that I was to get a generous supply of Hope Cheese—which is what they still call it—for the rest of my life. So I get a care package Purolated to my front door every Friday. Cool, huh?"

Kevin laughed.

When Kevin reached Burnham's woodlot, he turned off the road and stopped even with the cedar trees crowding the entrance. He shut off the engine and they got out.

"Well, here you go." Heather walked up to the sign nailed to the nearest tree. "'By order of the Minister of the Environment, Conservation and Parks pursuant to the *Endangered Species Act*, S.O. 2007, chapter six, access to this property is forbidden until a habitat assessment is completed and a strategy enacted to recover an identified species at risk on this property.' Signed by the minister and so on and so forth."

"Another one here." Kevin walked over to an identical sign posted on another tree. He took a picture of it with his phone.

"So what's going on? Did they find those funky blue frogs that people lick to get high or something?"

"I don't know." Kevin walked under the archway of cedar boughs and into the clearing that had served as Burnham's parking area. His truck and equipment were gone, having been removed by Ident for further processing in their garage and lab, but everything else looked the same as it did when he was here before.

Heather walked behind him and up the deer trail a few paces. "This is where he bought it?"

"Yeah."

"Grim stuff."

"Yeah."

She came back to him, arms wrapped around herself. "Maybe the guy across the road saw them putting up the signs. Maybe he knows who it was."

Kevin nodded. "Good idea. Let's go ask him."

They walked across the road. Kevin went up the cement steps and pounded on the front door while Heather looked through the window into Max's Hyundai before mooching around the side of the garage.

Kevin pounded again. There was no traffic passing on the road behind him. The entire place was completely silent except for the ringing in his ears and the sound of Heather's receding footsteps. Nothing at all came from inside the house.

He pounded one more time, and then turned to go down the stairs.

"Kevin!"

It was Heather, her voice high and shrill.

He ran around the side of the house into the back yard.

Past a picnic table on patio slabs. Past a lawn mower sitting at the end of a narrow strip of mown grass.

Past Heather, who was staring at a large tree at the back of the lawn, just in front of the bush line.

To the body of Max Macdonald, hanging suspended by an orange extension cord from a limb of the tree.

Chapter

51

"What do you think?" Sonja asked.

"I won't be able to say definitively, of course, until the autopsy is complete, but my preliminary examination finds nothing that would contradict a verdict of suicide." Dr. Phong looked at Kevin.

"I agree," he said. "How long was he there?"

"Only a couple of hours."

The body had been lowered from the tree and placed on a gurney, and the coroner had declared it ready to transport.

Sonja looked at Bob Pierce. "Stay with it."

"Will do." Pierce nodded at Kevin and followed the gurney around the side of the house to the hearse that was parked behind Max's Hyundai.

Sonja looked once again at the piece of cardboard that had been placed in an evidence bag when the victim's clothing was being examined. It was a scrap torn from a package of sandpaper that had been found in the left hip pocket of Max's jeans. On the back, handwritten with a black permanent marker, was a message:

I'm sorry for what I done.

"It doesn't leave a lot of doubt," she said.

"You think he's confessing?" Heather asked. "That he killed Grant Burnham and then killed himself because he couldn't handle the guilt?"

"I think it sure looks like it." She handed the evidence bag to a SOCO who was on his way out. "I know you've handled a number of homicides," she said to Kevin, "but I worked North East for a long time, and I saw dozens of suicides, a lot of them out of remorse for something. This definitely has all the earmarks of another one."

"I still don't think he's good for it," Kevin said. "We need to go over the physical evidence again. Especially the footprints. I thought Dave had proven that Macdonald's footprints were over top of the prints from the Gore-Tex hiking boots worn by the killer."

Sonja nodded. "We'll look at everything again."

"We already put this guy under the microscope," Heather said, "and came up with zip."

"Well, we'll just put him back under it again."

"Sure."

Kevin sighed.

"I want you two to notify the ex-wife. If I remember correctly, she was interviewed once before, but maybe the news of his death will shake something else loose."

"Maybe."

"Did he have any pets?"

Kevin looked at the house and shook his head.

"Well, that's one less thing to worry about."

"This is really sad," Heather said. "Really, really sad."

Chapter

52

Carole Kerr lived in a small bungalow on a side street in the north end of Perth. She came to the door in a beige skirt suit that matched her copper-coloured hair and hazel eyes. She looked tired.

"Come in," she said, holding the screen door open for them. "I just got home from work. I haven't had time to change yet."

Heather led the way inside, having contacted Carole to set up the appointment. She'd also insisted on handling the notification, which responsibility Kevin had gladly yielded.

They sat down in a modestly furnished living room. She offered them tea or coffee, which they both declined.

"You said you needed to talk to me about Max. I already talked to someone about him and Mr. Burnham. I forget the man's name. I have his card around here somewhere."

"I'm afraid we have some bad news for you," Heather said. "Max is dead. He took his own life earlier today."

Carole's eyes widened and her mouth opened. For a moment it seemed as though she thought Heather had said something absurd, or had spoken in another language. The moment passed and she began to cry. Soundlessly, a few tears sketching down her cheeks.

"I'm very sorry, Mrs. Kerr."

Carole nodded, pulling a handkerchief out of the pocket of her jacket to dab at her face.

"Can we get you a glass of water?"

When she nodded, Kevin got up and left the room. The kitchen was down the hall to the right. He opened cupboards until he found a glass tumbler. He took his time filling it, then took a quick look around, checking the freezer, the fridge, and the other cupboards. There was no alcohol in sight.

He took the glass of water into the living room and gave it to Carole.

"Thanks," she said, putting it down on the side table without drinking from it.

Kevin was relieved to see that the tears had stopped. He sat down and took out his notebook.

"I suppose there always was that possibility," she said to Heather. "He was never a happy man. He had absolutely no self-confidence, and without any post-secondary education he was always going to be stuck in unskilled labour, which he hated. On top of that, he suffered from depression. He had medication he was supposed to take, but he always found a reason not to. I guess it was just a matter of time, really."

"Did he ever make any attempts while you were living with him?"

She shook her head. "When we were married it was the drinking that was the problem, not self-harm or suicide threats or anything like that. It was the drinking."

"How much did he drink?"

"A pint of Johnny Walker every night during the week, and a forty-ouncer every day on the weekends. It was awful."

Kevin winced as he wrote it down. His father's nickname was "Johnny" Walker for the same reason, and although calluses had grown over the wounds in the years since he'd left home, it still hurt to be reminded, even indirectly.

"Is that why you left?"

She nodded. "He wasn't a bad drunk, don't get me wrong. He was never violent or angry or any of those things. He just cried a lot, and when I tried to talk to him about what was upsetting him, he wouldn't listen to anything I said to try to help. After a while I'd just make sure he didn't burn the place down with dropped cigarettes and wait for him to pass out. We were out in that awful place in the country, with no friends and no neighbours. It was very lonely. Finally, I couldn't take it anymore."

Heather said, "You told the other detective you didn't know Grant Burnham."

"Yes. I knew who he was, of course, and shortly before I left I heard he'd bought the lot across the road from us, but I never met him."

"After you divorced, did you have much contact with Max?"

"No. I didn't see him at all for the first year or so after I left. He switched oil companies, which I was very relieved to find out, so he didn't come in to the office anymore."

"Oil companies?"

"Yes. I'm a secretary at Cromwell and Sons Fuels, here in town. Max would come in to the office to pay his oil bill every month, and we became acquainted. He was very shy, but seemed nice. I was coming off a bad relationship with a man who was obsessively possessive—I think there's a term for it."

"Obsessive love disorder," Heather said.

"Could be. Anyway, I guess you could say it was a rebound thing. I needed to be involved with someone new, to create some distance from the previous relationship, and Max seemed like a harmless choice. When he finally got up the nerve to ask me out, we started dating. I didn't realize he had a drinking problem until it was too late."

"After you remarried, did you see Max at all?"

She nodded. "Once. A week after the wedding he came around with a present for us." She laughed sadly. "A hundred-dollar gift certificate for maintenance at the car dealership. You know, where he works. Worked. Gavin was very polite and thanked him. He didn't stay. He just shook Gavin's hand and left. That was it."

"You were aware that he'd stopped drinking?"

"Through mutual friends. I was proud of him."

"Did you tell him that?"

"We'd stopped communicating by then."

"One more question. Do you think Max was capable of harming someone?"

"No. Absolutely not. Max was the most passive, least aggressive person I've ever met in my life. This is a guy who'd catch house flies in his hand and release them out the back door instead of swatting them. If someone tried to pick a fight with him, at work or in the grocery store parking lot or wherever, he'd always back down and then turn it in on himself afterward, as a kind of self-loathing. No. He was a quiet, sad, depressed man, and I'm very, very sorry to hear that he's finally gone."

"Thanks for your time," Heather said, getting up. "We'll see ourselves out."

Chapter

53

The following Wednesday, Kevin spent the morning finishing up his reports on the interviews he'd conducted at Sonja's direction on co-workers and acquaintances of Max Macdonald. He'd received mixed feedback on Max's recent state of mind. Some had commented on his increased depression while others hadn't noticed much change at all in his demeanour. Everyone agreed he was not a very happy person, but most were surprised that he'd taken his own life.

Kevin, Heather, and Sonja visited the lab on Monday, and Dave Martin once more walked them through the physical evidence collected at the woodlot. He admitted that the footprints matching shoes owned by Max Macdonald had been found all over the place, including up the deer path to the spot where Burnham had died, but he was at pains to point out that so also had been the prints left by the Gore-Tex hiking boots. Not to mention the victim's footwear impressions, of course. And all of the prints had been left at various times over the past month or so. Some mostly eradicated by weather, but others reasonably legible.

When Sonja pressed him, Martin insisted he would testify in court that the individual wearing the Gore-Tex hiking boots had had the closest proximity to the body, and the impressions clearly demonstrated movement consistent with rapid pursuit and vigorous activity around the base of the tree where the victim was struck and killed.

In other words, the evidence failed to support the theory that Max Macdonald had killed Grant Burnham.

Kevin left the meeting convinced that he'd been correct to interpret the remorse Macdonald expressed in the handwritten note as having been connected to his theft of the chain saw, and not to the murder.

Sonja continued to harbour lingering doubts, however. She made it clear to him afterward in her office that unless he came up with an alternative suspect, they would be forced to accept Macdonald as the most likely perpetrator of the murder.

As Kevin finished up a final report and got up to visit the washroom, he bumped into Doug Skelton walking down the corridor.

"Hear it turned out to be my man after all," Skelton said, looking up at him with a smug expression on his face.

"It's not conclusive, Doug."

"Not what I hear."

Kevin opened his mouth to argue but quickly closed it again, compressing his lips to keep the words from being spoken. He didn't want to get into it with him, didn't want to rise to the bait, didn't want to discuss a case with him that no longer involved Skelton.

Instead, Kevin patted him lightly on the shoulder, moved around him, and pushed through the door into the washroom.

Back in his little cubbyhole, Kevin took a few moments to compose himself. He'd spent his time in the washroom stall fuming about Skelton and Sonja and the whole perception by everyone that Macdonald had killed Burnham and that he, Kevin, was somehow misjudging the evidence, or not seeing what was right in front of him, or was committing some other egregious rookie move. It was foolish and juvenile, but he couldn't help himself. He just didn't seem to fit in around here.

Back at his desk, he forced himself to calm down and focus. Find an alternative suspect, eh?

Okay, then. Fine.

He trawled through various elements of the case in his mind and soon found himself thinking about the sudden closure of the woodlot. What the devil was that all about, anyway?

He took out his cellphone and called up the photograph he'd taken of the sign. He studied it for a moment and then, logging back into the OPP intranet, found a link to the *Ontario Endangered Species Act*. He wasn't familiar with this particular piece of legislation, so he took a few minutes to read through it.

Section 10 of the Act contained a prohibition against causing damage to the habitat of an endangered or threatened species. The section that followed outlined recovery strategies for the species including a report to the minister that identified the species, described the threat to it, and recommended action to be taken to protect and help it recover. He figured that this must be what was going on at the moment on Burnham's woodlot.

Accessing the provincial government telephone list, he punched in the general inquiry number for the Ministry of the Environment, Conservation and Parks, and waited in a queue for his call to be answered. After several minutes he explained to a human being that he was looking for information about a species at risk assessment in Drummond Township, Lanark County. He was promptly put on hold again.

After several minutes, the line rang through and a pleasant female voice answered. "Environmental Sciences and Standards Division, Glenda speaking. How may I help you?"

Kevin ran through his spiel again.

"I'm sorry, sir, this is the lab."

"The lab?"

"Yes. On St. Clair Street?"

"In Toronto?"

"Yes, sir."

After a few minutes of back and forth, Glenda thought she might know the person he needed to talk to, so she put him back on hold. In only a few seconds, the line rang through and a male voice answered.

"John Carpenter, EAP Division."

Kevin delivered his speech again.

"Please hold." The line went dead for several very long minutes until it finally rang through again.

"Marilyn Sands, speaking. How may I help you?"

"Hi there, this is Detective Constable Kevin Walker, OPP, Lanark detachment. I'm trying to get some information about a species at risk assessment underway in Drummond Township."

"Uh, I'm sorry, we don't deal with that sort of thing."

"I'm still talking to the Ministry of the Environment, right?"

"Yes, sir. But this is the Environmental Permissions Branch. We don't deal with species at risk specifically. We review applications for environmental compliance approval. I work specifically with the *Safe Drinking Water Act*."

"Sounds like I was probably forwarded to the wrong person. Do you have any idea who I should be talking to?"

"Describe again what you're trying to find out."

Kevin did so.

"That sounds like a regional issue. You should be talking to your local district office."

"Do you have any idea what district I'm in?"

"Where are you located, sir?"

"I'm calling from our detachment office in Perth, and the site in question is in Drummond Township, Lanark County."

"Just a moment." The line went silent for a few moments before Marilyn came back on. "You'll want to call the Ottawa MECP office on Don Reid Drive. There's a toll-free number I can give you."

"Do you have a direct number?"

She rattled off both numbers to him.

He thanked her, ended the call, and punched in the direct number.

"District Manager's Office, Tawnya Hill speaking. How may I help you?"

Cautiously, Kevin asked, "Is this the Ottawa MECP office?"

"The office of the Ottawa district manager, yes sir."

Kevin identified himself and repeated his spiel.

"One moment and I'll transfer you to the regional manager's office."

The line went dead for a moment, then Kevin found himself listening to James Taylor singing about sweet dreams and flying machines lying in pieces on the ground.

There was a click, and a voice said, "Manjeet Singh."

Once more, Kevin patiently identified himself and

explained his mission.

"Yes. I'm familiar with the assessment you're referring to. Unfortunately, the officer looking after it, Melissa Yan, is currently on leave."

Kevin felt his hopes rise. "But you're familiar with the file?"

"Yes, Detective Constable Walker, I am."

Finally!

"Can you explain to me what it's all about?"

"About? Well, it concerns *Woodsia obtusa*, actually."

"I'm sorry, Mr. Singh. What's that?"

"Blunt-lobed woodsia. It's listed as an endangered species."

"Okay. What does it have to do with the woodlot that's part of the estate of Grant Burnham?"

"Well, as I understand it, the fern's been identified on the property, and recent activity has been damaging the habitat. Access has been restricted until a report can be completed and forwarded to the minister for approval."

"It's a fern we're talking about?"

"Didn't I say that already?"

"Okay, yes. Sorry. So, is Ms. Yan conducting this assessment?"

"No, she's the officer responsible for the file. The assessment itself has been contracted out."

"Who's got the contract for it?"

"Just a moment while I check. We have a number of them on the go right now."

The line went silent for a moment, and then Kevin found himself listening to Jackson Browne singing about having heard the word that Adam jumped, but he was thinking that he fell. Finally, Singh came back on.

"That would be GAEA."

"Sorry, who's that?"

"Gallagher and Allen Environmental Associates. GAEA.

Is that everything I can do for you today?"

"You wouldn't have a phone number for them, would you?"

"Not in front of me. Check their website; they'll have it there."

"Thanks for your help, Mr. Singh."

"Not at all."

Kevin hung up and put down the phone, badly in need of coffee. He briefly considered getting up and checking the lunch room in case someone had brewed a pot, no matter how bad it might be, then decided to ride the wave of momentum he'd built up after forty-five minutes of navigating the rocky rapids of provincial public service.

GAEA did indeed have a website. It began to load on his screen, taking a long time because, like many sites, it was image-intensive and the graphic card in his ancient desktop computer had been designed when dot-matrix printers were still the peripheral of choice.

While he waited, someone knocked on the doorframe of his cubicle.

"Hey, Kevvy. Whatcha up to?" It was Heather, wearing a black T-shirt with the promotional poster for the Kurt Russell movie *Big Trouble in Little China* prominently displayed on the front.

"Spinning my wheels. How about you?"

"The same." She looked around his arm at the monitor. "GAEA? Really? The earth goddess? Are you going all pagan on me, now?"

Kevin got up and offered her his chair. "Why don't I tell you about it?"

Chapter

54

"While everyone's been mesmerized by the whole Max Macdonald phenomenon, I've been trying to follow up on some other stuff."

"How dare you." Heather crossed her legs at the ankles and grinned up at him as he settled down on the corner of his desk.

"Yeah. But let me go back a step. Maybe I mentioned before that I interviewed Clarisse De Witt on Sunday?"

"Nope. Not to me, anyway."

"Sorry. I must have just talked to Sonja about it. Anyway, the report's on file. She was Burnham's lawyer, and her father told me before that she and Burnham were an item when they were in high school, so I wanted to get her perspective on things."

"Perspective's good."

"Yeah. She's a typical lawyer. One-word answers

whenever possible. She admitted that she and Burnham went back a long way, that she continued to have contact with him while he was still married to Roxanne, and that she handled the divorce, but I was getting all these weird vibes from her. She told me Burnham had been aware before he died that there was some kind of government problem with his woodlot, but she wouldn't elaborate. Then I was just about to ask her if she'd had an ongoing affair with him when her husband came in and put an end to things."

"Oh? Saved by the bell, eh?"

Kevin shrugged.

"What's he like? The husband?"

"Aggressive. Protective. Weather-beaten guy, around fifty. Lanky. Pretty sour disposition."

"Sounds like a charmer."

Kevin snapped his fingers. "She said he was a biologist. That he works for a consulting company in Ottawa. Has a desk job as a middle manager but spends his weekends doing field work. I wonder."

Heather's eyes went to the monitor. "No. Couldn't be."

Kevin stood up, but she beat him to the mouse. He watched the screen as she clicked through the website, going through their Contact Us page to a list of employees.

"Omigosh," she said. "Lookey there."

They stared at Dexter Trowbridge's name on the list of people working for the consulting company that was conducting a species at risk assessment on Grant Burnham's property.

"Bingo," Kevin said.

Chapter

55

"Nice one, Kev." Heather stood up. "Unfortunately, I can't hang around to watch the fun."

"Where are you going?" Kevin slipped into his desk chair and spun it around.

"Dentist. Root canal. Been putting it off since before the pandemic." She made a face. "They're gonna sedate me, like a little kid. I'll be worthless to the world for the rest of the day. See ya tomorrow." She waved and was gone.

Kevin telephoned Clarisse De Witt's home phone number. A housekeeper answered, and when he asked for Dex Trowbridge, she told him he was at work. He called the work number that was listed for him on the employee web page, but it went straight to voicemail. He then called GAEA's main number, and when he finally spoke to a human being he was told that Dex was out of the office.

"Where can I reach him?"

MICHAEL J. McCANN

"I'm sorry, sir. Did you try his cell?"

"Yes, it went right to voicemail."

"I'm sorry, he didn't leave any other contact number."

Kevin disconnected and called the De Witt law office. He was transferred to Clarisse's line, and when she answered he asked if she could tell him where to find her husband.

"Why?"

"I need to talk to him, Ms. De Witt." Kevin was getting a little tired of her taciturn evasiveness.

"Well, I don't know where he is. Did you call the house?"

"Yes. He isn't there. He's not at work either."

There was silence on the line for a moment. "I see. I'm sorry; I don't see how I can help you. Goodbye."

She hung up on him.

He dropped the phone into his jacket pocket and went to see Sonja. She wasn't in her office. Shrugging, he left the building. Jumping into the Charger, he headed off for Burnham's woodlot to take another look around.

On the way, his thoughts strayed to Max Macdonald. A sad, unhappy, recovered alcoholic with nothing in his life beyond a tenuous friendship with a former professional hockey player.

Thoughts of alcoholism inevitably brought his father to mind once again. Someone told him the other day that they'd seen John Walker at the hospital, in the waiting room of the Imaging department, apparently there for an x-ray or ultrasound.

"His head was down and he didn't see me," the man said. "I didn't want to bother him."

"I understand."

"He was awful grey in the face. Didn't look well at all."

Kevin didn't know how to react to this information. His father had cut him completely out of his life and had made it abundantly clear that further contact would be met with hostility. It was a situation Kevin couldn't understand but had decided to respect. As a result, he wouldn't call him up to see if he was all right. He wouldn't reach out.

Not that he didn't feel antipathy toward his father in his own right. They'd never gotten along, not since Kevin was a boy, the only child in a household filled with discord fuelled by alcoholism and jealousy. They'd had their fights, and words had been spoken that couldn't be unsaid.

Just the same, Kevin felt a hollowness in the pit of his stomach at the thought that his father might be seriously ill.

When he reached the woodlot, he saw that caution tape still cordoned off Max's house. He'd died without a will and without a lawyer to represent his interests. The house was a rental, so there was only Max's personal property to be dealt with. It was a task that wouldn't take long. Max had owned very little other than an assortment of tools, cheap furniture, a television, cellphone, and a few other miscellaneous items.

Feeling depressed, Kevin turned into the woodlot entrance and drove past the signs, right through to the clearing that had been used as a parking area. He got out and slowly moved around the scene, scanning the ground, not sure what he was looking for.

It was a bright, late-summer day, and the sun warmed his back from its vantage point above the line of cedar trees along the road. He walked through the area where Grant had been cutting and piling his firewood. He could smell it, the odour of drying maple, ash, and birch. He heard crows raising a fuss and, looking up, saw several of them swirling and dipping around in the distance. As he watched, they disappeared beyond the tree line, calling out to one another until their voices faded into the gentle buzzing in his ears.

He decided to see what was down the path that Grant had cut toward the back of the lot. The ground was clear for a hundred metres or so except for scattered shrubs, mostly buckthorn, and tall weeds. He remembered that Dave Martin's team had been back here, taking photographs and searching in vain for physical evidence connected to the homicide, but he wanted to see for himself where it led.

Kevin studied the trail as he walked. It consisted of a pair of well-worn wheel tracks leading more or less straight back to the trees. Although rain had smoothed out much of the hard-packed dirt, he could see evidence that Grant had driven his pickup truck and trailer back and forth along here many times.

He wondered why Grant hadn't used a four-wheeler instead of his pickup. It didn't seem to be a very important point, all things considered, but he'd always been under the impression that woodlot owners preferred a smaller vehicle to move around the trails that wound through the back of their property.

As he studied the ground in front of him, Kevin also saw boot prints crossing the trail diagonally, heading away from the forest. They looked fairly recent, certainly made after the rain that had eroded the truck tire impressions.

He took out his cellphone and texted Sonja:

Are you in your office?

While he waited for a response he moved out of the wheel track he'd been following and into the grass alongside it. After a moment, his phone pinged:

Yes. Where are you?

He stopped moving and turned his back on the sun in order to see the phone's screen more clearly.

At Burnham's woodlot. Can you send me the pic of the Gore-Tex boots worn by the killer?

Yes. Wait one.

He lowered the phone and looked around. The path disappeared into the trees about thirty metres ahead of him, and the ground seemed to rise beyond that. Far above, in the blue sky, he could see a vulture riding the air currents, slowly patrolling its territory, and beyond that, now that he was looking, another one, farther away. Perhaps that was what had disturbed the crows.

Like many city boys, Kevin had come to appreciate the peacefulness of rural settings as a break from the traffic, the impatient and impolite people, and the lack of open spaces in an urban environment. And the fresh air. He filled his lungs. It smelled so good.

His phone pinged. He opened the image Sonja had sent and got down on his knees so he could compare it to the prints he was looking at now. They matched. He texted:

Our guy was here recently. I'm going back for a look.

He stood up and resumed walking.

Be careful. Call for backup ASAP if necessary.

Will do.

He put the phone away and left the clearing. After a few metres the ground did indeed begin to rise, and he saw spots on both sides where Grant had brought down trees, cut them up, and hauled them out. From the look of the stumps left behind, and the nearby piles of branches, he must have been culling out deadwood. Kevin was aware that certain types of trees, such as ash, provided good firewood even after dying, and he also knew that harvesting them brought the wood out of the forest, removing a potential fire hazard in the instance of a lightning strike, for example.

As he kept going, the trail continued to rise, and the

terrain on either side was becoming more rugged. He could see outcroppings of rock and the dead skeletons of saplings that had sprouted in the past and failed to survive.

He reached a spot where the wheel tracks ended. Grant had cut a spur into the brush to use as a turn-around for his truck when he wanted to head back down with a load of wood. Beyond the spur was a walking trail leading further up the incline.

As he began to follow this path, he reminded himself that some sort of endangered species of fern was supposed to be here, so he began to look for it. The rock around him was exposed in many spots, and the soil was thin and mossy. The trees that had persisted here were scattered, undersized maples, their leaves beginning to turn red, and oak trees, thin and stringy. Here and there he could see plants that looked like trilliums, a few juniper shrubs, and a scattering of ferns in the shadier areas. Were they the endangered kind, or merely everyday, ordinary ferns? He had no idea.

A movement above him on his right drew his eyes. A chickadee hopped from branch to branch in a tree, peering down at him. Another sang its distinctive song from a branch nearby. At least he had company, he thought.

He reached a flat ledge and decided to take a short rest. This side of the ridge faced south, and as he'd climbed he'd received more of the sun's direct rays on his back, so he was perspiring and thirsty. He wasn't much of a hiker. A more experienced person would have dressed better, worn appropriate footwear, and brought water, no doubt. Maybe even a granola bar for an energy snack.

Oh well. He was a cop, not a hiking enthusiast.

He followed the trail upward with his eyes, wondering if it was worth it to keep climbing, or if he should just turn around and go back. Like Martin's SOCOs, he hadn't spotted anything notable.

There was a sudden noise behind him.
A voice snarled, "What the hell are you doing here?"

Chapter

56

Startled, Kevin whirled around.

"I asked you a question," Dex Trowbridge snapped. "Didn't you see the signs back there? 'Access forbidden'? Or can't you read?"

"What are you doing here, Mr. Trowbridge?" Kevin shifted his weight to face the man squarely. He was about four metres above him on the ridge, looking down.

"My work. Which you're interfering with. Can't you people understand there's an endangered species at risk here?"

"Some kind of fern?"

Dex huffed with disgust. "Not 'some kind of fern.' *Woodsia obtusa*. Otherwise known as blunt-lobed woodsia. There are fewer than fourteen hundred mature plants in all of Canada, for heaven's sake, including the forty-four I've counted here. Not to mention the twelve I've managed to record as having been destroyed by that careless idiot Burnham."

"So you're the one conducting the habitat assessment for GAEA?"

"Yes. Since you know about it, you should know enough not to blunder into a critical work in progress."

"Is that what Grant Burnham was doing? Blundering into your work?"

"I told him a dozen times, in no uncertain terms, that I would do whatever it would take to get him to stop clearing the brush back here and destroying this species."

"But it was his property. He had every right to be here."

"Doesn't matter. If it's proven to be the habitat of an endangered or threatened species, then the legislation's very clear. The province has complete authority under the *Endangered Species Act* to restrict all access to the habitat until an assessment is completed and a report's submitted to the minister with an appropriate recovery strategy. Burnham flouted the law repeatedly, as are you at this very moment."

"There weren't any signs posted a week ago Saturday," Kevin pointed out. "The day he was murdered."

"He was given verbal notice, multiple times."

"By you?"

"By me. I made it very clear, in language even a lout like him could understand, that he was not to enter this woodlot until the minister finished dealing with the situation and gave her orders on how to proceed. But he wouldn't listen."

Kevin stood with his hands on his hips, staring down at him. Dex was dressed for the outdoors, with a green vest covered with bulging patch pockets, a plaid shirt, khaki cargo pants, a floppy hat, and . . . Gore-Tex hiking boots. He had a knapsack slung on his back with a large water bottle sticking out of a side pocket, a monocular and a digital camera slung on lanyards around his neck, and a satellite phone clipped to his belt.

His hands were closed into fists at his sides. His expression was grim, belligerent. Kevin decided to push him.

"You've known Grant Burnham for quite a while, haven't you? This isn't just some stranger you were dealing with here. You had a bit of a history with him already."

"I don't know what you're talking about. And it's totally irrelevant."

"No, it's not. You knew, didn't you, that he was carrying out a long-standing affair with your wife. High school sweethearts who never strayed from each other for very long, even though they both were married to someone else."

"My only interest," Dex said, "is, and has always been, Clarisse's welfare. Whatever's best for her. Whatever makes her happy. Keeps her calm and stable. Can't you see that?"

"So you flew into a rage, confronted Burnham here on his woodlot about his relationship with your wife, and killed him with one of his own baseball bats."

"No, no, no. You're not listening to me. I hated him for cuckolding me, yes. Hated him with a passion. But he made Clarisse happy. In a way that I couldn't. They were old friends as well as old lovers, and that made me something of a Johnny-come-lately, yes. But I wouldn't take that away from her."

"You did, though."

He made a face. "Yes, I suppose I did."

"Dexter Trowbridge, I'm arresting you for the murder of Grant Burnham."

"He wouldn't listen! He was so goddamned arrogant, thinking I was a damned fool for giving a shit about a bloody plant, for chrissakes!"

"You have the right to retain and instruct counsel without delay."

"He swore at me, called me a loser, and told me to get off his property. I grabbed a bat to protect myself. He started walking toward me."

"You also have the right to free and immediate legal advice—"

"Shut UP! Everything went all red, I tell you! I lunged at him with the bat and hit him on the arm. I was going to hit him again and he started to run away from me."

"Do you understand these rights?"

"Shut up! You're just like him! I won't take any more of your bullshit!"

He raised his right hand. Too late, Kevin saw that he was holding a rock. Dex wound up and threw it with all his strength.

It struck Kevin on the left side, knocking the wind out of him. He dropped to one knee, gasping. He groped for his sidearm, but the pain in his ribs was so intense he couldn't seem to find it with his fingers.

Struggling for breath, he looked up as Dex closed the distance between them, a much larger rock raised above his head.

There was absolutely no doubt in Kevin's mind what he intended to do with it.

Chapter

57

"Stop right where you are," a new voice said.

Dex kept coming, the rock above his head, his shadow falling across Kevin, who was now down on both knees.

A gunshot ripped through the air behind them.

Startled, Dex stopped and whirled around, still holding the rock.

Doug Skelton stood a few metres below them on the trail, his gun pointing skyward.

Dex froze in place.

Skelton lowered his weapon until it was pointed directly at him. "Toss the rock away, right now, or the next one's gonna cause you considerable pain."

Dex hesitated.

"Now!"

He tossed the rock aside, his eyes still on Skelton. They listened to it roll down the incline and thump against the trunk of a tree.

"Hands on top of your head. Down on your knees. Move!"

As Dex slowly complied, Kevin lurched to his feet. He fumbled for a zip tie in his jacket pocket and, as Skelton continued to cover him with his gun, he secured Dex's wrists behind his back.

"Glad to see you," Kevin said, looking at Skelton over the top of their prisoner's head.

"I was driving by and saw the vehicles parked in the clearing. Thought I'd take a look."

"Good timing."

"Called it in. Backup's on the way."

Kevin tugged on Dex's arm, forcing him to his feet. Ignoring the surge of pain in his side, he thumped the man's back to start him moving down the trail.

Skelton retreated a few steps and lowered his weapon. "If you can cover him, Walker, I'll take him from here."

"Sounds good."

Skelton holstered his sidearm and stepped up to grab Dex's arm.

"Fascists," the man snarled.

Skelton rolled his eyes. "I love you too, dear."

As Kevin fumbled out his weapon, he heard a vehicle pulling into the parking area below, followed by another immediately after it. The cavalry had arrived.

Dex suddenly stopped moving. "There. Right there. That's what we're fighting for." He pointed with his chin, looking off to the right.

Following his gaze, Kevin saw a pool of shadow about a metre in from the trail that was surrounded by trees. Within the pool was a large fern.

"Woodsia?"

"Exactly. We're supposed to be the custodians of this world. We're supposed to look after things, nurture all forms of life, be the ones responsible for the continuation of life on this planet. Instead, we carelessly trample it into the ground. I can't stand by and let that happen. I can't."

"Save it for court," Skelton said, jerking him forward. "I'm sure everyone will be really impressed."

Following them down to the wheel tracks, his gun held in a low ready position, Kevin listened to a vehicle bouncing up the trail toward them.

Skelton glanced over his shoulder. "Looks like you can ride the rest of the way, Walker."

"I'm all right."

"Yeah. You're a tough guy."

Skelton tugged Dex onto the grass beside the wheel tracks as an OPP off-road vehicle stopped in front of them and uniformed constables tumbled out, weapons drawn and ready.

Kevin put away his gun, thinking that a ride down to his car might not be all that bad an idea, after all.

He could also use the time to think about what Dex had said, and to deal with the uncomfortable feeling that he agreed with him.

About the custodians of the planet part, anyway.

Chapter

58

Three days later, on Saturday morning, Ellie drove to the hub office of the Leeds county detachment at Spring Valley, in Elizabeth-Kitley township. It was the day of Dean Othman's ride-along, and she was a little apprehensive. Having suggested it, and made all the arrangements for it to happen, she felt responsible for its success or failure. She wasn't, of course, but she liked the boy and wanted to see it go well.

Dr. Othman would accompany his son on the excursion, and he'd insisted on driving to the detachment office himself rather than ride with Ellie. She understood his motive. It gave him the ability to pull the plug on the whole thing at any point and whisk Dean back home, out of harm's way.

In many ways, Ellie thought, this ride-along was as much about Dr. Othman and his over-compensation for earlier mistakes as it was about Dean and his desire to experience the world of law enforcement at close hand.

She reached the detachment office before the Othmans, and it gave her a chance to talk to Leung to make sure everything was lined up. He introduced her to Constable Donna Kline, who'd agreed to assist Leung in a tour of the office and to take the boy outside to show him a police cruiser. He explained that after Donna did her thing, he'd show the Othmans a bit of the dull routine carried out by detectives at their desks before embarking on the actual ride-along. He planned to drive by a house construction site north of Mallorytown where someone had stolen a Caterpillar tractor and driven it away on a flat-bed trailer. Then he'd work his way west to a former grow-op that had recently been cleaned out in a joint-forces operation that had included Leung as the OPP participant.

"I'll keep the radio on as we go, so he can hear the calls and I can explain what's going on. It'll give him something to concentrate on between stops."

"That sounds fine, Dennis." She looked at her watch. "They should be here soon."

Ten minutes later, she came out of the washroom to find Donna Kline in the doorway of Leung's cubicle, introducing herself to the Othmans. She was explaining her job as a provincial constable assigned to Traffic, and when she was finished she said to Dean, "Would you like to go out back now?"

"Sure!"

Donna led the way, followed by Dr. Othman. Ellie stepped back to let them pass, and as Dean came out of the cubicle he said, "I get to sit in a real police car!"

He was trying very hard not to show his excitement and was doing a rather poor job of it.

Ellie nodded. "I have some stuff to do in here, so I'll see you when you and Constable Kline are done."

She figured Donna would spend about fifteen minutes

with Dean, and then revised it to twenty when she factored in the questions the boy would be asking her. She walked down to the detachment commander's corner office and talked to Kirk Rousseau for a few minutes. Leung had introduced the Othmans to him when they first arrived, and he thought that Dean seemed like a nice kid.

"He's in good hands with Dennis," Rousseau added. "A real family man."

She then chatted with Prez Raintree, who was scheduled to meet Dean and his father after they came back inside. His assignment was to explain to Dean the purpose of the crime unit, to mention a few statistics, given that Dean had a head for numbers, and to set up Leung for his part of the visit. While they were talking, she heard the sound of a cruiser's siren in the parking lot.

Dean was trying out the equipment.

Ellie was pleased at the level of co-operation everyone was showing. It was something out of the ordinary for them, a break in the routine, and she could see that Dean was making a good impression, despite his shyness.

"I hear our boy Walker did himself proud up in Lanark," Raintree said.

Ellie nodded. "He and Detective Constable Skelton arrested a suspect who's been charged. The man's given a confession witnessed by Kevin and Skelton, and he hasn't retracted it."

"I hear he's going to claim temporary insanity. 'A red haze came over me.' The usual."

Ellie shrugged. "Susan's handling it. We'll see how it turns out." Susan Mitchum, the Crown Attorney, was now in charge of the case as it made its way into the court system. Ellie felt confident that she would see it through to an appropriate conclusion that would afford Burnham's father, his business partner, and others a sense of closure. They'd built an iron-clad case against Trowbridge, and now it was a matter of dealing with his defence attorney's attempts to influence the court's perception of his client's guilt.

The Othmans came back inside, and Ellie retreated to allow Raintree to bring them into his office, along with Leung, and carry out his part of the tour. Dean's face, as he passed her through Raintree's door, was glowing.

It made her feel good to see it.

She grabbed a coffee in the lunch room and took her time with it, knowing that not only would Dean's endless supply of questions keep Raintree busy, but also that the affable detective sergeant's love of conversation would make his answers much longer than normal.

Finally, it was time for them to pile into Leung's motor pool vehicle and hit the road for the actual ride-along. Ellie was grateful that Raintree had allowed Dennis to combine his desk presentation with his own, the two of them walking through typical after-action reports and other necessary paperwork and routine matters, and they were thankfully able to move on with things before Ellie reached retirement age.

With his father's permission, Dean sat up front. His father sat on the driver's side in the back seat so that he could see Dean at all times. Ellie sat on the passenger side so that Leung could see her.

As promised, Leung turned on the radio as they pulled out of the parking lot, and as they drove on County Road 46 toward Seely, he kept up a running commentary on what they were hearing.

"That officer's requesting a ten-minute coffee-and-washroom break. He's patrolling the Four-Oh-One. The dispatcher acknowledged and recorded his location."

"It's hard to tell what they're saying," Dean said. "They talk fast and it's a little blurry."

"You develop an ear for it."

At Seely, Leung turned right and followed a series of daisy-chained back roads past Caintown. Just north of Mallorytown, he pulled over onto the narrow shoulder, shifted into park, and turned on his hazard lights.

"You see this house we're parked in front of?"

Everyone looked out the passenger side at a two-storey frame house that was still under construction.

"Is it a crack house?" Dean asked.

Leung laughed. "No. When they were working on the foundation, before the walls started to go up, they left some heavy equipment here overnight. This was in the second week of May. One of the pieces was a Caterpillar Crawler Dozer, a thing with a big blade on the front they use to push back the debris as they clear the lot."

"You mean a bulldozer with metal tracks like a tank?"

"Yeah, that's it. A smaller-sized one. Anyway, one night a couple of guys backed a flatbed trailer in here and got the dozer onto it. They took off up the road the way we just came."

"Wow. They stole it."

"Yep. Now, you remember that sharp curve we came around, about a kilometre back?"

"Yes."

"Well, they took that curve a little too fast and tipped over, dozer and trailer and truck and all. Ended up in the ditch. Both guys were knocked out. A passing car saw them and called it in."

"Wow. Did they have to go to the hospital?"

"Yeah, overnight because they had concussions. After that, it was off to jail."

"So what did you do?"

"I talked to them a couple of times once they were behind bars. Separately, of course. I wanted to know, first of all, how they managed to start the dozer up so they could drive it up onto the trailer. Second, I wanted to know if they'd done it before. Heavy equipment theft is an ongoing problem."

"Did they talk?"

Leung smiled. "Eventually. Part of a detective's job is to get people to tell you things they might not want to if they thought about it long enough. You try to get them to relax a bit and talk about stuff. A lot of guys like to brag. They lack self-confidence and want you to think they're smarter and slicker than they really are, so you encourage them to tell you little stories about things they've done, and before you know it they've said something you can use. You go with that, and they'll start talking about more things, important things that help open up your case, and away you go."

Dean stared at the house. "How did they move the bulldozer?"

"Turns out one of the guys had a buddy who works on construction sites, including this one. He made a copy of the key and gave it to our suspect. I went to the other guy and used this information to get him to admit this buddy had helped them with other thefts before."

"For a percentage of the take, right?"

Leung chuckled. "Yes, sir. Before long they told me about six other thefts they'd carried out in the last two years or so, including a backhoe, generators, ATVs, and a bunch of other stuff."

"That's real detective work."

"That's what they pay me the big bucks for," Leung said, winking at Ellie before pulling back out onto the road.

Eventually they pulled up at a T-intersection a few kilometres northwest of Lansdowne. The radio had come alive as a patrol officer reported in to dispatch, and Leung shifted into park a few metres from the intersection so that they could listen to the exchange.

"The constable's on patrol," Leung said. "He's doing a drive-by on the site I was actually coming to show you. It's right around the corner from here."

"Another robbery case?"

"No, this time it actually is a drug case. A cannabis grow-op. They were using an old farm house about half a kilometre from where we are, down to the right. On Bullfrog Bay Road. I was working as part of a JFO, a joint-forces operation with Customs and the RCMP, and we got a tip to take a look at the place. Two of us, myself and a Mountie, conducted surveillance for a week, taking pictures of the vehicles coming and going, logging the times of whatever activity we observed. We co-ordinated with Customs on the licence plates to find out how often they were crossing the border, and that sort of thing. Finally we raided the place and grabbed three hundred and fifty kilos of marijuana, seven kilos of hash, half a dozen firearms, and a bunch of paraphernalia. Arrested nine people altogether."

"Gee. Out here in the middle of nowhere?"

"It's surprising, isn't it, Dean? Crime doesn't stop to admire the pretty scenery."

The radio chucked again. "The constable's approaching the house right now," Leung said. "He'll pass right by us in a moment or two."

"Will you tell him we're here?"

"No, but he'll see us as he goes by. He may want to stop and check us out."

Dean looked worried.

Leung said, "I know him. It's okay. He's cool."

The radio suddenly blared, "An ATV and grey four-door sedan in the driveway. Slowing for a look."

Ellie leaned forward to listen.

"Tag obscured by the four-wheeler. I—"

Everyone heard the sound of glass shattering. "Shots fired, shots fired! From the sedan. ATV's pulling out of the driveway and proceeding east."

"Dennis," Ellie said.

As he reached for the gear shift, the four-wheeler suddenly flew past the intersection. The driver reacted as he saw the car parked there. Before he could bring his eyes back to the road, his inside wheels caught the gravel shoulder and he went barrelling down into the ditch.

"Get them out of here," Ellie said, opening her door.

She stopped and tapped on Dean's window. "Get that seatbelt back on, mister, and don't move from this car."

She saw him nod, and immediately she took off across the intersection. Just as she reached the spot where the ATV had cut through the tall grass and weeds on its way into the ditch, the driver boiled up at her with a knife in his hand.

She skidded to a stop and shouted, "OPP! Drop your weapon and put your hands on top of your head!"

He lunged at her before she could draw her sidearm.

She side-stepped the knife, grabbed his wrist, spun him around, and threw him down in a jiu-jitsu move onto his stomach. She twisted his knife arm behind him, squeezed a pressure point to force him to release the weapon, knocked it away, reached into her jacket pocket for a zip-lock restraint, and quickly secured both hands behind his back.

Keeping her knee on his right shoulder blade, she brought out her cellphone and called it in. Dispatch told her that backup was en route with a five-minute ETA. She asked about the status of the drive-by check and was told that the responding officer reported a 10-92, which meant a person or persons in custody.

She recited to her prisoner his rights under the law and chatted back and forth with him as they waited for backup to arrive. He begged with her to let him go, claiming he was only doing what his brother-in-law told him to do. She listened sympathetically until the backup cruiser arrived and the constables took custody of her prisoner.

Turning around to look up Russell Road, wondering whom she would ask to get a ride back to the detachment office, she saw that Leung was still sitting there. He'd backed up about a dozen metres, but he was still there, idling in park.

Frustrated that he hadn't obeyed her order to take the Othmans away from the scene, she strode up to Leung's window. As he lowered it, she put her hands on her hips.

"What the hell are you still doing here?"

As Leung opened his mouth to respond, Dean leaned over and grinned up at her.

"Holy cow, Ellie! I saw the whole thing! You were incredible! You captured that guy all by yourself without drawing your gun!"

She looked in the back window. Dr. Othman stared up at her, an odd, crooked smile on his face.

Leaning down, she pointed a finger at Dean.

"Time to get you home, young man."

Chapter

59

The following morning, which was Sunday, Ellie fixed herself a cup of coffee in the kitchen and took it in to her desk. Picking up her cellphone, she called Sonja Freeling.

"I understand that congratulations are in order," she said, hoisting her feet up onto the corner of her desk.

"Thanks, Ellie. I'm really happy about it."

"And at the top of the list, as rumoured. Colleen's gloating about getting to draft the first-overall pick."

"I'm flattered."

"I also hear, Detective Sergeant Freeling, that you're already making moves to rebuild the crime unit up there."

"Yes, I am. If you know of an experienced file co-ordinator who'd like to transfer in, let me know."

"I'll do that." Ellie sipped her coffee. She'd been informed yesterday that Constable Stephen Downey had confessed to Staff Sergeant Dunn that he'd been the leak within Lanark detachment, passing on inside information about the Burnham investigation to the Member of Provincial Parliament for Lanark-Frontenac-Kingston, William F. Hollingsworth. Turned out that Hollingsworth was his uncle, and Downey had been coerced into talking about the case by his mother and her loudmouth brother. A disciplinary hearing was forthcoming.

Meanwhile, Constable Annette Perreault, who normally served as file co-ordinator for major cases, had experienced complications after her appendectomy and was expected to be on leave for quite some time.

"I hear that Colleen and Joe Fleishman have agreed to let Pierce transfer in."

"Yes! He's going to make a great addition to the unit."

"Seems like you're getting your own way at every turn."

Sonja laughed. "Well, I still have to convince Walker to come over. Kirk Rousseau and Colleen are dickering about it right now, but Kevin still hasn't given it the green light."

"He's got a family to take into consideration. That's a top priority for him."

"Yes, it is. But if I add him then the unit takes a big step forward. He's a steadying influence on Hope, and a good counterbalance to Skelton."

"Who seems to have vindicated himself after all."

"Looks like. He wasn't the leak, and he was Johnny-on-the-spot when Kevin needed backup."

"Well, best of luck going forward, Sonja. I'm very pleased for you."

"Thanks, Ellie."

After ending the call, Ellie jumped in the shower, got dressed, and drove into Brockville for her doctor's appointment.

Over the past week or so she'd endured the inevitable lab visits for blood tests, urine donation, and all the rest of it, and now it was time to hear the diagnosis.

Ellie wasn't in a good mood as she sat in the waiting room for her name to be called. She liked her doctor, Sulari Kay, but disliked the process, hated being poked and prodded, and dreaded the moment someone would solemnly inform her that she had cancer or emphysema or tuberculosis or some other damned thing.

Better to die a quiet death in her recliner with a cigarette in one hand and a Jack Daniels on the rocks in the other, Reggie dozing at her feet and *Die Hard* playing on the TV.

Instead she had to shuffle after the nurse like a docile sheep, submit to being weighed and measured, passively nod when she was told her blood pressure was too high (well, duh), and then sit like a rock waiting to find out what was wrong with her.

"Good news," Dr. Kay said as she bustled into the examination room and closed the door. "All your tests came back just as I expected them to."

"I see."

Dr. Kay set down her iPad and fiddled with it. "Blood sugar's a little high and so's your bad cholesterol; good cholesterol's too low; and your estrogen has dropped through the floor. It all adds up. Explains the hot flashes, irritability, disappearing periods, urinary problems, insomnia, and all the other symptoms you've described."

"Cancer?"

Dr. Kay laughed. "You're so funny. I always enjoy your visits. No, no. Just simple, straightforward menopause."

Ellie sat there for a moment, at a loss for words.

"The thing to do at this point is to begin restoring your estrogen levels to what they were before. Hormone therapy is okay for women in your age group. It's only after the age of sixty that problems can start, like blood clots in the legs and a higher risk of breast cancer. Or if the treatment exceeds five years. So we'll start with a low dose and monitor how your body reacts to it."

Elllie said nothing.

"There are both natural and synthetic products available," Dr. Kay rambled on, "but we'll start you on a natural one because the others are way too potent for what you need. Would you prefer a tablet or a patch?"

"You're telling me I'm old. I've gotten old."

"Well, dear, we all reach that point in our lives when our body decides it's time for a change."

"I'm old. What the hell."

"We'll start you off with a modest dosage for the next two months, as I say. I'm guessing you'd prefer a tablet."

"Sure. Why not. What the hell."

Dr. Kay filled out the prescription form on her iPad and printed it out. She got up and handed it to Ellie. "It's important to remember this is a natural process, and we all must deal with it gracefully. We're not getting old; we're getting mature, like a really good single-malt scotch."

Ellie opened her mouth and then closed it again. After a moment, she took the prescription form.

"You know what? You're right. I'm not old yet. Just the other day I whipped some young guy's ass, took away his knife, and hog-tied him inside of ten seconds. Never knew what hit him."

"My. You're not joking this time, are you? A knife?"

Ellie stood up. "Better watch, Sulari. Next time, I might be coming after you."

Dr. Kay picked up her iPad and opened the door, shaking with laughter. When she glanced over her shoulder on the way out, Ellie winked.

Epilogue

"Are you sure this is it?"

Kevin shifted the car into park but left the engine running. "Yeah, it's the right one."

"Holy crap." Janie put her hand on his thigh as she leaned down to stare at the house across the street. It was incredible: two-storey red brick, six windows on the front with white frames and black shutters, and a short sidewalk leading to cement steps with black, wrought-iron railings. "Look at the front porch."

White columns on white pedestals, topped by a triangular roof with fancy carving and triangles within triangles. On the left-hand column was a discreet white sign that said, in black serif lettering: "Nicholas Rush Investigations." The column on the right had a similar sign with nothing on it.

When the possibility of relocating to Perth had come up, they'd discussed the matter between themselves and then convened a family meeting with the kids. Brendan brought out his laptop and they looked up the schools, and Caitlyn used her tablet to browse for houses for sale in town and the surrounding area. Josh, meanwhile, monkeyed around with his Game Boy, oblivious to the whole thing.

Kevin was astonished at how quickly they took to the idea of a new start in a new town with new schools, new friends, and new neighbours. It wasn't what he'd expected.

"I think you can park around the back," he said, shifting into drive.

"Let's take a look."

He turned into the driveway that ran alongside the house and followed it to a parking lot with enough space for six vehicles. There was one car parked in the lot at the moment, a dusty brown Kia SUV that looked more than ten years old. Next to it was a motorcycle, a Harley Davidson Fat Boy. Kevin parked in the slot on the other side of the bike and they got out.

As they strolled along the driveway up to the front, Janie said, "What do you think, Kev?"

"I don't know. Could be good."

"Could be way out of my league, too."

They stood for a moment looking around. Perched on a neatly tended corner lot, the house faced out onto Drummond Street East. Across the way were the provincial court house on the right and a large Anglican church on the left.

Justice and mercy, Kevin thought. Side by side.

Or something like that.

"All right," Janie said, taking a deep breath. "Let's go take a look."

They went up onto the porch. The front door was wooden, painted white, with frosted glass and a brass bell handle that you twisted to make it ring.

Janie twisted. The bell made a purring sound, like an old-fashioned alarm clock winding down.

After a moment they heard footsteps on the stairs. The door opened and a nondescript, middle-aged man stood there smiling at them.

"Hi," he said, "come on in." He stuck out his hand. "You must be Janie."

She stepped inside and shook his hand.

"And you're Kevin Walker. I'm Nick Rush. Glad you could come over."

"I hope it's not a bad time for you," Kevin said, shaking his hand and closing the door behind him.

"No, no, I don't have any appointments this afternoon. Come on, let me show you around."

Rush was the kind of guy you'd walk right past without a glance on a busy sidewalk. He was medium height, about five-ten, with a slightly stocky build. Somewhere in his early forties, he looked like a high school shop teacher or the guy you'd call to clean your oil furnace in the fall. His mousy brown hair was trimmed short and receding at the temples. His glasses had thick, black frames.

He led them down the hallway. The staircase was on the left, with a sign on the wall featuring an old-fashioned arrow and "Nicholas Rush Investigations" pointing the way upstairs. On the right was a doorway, through which he took them into a smallish, high-ceilinged room.

"This was originally the front parlour," Nick said. "I had a mom-and-pop insurance company in here before the pandemic hit, and they used this to keep their files and stuff. I figure it would be great for your front counter and waiting area."

Kevin watched Janie nod absently as she drifted around, eyes moving everywhere at once. He knew immediately she wanted the place but was worried about what the rent would be.

"This was the dining room," Nick said, leading the way. "I thought you could have your haircutting stations in here, or whatever you call them. How many chairs did you have in your old place?"

"Three."

"There's plenty of room in here for six. Plus wall space for shelves to display hair products and all that sort of stuff."

Kevin kept his eyes on her. Normally she hated other people telling her what she could or could not do, especially when it came to her business. But she was clearly in a zone right now where everything Nick Rush said happened to agree exactly with what she was thinking. He fought to keep a smile off his face.

"This was the kitchen," Nick said, taking them through another doorway. "I've already gotten a quote on what it'll cost to have four sinks installed, and the guy can do it for me next week. It's big enough for your hair dryer chairs, or whatever you call them, and so on."

He pointed to a door at the back. "Washroom."

Janie came to and put her hands on her hips. "Okay. How much?"

Nick smiled. "Why don't we go upstairs to my office and we can talk about it."

"All right." Janie glanced at Kevin, a little worried she was being prepared to receive bad news.

"You can meet my assistant," Nick threw over his shoulder as he led the way up the staircase.

At the top was a small room set up as a reception area with filing cabinets, a few wooden chairs, and a big oak desk. The guy sitting behind the desk was typing something on the computer, his fingers flying over the keyboard at a pace that sounded to Kevin as though it was at least seventy words a minute.

"Luke," Nick said, "this is Janie Walker. Janie, meet Luke Ferguson."

He stood up and limped around the desk to shake her

hand. "Nice to meet you, Ms. Walker."

"Mrs.," Janie said. "Um, Janie."

"And you're the cop."

"Kevin Walker."

He found himself staring. Luke was a few inches taller than his boss and about a decade older. His handlebar moustache was iron grey, as was his short-cropped hair, and his face bore several scars, one on his left temple, another on his chin, and a third at the right corner of his mouth. He was missing an earlobe. He wore a Harley Davidson T-shirt that showed off tattoos on both well-muscled arms.

Kevin remembered the motorcycle parked outside, and thought it likely belonged to him.

"Would you folks care for a cup of coffee?"

"I'd love one," Janie said. "Cream and two sugar."

"How about you?"

Kevin shook his head. "I'm fine, thanks."

"I thought you cops drank coffee non-stop."

Kevin smiled faintly. "All caffeinated out this afternoon, I guess."

"Come on in and sit down," Nick said, leading them into his office. "Let me get the file out and you can take a look at what I've drawn up for us.

It was a nice office, Kevin thought, looking around. Neat and clean, with non-intrusive furniture and a large window facing out onto Harvey Street.

As they sat down, Nick pulled open a drawer and took out a file folder. "When Wally called to let me know you might be interested in the place, I took the liberty of doing a little research. At one point there were six different hair salons in town, but after the pandemic there are only two left, and they're both chain franchises."

"Yes," Janie said, having done her homework as well.

A few days ago Kevin had stopped into the Red Anvil to

pick up some muffins for the kids on the way home. Wally happened to be there, and they talked. It soon became evident that Wally bore him no malice for the tone of his interrogation, the actual murderer having been caught and justice for Grant Burnham having been achieved. When Kevin mentioned that he and Janie were considering relocation to Perth, if she could find an affordable place to open her hair salon, Wally had given him Nick's phone number.

Kevin looked at the name plate on the desk: N.O. Rush. "N.O."

"Nicholas Oliver," Nick grinned. "Of course, in high school everybody called me No Rush, because I always like to take my time with stuff and not make the kind of unnecessary mistakes people make when they hurry."

"No Rush," Janie said.

"You can call me Nick." He opened the folder and sorted through the documents inside. "Something else to keep in mind is the location. The court house is perfectly situated for me, of course. Crazy convenient, not only for ongoing stuff but as a source of new clients, too. The church, though, not so much. Over there, it's either too late or too early for me."

Janie smiled, tentatively.

"Now in your case, I can see a lot of walk-in trade. Lawyers grabbing a last-minute trim before approaching the bar, or forcing their clients to clean up before an appearance in front of the judge. And the church. People want to look good before a wedding or funeral, right?"

"I see what you mean," Janie said.

"Here's what I had Luke type up for us this morning." He passed a three-page document over to her.

She read it carefully, a frown on her face. When she was finished all three pages, she went back to the first page and read it again before sliding it over to Kevin.

Nick had listed a rent that was only 15 per cent higher than what she'd paid the hated Harry Bridges for her storefront in tiny Sparrow Lake.

Luke limped in, gave Janie her coffee in a nice china cup and saucer, and limped back out. He left the door open, as he'd found it.

"Motorcycle accident," Nick whispered. "Guy was passing him on Seven and cut back in too closely. Luke went into the ditch and spent the next month in hospital. Since he was already past forty, they talked him into retiring after that."

Kevin raised an eyebrow. "They?"

"You know." He turned back to Janie. "You probably saw that I've included a clause freezing the rent at the stated amount for the first five years. Are you okay with that?"

"Hell, yeah."

"I think you'll like it here. Luke and I don't make a lot of noise, and you'll have lots of room to handle the steady flow of customers. What do you call your business?"

"Skiz—"

Kevin watched her eyes slide sideways as she clamped her mouth shut and thought quickly. He knew her as well as he knew himself, and there was no doubt in his mind that she was thinking about the look of this place, the increased traffic in a much larger community, and a chance to give her business a new and different tone.

"Jane Walker Salon," she said. "No. The Jane Walker Salon. *The* Jane Walker Salon."

"Once everything's finalized I'll have some signage done up for you. My treat. For the front porch, and something in the side window, if you like."

"That would be nice."

"I'm glad to be getting a tenant downstairs again. Keeps the place looking busy. Which reminds me, I'll have to show you the security system. It's a little more advanced than what you might be used to."

Janie glanced at Kevin, who smiled reassuringly.

"You're an investigator?" she said, watching Nick scribble his signature on two copies of the lease.

"Yeah. Private eye." He spun the copies around and slid them forward, along with the pen. "Keeps me busy."

Janie looked at Kevin.

"I'm signing this," she said. "We'll find a house. The kids are on board. This place is terrific. Lauren will come over with us. She's been talking about a fresh start ever since she kicked Brad out. I'll hire more staff. Get three more chairs. There's a line of hair products I've been wanting to get into for a while now. It'll be perfect for here. I love it. I want this. I'm going to sign."

Kevin shrugged, struggling with a grin.

"Sounds good to me," he said.

Oxford Station, January 5, 2023

Acknowledgments

As always, it's important to note that this novel is a work of fiction. Although the Ontario Provincial Police, the Leeds County Crime Unit, the Lanark County Crime Unit, and most of the locales actually exist, their portrayal, along with the characters and events included in the story, are entirely the invention of the author. All resemblances to actual people or occurrences are strictly coincidental.

The following publications were helpful in the writing of this novel: John E. Douglas, Ann W. Burgess, et al., *Crime Classification Manual: A Standard System for Investigating and Classifying Violent Crimes* (San Francisco: Jossey-Bass Publishers, 1992); *Bernardo Investigation Review: Summary. Report of Mr. Justice Archie Campbell, June 1996*, p. 9; Alan W. Watts, *The Way of Zen* (New York: Vintage Books, 1957); "Lanark, Ontario," Wikipedia, accessed 7/10/2022; *R. v. Sinclair* (2010) 2 S.C.R. 310; and Gino Arcaro, *Criminal Investigation: Forming Reasonable Grounds* (Toronto: McGraw-Hill Ryerson Limited, 1997).

Finally, where would I be without my life partner, editor, and best friend? Thanks, Lynn.

About the Author

Michael J. McCann lives and writes
in Oxford Station, Ontario, Canada. A
graduate of Trent University (Peterborough,
ON) and Queen's University (Kingston,
ON), he served as Production Editor of
Criminal Reports (Third Series) and Law
Reports Co-ordinator for Carswell Legal
Publications (Western) before spending
fifteen years at the Canada Border Services
Agency as a project officer and national
program manager. He's married to author
Lynn L. Clark. They have one son.

If you enjoyed this crime novel, you'll also love the debut of retired detective Tom Faust in

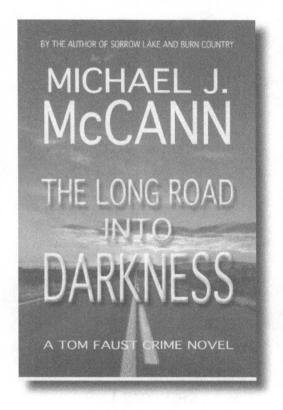

The Long Road Into Darkness
Michael J. McCann
ISBN: 978-1-927884-17-1

Ask your local independent bookstore to order it today!

Finalist for the
HAMMETT PRIZE
Best Crime Novel in North America

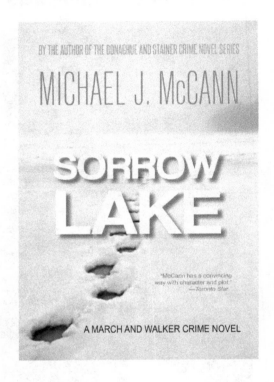

Sorrow Lake
March and Walker #1
Michael J. McCann
ISBN: 978-1-927884-02-7

Ask your local independent bookstore
to order it today!

Maddie Hubbard must face her greatest fears before they drive her mad.

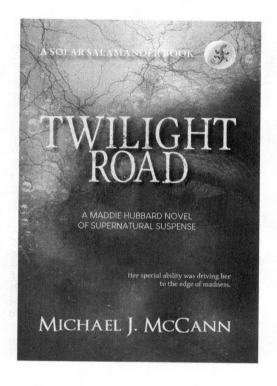

Twilight Road
A Maddie Hubbard Novel
Michael J. McCann
ISBN: 978-1-927884-23-2

Ask your local independent bookstore to order it today!

Stuck in a snowed-in village
with dangerous criminals
locked in a bitter internal feud!

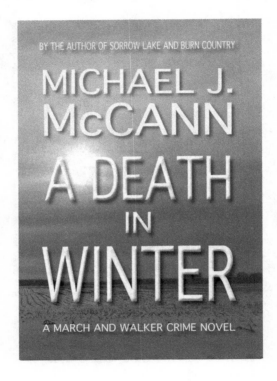

A Death in Winter
March and Walker #5
Michael J. McCann
ISBN: 978-1-927884-19-5

Ask your local independent bookstore
to order it today!

Printed in the USA
CPSIA information can be obtained
at www.ICGtesting.com
JSHW081957261123
52533JS00001B/19